The Historian

Michael Peron

Dedicated to my parents, who continue to put up with me.
I'm not sure why.

Michael Peron

Part I: Primus

Arbitration

A ray of light danced over the procession, and Sev of Primus shot a hopeful glance at the greyed sky above—perhaps Olius would shine down upon the ceremony after all. But just as his eyes reached the atmosphere, the clouds thickened, erasing any trace of light attempting to meet them.

Sev returned his attention to the marching group of people and frowned. All around them was the familiar environment of Primus—an arid, almost infertile world—yet here and now, of all places and times, the sky threatened rain.

None of the Scholars showed any sign of recognition—no doubt worried such distractions would be seen as disrespectful—but the peasants on the sidelines made their confusion clear: conversations of the lowest quality permeated the air around them, and Sev's frown deepened.

He searched his mind for meaning, for some kind of answer. Perhaps Olius mourned by blocking its light and casting a shadow across the land? This was not a celebratory parade, after all. This was the Walk of Respect, the final goodbye to High Scholar Dren, a man of incredible wisdom whose passing marked a terrible loss for the Scholarship.

But Sev didn't agree with this line of thought. At other, less significant Walks, Olius had shone brightly, as if to bless the fallen. So why was it absent now?

He frowned a second time. He should not think of his other Walks as less significant. A High Scholar held a position of great importance, but Sev knew such things were relative. Every being was graced with the light of Olius, and every being deserved respect. It was a mindset he was still working to ingrain, the habits of his past life at odds with the present.

A stir toward the front caught his attention, and Sev saw their destination up ahead: a thick slab of iron jutting out of the barren hillside, pockets of rust betraying its age. Stairs led up to the platform, which was occupied by a small craft: the Vessel of the Fallen, where the remains of High Scholar Dren awaited them.

At the base of the stairs stood two men draped in purple and black—soldiers of the Palace, sent as crowd control. Already they flashed their hotswords at the nearest peasants, threatening those who stepped too close. Sev watched them slash through the air, laughing as their victims stumbled to the ground.

For the third time, he frowned. This was far more disrespectful than any conversation about the weather. He wanted to voice his opinion to Scholar Folin, the man standing next to him, but all he could do was turn and share a knowing glance. In that glance, an ocean of meaning passed between the colleagues, and Sev knew their thoughts aligned.

As the head of the procession approached the base of the stairs, the peasants made way of their own volition. The contrast was not lost on the two soldiers, who watched leaders of the Scholarship with a sort of begrudging respect, stepping aside to grant them access to the platform.

The men walked up the staircase, the Elder Scholar followed by the surviving High Scholars, and Sev took a moment to study the crowd. There were at least a hundred people here—the most he had ever seen on a Walk. He had expected a large showing, but these numbers were surprising. And this didn't even take into account the other Scholars who were walking in solidarity all across Primus, separated by distance but not in thought.

"Scholars of Primus, it is with a heavy heart I greet you on this rotation."

The Elder Scholar had taken a position just ahead of the other ten, addressing the crowd. Though his scalp was barren, his beard grew long and white, dangling down to his chest. His was a face Sev knew well, one of supreme authority and wisdom, and one clearly troubled on this occasion.

"High Scholar Dren was a man of great wisdom and intelligence, someone who dedicated his life to the pursuit of knowledge in the name of Olius and the Historian. On the previous rotation, his worldly life came to an end, but his legacy will live on, carried by each of us, his brothers in Scholarship."

The Elder Scholar reached his arms out toward the crowd and looked up at the clouds.

"The Vessel of the Fallen stands ready to take High Scholar Dren to Olius, ending his worldly journey. Let us take a moment of silent thought and remembrance as this Walk of Respect comes to a close."

As the Elder Scholar dropped his arms and brought his head down, the other High Scholars and everyone in the crowd followed suit—everyone except the soldiers. They watched the proceeding, trying to seem amused, but their expressions betrayed the awe they felt: they couldn't believe the peasants were observing this silence, submitting to the will of the Scholars.

Only now, in this brief interlude, did Sev feel the oppressive heat surrounding them, and he fought the urge to shift his weight. Perhaps it was better the sky was obscured.

"Thank you."

Everyone looked up, and the High Scholars turned to face the Vessel. This part caught Sev's attention, as it was new to him; most Walks ended with the spreading of the mortal ashes, as a Scholar's remains joined the soil of Primus. But a High Scholar wasn't meant to return to Primus, he was meant to travel to Olius.

The Vessel stirred, seemingly of its own accord, and began to lift off the platform. It was a small craft, large enough to hold the High Scholar's ashes and some rudimentary propulsive systems, but for a Scholar, any exposure to space-capable vehicles was cause for wonder—and even more so for the peasants. There were never any common folk at the other Walks, and while Sev believed some had come to pay their respects, he wondered how many were there just for the show.

The crowd stared at the device as it rose ever higher, accelerating toward the clouds. Then it penetrated the darkened sky, disappearing from view, and the ceremony came to a close. The Walk was over, and High Scholar Dren's duties were complete.

Here, at least, Sev could find some solace: once the Vessel broke through the other side of the clouds, the light of Olius would shine on High Scholar Dren once more.

***

As the procession made its way back to the Scholarship, the clouds began to clear, but Sev knew the shadow would never truly depart. This was a heavy loss, one that would be felt for many rotations to come.

"I have never seen so many attend a Walk," he commented.

Scholar Folin nodded in reply, eyes fixed on the ground before them.

"The numbers I expected, but the soldiers…"

He let the sentence hang in the dry air, shooting a glance at Sev.

"I wonder if the Council requested their presence," Sev replied, disturbed by the memory of their behavior.

Folin sensed his friend's discomfort.

"What tasks await you?" he asked.

Sev almost flashed a smile. Folin was well-versed in reading others.

"A new batch of tomes need organizing. I should be able to finish before nightfall." Then, after a pause, "High Scholar Zoph was kind in his orders on this rotation."

Folin nodded.

"Indeed he was."

They rounded the final curve of the path, bringing the Scholarship into view. Before them lay a grand campus of weathered buildings, each one a nondescript, grey rectangle lacking windows or doors. Strategically placed openings, some small and some large, channeled wind into the halls, giving the occupants a mild respite from the planet's heat.

This was home, Sev thought, but the sentiment lacked conviction. He frowned, wondering how long it would take him to truly accept this place. Still, it felt more like home than the Palace ever did. Perhaps that was enough?

A thought came to him suddenly, and he turned to Folin.

"What of the future?"

Folin gave him a curious glance.

"What do you mean?"

"We have lost one of the Council, this brings significant consequences."

Folin nodded.

"Indeed it does. And while High Scholar Zoph was kind on this rotation, there is no doubt the coming rotations will be far more challenging."

Sev processed these words, realizing how right he was—one of the High Scholars was gone, but the Scholarship's workload went unchanged.

"But there is no reason to worry," Folin continued. "A successor will be chosen in due time, and the Scholarship will heal and grow, as it has so many times before."

This time, Sev allowed himself to smile. Folin was a great friend, and an even greater Scholar. There was a maturity about him beyond that of his peers—and Sev would be one to know. Perhaps he would be the chosen successor? But these were premature thoughts—disrespectful, even.

Their path reached one of the larger openings, and they crossed the threshold into the Scholarship. The familiar grey halls calmed his wandering mind, their oppressive austerity focusing his thoughts on the job ahead. When they reached one of many forks, Folin gave him a parting nod.

"Go with Olius, brother."

"And you."

Sev turned, remembering the words he had read on his morning parchment. The room he was looking for was near the western end of the campus, where most of the new data was taken.

As he made his way over, Sev nodded to every Scholar he passed, noting, as always, how a handful of them made no reply. This rudeness might have frustrated him were the evening not so pleasant—he could feel the cool air flowing through the halls, propelled by the cleverly engineered openings in the walls. But when he rounded the final turn and entered the chamber to which he had been assigned, Sev couldn't hide his frown.

Before him were what looked to be a hundred data tomes, strewn across several sets of shelves in no discernible order. Whoever had placed them here had done so with little care, and now it was up to him to categorize and order this small subset of Priman knowledge.

Sev let out a sigh and grabbed the closest tome, opening to the first page. Inside was a table of contents describing food distributions of an agricultural shipment to a specific district. He leafed through the pages and saw more detailed explanations of what food was going where, then placed it on an empty shelf to his right.

His hands went to the next volume and hesitated. How would this night unfold, he wondered. Either the mess before him was on purpose, in which case he would be here for quite some time, or it was simply the product of haste, in which case he might actually get some rest. He opened this second tome and saw a very similar layout, this time specific to a neighboring district.

He closed the cover and smiled. Haste, not hate. Sev put the second tome next to the first, arranging them with care on one of the shelves.

It made sense, of course—perhaps the Scholars were in the midst of unpacking the volumes when they rushed to make the Walk. He too had almost missed the event, having been so engrossed in his duties.

He checked the next four volumes and arranged them along the same shelf. Sev wasn't a huge fan of these organizational jobs, but he knew they were an integral part of the Scholarship's functions: not just maintaining the records of Primus, but keeping them in order. After all, no one really knew when the next Visit might occur…

"Scholar Sev, do you need assistance?"

Sev glanced at the man in the doorway and had to stifle a smile.

"No, Scholar Ro, thank you."

A flash of relief crossed the man's expression before he turned around and left. Sev watched him walk away, sharing in his relief. Ro was one of the Scholars who would have made it a point to ignore his greetings.

In truth, Sev felt some pity for his spiteful peers. Yes, some of their frustration stemmed from his past, but it was more a combination of his past and his present: to work in the Scholarship itself under the direct tutelage of one of the High Scholars was the most distinguished position available besides that of the coveted twelve. In fact, his status put him in the same spot as Scholar Folin: next in line for a promotion to the highest ranks of the Scholarship—a promotion that was now possible given the passing of High Scholar Dren.

It was something he had considered in the past, but then as now, he repressed these thoughts as selfish. This was another vestige of his past life, the never-ending quest for glory, but glory was not a Scholar's purpose —quite the opposite. A true High Scholar, Sev thought to himself, would not crave the position.

He stared at the volumes before him, trying to clear his mind. Why had he let his thoughts wander? There was so much to get done, and he knew this idea wouldn't give him peace—not once it had taken root. It would eat at him, diminishing his ability to focus and deteriorating his ability to perform his duties.

No, Sev thought to himself, he could not let this poison linger. There was only one person who might have the antidote, but Sev knew it would have to wait until the following rotation. Besides, he could stand to work on his patience.

***

"Sev, what is troubling you?"

They sat side by side on the stone bench lining the Hall of Nourishment. Other Scholars passed before them, the hungry in one direction and the satisfied in the other.

"Thank you for taking the time to speak with me, High Scholar."

High Scholar Zoph smiled at his pupil. This was a difficult time for everyone, and he supposed he had an idea of what was going through the young man's mind.

"Of course, Sev. Speak your mind, Scholar."

Sev took a breath to clear his head, trying his best to ignore the voices around them.

"I am struggling with my past again."

Zoph frowned. This was not what he had expected, though he had talked to Sev many times about his connection to the Palace. Still, he thought they had moved on from these issues, at least for the time being.

"Are the other Scholars excluding you?"

Sev turned to his mentor and shook his head.

"No, High Scholar. It's not that."

Zoph saw that Sev was gathering his thoughts, and waited for him to continue.

"It's the loss of High Scholar Dren."

This made more sense to the High Scholar, though he still didn't see the connection. He waited for Sev to build the bridge.

"I've had thoughts of greed and glory, High Scholar."

With these words it clicked, and Zoph nodded.

"I understand, Sev."

He sighed, looking up at the other Scholars moving to and fro.

"This is not a product of your past, Scholar. This is a product of our lasting imperfection."

He turned his eyes back to his pupil.

"You are not the only one who has gazed longingly at the chairs in the Room of Council, and you are certainly not the only one now pondering their future."

He paused and Sev nodded.

"Be that as it may, High Scholar, I am ashamed of these thoughts."

Zoph couldn't help but smile. This young man was an outsider, there was no doubt about it, and yet he seemed to understand the word of Olius better than most. A cruel twist of fate? Or perhaps the most sensible one yet?

"Sev, do not let this shame consume you. It's right of you to avoid greed, but you ought to channel your energy into positive thoughts. Don't waste effort fighting your natural imperfections. This is a battle you'll never win."

Sev looked at his mentor expectantly.

"How can I channel my thoughts positively, High Scholar?"

Zoph held his gaze for a few moments then cocked his head.

"How? You know how, Sev. Focus on your duties. We both know this is easier said than done, but it's what we must do. It is our purpose and our mission."

Sev nodded, contemplating the man's words. As he made to respond, a presence before them caught their attention.

"High Scholar. Scholar. My apologies for interrupting."

The Scholar's eyes darted between them and landed on Zoph.

"The Elder Scholar requests your immediate presence in the Room of Council," he announced.

Zoph nodded and stood.

"Thank you, Scholar. I'm on my way."

Sev stood in turn, and Zoph placed a hand on his shoulder.

"Don't let it consume you, Sev. Take care."

With that, the High Scholar left the Hall of Nourishment, and Sev stood alone amongst the moving bodies, lost in thought.

***

Following their meeting, Sev noticed several changes in his routine. Duties he was not accustomed to performing were added to his plate, and he wasn't the only one: the entire Scholarship seemed to buzz with increased activity, and it wasn't hard to guess the reason.

The High Scholars spent most of their time locked in the Room of Council, going so far as to skip meals and cancel appointments. The individuals directly beneath them—Sev included—were made to pick up the slack, and this process continued down the line all the way to the servants. As one rotation rolled into the next, the sadness of Dren's passing dissipated, replaced by an unavoidable frustration at incredibly demanding loads.

How long would it take to decide a successor? Though Sev was not yet a Scholar at the time of the last High Scholar's passing, he knew the procedure well: the remaining High Scholars would choose a number of candidates, typically three, from the most qualified Scholars. These choices would be shared with the Palace, and the Elector would have the final say.

At this innocent thought, memories flashed before Sev's eyes: various passing encounters with the supreme leader of Primus, never close enough to see his face but always close enough to feel his presence. The man had been his master and commander for so many revolutions, but Sev was never important enough to meet him. Few were.

In a way, he didn't mind. Even from a distance, there was something menacing about the Elector—his power, his mythos, some combination of the two. Sev did not want for such a meeting, it seemed a dangerous thing to hope for. In fact, at the first sign of his potential promotion, he had done the unthinkable, and that had brought him here, to the Scholarship.

His mind shifted to the Elder Scholar, the master and commander of his new path. This man, he had met several times. This man, he hoped to meet again. There was no menace in his presence—his was an authority cemented in wisdom, not fear.

Of course, the Elder Scholar was not the supreme leader of Primus—the Elector was. Still, the Scholarship and the Palace maintained a working relationship, a difficult but important equilibrium in the planet's governance. This had always confused Sev in his rotations as a soldier: why did the Elector give this entity, one with no military might, so much power?

In hindsight, the answer was clear, embedded in the fabric of the Scholarship itself, the very reason for its existence. When the Historian returned to Primus, he wouldn't seek the audience of the Elector, or a visit to the Palace—he would seek out the Scholars, and the knowledge they had compiled for him.

But when would this next Visit occur, Sev wondered. Even the Scholarship didn't have the answer to that question. The last one was over a hundred revolutions ago, well before Sev's birth. Was it just around the corner, or another hundred revolutions away?

"Sev?"

Sev snapped out of his train of thought, turning to the familiar voice.

"Scholar Folin."

Folin smiled.

"Are we yet so formal?"

Sev found the smile contagious.

"My apologies, the past two rotations have been difficult—as you predicted."

Folin shrugged.

"All of us labor, including the Council. I'm not sure I'd prefer to be in their spot."

"Yes, theirs is a difficult decision," Sev replied, but even as the words came out, they rang false.

Indeed, theirs was a difficult decision, but looking at his friend, Sev knew they were not lacking in qualified candidates.

"Unfortunately I'm here to add to your burden," Folin said, handing Sev a parchment. "High Scholar Zoph has an urgent task requiring our attention."

Sev took the paper and looked it over, frowning.

"You're right, this is unfortunate," he replied, handing the orders back to Folin.

Folin gave him an encouraging smile.

"It is our duty," he said, turning to lead the way.

As Sev made to follow, he wondered how much longer the Council might need to debate—the choice seemed more than clear.

***

The two Scholars walked side by side along the familiar path, sweat clinging to their robes. Olius was already on its downward journey, but its heat had not yet dissipated—in fact, Sev thought with a grimace, this was the hottest part of the rotation.

He glanced up and saw their destination just ahead: the Hall of Arbitration, a rather dubious name for such a small structure. Its grey walls bore a resemblance to the Scholarship, but it lacked any clever openings for air-flow—this building was not situated in a wind tunnel like their campus, its location being more symbolic: the halfway point between the Palace and the Scholarship.

"I trust the Palace won't delay," Sev commented, unable to contain his indignation. This was the last thing he wanted to deal with right now, knowing the number of tasks awaiting his attention.

"We can only hope," Folin answered, choosing to ignore his friend's dry tone.

Sev felt a pang of shame at his immaturity, but it was short-lived in the unbearable heat. How could Folin keep a cool head out here?

They finished the trek in silence, stepping through an opening into the small shelter. Inside were two patriarchs: leaders from local villages come to represent their tribe in this disagreement. Sev saw their tattered robes, smelt their odor even from a distance, and had to fight the prejudice within him. Yes, these were peasants, but this was the population of their planet, a population he had sworn to serve.

"Scholars," one of them began, but the other shot him a deathly glare.

"Silence! One Arbiter is still missing."

The first patriarch—the taller of the two—sighed, then looked to the Scholars.

"Do I break the rules of Arbitration in addressing you two?"

Sev found himself surprised by their eloquence. These men must have been Pupils in their youth.

"No," Folin answered, "Both of you may speak freely, but nothing will be settled without the third Arbiter."

The shorter man scoffed.

"This matter doesn't concern the Scholarship. A quick trip to the Palace would have fixed our problems long ago."

There was a disdain in the second patriarch's eyes that put Sev on guard —this man had little respect for them, a dangerous prospect given the nature of the third Arbiter.

"I disagree," the first man replied. "This is the very reason for this Hall."

The shorter man scoffed again, then turned his back to them. The taller patriarch took the opportunity to address Sev and Folin.

"Scholars, our dispute comes from a recent food shipment. One of our families just had twins, but they haven't been added to the census. The father asked for a larger share from the soldiers, but they refused. He argued with them, and as punishment, the soldiers gave his share to someone from another village."

He paused, glancing at the other leader.

"Unfortunately, this was not the end of it. The father followed the man to the other village, pleading for his share, but the man refused. At some point, an altercation occurred—"

"Have you started proceedings without full committee?"

All eyes turned to the opening, where a soldier of the Palace stood draped in his purple and black. There was an arrogance in his stature, an assumed superiority derived no doubt from the hotsword on his left hip.

Sev's eyes locked on the weapon, memories flashing before him: there was once a time where he wore the same protection, carried himself in the same manner…

"Sir," said the shorter patriarch, dropping his right knee and right hand to the ground in the symbol of obedience and gratitude.

At the sight of this show of reverence, coupled with the soldier's demeanor, Sev tensed. There was danger here, and as had happened so many other times since his departure, he felt naked without his blade.

"Rise, peasant," the soldier replied, but his eyes were locked on the taller patriarch—the one who hadn't shown his respect.

"Sir," this man said, fear passing over his expression. He too, saw the danger before him.

"Welcome, sir," Folin added, smiling at the soldier. "Shall we begin the proceedings?"

The soldier eyed him with distrust.

"What were you talking about earlier?"

Folin gestured to the taller man.

"This patriarch was explaining the situation to us, but as you said, we were not in full committee. He will have to start over and do it officially."

"Of course," the taller man said, his eyes jumping from Folin to the soldier.

But the soldier's eyes didn't leave Folin.

"Officially? So this man has attempted to corrupt the proceeding?"

Sev felt a punch of adrenaline and watched the soldier intently.

"Indeed he did, sir! I told them to wait but they didn't listen!"

The shorter man jumped in excitement, and Sev watched the soldier's hand drop to his hilt.

"Quiet, peasant! You will speak when spoken to."

The shorter man took a step back and Folin took the opportunity to speak.

"There was no corruption, sir, only conversation. And per the rules of Arbitration, such conversations are wholly permitted."

Sev could see the contempt in the soldier's expression—the man did not enjoy Folin's tone—but he was more concerned by the hand: it had not left the hilt. Something needed to be done.

"Sir," he announced, a bit louder than expected, and all eyes turned.

The soldier looked him up and down, as if seeing him for the first time, but Sev persisted.

"Does your general want you to waste your time here? Let's hear each of their cases and be done with it."

It was a reflexive action, this speech, and his own disdain trickled between the words. The man of the Palace seemed to notice, and confusion replaced disgust. He looked Sev over once more, then let his hand relax.

"So be it," he replied. Then, pointing to the taller man, "Start your story over."

The patriarch shot a glance at Sev before addressing the soldier.

"Yes, sir. As I was telling the Scholars, this dispute comes from a recent food shipment."

He paused, as if waiting for the soldier to interrupt, but no response came.

"One of the families in our village was blessed with twins, but the census hasn't added their number. When the father went to get his share of the shipment, he asked the soldiers for more—enough to feed the new additions. The soldiers denied his request, and…"

He paused a second time, glancing at the Scholars.

"And?" the soldier asked, irritated.

"Sorry, sir. After they denied his request, he argued with them. As punishment, they gave his share to someone from his village."

He pointed at the shorter man.

"This is the reason we've been called here?" the soldier asked, incredulous.

"No, sir," the shorter man cried out. "One of my people was killed!"

16

Anger came over the soldier's expression, and his hand returned to his hip, clasping the hilt of his hotsword.

"You were not given permission to speak!"

The man stepped back, cowering at the threatening tone. This display of fear seemed to appease the soldier, who turned to the taller man.

"Finish your story."

Sev shot a glance at Folin and saw the frown on his friend's face—this was far worse than they had expected. Who was this hot-head the Palace had sent? And what was this about a man being killed?

"Yes, sir. The man from my village followed the other man, pleading with him to give his rightful share."

"Rightful?" the soldier barked, "Was it not denied him by the authority of the Palace?"

The patriarch lowered his gaze.

"You're right, sir. It was not his to take, but he asked for it all the same."

The soldier eyed the village leader, disappointed by his collected manner.

"Continue," he commanded.

"Yes, sir. When the two men could not come to an agreement, an altercation occurred, and the man from my village killed the man from his."

Sev saw the shorter man take a step forward as if to speak, but a quick glare from the soldier kept his mouth shut.

"Is this all?" he asked the taller man.

"Almost, sir. As soon as this happened, he came to me and reported his crime. According to him it was an accident, and he left both shares of food with the man's family."

He glanced at the Scholars then back to the soldier.

"That's all, sir."

The soldier nodded slowly, then turned to the shorter man.

"Now, peasant, you may tell your side."

The man glared at the other patriarch then spoke.

"Thank you, sir. Part of what this man says is true: one of his people killed one of mine. All else is distraction. This crime must be punished."

"Is this all?" the soldier asked.

The man nodded.

"Yes, sir."

The soldier studied both men for a moment, frowning.

"Why do you waste the Palace's time on such trivial matters?"

Fear came to the shorter man's eyes, and the taller man glanced at the Scholars.

"You," the soldier barked, catching the taller man's attention. "Do you admit one of your men killed one of his?"

"Yes, sir, but—"

"But? This peasant is right: all else is distraction. Your man must be executed for murder."

Folin could stand idle no longer.

"Sir, we should discuss this matter away from the affected parties…"

The soldier stepped toward him.

"Do you disagree?"

Folin held his gaze for a moment, then turned to the two men.

"Citizens, please wait outside while we come to a decision."

Sev almost expected the soldier to tell them to stay, but he said nothing. Folin watched the village leaders leave, then addressed the man of the Palace.

"Yes, sir, I disagree."

The soldier scoffed.

"On what grounds?"

"On the grounds of context: the man was a father with two newborns, and he acted in desperation. If you execute him for his crime, you deprive two newborn children of their father."

The soldier shook his head contemptuously.

"This is irrelevant. A man was killed."

Sev watched the soldier with a frown. This black and white type of thinking was typical of the Palace, and he himself had adhered to it for many revolutions. Even now, as these two argued, he felt torn between the two sides.

As if reading his thoughts, the soldier turned to him.

"And what do you think?"

Sev looked from one to the other: the soldier eyeing him with a mix of eagerness and agitation, while Folin's gaze was calm, almost pleasant.

"I agree with my colleague," Sev answered.

The soldier scoffed again.

"Context is always relevant," Sev continued. "This man had a family to feed, and he went out of his rights to fulfill a primal need. That being said," he turned his attention to Folin, "a man was killed, and just punishment is necessary."

"What do you propose?" Folin asked.

Sev saw both sets of eyes on him, each one curious to hear his solution.

"I propose a life-debt on the accused to the other village, specifically to the family of the victim."

As expected, both men frowned at the suggestion.

"This is a waste of time," the soldier replied. "Who will ensure he fulfills his life-debt? The Palace doesn't have time to police the affairs of peasants."

Isn't that part of your job, Sev thought, but he kept the question to himself. Besides, he knew the answer from experience.

"Even if the Palace was able to monitor the punishment," Folin added, "a life-debt would be the same as execution: you would deprive these twins of their father."

Sev shrugged.

"You are welcome to your own proposals."

"I've already made my suggestion," the soldier barked in reply. "And you? You would have him walk free?"

Folin frowned.

"We do not know enough about the situation to pass such harsh sentence. What if it really was an accident?"

"We can call for witnesses," Sev suggested.

The soldier groaned.

"You want to drag this on?"

Folin shook his head.

"Witnesses from either camp could be unreliable. The villagers might side with their own."

Sev almost wanted to laugh at the absurdity of their existence. The Scholarship was a beacon of truth, meant to spread the ideals of Olius throughout Primus. How well had they fulfilled that mission if every villager was untrustworthy? They had tried, of course, but the peasants were mostly uneducated. Trying to get them to be honest and moral when they struggled to put food on the table… it was a losing battle.

"If you propose to let him live, I will not accept," the soldier announced.

Sev turned to him, anger seeping into his words.

"Now it is you who will drag this on."

The soldier took a step toward him, hand dropping to his hotsword.

"Is this how you address a man of the Palace?"

Sev stood up straighter, holding his ground.

"Enough!" Folin snapped.

The two men turned in shock, as if to verify the source of the outburst.

"I will accept my colleague's proposal," he continued, gesturing to Sev. "Will you?"

The soldier looked him up and down, hand on his weapon, then looked back at Sev. The Scholars saw his hesitation, the gears turning: was this admitting defeat? Would his pride remain intact?

Finally, the soldier relaxed his grip.

"So be it."

Sev let out a sigh of relief.

"So we are in agreement?" Folin asked. "The accused will have a life-debt to the accusing village or the victim's family if there is one. All in favor say aye. Aye."

Sev glanced from one to the other.

"Aye."

The soldier's eyes remained on Sev.

"Aye."

"Good," Folin said. "I will let the citizens know we have come to a decision."

But as his friend made his way out of the opening, Sev caught a sly satisfaction in the soldier's expression—one that brought a sickness to his stomach. There was something he was missing, something that had slipped by both of them, but what it was, he didn't know.

***

Their walk back to the Scholarship was a silent one. The patriarchs had reacted unpleasantly to the verdict, although that was to be expected—in the handful of times Sev had been called to the Hall of Arbitration, only once had he seen a leader leave happy.

It was a strange custom, this Arbitration, as it only dealt with tribal matters. Everyone knew where the real decisions were made, where the real judgements were passed down: the Palace. The Elector's title was not just a word, it defined his very existence. The man decided the fate of the planet far more than any of these Arbitrations.

So why bother with them at all? Why not have the tribes do as the short man had wanted and bring their concerns to the Palace? Here again, Sev's experience gave him the answer: the Palace didn't care to deal with such trivialities. Even the hot-headed soldier, one of the lowest-ranked members of the black fortress, had considered his time wasted.

But this was not what occupied Sev's mind on his walk down the open path. No, his thoughts were on the man walking next to him, on his friend and colleague. Sev had never heard or seen Folin be anything other than calm, and while his outburst was short-lived, it represented a very real change in his character—or at least Sev's perception of it.

Was it the load on their shoulders? He had been shocked by Folin's initial attitude toward the assignment, perhaps it was just for show? They were both returning to a large list of unfinished duties, and such stress—repeated rotation after rotation—could eat at someone. Sev thought to ask his friend on his feelings, to try to help him through whatever was bothering him, but by the time they reached the Scholarship entrance, he had neither the words nor the courage.

"Go with Olius, brother," he managed to say.

"And you," Folin replied, though the Scholar didn't look him in the eye.

Before this strange behavior could take any more of his attention, a servant came to Sev with a parchment.

"For you, Scholar Sev."

Sev nodded, grabbing the paper and looking it over. By the end of the message, he had all but forgotten the situation with Folin.

***

Sev finished his remaining tasks in record speed, nearly catching up on the time he had lost in Arbitration. Unfortunately, time was the last thing he wanted right now. In fact, he'd rather have more work to keep himself busy.

High Scholar Zoph had requested a meeting at the mid-rotation meal. A personal meeting, in his chambers. And now, as Sev made his way to the Hall of Slumber, only one question was on his mind: what could be so important to take time away from the Council's current task?

He searched the Hall for Folin, eager to discuss this matter with someone, but his friend was nowhere to be found. Other Scholars took to their bunks, yet Sev was in no rush to sleep—at this point, he doubted he could.

There was a battle raging in his mind, a futile struggle against the one answer he could come up with, the one possibility he had just managed to forget: what if the High Scholar wanted to inform him of his candidacy?

Sev cursed both his shameful hypothesis and his lack of discipline. How could he consider himself worthy of the Council when he hadn't even mastered his impatience?

In the first few revolutions at the Scholarship, Sev had found their pace of life painfully slow. At the Palace, things happened with alarming speed, and one had no choice but to adjust to their unpredictable nature. In the military service of Primus, it was a matter of life and death.

Life and death. Sev thought back to the rotations's Arbitration, to the arrogant soldier. Would he have acted the same way, back in his time? He had never been called in for an Arbitration, and for that he had been grateful: who wanted to waste time with the Scholars debating the trivial matters of peasants? Still, if he had been called, would he dare threaten a man of the Scholarship?

Sadly, Sev had trouble denying it. The Palace did not hold the Scholarship in high regard, except for the Council and of course the Historian. After all, who held the weapon? Who held the power? He thought back to the balance between the institutions of Primus and wondered how much longer it might last, how much longer until the Elector decided to rule without checks and balances, without the need for patience.

Patience. It had taken Sev quite some time to adapt to life in the Scholarship. He had realized, reluctantly, that patience was a valuable skill, one that helped a Scholar think through things rather than react to them. But as he stood in the Hall of Slumber, surrounded by the sounds of other Scholars drifting into their dreams, he felt the old restlessness within him, overpowering any degree of discipline he might have built up.

The lights dimmed with the extinguishing of the candles, and Sev made his way to one of the remaining bunks. It was no use standing around, the best he could do was take his training to heart, to calm his mind and get some rest.

After all, if this was what he thought it was, he had better get his act together.

***

Sev stood outside his mentor's chamber, trying to maintain his composure. Not only had he failed to get any sleep, the compounding fatigue and a lack of focus on his morning tasks had made the first half of the rotation a nightmare.

And yet, now that he was here, standing in front of the door, he hesitated. What waited for him on the other side?

"Sev?"

Sev whirled around to see his mentor approaching from the hall.

"High Scholar," he blurted out, surprise slipping into his tone.

Zoph looked him up and down.

"Thank you for coming to see me," he said, stepping past Sev and opening the door. "Will you come in?"

Sev nodded.

"Of course, High Scholar."

Zoph stepped aside and let Sev walk past.

Where the Scholars spent their nights in the Hall of Slumber, the High Scholars had their own private chambers—possibly the most distinguished of perks. Sev had been in Zoph's a handful of times, and each time he felt a pang of yearning—another hint of greed he had to fight to repress.

"Another busy rotation?" Zoph asked, closing the door.

"Yes, High Scholar."

Zoph stood in front of Sev, noticing the fatigue in his eyes, and flashed a smile.

"I trust you've been able to take my advice to heart?"

It took a moment for Sev to remember their earlier conversation.

"Yes, High Scholar."

It was true: before the parchment, Sev had managed to focus his attention on his duties, though how much of that was self-control and how much was simply the incredible load, he couldn't say. Of course, this meeting reversed all progress he had made, and now the forbidden topic was front and center: was this it? Why else would the High Scholar want to see him in private?

"Please, take a seat."

Zoph gestured to one of two chairs around a small table, and Sev followed his command.

"I promise to keep it brief," his teacher added, taking the seat across from Sev.

"Yes, High Scholar," Sev replied, unsure of what to say.

Zoph eyed him intently for a moment, then leaned back in his seat.

"Sev, I won't lie to you. What I'm about to ask you may make you uncomfortable, and for that, I apologize."

Sev's curiosity grew. Uncomfortable?

"But remember: all knowledge falls within the light of Olius, there is nothing that is off-limits."

Now Sev was truly lost. Perhaps this wasn't what he had expected.

Zoph looked away for a moment, deep in thought, then brought his attention back to Sev.

"Sev, what do you know of Secundus?"

Sev's intrigue vanished, replaced by a mix of concern and fear.

"Secundus?" he asked, as if he hadn't understood.

Zoph stared at him for a moment, a frown spreading across the familiar face.

"Yes, Sev. Secundus."

Secundus—the other planet of the system and de-facto enemy of Primus—was not a subject brought up lightly. In most cases, it was not a subject brought up at all.

"What do you mean, High Scholar?"

Zoph's frown deepened, and Sev saw a hint of frustration in his mentor's expression.

"Sev, remember your duty. You are a Scholar of Olius now, a man of knowledge. No subject is off-limits."

Except Secundus, Sev thought to himself. That subject was always off-limits. Zoph may claim it was open to the Scholars, but Sev had been here for eight revolutions and could count on one hand the number of times it had been mentioned.

"Sev?"

He met his mentor's eyes and saw frustration turning into anger, so he stumbled a reply.

"Secundus is a planet rich in agricultural resources, and their people harvest the land for crops. In ancient times, we had an open and peaceful relationship, but this ended with the Great War. During the Historian's last Visit, he brokered a ceasefire, ending the conflict. In the aftermath, there was hope for renewed peace, but Secundus attacked soon after, and since then our borders have remained shut."

This was the full extent he felt comfortable conveying in that moment, but it was clear High Scholar Zoph was unimpressed. Still, Sev had to wonder what his mentor was getting at: there wasn't much more knowledge available, at least not in the Scholarship.

"Our borders are not completely shut, Sev."

Here, the High Scholar had a point: soon after Secundus's unprovoked assault, when it became clear both planets needed one another's material resources, trade was opened up again. The planets exchanged what they had for what they needed—Primus received vegetation and agricultural goods, exporting its rich mineral resources in return—but the process was made to be as closed-off as possible, and no citizen of one planet ever set foot on the other.

"You are right, High Scholar. There is the trade, though it is limited by design."

In fact, Sev wasn't sure if anyone on Primus had ever seen the surface of Secundus: the trade ships—all operated by Primus—were windowless, guided by blind faith in ancient technology derived from Olius itself.

Zoph sighed, leaning forward and putting his elbows on the table.

"Sev, I will not dance around the point any longer. In your time at the Palace, did you learn anything else about Secundus?"

Sev stared at the man for a moment, shocked by the words he had heard. An odd sensation came over him—a discomfort he had never felt in any of his previous interactions with Zoph, which only served to deepen its effect.

For his part, Zoph noticed this abrupt shift in demeanor, and a sadness came into his eyes.

"Sev, I apologize. I knew this subject would make you uncomfortable, but I assure you I bring this up only out of urgent necessity."

These words served to temper Sev's unease, piquing his curiosity. Yet he knew it was no use prying—if the High Scholar had meant to explain the reason for this line of inquiry, he would have already done so.

"I—"

In trying to answer, Sev's discomfort returned, and he cursed the situation he found himself in. Not in a thousand revolutions had he expected his mentor to ask him about the other planet, and not in a thousand revolutions had he expected to test the dreadful oath he had taken, the one before he was permitted to leave the Palace...

Zoph sighed once more, leaning back into his chair.

"Sev, I'm afraid I've made a mistake. I didn't expect this conversation to affect you so deeply, and I don't wish to distress you any further. I think perhaps it would be best if you took some time to process what I'm asking and approach me when you feel ready."

Sev watched his mentor with a mix of gratitude and concern. What was this urgent necessity he spoke of?

"Sev, there's something else I feel I should let you know…"

Zoph's sentence trailed off, and Sev could see the High Scholar searching for the right words. Before they could come out, however, there was a knock at the door.

Both of them sat up straight, turning to the noise.

"Could you open it, Sev?"

Sev nodded, getting out of the chair.

"Yes, High Scholar."

He opened the door and saw a man draped in purple and black, an envoy of the Palace. Instinctively, he stiffened, standing at attention, then relaxed—this man was not his superior, not anymore.

The envoy eyed his reaction with interest.

"Scholar Sev of Primus?"

"Yes?"

"You are summoned to the Grand Palace for an audience with the Elector."

***

Sev paused at the top of the dune, the light of Olius warming his back. Before him lay the Grand Palace, a fortress of black stone in a sea of orange sand. He had never seen the Palace from this vantage point, but the impression it made was no less fearsome. As he stared at those imposing black walls, he wondered if he should be enthused or terrified.

He made his way down the dune, careful not to lose his footing. No matter what awaited him, he could not delay. Normally, the journey from the Scholarship to the Palace was made by paved road, but Sev had elected to cut through the dunes to save time. Now that the wind had picked up, whipping his robe and threatening to throw him into the sand, he began to regret his choice. He could not afford to soil his garment—not before this audience.

Summoned by the Elector himself? From almost every perspective, it made no sense—there was no reason for the supreme leader to see a Scholar, even one just below the twelve. But the envoy had handed him the parchment with the official seal—the summons was clear, and it was real.

Sev couldn't help but wonder if the conversation with Zoph was somehow related. Why had his teacher brought up Secundus, Primus's enemy? And the way their meeting had ended: Zoph was on the verge of saying something important, Sev knew it, but after the interruption, a shadow came over the man's expression, and Sev saw anger in his eyes—something he had never seen before.

What did it all mean? And why was it happening to him? Sev was burning to know the answers, the Scholar within him struggling once more to be patient. At least now he had something to distract himself, and it was something he had to give his full and undivided attention: one did not take a summons by the Elector lightly.

Sev reached the bottom of the dune and walked toward the nearest entrance, a large arched door with soldiers on either side. The black mouth loomed over him, threatening to swallow him whole, but he marched forward, almost in a trance.

At his approach, the guards gave him curious looks, but he made an effort to ignore them, channeling an outward confidence.

"Greetings, Scholar," one of them declared, opening the door.

"Thank you, sirs," Sev answered, hiding his relief.

He crossed the threshold into the Palace, taking a deep breath of the cool indoor air. He envied the Palace's self-contained atmosphere, a far cry from the sweltering heat just steps behind him.

A servant approached him almost immediately, and Sev came to a halt.

"May I help you, Scholar?"

The servant eyed him as the guards had, with a mix of curiosity and disdain.

"Yes," he answered. "I have an audience with the Elector."

The servant straightened, a newfound respect in his eyes.

"Of course. This way, Scholar."

He was led through a large hall into an even larger one, surrounded all the while by the black and purple of Primus. Though the Palace's facade was stark, its innards were ornate, an intricate testament to the wealth of its inhabitants. In his past life, Sev had visited the Palace on many occasions, but it was never his place of residence—the only occupants were the top echelon of the Priman military, the Elector and his generals. Even in those rotations, the decor was overwhelming, but now in contrast to the Scholarship…

"Scholar, please wait here."

They reached the end of the hall and Sev waited while the servant entered a large set of doors. He continued his admiration of the surroundings, wondering how it was all maintained in such impeccable order. The staff must be quite busy, he thought.

"Thank you for your patience, Scholar. The Elector will see you now."

The servant held one of the doors open and Sev walked inside.

The audience chamber was a spacious room of carpets and columns completely devoid of furniture with the exception of one raised chair in the center. The Elector, supreme leader of Primus, sat upon this high chair, draped in purple and black. His figure matched that of the Palace itself: outwardly imposing, with harsh lines in his expression—a man that had seen battle. On either side of the high chair stood his personal guardians, hands tight around the hilts of their hotswords.

Sev approached the base of the chair, surprised by the size of the chamber—every other time he had been inside, it was with a regiment, their numbers filling most of the room. Now, alone in the robes of a Scholar, Sev felt more out of place than ever.

"Welcome, Sev of Primus," the Elector said, his voice echoing through the emptiness around them.

Sev brought his right knee and right hand to the ground in the symbol of obedience and gratitude.

"Thank you, Elector."

Though he was no longer under the Palace, every citizen of Primus was under the Elector.

"Rise, Scholar."

He stood once more, and the Elector studied him for a moment, a hint of curiosity in his hardened expression.

"Sev of Primus, do you know why you are summoned?"

Sev's eyes darted to the supreme leader—as a soldier, one was never permitted to look into the Elector's eyes unless asked a direct question.

"No, Elector."

He gave a half-nod then leaned forward slightly.

"Sev of Primus, whom do you serve?"

There was an eagerness in his expression that was almost off-putting, but Sev knew the correct answer. It was the answer that had been drilled into him time and time again, for all those revolutions.

"I am a servant of Primus, Elector," he replied.

The Elector nodded again, leaning back in his chair and eyeing Sev with the same curiosity as before.

"A wise answer, but as a Scholar, are you not bound to the word of Olius?"

Sev hesitated. There was an unfathomable amount of power sitting in the chair above him, and he dare not speak without total conviction. Still, this was another answer he knew, one that had been explained to him time and time again in the past few revolutions.

"All are bound to the word of Olius, Elector."

For a moment, the Elector didn't respond, and Sev felt his heart beating in his chest, louder and louder. Finally, the supreme leader spoke.

"Another wise answer. I expect nothing less from a Scholar."

Sev could feel the tension fall out of his body, but he was quick to hold his posture.

"Sev of Primus," the Elector continued, "I will tell you why you are summoned. One of the High Scholars has passed on. You will take his place."

The Elector's words caught Sev off-guard. Had it really happened? Had he been selected as one of the candidates? Was that what Zoph had been meaning to tell him?

"There is an Arrival imminent, Sev of Primus. In eight rotations, the Historian will join us on Primus. We need the ranks of the High Scholars to be full in preparation for this historic event."

His confusion vanished, replaced with excitement. An Arrival in eight rotations? This was amazing news, wonderful news.

"Sev of Primus, do you accept the position of High Scholar?"

He dropped his knee and hand once more.

"Yes, Elector. Thank you."

Adjustment

Sev cut through the dunes on his return, eager to speak with High Scholar Zoph. The wind had picked up during his visit, but he hardly noticed. The Elector had made him a High Scholar, and the Historian was on the verge of Arrival. Never in his life would he have expected anything like this to occur, and neither the sand biting at his skin nor the heat radiating from the sky could temper his elation.

He reached the Scholarship in record time and made his way inside. Gone were the excessive decorations of the Palace, replaced with the familiar austerity, but the walls did nothing to calm his mind, not now. His thoughts swirled in unchecked chaos, and he tried in vain to relax his beating heart.

Still, his surroundings served to do what the outdoors could not—the familiar halls tempered his elation, and Sev found himself questioning the Elector's decision. While he wasn't in any position to dispute the supreme leader's will, he wondered why the most qualified candidate had not been chosen. Not that he didn't believe in himself—he did—but he knew there was someone better.

How would Folin react, Sev wondered. But he didn't need to wonder, he knew: the man would share in Sev's delight, supporting the decision with zeal. Would Sev have been able to do the same, if the situation were reversed?

He shook his head in an effort to clear it. It didn't matter, the situation wasn't reversed, it was as it was. How and why weren't important right now, what was important was speaking with the High Scholar, thanking him for his contribution, for his unwavering belief in an outsider. But when he reached Zoph's chambers, Sev found them empty.

The Room of Council, he thought to himself. And then another realization came to him: of course the High Scholars had been incredibly busy. Not only did they have to manage the replacement of High Scholar

Dren, there was an Arrival around the corner. It was a wonder they had any time to eat!

Sev turned away from the chamber and headed down the hall, barely noticing the Scholars around him. The events at the Palace seemed no more than a dream, yet here he was, a High Scholar of Primus, walking toward the Room of Council. No doubt the rest of the High Scholars were inside, preparing for the coming of the being of Olius. So how could he speak to Zoph? He would need permission—

He paused a few paces from the Room, almost laughing at himself. Permission? He was a High Scholar now. These were his peers. Still, he hesitated, eyeing the door before him. There were no guards here, no sentries. This was the Scholarship, its members were expected to follow the rules. No one would enter the Room of Council without approval, this would be a grave breach of protocol.

As he stood just outside the door, more doubts crept into mind. He looked down at his robes, the robes of a Scholar, and wondered where and how he would receive his new ones. And shouldn't there be a ceremony? A welcoming?

The Arrival, he told himself. That was more important than anything, more important than even the promotion of a new High Scholar. The Arrival had to be the reason for their silence, the reason he didn't have new robes or a ceremony. Still, it felt wrong barging in on the others without any sort of introduction. What should he do? Where should he go?

"Scholar Sev, do you need something?"

He turned at the familiar voice, one of his peers approaching from behind. The man eyed him with a hint of suspicion, but it was not his expression that worried Sev—it was the words that had come out of his mouth: Scholar Sev. Did no one know?

"Are you summoned to the Room of Council?" Sev managed to ask.

The man came to a stop next to him.

"I am."

The suspicion grew, but Sev ignored it.

"Can you pass a message for me?"

The man hesitated, glancing at the door then back to Sev.

"What is it?"

Now it was Sev who hesitated, wondering what he ought to say. Was it wise to reveal everything to this man, someone who might have been another candidate?

"Can you tell High Scholar Zoph I await my change in duties."

The man peered at him for a few moments before nodding.

"Very well."

Sev watched him enter the door before them, uncertain of his choice. His earlier elation had all but disappeared, and his old shame threatened to return. Of all these lifelong Scholars, he had been chosen to take Dren's place. It didn't seem fair, even to him, but who was he to doubt the Elector?

Before his thoughts could wander too far, the door opened once more, snapping him out of his daze. The man came toward him, a hint of anger veiled beneath his expression.

"Congratulations, High Scholar."

Hearing the words brought a wave of relief, but it was short-lived. Clearly, his peer found the news unpleasant.

"High Scholar Zoph has asked me to guide you to your chamber, where you will find your new robes."

The man strained to keep his composure, and Sev looked away with shame. Then, remembering the new hierarchy of the interaction, he made an effort to look him in the eye.

"Thank you, Scholar."

There was no malice in Sev's tone, but the man grimaced.

"Follow me."

Sev hesitated, wondering whether to remind him to call him by his title, but decided against it. This was not a battle worth fighting—there were far more important things to take care of.

***

For the past eight revolutions, Sev had shared a bunk in the Hall of Slumber and taken his meals in the Hall of Nourishment. Now he stood in his private quarters, eyeing the dinner waiting on his table, unable to comprehend the situation.

His colleague had taken a quick leave, and Sev didn't blame nor delay him. The last thing he wanted to do was create friction right now—a High Scholar had just passed, and the Arrival was imminent.

The Arrival! A rush of adrenaline came over him, and suddenly he wondered who else knew. The Elector had ordered him to keep the news a secret, though it was certain the Council was aware. Still, his colleague wasn't, otherwise even Sev's promotion wouldn't have soured him.

But why? Why hadn't the High Scholars let the Scholarship know? The Arrival was the very reason for the Scholarship's existence, and the sooner its membership knew what was coming, the better. There was so much to do, so much to prepare...

In that moment, standing awkwardly in his new chamber, Sev felt more restless than ever. Patience be damned! He scanned his surroundings again and saw a parchment placed neatly by his dinner. He stepped forward and lifted the document, unrolling it and reading its contents. As he read, his restlessness disappeared, but a frown spread across his face.

Nothing. He was meant to do nothing.

He put the parchment down and stared at the meal before him, knowing full well the other High Scholars would be eating in the Room of Council. Why did this piece of paper ask him to familiarize himself with his new quarters and robes? Why didn't it order him to change and report immediately?

Sev took a deep breath in an effort to think clearly. He was overwhelmed and underprepared, of course they had asked him to slow down. There was no need for him to enter the council now, especially when the appearance of a new face might slow down the process. Not in such a critical moment, not at such a crucial time. He needed to take stock of where he was and truly understand his new position before he could step foot in that room.

He walked to the cot, where his new robes were laid out for him. Of all the distinctions separating a High Scholar from a Scholar, it was the change in wardrobe that pleased Sev the most. The Scholar's robe tried to blend the colors of Primus and Olius in a manner Sev had never truly endorsed. Purple and black with white and gold didn't match—they clashed. But the High Scholars had robes of pure white with gold accents, a design he found much more tasteful.

He changed into his new garment, trying to ignore whether they were new or simply passed on from their previous owner. Whatever their origin, they were his now, and he needed to accept this fact before he could be of any use to the others.

A knock on the door caught his attention, and he hesitated, unused to this practice: the Hall of Slumber had no doors, and Scholars entered and exited as they pleased. Privacy was a privilege he had all but forgotten.

He walked over to the door and opened it.

"Greetings, High Scholar."

At the sight of his old friend, Sev felt a strange stab of shame: here was the person who deserved this position, this chamber, these robes.

"Folin."

There was a moment's hesitation—one that exacerbated Sev's strange guilt—before Folin flashed a smile.

"Congratulations."

His friend's demeanor helped calm him, and Sev gestured inside.

"Come in, please."

Folin stepped inside, closing the door behind him. His eyes scanned the chamber then settled back on Sev.

"How do you feel?"

Again, Sev hesitated. Here was his oldest friend, someone he had always opened up to, and yet now, when he needed an ear to hear him out, something felt off. Was this still guilt? Did he simply refuse to accept the honor?

"I'm… humbled," he replied.

Folin stared at him with an odd intensity, and Sev's discomfort grew.

"How did you find out?" he managed to ask.

Folin shrugged.

"The news is getting around. I came as soon as I could."

He looked up and down the High Scholar robes, and again Sev felt out of place.

"You met with the Elector, yes?" Folin asked.

Sev nodded.

"Earlier this rotation."

"How was that?"

Sev looked away, trying to suppress these bizarre feelings. Here was his opportunity to speak, his opportunity to share his worries.

"Disconcerting," he replied.

"Disconcerting?"

Something in Folin's tone caught his attention, but Sev couldn't put his finger on it.

"Yes, well…"

Sev paused, thinking on how to express himself.

"One must be careful in the Elector's presence," he said.

Folin nodded, still eyeing him with unsettling intensity.

"Sev…"

Now it was Folin who chose his words carefully.

"Why hasn't there been a formal induction?"

At this question, Sev felt both a surge of relief and a wave of concern: relief in understanding why his friend was acting so strangely, but concern in the realization that he couldn't answer—if the Council hadn't announced the Arrival, he certainly couldn't share the news with Folin. Which only begged his earlier question: why hadn't they?

He realized he had remained silent for too long and stumbled a reply.

"I… I can't say."

Sev gave his friend a sad smile, which Folin returned.

"I don't mean to sully your promotion, but I thought it best to let you know: these extenuating circumstances have gotten others talking."

Sev frowned. He hadn't considered it, but this situation was bound to worsen existing tensions. Should he do something about it? Could he?

No, he thought to himself, he couldn't, and frankly he didn't need to. Once word got out about the Arrival, his promotion would be all but forgotten. Or so he hoped.

"I apologize if I've offended you, High Scholar."

Sev's stared at Folin, surprised by his tone.

"Folin, you don't need to use that title with me. Not now."

Folin's intense gaze came back, but before he could reply, there was another knock at the door.

Sev turned and opened it, still surprised by the newfound privacy. Outside stood a servant, scroll in hand.

"Greetings, High Scholar. I have a message from the Elder Scholar."

Sev nodded, taking the parchment and reading the message. As he processed the words, another rush of adrenaline came over him, and he turned to Folin.

"I am to report to the Room of Council on the following rotation, at Olius's first light."

Folin smiled.

"Your first council. An exciting moment."

He put his hand on Sev's shoulder.

"Thank you for seeing me, Sev. I wish you luck on the following rotation, and every rotation after that. Go with Olius, brother."

"And you," Sev replied, almost automatically.

With that, Folin left, but Sev's eyes lingered where he had stood.

Why had he been chosen over that man? And why hadn't the Council told the Scholarship of the Arrival?

Sev closed the door and shook his head. He would address these questions later. Right now, he had more pressing matters: specifically, how he would prepare himself for his new role in just one night. He glanced once more at his quarters, taking it all in. Was one night enough time? Would he be ready for whatever was in store?

Yes, he thought to himself, he would be. He was a High Scholar now, and this was his duty.

***

The following rotation, Sev of Primus woke to a knock on the door and was surprised to find a servant carrying a meal: his breakfast. The servant left the food on his table with a candle for light, grabbing the remains of last night's portion on his way out. Sev watched with fascination, shocked by the level of accommodation his new position afforded. Was this the norm? It couldn't be and he knew it—he had seen the High Scholars in the Hall of Nourishment almost every rotation, eating with the rest of the Scholarship. Perhaps this was a special luxury specific to this pressing time?

A quick glance through one of the wall openings told him Olius would be rising soon, so Sev ignored these questions and sat to eat. The meal, at least, was no different from what he received as a Scholar—only its delivery was unusual.

With his new robes on, Sev exited the chamber, making the walk to the Room of Council by the lights of the torches along the walls. The events of the previous rotation, particularly his audience with the Elector, seemed like a bizarre dream. Was this really happening? Was he really a High Scholar now?

He reached the same spot he had stopped the rotation before and hesitated. He could hear the muffled voices of the other High Scholars already inside, and he wondered how long they had been meeting. Had they even slept? Again Sev felt a pang of guilt, questioning why he hadn't been asked to come in the night before, to help right away.

He took a deep breath to calm his mind. While there might be a storm raging inside of him, it would be in poor form to display these feelings. With concentrated effort, Sev stepped forward and opened the door.

The Room of Council sat at the heart of the Scholarship, the very center of the grounds. It was the only room whose walls showed even a hint of decor: its rotunda of polished stone was painted white with subtle gold accents.

A half crescent stone table dominated the interior, with thirteen stone chairs lining the outside. The High Scholars filled eleven of the chairs, leaving two empty. One of these two—the furthest on the right, outlined in white—had been vacant for just four rotations. But the other—the middle one, raised slightly above the rest and outlined in gold—had been empty for over a hundred revolutions.

Sev's eyes were fixed on this middle chair. He had trouble believing it would be filled in his lifetime, let alone in seven rotations.

"Welcome, Sev of Primus."

He closed the door and turned to face the Elder Scholar. For as long as Sev had been a Scholar, and many revolutions before that, this man had been the leader of the Scholarship. But in seven rotations, their true leader would arrive.

"The Elector has promoted you to the rank of High Scholar," he continued.

There was a harshness in the man's tone that surprised Sev, but he caught himself before he displayed his confusion.

"Unfortunately, this promotion comes at an inopportune time. As you know, the Arrival is in seven rotations. We are in the midst of frantic preparation, and there is no time to formally induct a new High Scholar. We ask for your patience and understanding so we may focus on the matter at hand."

Sev shot a glance at Zoph. He, at least, must feel some pride. He, at least, would share in Sev's joy.

"With that in mind, we ask that you sit at the Council as an observer, until such a time that we can properly address your induction. Is that understood?"

But Sev barely heard the Elder Scholar's question, as his attention was on his former teacher: there was neither pride nor joy in his mentor's face. Only pity, mixed with a hint of shame.

"Sev of Primus?"

Sev whirled to face the Elder Scholar, unable to contain his embarrassment.

"Yes, Elder Scholar. I understand."

The Elder Scholar eyed him with a hint of disdain, and Sev cursed his distraction. What a horrible first impression.

"One further question, Sev of Primus: have you shared the news of the Arrival with anyone?"

As much as he should have expected it, Sev was surprised by the question, and once more he found himself wondering why the Council had decided to keep it a secret thus far.

"No, Elder Scholar."

The Elder Scholar peered at him curiously, then nodded.

"Very well. The announcement will be made later this rotation. Please take your seat and remember: you are acting only as an observer at this time."

Sev gave a short nod then walked over to the empty chair. His hand felt the cool stone backing, his eyes taking it all in. This was it, he thought. He was about to sit on the Council as a High Scholar. For all intents and purposes, it ought to be a moment of great pride.

But as he took his seat and the other High Scholars dove into lively discussion, reality came to him in a series of stark reminders: the lack of formal induction, the disdain of the Elder Scholar, the pity and shame in Zoph's expression...

Zoph. He watched his teacher converse with the other council members, each one making suggestions for the coming announcement. Though he knew he ought to focus on their conversation, the sight of his mentor and the memory of their meeting led to a terrible revelation.

Could it be? Had he asked about Secundus because of the upcoming Visit? Did the Scholarship know what the Palace was doing? Even if they didn't, surely the Historian would find out...

Sev shuddered, unable to contain his discomfort. Suddenly, things were a lot less clear—maybe he should have told Zoph everything? No, his parting oath forbid it, but what were the consequences of silence?

With supreme effort, he buried these questions in the back of his mind. This was not the way to spend his first time in the coveted chair. Besides, brooding on these issues would not help—there was really only one answer.

***

That evening, Sev stood with the other members of the Council at the front of the Hall of Nourishment. The entire Scholarship had been called in for a celebratory meal, and there was a collective excitement among the Scholars gathered before them. But despite the smiles surrounding him, Sev was in a sour mood.

He had spent most of his first rotation on the Council as a silent observer. His peers had debated and delegated the enormous list of tasks the upcoming event necessitated, assigning different jobs to different members of the Scholarship. At no point in time did they so much as acknowledge his presence, and while he tried to look past it, the exclusion ate at him.

He knew he shouldn't take their neglect personally—it was no surprise that in the rotations leading up to the Arrival, its leadership would be tremendously busy—but he felt more useless as a High Scholar than he had as a Scholar. Worst of all, he couldn't help assuming this neglect was directly related to the Palace's operations…

In his time at the Scholarship, Sev had always been told knowledge and truth were paramount, that no question should go unanswered. Yet he knew there was at least one path the Scholarship refused to explore, a path the Palace had decided to take in secret and one related to their enigmatic neighbor. Ever since he switched his robes, he assured himself he would never have to reveal what he knew, but now? Was this the only way to get the Council's blessing?

These rhetorical questions were of no use—he needed to speak to Zoph. True, there was something off-putting about the way their last meeting had ended, and of course there was the way the man had reacted that morning, but Sev didn't know where else to turn. For eight revolutions, Zoph had been the man to give answers, especially to his most important questions. During the council, he hadn't had an opportunity to speak with him, but he hoped he might be able to after the announcement.

The announcement. Sev should be excited for what he was about to witness, but he knew all of the Scholars gathered before them were expecting something entirely different.

"Greetings, Scholars."

The Elder Scholar began his speech, and the hall went quiet. Sev tried to ignore the hundreds of furtive glances in his direction—they only made this worse.

"There is news this Council wishes to share—news the likes of which our Scholarship has not experienced in an extraordinary amount of time."

A murmur among the Scholars made Sev frown. This introduction seemed over the top to them, given the expectation. But their presumption was about to be subverted, and Sev's time as the center of attention was at its end.

For a moment, he wondered what Folin was thinking, standing out there in the crowd. But it didn't matter. This was not what his friend expected either.

"I want to remind us all of why we are here. You and your predecessors have spent revolution after revolution collecting and recording the knowledge and history of Primus, organizing and cataloging massive amounts of information... and for what?"

The murmur was gone, and Sev looked up at his peers. Some were confused, and a few shot glances in his direction, but most had their eyes locked on the Elder Scholar, a mix of disbelief and hope in their expression. These individuals had no doubt guessed, though few would dare to believe.

At the sight of these wide-eyed colleagues, and knowing the news they were about to receive, Sev felt his anger fade. Frustrated as he might be, this was a wonderful moment, one no one would ever forget.

"We all know the answer to that question, no doubt. The Scholarship exists to serve the Historian, to prepare for his Visit."

The Elder Scholar paused, allowing himself a rare smile, and Sev saw that all eyes were on their leader.

"Scholarship of Primus, the next Visit is on the horizon. In seven rotations, we will gather at the landing site of the Vessel to celebrate his Arrival."

The Elder Scholar barely managed to finish his statement before the entire hall was on its feet, cheering. Scholars turned to their brothers in disbelief, embracing each other with unbridled joy. It was an incredible sight, and Sev couldn't help but smile, feeling the collective excitement around him.

After a while, the noise subsided, and the Elder Scholar took the opportunity to close his speech.

"Eat well, Scholars, for the next few rotations will be the busiest we've ever experienced. Your assignments will come before Olius's first light."

The crowd sat back down, chatter filling the hall. Sev was so absorbed in the scene, it wasn't until he felt a tap on his shoulder that he knew it was time to go—or so he thought.

"Your orders, High Scholar."

Sev turned at the unfamiliar voice to find a servant before him, parchment in hand. He searched his surroundings for the other High Scholars and saw them leaving the Hall of Nourishment, heading back to the Room of Council.

Anger and embarrassment took hold, and a cold chill swept over him. How many of the Scholars were watching right now? How many had seen this public disavowal?

He snatched the parchment from the servant's hand, but the man's shocked reaction only angered him further. For a moment the two stared at one another, and Sev wondered why he hadn't left.

"Something else?"

"High Scholar, y—you have a visitor."

Sev peered at him, confused. A visitor?

"Who?"

Seeing the anger fade, the servant relaxed.

"The patriarch of the eastern fork. He waits outside your chamber."

Sev nodded.

"Is that all?"

The servant nodded.

"Yes, High Scholar."

Sev watched him walk away, then opened the parchment. Inside were orders to rest the night and rejoin the Council at first light. No surprises there—though this visitor was a surprise. What did a village leader want from a High Scholar?

Sev marched toward his chambers, thankful he was far enough behind the rest of the Council that he could neither see nor hear them enter the Room without him. His initial anger had faded, mostly at the realization that few Scholars would have noticed what had happened—after the announcement of the Arrival, who could pay attention to anything?

Still, the manner in which he had been left up there, by himself, was concerning. It was one thing to ask him to act as an observer, and even to postpone his induction, but to humiliate him in front of the rest of the Scholarship?

No, Sev thought to himself, humiliate was a word his past self would use. This was not the intention of the High Scholars, and he was not a soldier any longer. Here, things were out in the open, and he had to accept it—he had thought perhaps his lack of induction might be a secret for only the rest of the Council, but that wasn't how the Scholarship worked: truth was paramount, and knowledge was shared by all. Even if it made Sev unhappy or uncomfortable, the rest of the Scholars had a right to know his promotion was pending.

But was it really? Was he not wearing the robe and living in the chambers? And why hadn't they tossed his induction in at the beginning of the announcement? There was no need to make it a grand ceremony, and the Arrival could immediately overshadow it.

Sev frowned. It seemed as if the questions kept piling on, and his one solution—talk to Zoph—had slipped away, at least for the rest of the rotation. Would he have a chance on the next one?

His thoughts were interrupted by a familiar face just outside his door: the taller man from the Hall of Arbitration. The face was not a happy one, and Sev knew right away this was going to be a difficult conversation— though he wondered why the man was here at all.

"Greetings, citizen," Sev said.

The man looked him up and down, a hint of surprise crossing his expression. No doubt he knew what the change in robes signified, and Sev could see the hesitation take over.

"High Scholar," he managed to say, disbelief and respect clear in his tone.

Sev stepped past him, opening the door to his chamber.

"Please, come in."

The man bowed his head in deference, then stepped inside. Sev followed, closing the door behind him.

"How can I help you?"

Again, the man hesitated, shifting his weight and avoiding eye contact.

"High Scholar, I apologize, I didn't know…"

Sev felt a hint of impatience but repressed it. Where else did he have to go?

"Please, citizen, speak your mind."

The man met his gaze and nodded.

"High Scholar, I come to you with news regarding the Arbitration."

Sev thought back to the tense gathering, and he wondered when he would next see Folin.

"Yes?"

"My comrade—the father upon whom the life-debt was placed—was killed last rotation."

Sev frowned.

"I'm sorry to hear that."

But the man wasn't finished.

"High Scholar, after the Arbitration, the soldier followed me to my village and asked to see the man. I tried to deny him, but how can I deny a soldier of the Palace?"

Sev's frown deepened, and a discomfort came over him.

"I thought he might kill him then and there, but he didn't even speak to him. He just… looked at him."

The man's hesitation was gone, and Sev could feel the rage bubbling beneath his words.

"The next rotation, I made the trek with him to the other village to begin his life-debt. When we reached our destination, the other patriarch was not alone—no, the same soldier was there, waiting."

He paused, and he gave Sev a piercing look—one that made him reassess many of his thoughts on the peasant populace. There was no doubt this man was educated.

"High Scholar, he was only one rotation into his life-debt when he was cut down. Allegedly, he incited violence against a solider. This is not only a lie, it is a farce. The Palace is making a mockery of Arbitration!"

Just as he concluded his speech, the man noticed the aggression in his tone and lowered his head in shame.

"My apologies, High Scholar."

This final bit of deference sent Sev over the edge, into a dangerous empathy. Here was a man facing a situation he felt unjust, searching for recourse in any way he could. And though he would never admit it outwardly, the man was almost certainly right: of course the soldier would take matters into his own hands. After all, there was no direct proof, and there never would be.

"Patriarch, this must be addressed."

The man looked up, startled at the reply, and Sev himself wondered what had gotten into him—it was as if the man's frustration was contagious. Still, what was he thinking? This couldn't be addressed—to do so would be to contradict the Palace, and such contradiction might lead to death. But right now, with so much pent up resentment, Sev was lashing out.

"I will look into the matter personally. What is your name?"

The man stared at him in awe, clearly not expecting such an answer.

"Hibbon of Primus, High Scholar."

"You were a Pupil once, I take it?"

Hibbon nodded.

"Yes, High Scholar. I thought to take the Olian oath but a woman—and then family—took precedence."

Sev smiled. The man would have made a good Scholar.

"High Scholar, if I may ask…"

"Yes?"

"I heard quite a commotion while I waited—what was that?"

Sev almost chuckled. How long would it take for this news to reach the farthest villages? Three rotations? Four? The man's villagers no doubt already knew.

"The Historian comes, Hibbon. The Arrival is in seven rotations."

The man's eyes widened, and he stepped toward the door.

"High Scholar, I have made an error. I cannot take your attention away from this historic event. Please accept my apologies, for I didn't know."

Sev frowned. In most circumstances, the man would be right—a High Scholar had no time for distractions with a Visit on the horizon. But given his ongoing ostracism, Sev needed a task to occupy himself with.

"Hibbon, there is no need to apologize. I will help you."

The man shook his head emphatically.

"High Scholar, I cannot, in good conscience, accept your help."

The man's insistence frustrated Sev.

"Then don't take it in good conscience, but I am helping all the same."

Hibbon heard the anger in the High Scholar's voice and lowered his head once more.

"I did not mean to anger you, High Scholar."

Sev sighed, shaking his head. Frustrated though he may be, this emotional turmoil he was experiencing was not befit a High Scholar.

"Hibbon, no apologies are necessary. I am allowing my personal feelings to get the better of me. Please, return to your village, as I am sure the news of the Arrival will necessitate your presence. I will reach out to you about this matter when I am able."

Hibbon hesitated, then nodded.

"Yes, High Scholar. Thank you for your time."

He opened the door and left Sev alone in the chamber, wondering how in the world he would fulfill this promise.

***

Sev's second full rotation as a High Scholar started much like the first, with one exception: the mood in the Scholarship. Though the loss of High Scholar Dren was not forgotten, Sev would be lying if he said it wasn't overshadowed. In reality, Dren himself wouldn't mind—this was the Arrival after all.

It was every Scholar's dream to live through such a Visit, but to simultaneously hold the position of High Scholar? Sev knew he ought to feel overwhelming excitement, that he should be supremely thankful for the opportunity he had been afforded, but these feelings were eclipsed by the doubt and frustration clouding his mind.

He knew he had to speak to Zoph, and soon. Patience was useless here, as things would only worsen with time. Still, he sat through the morning council as an observer, trying to pay attention to the proceedings before him rather than brood on his misgivings. What he needed was an opportunity to catch his mentor alone, something that was easier said than done.

The mid-rotation meal was taken in the Room, and short of following him on an alleviation, Sev had no options. As the evening council came to an end, Sev worried he would have to wait yet another rotation—if the Elder Scholar dismissed him but everyone else stayed, there would be no chance to see Zoph alone. But to his surprise, the Elder Scholar dismissed everyone, asking them all to catch up on much-needed sleep.

Sev tried to linger, to catch his mentor on the way out, but the other High Scholars left in haste—no doubt eager to spend some time alone and catch their breath. He watched them rush to their chambers and frowned. Now was not the time to interrupt Zoph, the man needed a few moments to himself. But he couldn't wait forever.

Inside his own chamber, Sev found dinner but no parchment—the Elder Scholar had asked to see them all at first light on the next rotation, so he knew his orders. He sat at the table and stared at the meal, wondering what Folin was doing. It was strange not to have seen him for so long, but given Sev was locked in the Room of Council most of the last two rotations, it wasn't surprising.

Actually, Sev thought, he knew exactly what Folin was doing—the Council had discussed it in detail. Yet it was a vague memory, one clouded by his own frustration, and he realized just how poorly he had been paying attention. The opportunity of a lifetime—to be on the Council in the rotations before an Arrival—and Sev was more concerned with his own problems.

He slammed his fist on the table in anger. What was wrong with him? Why couldn't he focus on the priorities here? The Historian was on the verge of a Visit and this was what worried him?

He closed his eyes and took a deep breath, leaning back in his chair. These questions were futile, and try as he might, he did not have the patience of a man like Folin. He needed to speak with Zoph, it was the only way to clear his conscience. Besides, there was also the other matter, the matter of the Palace's secrets…

He opened his eyes and stood. It was now or never.

Sev exited his room and walked three doors down, stopping in front of the familiar stone entrance. For the first time in his eight revolutions at the Scholarship, he felt anxious at the thought of the person he was about to see. Why?

He ignored this bizarre feeling and knocked. The stress was getting to him, that's all.

The door swung inward and he stood face to face with his mentor.

"High Scholar Zoph, may I speak to you in private?"

A shadow of anger came over the man's face, and for a moment Sev thought his unannounced visit had been a mistake. But just as quick as it had built, the anger faded, replaced by the same look of pity he had seen in the Room of Council.

"Come in, Sev."

Zoph stepped aside and Sev walked in. His former teacher's private quarters matched his own in almost every way: the layout was identical, as were the furnishings. And yet, at a glance, Sev could tell that these quarters had been occupied for far longer than his own.

"I'm sorry I've been avoiding you."

Sev turned to face his mentor, surprised to hear him openly admit it.

"I assume you're wondering why I have acted this way, why I haven't congratulated you on your promotion?"

Sev nodded.

"Yes, High Scholar."

Zoph stared at him for a few moments, and for a third time Sev saw the man's pity. Then his former teacher looked away and sighed.

"Sev, do you know our purpose?"

This question caught him off-guard.

"The Scholarship's purpose?"

"Yes."

He eyed his mentor curiously before responding.

"We are the bridge between Olius and Primus, charged with the collection of knowledge between each Visit. We document the history of Primus until we are able to pass along this knowledge to the Historian."

Sev had known the answer to this question since before his rotations as a Pupil. Why was Zoph asking him this?

"Precisely. We are the bridge between Olius and Primus. A Scholar's robe combines the colors of the star and the planet, symbolizing this bridge. And these—"

His mentor grabbed a fold of his own robe.

"These shed the colors of Primus altogether. Though we are all of Primus, we are the servants of Olius, first and foremost. And that is why I have not congratulated you, Sev. That is why the rest of the Council eyes you with suspicion."

A coldness came over Sev, one of sharp discomfort deep in his chest. Was this what he thought it was?

"But, High Scholar, I do not understand. I wear the colors of Olius just as you do. I am a servant of Olius just as you are."

There was pain in his voice, and he made no attempt to hide it. To even consider that his trusted mentor held the same prejudices as some of his peers… it was almost too much to bear.

Zoph, for his part, sensed his pupil's fear and frowned.

"Sev, this is not what you think it is…"

Sev stared at him expectantly, begging for an explanation, but Zoph hesitated in his reply, choosing his words carefully.

"Do you know how a new High Scholar is selected, Sev?"

The question caught him off-guard, as had the last one.

"The Council select a number of candidates and the Elector chooses among them."

Zoph smiled, but there was a sadness in the expression—one that ignited an entirely different dread in Sev's mind.

"Indeed that is the technical procedure. But that's not what happens in practice. In practice, the Council presents only one candidate to the Elector, whom the Elector then approves. The Elector's role is largely ceremonial."

As he listened, the dread grew—a premonition of where the conversation was heading, an intuition that had already connected the dots.

"When High Scholar Dren passed away, we began the process of determining our candidate. But before we could make any definite progress, news of the Arrival came to us, and we decided to deal with his replacement after the Visit."

Finally, the fog was cleared, and he understood.

"Sev, the Elector promoted you without any input from the Council. This came as a surprise to us, but once again, we were too busy to properly handle the situation. Besides, eight rotations before the Arrival is not the time to divide the Palace and the Scholarship. That is why we have temporarily recognized your promotion, at least until the Departure."

The two shared a silence, and the mentor's sadness passed on to his student. Sev felt the weight of this new knowledge and retreated into his thoughts.

"My promotion…"

Zoph sighed.

"You would've been my choice, Sev. I would've argued in your favor. I cannot say the Council would've selected you, but I can say you were always an option."

Sev looked at his mentor once more, a spark of hope emerging to fight the dread.

"High Scholar, is there a way I can prove myself worthy of this position?"

Zoph frowned.

"I do not mean to give you hope, Sev. It would be almost impossible for you to fill the role you have been given. Though your robe is white and gold, your promotion was purple and black. To make matters worse, not all eye you without prejudice, as you already know."

Here, Sev saw sincere sympathy, and he was glad at least to have one fear vanquished.

"This is a complicated issue that will be dealt with in due time. For now, we must concentrate on the Arrival and the duties we are assigned. After the Visit, perhaps we can address these questions."

Zoph sighed, and Sev saw some of the tension leave his mentor's body.

"We do not know why the Elector has acted in this manner, but it is worrisome."

Now it was Sev's turn to tense; though he understood Zoph's message, it was dangerous to make such remarks.

"High Scholar, what are you saying?"

His mentor seemed to catch his suspicion, and the wall came back up, a shadow of anger returning to his expression.

"That's enough, Sev. The Arrival approaches and I must prepare. I suggest you do the same, especially if you wish to prove yourself a High Scholar."

He opened the door and gestured for him to exit. Sev looked at the open door then back to his former teacher.

"My apologies, High Scholar Zoph. I do want to thank you for what you have said—that I was your choice. I appreciate everything you have done for me."

He saw some of the anger fade away, but there was no reply from his mentor. He left the man's quarters, the door closing behind him.

***

Sev woke the next morning surprisingly well-rested. As he took his morning meal and prepared for another rotation of exclusion, he realized just how much his conversation with Zoph had helped. Yes, it had been somewhat contentious, and yes, the implication of how his promotion had unraveled brought him great distress, but now he understood why the Council treated him so. Most of all, Sev was relieved it had nothing to do with Secundus.

Perhaps that was a stretch—after all, it had everything to do with his time at the Palace, which included the secrets he knew—but he was glad Zoph hadn't mentioned their neighbor. If the price of acceptance had been the knowledge of Secundus, he wasn't sure what he would have done. Unfortunately, this also meant the path to induction was far less clear: how could he erase the purple and black from his promotion?

At first, he had briefly considered renouncing the robes and returning to his previous position, but the thought was short-lived: beyond his own vanity and pride—reasons he tried so hard to deny—there was the Elector to consider. Open rejection of his promotion was ill-advised, to put it lightly. After all, why else had the other High Scholars tentatively accepted his role, if not to appease the most powerful man on Primus?

But in five rotations, the balance of power on their planet would turn upside down. The Council knew it, Sev knew it, and the Elector knew it. Did the Council mean to undo his promotion with the approval of the Historian? A complicated proposal with its own set of political consequences, but Sev could do little to prevent it. Unless, of course, he did what Zoph said was nearly impossible: prove himself worthy of the position, circumstances be damned.

So that morning, only five away from the Arrival, Sev entered the Room of Council with newfound purpose. Despite Zoph's revelation, he felt no shame, only hunger—hunger to be what he knew he was capable of, hunger to fulfill his dream. He paid even more attention to the words shared, the lines of inquiry followed... there was so much going on, so much to get done in preparation, it wasn't hard to feed that hunger, to occupy his mind.

He rode the wave through most of the rotation, absorbing everything he could from the proceedings before him, but it couldn't last forever. When the rotation came to a close, when the Elder Scholar singled him out for dismissal while the rest stayed, when there was no more frenetic activity to engage his thoughts... then, the questions threatened to return.

He needed a new diversion, and he knew just the thing. The only problem was finding Folin: there were more people in the halls than Sev had ever seen—every Scholar on Primus was on their way to the Scholarship in preparation for the Arrival. Already, the Hall of Slumber spilled into the adjacent corridors, and it was a struggle to get from one point to another.

Faces he had never seen before made way for his robes, greeting him with more respect than he had ever received from the campus regulars. It was refreshing, if not overwhelming, but he kept his eyes peeled for one in particular, one that had to be around here somewhere...

"High Scholar!"

He turned and saw the familiar smile, realizing as Folin approached just how much he had missed his friend.

"Folin."

The two shared a quick embrace.

"How are you?" Folin asked.

Sev shot a glance at their surroundings.

"Overwhelmed," he replied.

Folin nodded, still smiling.

"Aren't we all? The rotation's council is over?" he asked.

Sev nodded.

"I'm sure I was meant to rest in my chambers but I wanted to speak to you."

Folin gave him a curious look.

"What is it, Sev?"

Sev smiled, happy to hear the man use his name rather than his title.

"Do you mind if we go to my chambers? I prefer to speak in private."

Folin's curiosity grew, but he nodded.

"Of course."

They started off back the way Sev had come.

"I am not taking you from your duties, am I?" Sev asked.

"No. Surprisingly I managed to finish, though I'm sure I'll receive another batch before Olius's light returns. There are so many bodies here yet it's as if we don't have enough to get all the work done. But I'm sure you're well aware of that."

Sev nodded. The subject was indeed familiar to him, having observed the last few councils. The High Scholars were struggling to get everything in order, and while many things were going according to plan, just as many were seemingly falling apart. He had wondered, absentmindedly, what the councils were usually like: those on normal rotations, without an Arrival imminent.

They reached his chambers and stepped inside, Sev closing the door behind them.

"Have a seat," he said, gesturing to the table.

Folin did as asked.

"What is it you wanted to discuss?"

Sev took the seat across from him, hesitating. What was he thinking, bringing this up five rotations before the Arrival? Still, they had come this far, and he needed something to distract him.

"Do you remember the Arbitration a few rotations ago?"

Folin nodded, the curiosity back in his expression.

"Yes."

"One of the patriarchs came and visited me just after the Elder Scholar announced the Arrival."

Consternation mixed into the curiosity, but Sev continued.

"According to this citizen, the accused was sent to pay his life-debt and not more than one rotation later, he was killed by a soldier of the Palace."

Folin peered at him with surprising intensity, the same look he had given him just after his promotion.

"For what cause?"

"Apparently for inciting violence," Sev replied.

Again, Folin stared at him, to the point Sev felt uneasy.

"It was the leader of the accused who came to speak to you?" he asked.

"Yes."

"And what did he want?"

Sev hesitated.

"Justice."

Folin frowned.

"He thinks the soldier killed the accused without just cause?"

Sev nodded.

"He thinks it was related to the soldier at the Arbitration. According to him, the same soldier was with the other patriarch when the accused arrived for his life-debt."

"Does he have any proof?"

Now it was Sev who frowned.

"No."

Folin's gaze broke off, and the two shared a moment of contemplative silence.

"Folin…"

His friend looked up and Sev hesitated, searching for the right words, ones that wouldn't necessarily be treasonous.

"If this man is right, if this soldier acted in the manner described, it would be in violation of the Arbitration."

Folin leaned forward, the intensity back in his eyes.

"And what do you think, Sev?"

There was something surprisingly eager about Folin's tone, and Sev realized he had put himself in a corner. This was exactly the kind of conversation he had thought his mentor shouldn't have, and yet here he was having it. If he spoke the truth now and somehow word got out, he could face execution.

"I think these soldiers, as representatives of the Palace, are bound to speak the truth of their actions. If a citizen disagrees but has no proof, then there is nothing that can be done."

He felt a stab of shame as he spoke dishonestly—was this proving himself worthy of the robes he now wore?—but he didn't know how else to respond. What good was a High Scholar that got himself killed?

"I think the citizen is right, and I wouldn't be surprised if the soldier was involved in the accused's death."

Sev stared at his friend in shock. To speak such words outwardly...

"And," Folin continued, standing, "I think you agree. But I understand your hesitation, your struggle—especially given your past."

He took three strides to the door, and Sev watched with wide eyes, unsure of how to react.

"I only hope that now, as High Scholar, you remember there is no purple and black in your robes."

Folin smiled.

"Actions hold far more weight than words do, Sev. Choose your actions wisely."

And with that, he opened the door and left.

Arrival

Sev woke the next morning angry and frustrated. He had spent the night contemplating Folin's near-treasonous words—words he himself believed but dared not speak. Twice now Scholars he held in high esteem had shown hints of defiance toward the Palace, and it made him wonder how blind he could have been. Were they just now growing comfortable around him? Or perhaps the coming Arrival gave these men the courage to stand up for what they thought was right?

In either case, Sev couldn't help but feel ashamed. Folin was not afraid to speak the truth, yet it was Sev who wore the robes of the Council. Of course, given Zoph's revelation, these details only served to emphasize the insecurity looming in his mind. He didn't deserve this position, and he wasn't sure he could ever prove himself worthy.

The rotation's councils helped distract him, but he no longer felt the hunger he had before. In fact, he came to the conclusion that the hunger was simply a symptom of his denial, of his inability to accept the reality of where he was and why.

And yet, despite everything weighing him down, Sev managed to hold onto one thread of purpose: the Arbitration. By learning as much as he could about the death of the accused father, Sev thought he could bring justice to the situation—something that wouldn't prove him worthy of his spot among the twelve, but at least it would ease his conscience. So as soon as the Elder Scholar dismissed him, he left not just the Room of Council but the Scholarship itself, setting off toward the eastern ridge—toward the village where the supposed injustice had occurred.

The night sky was filled with stars, a beautiful view for any that cared to look, but Sev's eyes were on his surroundings, on the path ahead. It wasn't always wise to roam Primus at night—bands of criminals roamed the region—but he hoped his High Scholar's robes would protect him from all but the most brazen of peasants.

There—three figures walking the path, approaching him. The glow from their hips made it clear they were armed—soldiers with hotswords—and suddenly Sev had to ask himself: what if the criminals he encountered weren't peasants?

"Who goes there?" one of the soldiers barked, and Sev saw all three hotswords exit their sheaths, the lights of the blades revealing their faces.

"High Scholar Sev of Primus," he announced.

The soldiers looked at one another hesitantly, putting away their weapons.

"Does the High Scholar need an escort?"

Sev stopped a few paces from the men, eyeing the leader curiously. He could tell the question was not one of decorum—these soldiers wanted to know what he was up to.

"I don't wish to interrupt your duties, sirs."

This answer didn't please him, and Sev watched the man's contorted expression as he searched for the right response.

"The life of a Councilman supersedes our current obligation. Where are you headed, High Scholar?"

Councilman—a term used only by the Palace, one that could sometimes be taken derogatorily. In this instance, Sev chose to take it neutrally.

"I am headed to the village just before the grand ridge." Then, after a pause, "If you wish to join me, you are more than welcome, though I repeat I have no need for escort."

The soldier nodded, glancing at his colleagues. Sev knew what was going through his mind: is it worth it to follow this man all the way to the village, just to see what he's up to?

"Very well, Councilman. May you have safe passage."

Sev forced a smile.

"Thank you, sirs."

As he walked past the men, he felt their eyes on him, the curiosity in their minds. Truth be told, he himself wasn't sure what he was doing: once he got to the village, he planned to speak to the victim's family—the first victim, the one killed by the father—but he had no idea how to find them, and he wasn't sure if the patriarch would help him. In fact, he was a little worried about what the leader might do if he saw him, but if the position of High Scholar couldn't protect him from a typical citizen, it wasn't worth much.

After a few uneventful encounters with wandering peasants, Sev reached his destination. The village sat against a tall ridge that ran along Olius's path, giving it more shade than the surrounding areas. It wasn't enough for crops, but from the light of the remaining fires, Sev could see thick shrubbery surrounding the huts.

A few peasants stood around one of the fires, watching his approach. Two of them made to confront the intruder, but when they saw the robes of white and gold, they hesitated.

"Citizens," Sev began, taking the opportunity to speak, "I am looking for a family—the family of the man who was killed."

They looked at one another, then back at Sev. There was reverence in their eyes, but it couldn't mask an undercurrent of suspicion. Not that Sev could blame them: what was a High Scholar doing here, in the middle of the night, asking such questions? Particularly given what had just happened to the accused killer.

"What is happening?"

Sev looked behind the men to see the patriarch—the short man from the Arbitration—coming toward them.

"Sir, this master of the Scholarship has come to see Rivin's family."

The patriarch caught up to his men, shocked at the sight of the white and gold robes.

"High Scholar? What brings you—"

Recognition cut him short, and Sev saw reverence disappear, replaced by distrust.

"What do you want?"

There was venom in his voice, enough to surprise his two companions.

"It is as your men say. I am here to see the family of the man who was killed. The subject of the Arbitration."

The man peered at him through the darkness, and Sev cursed his own recklessness. What was he doing? What did he plan to accomplish?

"You were the one they promoted, then?"

There was no less malice in the tone, though Sev knew he used the question to stall. The man was trying to see through Sev's plan, or at least decide how much leverage he could have against a high-ranking member of the Scholarship. No doubt the man wished a soldier of the Palace would appear, someone to even the scales.

"Indeed. Now if you don't mind, citizen, it is late, and the Arrival approaches. Will you allow me to meet with the family?"

At the mention of the Historian's coming, the man stiffened, and Sev knew he had him. No one could balance the scales against the being of Olius, not even the Elector himself.

"Very well. Come with me."

The man turned in a huff, marching back toward the village, and Sev had to hustle to keep up. The other two peasants didn't budge, watching him pass with deepened curiosity. Though he knew the robes kept him safe, Sev couldn't help but feel the lack of weight at his hip—what he would give to hold a hotsword right now… but such was not the way of Olius, not the way of the Scholarship.

The patriarch led him to one of the huts closest to the ridge, then tapped on the outside frame. Sev had seen many huts like this before— they were the most common form of lodging built by the peasants—but each village had its own unique style. Here, curtains of thick hide were reinforced by the surrounding shrubbery, another layer of protection from the elements.

A hand pulled back the front flap, revealing a woman's head. She caught sight of the patriarch first, and Sev saw a flash of fear in her eyes.

"Sorry to disturb you, miss," he said.

The woman turned her attention to this unknown voice and looked Sev up and down. As she noticed the robes and understood their significance, her eyes widened.

"You're…" she began, then fell silent, glancing at the patriarch.

Sev frowned.

"Miss, I wanted to ask you about the man from the other village, the one sent here on a life-debt to your family."

The woman hesitated, shooting another terrified glance at the village leader.

"This is what you want to ask her?" he began. "I can—"

"Silence!" Sev shouted.

The patriarch recoiled, caught off-guard by Sev's ferocity.

"Miss," he continued, ignoring the village leader, "I want to hear from you what happened."

She stared at the High Scholar with a mix of admiration and fear, and Sev wondered if he had pushed it too far. Though his eyes were fixed on the woman, he could feel the growing anger in the man beside him, a man not used to being humiliated before his subjects.

"Master Scholar," she began in earnest, and for the briefest of moments, Sev thought he had her, thought his trip was a success—but another quick glance at the patriarch brought her guard back up, shifting her tone completely. "…there is not much to tell."

Sev frowned.

"All the same, I wish to hear it."

She nodded without making eye contact.

"The man came a few rotations ago and set to work. On the next rotation, he attacked a soldier and was killed."

There was no conviction in her voice, no truth.

"You saw this yourself?" he asked.

The woman looked at the patriarch then back at the ground.

"Yes, Master Scholar."

Sev's frown deepened.

"Very well. Miss, I want to let you know the Scholarship will provide for your family. I will see to it this situation is resolved."

The woman looked up at him, surprised.

"Th—thank you, sir."

Sev smiled.

"The Scholarship will do what it can. Go with Olius."

Before she could reply, he turned around and started walking back the way he had come, toward the fires in the middle of the village. It wasn't long before the patriarch caught himself up.

"You plan to return?" he asked.

Sev stopped, glanced around to make sure they were alone, then looked the leader in the eyes.

"Yes, and I plan to convey her story to the Historian himself, just to be sure."

Terror came over the man's expression, and Sev allowed himself to enjoy the moment, to soak in the man's horrific realization: the being of Olius always knew the truth. Always.

"But... but this is a waste of his time! You need not worry him with this matter!"

Unfortunately, not only was it doubtful Sev would ever have the opportunity to share any time with the Historian, this was a gross misuse of his rank. The Scholarship did not operate on subtle threats, nor did it use its powers as leverage against the citizenship of Primus. This was the old Sev coming out, the one from the Palace.

"The Historian will decide what is worth his time, citizen. Now as I have said, the Arrival is imminent, and I must be going. Thank you for your hospitality."

Sev turned and continued walking, but he only managed a few steps before the patriarch called after him.

"Do you walk alone, High Scholar?"

Sev hesitated, understanding the meaning underneath the man's words. He turned to face the leader.

"Yes, citizen. I spent several revolutions in the Palace before my time at the Scholarship. But I appreciate your concern."

And with that, he turned back and marched into the darkness, ignoring the hint of fear within him. Perhaps he should have taken the offer of escort?

***

The next rotation's councils were difficult. After spending most of the night walking the trails of Primus on high alert, Sev got less than half the sleep he was used to. He had lost the ability to focus, and had he been asked to participate, it would not have gone well. For the first time since his contentious promotion, Sev was relieved to be ignored.

Though he wished he could talk to Folin, to relate what had happened in the village, that would have to wait. After his dismissal, he rushed out of the Room of Council and went straight to his chamber, hoping to catch up on sleep. As he opened the door and stepped inside, only one thing was on his mind: would he eat his evening meal or skip it entirely?

"Good evening, High Scholar."

Sev jumped in surprise, staring at the man sitting by his table: the purple and black uniform, the weapon at his hip, the smug smile on his lips.

"How did you get in here?"

Sev looked back at the door, as if it held the answer, as if it would explain to him why the soldier from the Arbitration was in his private quarters.

"One of the servants said I could wait here."

Sev turned his attention back to the intruder and frowned. A servant would never allow such a thing, though a servant wasn't in any position to tell a man with a hotsword what they could or couldn't do.

"Why are you here?"

The soldier smiled again.

"Why, to congratulate you, of course. Promoted to High Scholar, that's quite an honor."

Finally, Sev took control of himself, remembering what kind of person he was dealing with, what kind of game they were playing. He took two steps forward and pulled out the other chair, taking a seat at the table.

"Thank you. It is indeed. The Elector gave me the news himself."

The smile disappeared from the soldier's lips, and Sev could see the gears turning once more, trying to plot the right course of action.

"I heard you visited one of the villages last night."

Now it was Sev's turn to smile.

"That's right, the village under the eastern ridge. I didn't realize the Palace was so invested in my comings and goings."

There was no more satisfaction in the soldier's expression.

"And why did you go the village?"

Sev hesitated, glancing at the sheathed hotsword. This imbecile had made a bold move, coming into the private chamber of a High Scholar. Too bold.

"That's none of your business."

The soldier stiffened, and Sev braced himself in turn.

"You dare speak this way to a man of the Palace?"

It took all of Sev's energy to maintain his outward composure. His heart was beating furiously in his chest, and he wondered how he could ever be so stupid? This whole situation was spiraling out of control, and for what? To pursue his vague idea of justice? To make himself feel accomplished, to make up for the humiliation he felt for his exclusion on the Council? This was not the way to prove himself a High Scholar—in fact, quite the opposite.

Still, he had dug a hole now, a hole he needed to get out of. And in that moment, he saw the way.

"If you'd like, we can take this issue up with the Elector. As I said, he promoted me personally."

This the soldier had not expected, and again Sev saw the gears turning, trying to decide how to get out of this with his pride intact. But where he would normally feel victory, or at least a sense of righteousness, Sev only saw a mirror.

"So be it," the soldier barked, rising out of his chair violently.

The outburst startled the High Scholar, who nearly fell out of his own chair, but the soldier barely noticed, marching out the door in anger.

Sev watched him leave, closing the door behind him, then frowned. What had he done?

***

Despite his lack of late-night wandering, Sev was no more rested the following morning. In fact, when he reached the council, he found himself even less focused, unable to follow almost any thread of conversation without getting lost in his own thoughts.

The fallout from the Arbitration was out of hand. A soldier breaking into his quarters? The threats he had made using both the Historian and the Elector? This was the opposite of a High Scholar's behavior, the opposite of him proving himself worthy.

Worst of all was his seeming inability to realize the magnitude of what was going to happen in two rotations: two mornings from now, they would gather to watch the Vessel of Olius on its final approach, and all he could think about was the death of a random peasant?

No, Sev realized, even that was giving himself too much credit: he didn't care about the man's fate, he cared about the implications it carried for him as a High Scholar, for him as a person in a position of authority—authority he had yet to earn.

Now Zoph's reaction made perfect sense. His mentor had known him better than he had known himself, and the man saw the purple and black was still deep inside of him, deeper than any white and gold.

He shot a glance across the table, watching his teacher say a few words to the other High Scholars without actually hearing them. He had let this man down, and in a way that was unforgivable.

Just then, a man entered the Room of Council and caught everyone's attention—even Sev's. His robes were the same color as the soldier's uniform, an unusual sight mid-council.

"Council of Primus, I have an urgent summons from the Elector."

The Elder Scholar eyed the envoy warily.

"For whom?"

"High Scholar Sev of Primus."

All eyes turned to him.

"He is requested at the Palace immediately."

A murmur would have been better than the silence that followed. Sev could feel their eyes on him, their judgements and assumptions, their distrust and suspicion. For six rotations now he had sunk further and further into obscurity, managing to make himself nearly invisible, but now he was front and center.

"Very well," said the Elder Scholar. "High Scholar Sev, you are dismissed for the rotation."

Sev felt another pang of embarrassment: the Elder Scholar was dismissing him for the rest of the rotation, even though it was only the morning council. If the meeting with the Elector ended early, he was not welcome back in the chamber.

"Thank you, Elder Scholar," he replied, standing.

He shuffled around the table's edge and joined the envoy on the floor.

"If you permit, we will go to the Palace now," the man stated.

Sev nodded, the eyes of the Council burning holes in his head.

"Yes, sir. Lead the way."

***

As the three of them walked down the official path—Sev, the envoy, and an escort soldier—a series of theories flashed through Sev's mind, each one as unlikely as the last.

Was this summons related to the soldier's visit? To the Arbitration? No, Sev assured himself, as hotheaded as the young man was, it was lunacy to take this matter all the way up the ladder, especially after what Sev had told him. But if it wasn't that, what was it?

The stark black walls of the Palace loomed ahead, their ominous presence growing ever closer. Inside was cool air, but for once Sev didn't mind the heat. Their entourage had made good time, and though they hadn't cut through the dunes, there was enough hurry in the envoy's pace to exacerbate all of Sev's latent fears.

The soldier broke off at the entrance, and the envoy led Sev through the interior, all the way to the audience chamber.

"The Elector awaits your presence, High Scholar."

His heart racing, Sev stepped into the familiar hall and walked toward the lone chair. The supreme leader sat on his throne, his personal guardians on either side. When he reached the base, Sev dropped to knee and hand.

"Rise, High Scholar."

Sev obeyed, realizing once more he didn't know whether to look the man in the eye or avoid his gaze.

"Sev of Primus, I have summoned you on this, two rotations before the Arrival, to ask what your role will be during the Visit."

A part of him relaxed, realizing the true reason for this appointment—this was not his end. But just as the tension began to fade, Sev found he had no answer.

"I—I do not know, Elector," he replied.

There was a pause, then a hint of a frown came over the supreme leader's expression.

"You do not know?"

A cold fear came over him. Warranted or not, a reply that made the Elector frown was a dangerous one indeed.

"I do not know, Elector. I have not been told anything about my role during the Visit."

His frown deepened, and Sev shot a glance at the guardians. Their swiftness was supposed to be unrivaled—it was said one could feel the heat of the blade before the eyes knew what was coming.

"They have not given you a role? Tell me, Sev of Primus, what have you done since your promotion?"

The Palace's atmosphere was much cooler than the Scholarship's, but Sev felt a strange warmth.

"I have sat as an observer at the councils, Elector."

The frown did not falter.

"An observer? What do you mean, an observer? Have they forbidden you from interacting?"

There was an undercurrent of anger in his questions, and Sev's discomfort grew. He knew the truth would only exacerbate the Elector's displeasure, and Zoph—treasonous though he might be—was right: now was not the time to divide the Palace and the Scholarship. But Sev didn't have much of a choice. His eyes drifted once more to the guardians and their weapons, a reminder of the consequences of omitting the truth.

"Elector, the Council has delayed my induction due to the tremendous workload related to the Arrival."

The Elector eyed Sev, and a tense silence took hold. He dared not look at the supreme leader, worried anger would ignite into rage. Finally, after an unbearable silence, the Elector spoke again.

"High Scholar, why is it that you left the service of the Palace?"

His tone had relaxed, but the question was no less difficult.

"Elector, I left the Palace to pursue the mission of the Scholarship, to commit myself to Olius and the search for knowledge."

Again, the man said nothing, and Sev wondered when this nightmare might end. Why was the Elector asking him these questions?

"You left just before a promotion, did you not?"

A quick glance at the supreme leader showed an unreadable expression. Was there a right answer to this question? More importantly, was there a wrong one?

"Yes, Elector."

For a third time, the man in the chair was quiet, and Sev had never before felt such longing for noise. The silence dragged on, as if tempting him to look up and try to read the Elector's thoughts.

"High Scholar, I would like an audience with the Historian. Can you arrange it?"

Sev hesitated, the change in topic catching him off-guard. Though he preferred this subject, he was not sure how he would manage to fulfill the man's request.

"High Scholar, can you arrange it?"

Sev did not need to look up to know the frown had returned.

"Yes, Elector."

A smile replaced the frown, but Sev didn't share the man's satisfaction. How would he arrange such an audience? How would the rest of the Council react? But now was not the time for these questions, he thought to himself. He would figure this out later, far from the heat of the guardian's blades.

***

There was no entourage to rush him, but Sev reached the Scholarship in good time. Olius seemed to grow brighter with each passing rotation, as if preparing for the Historian, and he wanted to avoid the mid-rotation heat.

At the outskirts of the campus, Sev hesitated, then turned toward one of the back entrances. His departure had been a bit of a show, and he had no desire to repeat the experience.

Still, given the swollen numbers in the Scholarship, even the least-frequented halls were alive, and Sev found it impossible to avoid his brothers. Most faces were foreign to him, their darker complexion hinting at a life spent outside the confines of stone halls. Many greeted him with reverence, some with curiosity, but Sev barely had time to acknowledge them.

He thought of the villages beyond the capital zone, where these Scholars acted as representatives of the Council. Sev knew these settlements had their own Arbitration practices, but he wondered if the will of the Palace was ever questioned so far away from home.

Enough, Sev thought to himself. That situation was no longer the main issue. The Elector himself had summoned him and expressed displeasure at his exclusion. On top of that, he had asked for an audience with the being of Olius—something that would have seemed reasonable had Sev not felt such a striking undercurrent of treason among his peers.

He stopped just short of his chamber, staring at the door before him. This was it, he realized. This was his opportunity to undo a little of what he had done, to prove himself worthy of the white and gold.

He turned around and walked to the stone door at the center of the Scholarship. Here he stopped once more, gathering his courage. Was this the right choice? Was this in line with the word of Olius?

Yes, he told himself, and opened the door.

Conversation came to a halt, and the eleven High Scholars locked eyes on Sev. A few paces ahead was another Scholar, who turned to see the intruder.

"Sev, what is the meaning of this?"

For a moment, Sev did not process the Elder Scholar's question, as he was busy processing the sight of Folin. What an odd coincidence.

"Elder Scholar, I apologize for the interruption, but I have urgent news."

The Council eyed him warily, and Sev wondered if he had gone too far.

"Very well," the old man replied. "Say your piece."

Sev glanced at Folin then back at the Elder Scholar.

"Elder Scholar, may I speak to the Council in private?"

The Elder Scholar raised his eyebrows then nodded.

"Scholar Folin, please wait outside."

"Of course, Elder Scholar."

Sev felt a stab of guilt, but Folin gave him a smile on his way out.

"Now, Sev, speak quickly."

The disdain was already seeping into his tone, but Sev did his best to project his position—to act as if he were indeed part of the Council.

"High Scholars, as you know I was just summoned for an audience with the Elector himself."

Some of the faces displayed unbridled suspicion, but Sev continued.

"The supreme leader asked me about my role during the Visit, and I answered truthfully."

"Truthfully?" the Elder Scholar asked.

"Yes, Elder Scholar. I told him I had no assigned role, and that my current role was that of an observer."

A few of the High Scholars exchanged concerned glances.

"Sev of Primus, is it your intention to threaten this Council?" the Elder Scholar asked.

Sev stared at the old man, surprised by his words.

"N—no, Elder Scholar." Then, after a pause, "Council, I came here right away to share this information with you because the Elector's reaction worries me. I have followed your command and sat as an observer, and this has not been an issue until now. I did not mean to complicate the situation, but as a man of Olius, I was bound to answer the Elector in truth. However, he made a request I feel compelled to share."

The Elder Scholar studied Sev, trying to read the honesty of his words.

"What did the Elector ask of you?"

Sev hesitated.

"Elder Scholar, the Elector asked me to arrange an audience for him— an audience with the Historian."

Again, the Council exchanged glances, and for a moment, all was silent.

"And what do you intend to do?"

Sev turned to the new voice, his mentor's voice. There was something different in his expression, something... hopeful.

"High Scholar Zoph, I intend to inform this Council, and I have done so."

Zoph nodded slowly, but Sev could see the hint of approval in his eyes.

"Very well, Sev," the Elder Scholar replied. "Is there anything else?"

Sev returned his attention to the leader of the Council.

"No, Elder Scholar. I apologize again for the interruption."

The Elder Scholar nodded.

"The Council thanks you for your commitment, Sev. Please tell Scholar Folin to rejoin us."

Sev nodded, shooting one more glance at Zoph before exiting the room. Folin stood just outside, waiting.

"My apologies, Folin. They wait for you."

Folin gave him another smile.

"No apologies needed, Sev. It seems those robes suit you more and more."

With that, his friend stepped past him and into the room.

***

Sev returned to his chamber and took a seat at the table, pondering what had just occurred. Yes, he had acted in line with his new role—or at least the one he was trying to prove he could fill—but one right did not undo a hundred wrongs. What of his promise to the woman? The Scholarship had the resources to help her, so much was certain, but at a time like this? Short of the Historian himself taking an interest...

Then it came to him: outside of the Room of Council, he was a High Scholar. Especially with the outsiders, he held a certain level of authority. Perhaps if he could find a few Scholars with lighter loads...

No, Sev thought, his enthusiasm fading. Light loads did not exist right now. And besides, if the Council found out he was abusing his position before a formal induction, it would undo all the work he had done. There was only one way to do it and gain the Council's approval: he had to bring it up in an official manner. But even if they agreed with him, even if they saw he was right, Sev knew they would table the matter until after the Visit.

A knock at his door interrupted his thoughts, and he hesitated. Was this Hibbon? Or perhaps the soldier?

"Sev?"

At the sound of Folin's voice, Sev hustled to the door.

"Folin, I'm glad you're here. I need to talk to you about the Arbitration."

His friend gave him a curious look.

"As much as I'd like to catch up, now is not the time. I've been sent here to tell you to return to council."

Sev digested the words, staring at Folin in disbelief.

"Return to council?"

Folin's curiosity deepened.

"Is that so surprising?"

Sev shook his head, regaining his composure.

"No…"

He stepped out of his chamber, closing the door. They were asking for him to come back?

"Go with Olius, brother," Folin offered, smiling.

"And you," Sev replied, turning toward the Room of Council.

On the way over, he felt a smile coming over his expression, and despite customary etiquette, he made no attempt to hide it.

"Council, you have summoned me?"

The Elder Scholar gave him an amused look.

"Sev, though you may not have been formally inducted, it is still our wish to have you observe the proceedings. Would you take your seat?"

Sev nodded, heading toward the chair, and shot a glance at Zoph. His mentor smiled encouragingly, and the discussions continued. Now, Sev listened much more intently.

***

The final rotation before the Arrival began with far more chaos than any of the previous rotations, yet Sev hadn't been in such a good mood since his promotion. During both morning and evening council, despite the rush to finalize preparations, the other High Scholars asked him for input on a handful of matters—matters related to his past and not necessarily matters at the level of a High Scholar, but this didn't bother him: he was participating in a council, rather than just observing.

At the conclusion of the evening council, there were still a few tasks to be done, but the Elder Scholar surprised them all with his closing words.

"Council of Primus, it has been an honor working with you for so many revolutions. The coming rotations will define our legacy and shape the history of Primus forever. This is a pivotal moment, one which will be passed down by future Scholars for revolutions to come. I know there are yet matters to attend to, but most of our job is complete. Please take the night to rest—we need everyone at full strength on the next rotation."

He paused, looking at the faces around him.

"Again, it has been an honor. We will convene at first light. Go with Olius."

"And you," came the choral reply.

Conversation broke out among the other High Scholars as they stood to leave, and Sev couldn't help but smile. The Arrival, less than a rotation away? If the Elder Scholar thought they were going to get any sleep this night, he was mistaken.

"Sev?"

Sev turned at the voice of his mentor.

"High Scholar."

Zoph smiled.

"Would you accompany me to my chambers? I wish to speak to you before things get out of hand."

Sev nodded.

"Of course."

The two left the room together, heading toward Zoph's quarters.

"I must say you impressed me on the previous rotation, Sev."

The halls were so full of Scholars, it was becoming hard to navigate. Greetings came at them from every direction, and there was no denying the excitement in the air.

"To prioritize the health of the Scholarship over the..."

Zoph glanced around and leaned toward Sev, whispering.

"...over the scruples of the Elector."

Zoph gave him a knowing look and Sev forced a half-smile. He had done what he thought was right, but already Zoph's words worried him. To speak of the supreme leader in such a way, and in public? Sev tried to shake the feeling, reminding himself of his goal, his mission. If he was to prove himself worthy of the robes he wore, he needed to follow the path of Olius. Still, one could never be truly free of the past...

They reached his mentor's door and entered his chamber, taking a seat at the table. It felt like a lifetime had passed since they last sat in these chairs, yet it was not even ten rotations ago.

"Sev, I will be brief, as the Elder Scholar is right: we both need to rest for the Arrival. I wanted to see if you had any more to say about our earlier conversation."

A sense of foreboding came over him, and while Sev hoped his teacher meant their most recent exchange, a part of him already knew that wasn't the case.

"I'm doing what I can to prove myself worthy of the position, High Scholar."

Zoph frowned.

"Not that conversation, Sev. The one about Secundus."

Sev stared at his mentor, trying to read between the lines. Was he asking about something he already knew, as a test?

"High Scholar…"

Zoph sensed the hesitation in his former student and his frown deepened.

"Sev, you disappoint me. As a Scholar, I had no right to push this information out of you, and I did no such thing. But now that you've been promoted to High Scholar, now that you yourself claim you wish to prove yourself worthy, you still hesitate?"

Sev took a deep breath, gathering his thoughts. He knew what he had to do, but it wasn't easy. He had gained so much ground in the past rotation, would this take all of that away?

"High Scholar, I am forbidden from speaking of my knowledge of Secundus."

Zoph glared at him, incredulous.

"Forbidden? By whom?"

Sev frowned, realizing this would only go from bad to worse.

"By the Palace, High Scholar."

There was a flash of fear in his mentor's expression.

"The Elector told you not to talk about it?"

Sev tried to ignore Zoph's change in tone, focusing instead on answering.

"No, High Scholar, not the Elector. The Palace. When I left the service of the Palace to join the Scholarship, I took an oath of secrecy. This oath covered all of my duties and time at the Palace, of which I am only allowed to speak again to generals or the Elector himself."

Zoph eyed him sternly.

"An oath of secrecy?"

Sev nodded, struggling to look his mentor in the eye.

"And what of your oath to Olius? The oath of a Scholar is one thing, but the oath of a High Scholar? Do you think you can be a part of the Council and hold a secret?"

Sev shook his head.

"No, High Scholar, but I have not taken this oath as I have not been inducted."

An anger came over his mentor's expression, and Sev realized he had misspoken.

"Is that what this is? Do you think the rotation before the Arrival is a time to be pedantic? You are about to serve the role of a member of the Council of Primus during a Visit in all but the most official of manners, and you wish to keep a secret from the other High Scholars?"

Sev felt the pressure rising, felt cornered in the small chair. He had never seen his former teacher so angry, never thought it possible.

"I don't wish to keep a secret, High Scholar…"

Zoph scowled.

"And yet you do."

Sev frowned.

"High Scholar, I don't understand. The knowledge I have of Secundus… it serves the Scholarship no purpose. Why does it matter so much to you?"

For a moment, Zoph said nothing, and Sev worried he had finally gone too far. But when the man spoke again, his tone was quieter, if not firmer.

"Sev, it is not up to you to decide what knowledge serves the Scholarship—all knowledge serves the Scholarship. If you do not plan on sharing everything you know with me—if you do not plan on proving yourself committed to the truth of Olius—then you are to leave my chambers at once."

A thought came to Sev—a specific question, one he had wanted to ask before. But asking it now would reveal too much.

"High Scholar…"

"I say again, Sev: if you do not plan on speaking the full truth to me, you are to leave."

Sev stood slowly, contemplating his options. He knew leaving the room now would negate all the goodwill he had so recently earned, but what choice did he have? He had made an oath to the Palace, an oath he had no reason to break—especially with the cryptic nature of this whole exchange. If Zoph had given him a reason, any inkling as to why this information might be important to the Scholarship, Sev might reconsider.

But he hadn't. So Sev turned around and walked out of the room.

***

Sev stood in formation with the eleven other High Scholars, staring at the empty sky above. A few paces away, a small depression in the platform marked the landing site of Olius's Vessel, the place where the Historian would greet Primus. Sev had noted the last-minute repairs the Scholarship had done, their attempts to bring the platform to its former glory, but the metal below them was riddled with rust, and it looked almost the same as it had when High Scholar Dren's ashes had lifted off just eleven rotations ago.

That was where the similarities ended, however. If Sev had considered Dren's Walk well-attended, the Arrival was another beast entirely. Below them, just behind the platform steps, every Scholar on Primus had gathered for the momentous occasion, a veritable sea of white and gold. Beyond them was a line of purple and black, a legion of soldiers flashing their hotswords to keep the peasants at bay. Of those citizens there were several hundred, more than Sev had ever seen in one place, and more than he might ever see again. But perhaps most important were the three individuals just in front of the Council: the Elector and his personal guardians, who had taken the spot nearest the depression.

Some of the High Scholars had whispered, had complained in quiet voices about the arrangement. But Sev did not join this chorus. He was closer than he ever imagined he might be, thankful to be standing among the twelve, thankful to be draped in the white and gold of Olius.

The white and gold of Olius. Sev had spent the night reflecting on his last few meetings with Zoph, and many questions remained. The man had emphasized the shedding of purple and black as a High Scholar, something that had made sense in the moment. Scholars, particularly High Scholars, are servants of Olius. But they were also servants of Primus, and it was dangerous to claim the two were exclusive. Between that and his discussion of Secundus…

A stir caught everyone's attention and cut Sev's thought process short. Above them, barely discernible against Olius's glare, was a small black dot —an object approaching from the skies. The crowd grew silent as it made its descent, and soon it was clear what they were looking at: Olius's Vessel, the Historian's ship.

Sev watched the grey sphere come to a hover above them, lining itself up with the platform before continuing its slow descent. He knew what it looked like, had read many descriptions, but Sev never thought he would see it himself. An Arrival in his lifetime—he was still having trouble believing it.

As the Vessel approached eye level, everyone on the platform took a step back—even the Elector. The sphere slowed to a stop, hovering just above the concave space, and Sev found himself as awestruck as the peasants—this technology was beyond anything he had ever seen.

Finally, with a controlled drop, the craft fell into the depression, landing on Primus. There was a moment's silence as the crowd stared at the alien craft, then a noise deep within the Vessel, like a faraway rumble of thunder, startled the lot of them. The Elector's guardians drew their hotswords, then the noise came again. A murmur went up behind him, but Sev ignored the sounds of the crowd, straining his ears to listen.

A third rumble, then a fourth. By the fifth, there was no mistaking it— each one was louder, each one was closer. It was both ominous and exhilarating. The murmur behind him grew with the rumbling, a steady crescendo that matched his own excitement. Soon, the Historian would emerge. This was the moment Sev had been waiting for, the moment his entire life had led up to.

A loud snap sent a gasp through the crowd, silencing Scholars and soldiers alike. There, in the surface of the sphere, a recession had appeared. And in that recession stood a man, his garment a radiant white with two thick lines of brilliant gold running up each side of his body and connecting behind his neck.

The Historian had arrived.

Assignment

When the Historian appeared in the recession of Olius's Vessel, the crowd went to knee and hand. The peasants, the soldiers, the Scholars—everyone showed their obedience and gratitude to the being of Olius.

Sev followed suit, as did the rest of the Council. Just ahead of them, the Elector's guardians put away their swords and mirrored the gesture, and Sev snuck a glance upward, knowing what would come next yet unable to believe it: the Elector himself, the supreme leader of Primus, dropped in reverence before the being of Olius.

"Rise, citizens of Primus."

The Historian's voice carried weight, its depth and volume commanding respect. Despite the clear nature of the command, Sev hesitated in standing. He did not feel worthy.

"I have come from Olius to collect your history, but I also come to share and spread the knowledge of the system. I thank you for both your hospitality and your help."

The Historian glanced down at the Elector and the High Scholars.

"Are you the Scholars?" he asked.

The Elder Scholar took a step forward.

"We are here, Historian. We await your command."

The Historian nodded.

"Thank you, Scholar. I wish to speak to the Scholarship."

"All of it, Historian?"

"All of it, Scholar."

"Of course, Historian. This way."

The Elder Scholar turned around to lead the way, and the rest of the High Scholars stepped aside, forming a path for the Historian. Sev watched the being of Olius step down from the recession and walk past the Elector without so much as a sideward glance. It was strange to see someone ignore the supreme leader, but as the Historian came within arm's length, even Sev seemed to forget the Elector's presence.

A closer look only emphasized his strange features: sure, he had the body of a man, but there was something about his skin, his face, his eyes... it all seemed surreal, almost alien. Sev was so mesmerized by the sight he nearly missed his cue to follow, shuffling to the platform steps with his colleagues.

Below them, the Scholars had parted down the middle, forming a path through the front of the crowd. Beyond that, soldiers flashed their hotswords to force the peasants aside, but it was no use trying to keep them away. As the Historian followed the Elder Scholar, the people did the same, an amorphous mob of Scholars, soldiers, and peasants walking in organized chaos toward the Scholarship. As they traversed the stretch of land between the platform and the campus, some of the peasants and soldiers slipped away, but others joined to take their place.

There was no chamber or hall within the Scholarship large enough to house all its members at once, so the Elder Scholar led everyone to the Garden—the Scholarship's courtyard, a large square of land almost completely surrounded by campus buildings. Despite its name, the Garden was more dead than alive, the same orange as the rest of Primus. Sev knew from his teachings it was once filled with vegetation, but that was many revolutions ago, well before the last Visit. Now a handful of plants dotted the plot, and the Scholars carefully avoided disturbing these islands of green as they arranged themselves for the speech.

The High Scholars took a spot near the pulpit, and only then did Sev noticed the Elector's absence. Somewhere along the way, the man had left the procession—or had he ever joined it? In normal circumstances, this might hold Sev's attention, but these circumstances were anything but normal.

While he couldn't spot the Elector, he did see a number of strangers in the crowd—peasants who had entered the campus to hear the being of Olius. He frowned, contemplating the many visitors they would receive in the coming rotations—a veritable pilgrimage of citizens all looking to speak to someone they considered a god. Oh well, he thought, such was the nature of the Visit.

It took some time for everyone to quiet down, and the collective excitement of the entire Scholarship managed to erase his frown. The Historian was here, the Visit had begun. This was their purpose, this was their mission.

"Scholarship of Primus, I thank you once more for your gracious welcome."

Now that Sev was closer he heard the voice more clearly. It carried the same weight as before, but there was something subtle between the words —an accent of some kind, almost imperceptible.

"Thus begins yet another Visit to Primus. Over the next revolution, we will work together to share and record this planet's great history, and we will use the lessons we learn to plan for its future. Together, we can achieve peace and prosperity for Primus and for the entire system."

Sev looked out at the crowd, soaking in every word. He didn't want to forget this moment.

"I know each and every one of you has contributed to this mission. Without the Scholars, a Historian would see but a fragment of the grand canvas of history. You all have your part to play, and I thank you for everything you have done and everything you will do... for the Scholarship, for Primus, and for Olius."

The Historian paused, scanning the crowd in front of him with a smile.

"And now, I plan to take a much-needed rest. I suggest you all do the same. On the following rotation, our work begins."

Laughter turned to cheers, and the Historian left the pulpit. Sev watched the being of Olius exchange some words with the Elder Scholar, then both men headed toward the Council living quarters. The rest of the High Scholars conversed among themselves, while the other Scholars formed their own circles. The voices of the Scholarship filled the Garden, but Sev's excitement waned, the frown threatening to return.

This rotation was one of celebration, but what of the next? He thought back to his most recent Palace summons, to the Elector's poignant question. What would Sev's role be during the Visit, this most important of events? Was he still meant to observe, to ride along as everyone else did the work? He knew it was shameful to want more than what he had—after all, he was a High Scholar during a Visit—but as Zoph had said, such feelings were human.

He glanced down at his robe, the white and gold shining under the light of Olius. Did his promotion matter? Was it justifiable? He shuddered at the treasonous thoughts permeating his mind.

"Sev!"

The familiar voice caught his attention and Sev barely had time to react as Folin took him into an embrace.

"Can you believe it?"

Folin's uncharacteristic excitement lifted Sev's spirits, and he smiled in turn.

"It's unbelievable."

His friend gave him a searching look.

"And you? I can't imagine what it's like to be in your shoes at a time like this."

Reality threatened to come back to him, but Sev kept his smile.

"It's hard to process it all..."

Folin gestured toward one of the openings nearby.

"Will you walk with me?"

Sev gave his friend a curious look.

"Of course."

The two of them shuffled through the raucous crowd, into the adjacent hall. There were dozens of other Scholars in the corridors, but it was quieter than the Garden.

"What did you want to discuss?" Sev asked.

Folin smiled.

"You know me too well, Sev. But I prefer to talk in private. Could we go to your quarters?"

Sev nodded, his curiosity piqued.

"Of course."

They walked side by side through the familiar campus, weaving past conversations and chatter. In all his revolutions at the Scholarship, Sev never would have thought the grey halls could be so cheerful, so alive. It was quite a sight to behold, and they made no effort to rush. When they reached Sev's chamber, both of them had a smile on their face.

"Have a seat," Sev offered, sitting down and gesturing to the chair across from him.

Folin did as suggested, and Sev noticed his friend's smile was already gone.

"Sev, I'm afraid this conversation will not be easy."

He peered at him, curious as ever.

"What is it, Folin?"

The man looked away, hesitating.

"Last night, High Scholar Zoph asked to speak with me."

Folin shifted his gaze back to Sev.

"He told me about your reluctance to break your oath to the Palace."

For a moment, Sev refused to process what he had heard. Not this, not now.

"I know this is a delicate subject, and I apologize for this rude interruption of what should be a rotation of celebration, but I had to let you know, I had to talk to you."

Folin paused, and Sev stared at his friend in disbelief.

"He... he told you?"

Several questions popped into Sev's mind. Why had Zoph told Folin? What gave Zoph the right to share a private conversation, one among two High Scholars, with another Scholar? Why did he feel ashamed that Folin knew? Did Folin think of him differently now?

"Indeed he did. Sev, I know you are no doubt angry at this breach of privacy, and that is understandable, but if you allow me to speak, I think I can explain the High Scholar's actions."

A pit formed in Sev's stomach, and even though neither of them had moved, it was as if the table had widened.

"Why did he tell you?" Sev asked.

Folin noted the cold tone and frowned.

"Sev, Zoph cares about you, you know this to be true. Eight revolutions of memory are there to prove it, and I daresay you need any reminding. Do you think he is acting this way out of malice? Out of spite? Ask yourself how that makes any sense, Sev. The man is doing everything he can to protect you."

Sev heard the conviction in his friend's voice, but he was unconvinced.

"Protect me? He asked me to break the Palace oath, to commit treason against Primus."

Folin nodded.

"You're right, Sev. He went too far. That much I agree. But I'm asking you to think on his motives. Just by asking you these things, Zoph puts himself in danger. Why would he do that, if not to help you?"

Something in the argument was making sense, but Sev had yet to put all the pieces together.

"How? How does breaking the Palace oath help me?"

Folin managed a small smile, and Sev couldn't help but be impressed by his friend's patience.

"Sev, you've been thrust into the middle of a dangerous and complex situation by the Elector's unofficial promotion. Zoph is trying to make it right, trying to undo what the Palace has done."

Sev shook his head.

"No, Folin. Zoph told me himself it was foolish to think I could prove myself worthy of the position."

"That's what he thought at first, Sev, and in some ways, he was right. As I said, asking you to break your oath to the Palace went too far, but he saw it as the only way to get the Council on your side. The only way to prove yourself worthy of the position, to dispel any doubt as to whom you serve."

With these words, Folin confirmed his greatest fear, and Sev found himself struggling to find a reply.

"Folin..."

Folin smiled a second time.

"I know. I know this is difficult, and I know this kind of talk is dangerous, especially for you. Sev, I am not asking you to do anything—at least not anything more than considering and understanding the circumstances. Because you're in the middle of this now, Sev, and we're all worried for you."

Sev stumbled for an answer, one that was honest yet safe, but he still couldn't find the words. Maybe Folin had a point? Maybe breaking the oath was the right thing to do? After all, if he wanted to be a High Scholar, he had to commit to the full truth, nothing less...

A knock at the door interrupted his thoughts, and both men turned. Before Sev could object, Folin was out of his chair, opening the door. Before him stood a man in purple and black, an emissary of the Palace.

"High Scholar Sev of Primus?" the man asked, looking from one to the other before settling on the one with the distinguished robes.

Sev stood from his seat.

"What is it?" he asked, making his way to the door.

"I have a message from the Elector," he answered, extending a parchment in his hand.

Sev looked at the paper then at Folin, who gestured into the hall.

"I'll be taking my leave, High Scholar."

His friend took two steps into the hall before Sev called after him.

"Folin."

Folin paused, looking back.

"Thank you," Sev said.

Folin nodded.

"Go with Olius, brother," he replied.

Sev smiled.

"And you."

Folin turned around and walked off, and Sev was left alone with the man from the Palace. He looked the emissary up and down, then locked his gaze on the piece of paper.

"A message from the Elector you say?"

The man nodded, and Sev fought the urge to frown, grabbing the parchment out of his hand.

"Does he expect a reply?"

The emissary shook his head.

"No, High Scholar. Do you have a message for me to convey?"

Sev shook his head.

"No. You may go."

The man nodded then turned around, and Sev closed the door, staring at the parchment. It felt so heavy in his hand, this small piece of paper...

Sev caught himself before his thoughts wandered too far. This was a message from the Elector, and he best open it immediately. He unraveled the parchment, reading the words inscribed. As he scanned the document, the frown he had hidden from the emissary made its way onto his face.

In the message, the Elector congratulated him and the Scholarship on the Arrival, then reminded him of his duty to arrange an audience for the supreme leader with the Historian.

Sev put the paper down on his table and sighed. How would he ever prove himself worthy?

***

The next rotation, Sev woke to the customary knock at his door and let the servant in. As usual, the man carried more than just his breakfast—there was a candle for light, and a parchment: orders from the Elder Scholar. As the servant took the remains of the previous night's dinner and left, Sev unrolled the paper and saw he was summoned at the usual time: first light.

Finally, a semblance of good news. Sev had barely slept the night before, and not just because of the festivities in the halls around him. After his last conversation with Zoph, and now the conversation with Folin, he had wondered if he might be excluded from council. Maybe the other High Scholars would deny him the chance to sit in the chamber with the Historian. After all, with the being of Olius present, the Scholarship had a measure of impunity. If there ever was a time to ignore the potential repercussions of their actions, it was now.

On the other hand, Sev wasn't all too surprised. While the balance of power had shifted, the Visit was temporary, and the Elector was not a man to forget. Once the Historian left, things would go back to normal… unless the Historian changed something while he was here?

Sev contemplated this possibility, but there wasn't much to contemplate. The being of Olius was a beacon of peace and truth, and how could one change the Palace with peace and truth? From his time in the black fortress, Sev knew the answer: it wasn't possible.

He took a bite of his meal and tried to focus on the more pressing matter. How was he supposed to arrange an audience with the Historian? He had only been allowed to speak on the rotation before the Arrival, and that was when he had the goodwill of the other High Scholars. After his latest meeting with Zoph, there was no doubt his privileges had been revoked.

At least he had warned them, Sev thought. He had told the Council what the supreme leader sought, and if he brought it up, it wouldn't be a surprise. Still, when he had brought it up, Sev had said his only intention was to inform the Council. What would happen when he actually did as the Elector asked? What would the rest of them think?

But Sev knew what they would think, because it weighed on him even now. He was the Palace's whipping boy, brought into the Scholarship to weasel his way up the ranks and report back to the supreme leader. How could he convince them it wasn't true?

If only he had never gone down that path, he thought. If only he had gone directly to the Scholarship, rather than the Palace. Would he have reached the same rank, but as a trusted colleague? Would he wear the gowns of white and gold with the full support of his peers?

He finished his breakfast and stood. His position was a difficult one, to be sure, but it was out of his hands for the time being. Right now, he just needed to do what the Elector asked, or he would find himself on the bad side of the Palace as well as the Scholarship—and the Palace dealt with their enemies in a manner far more dangerous than exclusion.

He stepped out of his chambers and walked to the Room of Council, his mood improving with every step. Despite the less-than-ideal circumstances, Sev was about to sit on a council with the Historian himself. Compromising missions from the Palace notwithstanding, this would be the ultimate dream of his Scholarly career. By the time he reached the door, he had managed to shelve his worries, at least for the time being.

As soon as he was inside, Sev's eyes darted to the thirteenth chair, the one that had sat empty for over two hundred revolutions. The Historian's presence brought him to a halt, and even though he had seen the man on the previous rotation, he found himself locked in a mix of disbelief and respect.

"High Scholar, please take your seat."

The Elder Scholar's voice, impatient in tone, snapped him out of his trance. Sev bowed his head with a hint of shame and went to his chair. Again, not the best first impression, he thought to himself.

"Thank you, High Scholars, for your gracious greeting at the Arrival. And thank you for affording me the much needed opportunity to rest. With that out of the way, I'm ready to get started on the daunting task ahead. So begins the first Council of Olius."

Sev had to force himself not to stare. Here he was, sitting in the Room of Council with the Historian just six chairs away. This was a dream, it couldn't be real.

"Our first order of business is categorization and prioritization. What is the current organization of the Scholarship's data?"

Where the previous councils had been guided by the voice of the Elder Scholar, this one was guided by the voice of Olius itself. The men no longer discussed matters of the Arrival, but matters of the Visit: how the knowledge would be passed on, what was more or less important, how things would be explained. The Scholarship had in its possession rooms full of volumes going into the most minute of details regarding the time since the previous Visit, but getting all that information into the Historian's head would take some sorting and summarizing.

Unfortunately, whether by the presence of the Historian or by consequence of his conversation with Zoph, Sev was once again excluded from discussion. He wondered what the being of Olius knew—had he been asked to ignore Sev as well?—but as frustrating as it might be, part of him was relieved: this was sure to be a defining moment in the history of the Scholarship, and even if he had been formally inducted, Sev wasn't sure he would've been ready for the responsibility of the Arrival in such a short time.

So, as he had done before, Sev listened intently, trying to learn as much as he could from the proceedings. In fact, his attention was at a higher level than ever, thanks not just to the presence of the Historian, but also by virtue of the Elector's request.

He waited in vain for some mention of the Palace, some segue that would make his interjection natural. By the time the light of Olius shone through the opening at the top of the rotunda, he knew he needed to act. The audience had to be arranged before the rotation's end, and this council would likely be the only chance he had to speak with the being of Olius.

When it became clear they were wrapping up their conversations in preparation for the mid-rotation meal, he ignored his trepidation and addressed the Historian directly.

"Historian, the Elector of Primus has requested an audience with you, if you would graciously accept."

Sev could feel the surprise and anger that permeated the Room of Council after the words left his mouth, but he remained focused on the being of Olius, ignoring the indignation that surrounded him.

The Historian eyed him curiously, then smiled.

"Of course, High Scholar. I will arrange it with you directly after this council."

The relief that came over him was immediate and overpowering—he could feel the tension leave his body. As an added bonus, he had orchestrated his first private interaction with the Historian—another event he had trouble believing.

As the Council stood to leave, Sev expected some sort of rebuke from one of his colleagues, but beyond a few uncomfortable glances, none came. Good, he thought to himself. Better those glares than the hotsword of a guardian.

"High Scholar?"

The voice of Olius stopped him in his tracks, and he turned to face the Historian. Over the course of the council, Sev had managed to shed his paralyzing awe, but now that he found himself face to face with the being of Olius, words escaped him.

"Did the Elector request a particular time or location?"

Sev snapped himself out of it, stumbling over his reply.

"He— at your convenience, Historian."

The Historian gave him an amused look.

"Please inform the Elector I will gladly see him on the next rotation at mid-rotation here, in the Scholarship."

Sev nodded.

"Yes, Historian."

"I also have a task for you, High Scholar."

Sev felt an overwhelming excitement come over him. During the council, each of the other High Scholars had been assigned their next role, but of course Sev was ignored. At least, until now.

"In preparation for my audience with the Elector, I will need a concise but thorough dossier on the supreme leader of Primus. Can you put one together before the end of the rotation?"

At the description of the task, some of Sev's excitement faded, though it was hard not to be excited about a request from the Historian himself.

"Yes, Historian."

The Historian gave him a knowing look.

"High Scholar, as I understand, this audience could be of monumental importance, so your dossier must be well-organized. Please skip the next council so that you may focus on this task."

Sev nodded again.

"Yes, Historian."

The man smiled.

"Thank you, High Scholar."

With that, the being of Olius walked past his star-struck admirer and continued to the Hall of Nourishment. Sev turned to watch him go, a smile spreading across his face. Yes, he had been asked to skip the next council, but frankly, what use was he sitting there with no input? Besides, the way the Historian had attributed such importance to his task... Sev couldn't help but hope this would prove himself worthy to the one who mattered most: the being of Olius himself.

***

Sev spent the rest of the rotation on the dossier, compiling as much pertinent information as he could find while discarding whatever he deemed irrelevant. At first, such additions and subtractions gave him a certain anxiety, especially with the words of the Historian fresh in his mind.

An audience of monumental importance... but Sev didn't need the being of Olius to spell that out for him. A meeting between the two most powerful individuals in the system? Of course it would be of monumental importance. Unfortunately, this was not the only source of his anxiety, as his wandering mind had allowed a different interpretation of the Historian's words.

What if this was somehow related to all the tension between the Scholarship and the Palace, all these questions about Secundus? What if, in making this dossier, Sev was indirectly deciding the future of Primus itself? It was an overwhelming if not disturbing thought, made worse by how true it rang. Still, this was his task, assigned to him by the Historian himself, and Sev would make sure he did it to the best of his ability.

But as Sev delved deeper and deeper into the Scholarship's archives, a new question came to him, one more problematic than what to include and exclude: was the Scholarship's data incomplete? There were copious files on the Elector's time as a Pupil, a soldier, a general, and finally in his current role, but what of the gaps? Certainly the Scholarship could not be expected to note down every breath the man took, but Sev had personal experience in the Palace, and he had a good idea of certain milestones an individual would need to reach to climb up to the position—milestones missing from the Scholarship's archives, milestones he himself had experienced and had been explicitly prohibited from sharing upon his departure.

Sev could feel the old frustration rising within him, the anger at his terrible position. Eight revolutions he had held onto knowledge the Scholarship didn't have, and not once had he considered the implications. Had his original placement under High Scholar Zoph been a ploy? Had they always intended to use him, to earn his trust and learn the Palace's secrets?

But Sev knew he was reaching. In eight revolutions, not once had he been asked to divulge or even acknowledge such information. Sometimes, he had considered the inconsistency of his position—this wasn't the first time he had heard all knowledge fell under the light of Olius—but in the past, this was easily explained away: anything missing from the Scholarship's tomes was related to the security measures of the Palace—there was no need for the Scholarship to know.

No, Sev thought to himself, this was an oversimplification. In its quest for power, the Palace had discovered many things, things the Scholarship probably ought to know. And now that the being of Olius was here? Could he, in good conscience, omit what he thought was missing from the dossier? Could he, in good conscience, keep the Palace's secrets from the Historian?

But he knew the answer to both of those questions, as much as he hated to admit it. He had chosen to prove himself worthy, to try to live up to the role he had been given, and there was only one way to do that. Sev only hoped the Historian would not ask for details, at least not yet.

***

Sev stood outside the Historian's private chambers, waiting for the evening council to finish. Given the sensitive contents of the dossier, he had opted to hand deliver it rather than entrust it to a servant or Scholar. Better safe than sorry.

Moments ago, he had penned a message to the Palace informing them of the audience and had passed it to a servant to see it delivered. Now, a part of him wondered if he should have admitted what he had done, explaining to the Elector his borderline treason.

No, he thought to himself, treason was not the right word. How could it be treason if it was for the Historian? Sev cursed his position once more, wondering how much longer it would take the being of Olius to arrive. But he knew his impatience didn't stem from the Historian, it stemmed from this whole situation. Folin was right, this was a complicated and dangerous spot he found himself in, and he saw no escape route, no way out. In trying to do the right thing, to follow the word of Olius, was he digging his own grave?

"High Scholar?"

A servant approached him, and Sev's reflex was to hold the dossier tighter.

"Yes?"

"You have a visitor."

Sev eyed him warily.

"Who?"

"The patriarch of a local village."

He felt the weight of the dossier under his arm and nodded.

"Thank you, have him wait outside my chambers."

"Yes, High Scholar."

Sev watched the man leave, his mind in disarray. Hibbon was here? He had all but forgotten the Arbitration, his nighttime visit to the other village, the confrontation with the soldier in his chambers... and the promise he had made to the woman, the promise he had yet to fulfill.

"High Scholar?"

The voice of Olius snapped him out of his thoughts and Sev stood up straight, watching the Historian approach with the Elder Scholar at his side. There was disdain in the latter's eyes, but Sev ignored it.

"Historian, I have your dossier, and the audience is set as you asked."

He held out the volume, and the Historian took it.

"Thank you, High Scholar. We will review it during our evening meal."

Sev felt a chill down his back, his eyes darting from the Historian to the Elder Scholar.

"Historian..."

The being of Olius gave him a curious look.

"What is it, High Scholar?"

Sev looked down, unable to hold his gaze.

"Historian, the contents of the dossier are of a sensitive nature..."

He scrambled to find the right words to say, to explain the importance of secrecy...

"High Scholar, do you intend to limit the reach of this knowledge?"

There was disappointment in the Historian's tone, a disappointment that brought Sev sudden and incredible shame. Without thinking, he dropped to knee and hand.

"Historian, I apologize. I..."

"Rise, High Scholar."

Sev did as asked, still avoiding the man's eyes.

"High Scholar, I understand your predicament, the complexity of your past."

There was a warmth to the words that caught Sev's attention, and he met the Historian's gaze.

"Trust that we will navigate this situation carefully, but you must remember all knowledge falls within the light of Olius. Nothing is off-limits."

Hearing him parrot Zoph's words only made things more difficult, but Sev kept his composure.

"Yes, Historian."

"Thank you for completing your task, High Scholar. Go with Olius, brother."

Sev glanced at the Elder Scholar and saw a hint of surprise in the old man's expression.

"And you," he replied, then took his leave.

Walking toward his chamber, Sev felt the questions multiplying, the worries compounding, but before he could process them, he saw the familiar face outside his door.

"Hibbon."

The patriarch's stern expression let Sev know this visit was not a happy one.

"High Scholar, I must speak with you in private."

There was anger in his voice, and Sev stepped past him, opening the door and gesturing inside.

"Of course."

The men entered the chamber and Sev closed the door behind him.

"What is it, Hibbon?"

The village leader hesitated, eyeing the door as if to make certain it was closed.

"High Scholar, I've come to ask you to remove yourself from the situation entirely."

Sev stared at the man, surprised by his harsh tone.

"Remove myself?"

"Yes. I understand your intentions were good, but whatever it is you have done, it has caused my village great pain."

He stared at the village leader, trying to read between the lines.

"Hibbon, have there been repercussions from the Palace?"

For a moment, a sadness came over the patriarch's expression, but it was quickly replaced by the same harsh lines.

"High Scholar, I thank you for your time, but I must go."

And before Sev could react, he opened the door and stepped out into the hall. Sev took two steps to follow, but stopped short of calling out after him. Whatever had happened, Hibbon was not going to tell him. Not here, not now.

***

The following rotation, after a morning council of continued exclusion, Sev joined the other High Scholars and the Historian in greeting the Elector at the entrance to the Scholarship. While his personal guardians were at his side, Sev was surprised by the lack of entourage—typically the Elector travelled with several servants and at least one of his generals.

"Historian."

The supreme leader dropped to knee and hand, and Sev felt a trace of shame. He knew the gesture was for the Historian alone, not for the High Scholars, but it bothered him nonetheless: there was something discomforting about the Elector showing such respect in their direction.

"Rise, Elector."

The men stood face to face, and Sev noted how vibrant each of their robes were: the Historian's white and gold gleaming in the light of Olius, and the Elector's purple and black both rich and aggressive.

"Thank you for granting me an audience, Historian."

The Historian smiled.

"Of course, Elector. It is important relations between the Scholarship and the Palace remain not only cordial, but friendly."

The Elector glanced at Sev before responding.

"I agree. Only through cooperation can we lead Primus to the future it deserves."

The being of Olius gestured into the Scholarship.

"If you would accompany me, Elector, we will convene in the Room of Council."

The Elector accepted the invitation, stepping forward to join the Historian. Sev watched the personal guardians file in directly behind their leader, a move that elicited a few stern glances from the rest of the Council. Still, no one dared say a word, and they took their place behind the elite warriors.

Sev was close enough to hear the Historian exchange a few words with the Elector, but too far to make out their exact conversation. Thankfully, they had chosen the entrance closest to the Room of Council, and soon they were inside the chamber, each of them taking their seats.

Immediately, Sev felt another hint of shame: the Council's table was raised so that they looked down on their audience, in this case the supreme leader and his guardians. It was an uncomfortable reversal to all his Palace visits, but he did his best to hide his unease.

"Welcome, Elector of Primus, to this Council of Olius."

The Elector managed a small smile, though Sev saw no warmth in the expression.

"Thank you, Historian. I trust your time on Primus has been fruitful thus far?"

The Historian nodded.

"Indeed it has, Elector, short though it may still be. I have gotten a glimpse of what lies ahead, and it's clear the Scholarship has done an excellent job of organizing and presenting the history of Primus since the last Departure. Thus far, the Scholars have been nothing but supportive. My job is only possible thanks to their efforts."

Sev's eyes darted from one to the other, and he had trouble believing what he was seeing. Had he been told even thirty rotations ago that he would sit in on a conversation between the two most powerful beings in the system, or that he would ever experience such an event in his lifetime, he would never have believed it.

"And you will be able to finish in time?"

The Historian smiled.

"Time is not an issue, Elector. The only issue is truth."

These words caught both the Elector and Sev off-guard.

"What do you mean, Historian?"

The Historian glanced at Sev before responding, a glance far more surprising than the previous statement had been.

"Elector, I am glad you asked for an audience. As Historian, I am a servant of Olius, in charge of the history and knowledge of our great system. I have done this many times, and I plan to do it many more, but there is a problem. Here on Primus, something unexpected has occurred. Something which has the potential to upset my entire Visit."

The being of Olius had their full attention, though Sev noted no surprise from the other High Scholars. Had they talked about this before, when Sev wasn't present?

"The Palace and the Scholarship have separated to the point where I am not certain the Scholarship has all the information I need."

After these words came a silence, and Sev felt a shift in the room's atmosphere.

"You believe the Palace is withholding information from the Scholarship?"

The Elector's tone made Sev uneasy, but the Historian betrayed no outward response.

"I do not know, Elector. That's why I am worried. There is one subject that remains mostly within the jurisdiction of the Palace, a subject that after only one rotation on Primus, I know will present the most difficulty during my investigations."

The Elector's expression hardened.

"What subject, Historian?"

The Historian smiled again.

"Secundus."

The word came out so calmly, so quietly, that it took a moment for Sev to register what had occurred. But one glance at the Elector was enough to make him want to leave this place, to renounce his promotion and everything that had come along with it. What was this cruel twist of fate? Why did it seem this subject was hunting him, chasing him even here, in this most sacred of places?

Thankfully, the Historian seemed to take note of his guest's disapproval.

"I see that I have upset you, Elector. That was not my intent. It seems the relationship between the planets has deteriorated farther than I had anticipated. I do not wish to upset you any further, I simply wish to express my concern. If there is any knowledge of Secundus the Palace holds which it does not share with the Scholarship, I would kindly ask it be shared with me. I am here for the truth, Elector. Nothing else."

Before the Elector could respond, the Historian stood.

"I'm afraid I've soured this audience enough, and I do not wish for our tempers to get the best of us. I look forward to hearing from you soon, Elector. Again, I apologize this meeting did not go as you had planned."

Sev watched the proceedings intently. The Historian standing was a symbol of closure, meant to indicate the audience was over. But Sev wasn't looking at the being of Olius, he was looking at the man in purple and black, the man with a trace of contempt in his eyes. Contempt aimed squarely at the Historian himself.

"Thank you for your time, Historian."

He did not drop to knee and hand.

***

As soon as the Elector stepped out of the Room of Council, the Historian brought up the next order of business, and it didn't take long for the chamber to fill with conversation. Sev watched his peers discuss the tasks related to the Visit and wondered how they could be so nonchalant, how they could ignore what had just occurred. Numerous Scholars were summoned to hear their duties, standing and listening where the supreme leader had stood, but each one of them left with a ceremonial touch of knee and hand to floor to symbolize their obedience and gratitude. Sev knew his peers understood the gravity of the Elector's gesture, yet that was not what bothered him most.

With the Historian's calm statement, Sev's worst nightmare was once again a reality, and it seemed as if there was no escaping that which he so desperately wanted to avoid: the secrets the Palace kept from the Scholarship.

He thought back to his conversations with Zoph, to the words of Folin, and for a moment he wondered if this was simply an informational coup. Until now, the Scholarship operated without knowledge of Secundus and had no way to obtain such knowledge. But with the Historian present, perhaps they meant to fulfill their role—after all, the Scholarship was meant to house every bit of information known to Primus, not just those the Elector saw fit.

Sev caught himself, surprised at his own heresy. Had he gone too far down this path? The Elector was titled such for a reason, he made all the most important choices. Choices such as the promotion of new High Scholars, or what knowledge was free and what wasn't. Did this conflict with the words of the Historian? Did this mean some knowledge didn't fall under the light of Olius?

These questions haunted Sev the entire council, and he heard nothing until the very end, when the voice of Olius addressed him.

"High Scholar Sev."

Sev stared at the Historian, confused and afraid. His mind was reeling from the rotation's proceedings, and by the way the being of Olius studied him, Sev worried all this turmoil was displayed in his expression.

"Yes, Historian?"

"I would like to meet with you privately in my quarters following this council. Is that acceptable?"

Sev hesitated, contemplating the absurdity of the Historian asking him permission.

"Yes, Historian. Of course."

Yet as they wrapped up the council and stood to leave, a part of him wished he had rejected the request.

***

The Historian's private chambers were adjacent to the rest of the Council, and were nearly the same as a High Scholar's. They were a little more spacious, and the view of the Garden was unique to the being of Olius, but otherwise they were identical.

The Historian gestured to a chair by the table.

"Please, Sev of Primus, take a seat."

They sat across from one another, and Sev fought the storm in his mind. He was sitting alone at a table with the being of Olius, the very epitome of a Scholar's career, yet he was far from happy. If anything, he was terrified.

"I take it you know why we are here," the Historian began.

Sev hesitated, contemplating his reply.

"I think so, Historian."

"High Scholar, I apologize for the discomfort this situation has brought you and will no doubt continue to bring. As I'm sure you know, the current predicament is unusual, though not without solution."

Sev glanced up at the being of Olius, noting once more the subtle accent. In these close quarters, it was more pronounced.

"I begin by asking you: why do the other High Scholars treat you as an inferior member of the Council?"

Again, Sev hesitated.

"I don't know, Historian."

The Historian frowned.

"Sev of Primus, at the meeting with the Elector, what did I say was of utmost importance?"

This time, Sev didn't hesitate.

"Truth, Historian."

The being of Olius nodded.

"Precisely. So why do you lie, and to the Historian himself no less? I have been told you wish to prove yourself a High Scholar. Do you think this is the proper way to do so, by lying to me?"

A wave of shame came over Sev, unbearable and unrelenting. He was right, of course. How could he lie to the being of Olius? All his upbringing, all his education... was he still a soldier of the Palace? Were they right to look down on him?

"Historian, I'm ashamed of my behavior. Please forgive me."

He made to drop to knee and hand, but the Historian stopped him.

"Enough. Let us try path of truth, shall we? Why do the other High Scholars treat you as an inferior member of the Council?"

Sev swallowed his pride and answered.

"Because I was promoted by the Elector without the input of the Council."

The Historian nodded encouragingly.

"Yes. And why did the Elector do such a thing?"

Sev hesitated, searching for a way to express his thoughts.

"I'm not sure, Historian."

The Historian shook his head.

"Ah but you are, Sev. You just refuse to accept it. The Elector promoted you to your position to use you as his liaison to the Scholarship, something he could never quite control. And you have played into his game."

Sev's shame disappeared, replaced by a deep and powerful fear. The Historian was nearing the heresy of his mentor… but was it heresy if it came from the Historian? Was he not above all others, even the Elector?

The being of Olius leaned forward, his frown replaced by a curious stare.

"Tell me, Sev, whom do you serve?"

Sev looked into the eyes of the Historian, thinking back to the last time he had been asked this question. Then, he had answered Primus, yet now, he was ready to say Olius. So which was the truth?

"A High Scholar would never hesitate to answer that question, Sev."

The shame returned full force and Sev dropped his head. The Historian was right. Perhaps he wasn't deserving of this position. Perhaps the other High Scholars were wise to exclude him.

"Do not be ashamed. You have been put into a difficult situation, one mostly beyond your control. But there are elements of this situation which you can control."

The Historian leaned back in his chair.

"Sev, is there knowledge you hold which you have not shared with the Scholarship?"

Sev took a deep breath, ignoring his racing heart.

"Yes, Historian."

"This knowledge, is it related to your time at the Palace, constrained by the oath you took upon leaving?"

"Yes, Historian."

The Historian nodded, then smiled encouragingly.

"Sev, are you willing to share this knowledge here and now?"

Sev tried to calm himself, in vain.

"Do you will it, Historian?"

"I do, High Scholar."

The being of Olius emphasized the title, and Sev knew there was no turning back.

"Then I will share it with you, Historian."

He took another deep breath, ignoring the terror in his heart. This was the path he had chosen eight revolutions ago, and now began the ultimate test.

"Historian, the Palace oath forbids me from speaking of the security measures put in place for the ongoing struggle against Secundus."

The Historian gave him a curious look.

"The ongoing struggle? Is Primus at war?"

Sev shook his head.

"No, Historian. But we were told of small, hostile encounters occurring from time to time."

The being of Olius continued to peer at him, intrigued. Something about this curiosity bothered Sev, but he was already past the point of no return.

"Did these confrontations take place on Priman soil?" he asked.

Sev hesitated.

"No, Historian. They occurred in space."

"Were you present at any of these encounters?"

Sev shook his head again.

"No, Historian."

"Have you yourself been in space?"

Sev frowned. This is what he was afraid of.

"Yes, Historian."

"And this was not aboard a trade ship, I take it?"

Sev's frown deepened.

"No, Historian."

The being of Olius nodded, deep in thought.

"So the Palace has made progress with the technology of Olius?"

There was no anger in his tone or expression, but Sev felt ashamed all the same.

"Yes, Historian."

The Historian eyed him curiously.

"How much progress has been made?"

"I—I'm not sure, Historian. I know nothing about their research, though I know most of their knowledge comes from the trade ships."

Again, the being of Olius looked away, lost in thought. Sev tried to decipher the man's expression, to read between the lines of their conversation, but the meaning was lost to him, beyond his comprehension.

Finally, the Historian looked up with a smile.

"High Scholar, I thank you for your time and of course your struggle. I know this was not easy for you."

Sev nodded absent-mindedly, the reality of what he had just done sinking in.

"Historian, if word reaches the Palace of my treason..."

The Historian gave him an incredulous look.

"Treason? High Scholar, you should not consider your actions treason, even if the Palace deems it so. For the time being, our conversation will remain between us, and I see no need to let the Palace know."

The Historian's reply was calm, almost nonchalant, but Sev felt no relief.

"Most important, Sev, is that you have made clear steps to prove your worth."

At these words, Sev perked up, attentive.

"Historian?"

The man stood from his chair, smiling.

"Get some sleep, High Scholar. The next council is an important one."

***

Sev was unable to follow the Historian's advice, as the potential repercussions for what he had done played through his mind over and over, denying him any chance to sleep. A vision of the Elector's personal guardians, hotswords drawn, dominated his imagination, and when he heard a knock at the door, he expected one of them to enter... but it was just the usual servant, bringing his morning meal.

He struggled out of bed, his muscles aching despite a lack of activity. The breakfast had little taste, but he scarfed it down, exiting his chambers and heading to the Room of Council. So great was the chaos in his mind, Sev almost didn't notice the Elder Scholar address him in the opening statement.

"High Scholar Sev of Primus," the old man announced.

Sev saw the eyes of the Council upon him and wondered if this wasn't some sort of hallucination; had his exclusion really ended?

"The Historian has requested you aid him in his quest to discover if there is any information the Elector is withholding from the Scholarship regarding Secundus. Do you accept this assignment?"

There was disdain in the man's words, but Sev hardly cared. Was this some cruel joke? Had he not already proven himself worthy? Their private conversation had bordered on treason, but accepting this task would spell his death.

"High Scholar."

Sev turned to the voice of Olius.

"The Council was adamant I do not ask this of you as they believe you are neither capable nor trustworthy, but I have assured them you are both. However, I understand this assignment brings with it great risk. You must choose, High Scholar, between your duty to Primus and your duty to Olius. Whom do you truly serve?"

Sev looked at the other High Scholars, most of them eyeing him the same way as the Elder Scholar. No doubt they had expected his continued exclusion, his eventual expulsion by some technicality. Now the being of Olius was putting him front and center, and Sev could tell it was causing a some frustration. And as much as he hated to admit it, he drew a certain pleasure from their reaction, from their anger.

"Olius, Historian."

He turned to the Elder Scholar.

"I accept this assignment."

The Elder Scholar nodded, no less contemptuous. It was clear he didn't believe Sev would succeed. Of course, Sev himself didn't believe it—this task was far more likely to fail than succeed. But he would do his best. This was his duty, as a High Scholar of Primus.

Admission

Sev's initial resolve was remarkably short-lived—even before the end of the morning council, he was cursing himself for accepting this assignment. Determine if the Elector was withholding information from the Scholarship regarding Secundus? Of course he was, and the Council knew it. But to get the supreme leader to admit to such a thing in an official manner? Sev thought back to the Elector's time in the Room of Council and wondered how he was supposed to succeed where the being of Olius had failed...

Either the Council had a skewed understanding of his past or this was a trap, a way to get him on the bad side of the Palace. If the Elector disassociated from Sev, the Elder Scholar could demote him, undoing this whole mess—a move that would destroy his reputation, but may well save his life. Still, there was a hole in this theory: the mission hadn't come from the Elder Scholar, it had come from the beacon of truth himself, the only man who seemed to believe in him.

Of course, the Historian's behavior brought its own set of questions. During their private meeting, the Historian had glossed over Sev's mention of hostile encounters, focusing instead on the progress the Palace had made with Olian technology. This part made sense: his mission was to learn as much as possible about Primus, and such research fell under the scope of his duty. So why was Sev's assignment to find information regarding Secundus?

If the Historian wanted information on their neighbor, he could get it firsthand—while no one knew the frequency or arrangement of the Historian's visits, Sev knew the man would at some point return to Secundus. If their Scholarship still existed, he would learn everything he wanted from them. So again, why bother with the Palace's data?

These thoughts overwhelmed his sleep-deprived mind, and he felt a measure of relief when the Elder Scholar suggested he skip the next few councils to focus on his assignment. Yes, this was another type of exclusion, but he needed to get his head straight before he'd be of any use in the Room of Council—assuming, of course, he'd still have his head for the foreseeable future.

He made a point to retire early that evening, before he had even had his evening meal, but just as he was falling asleep, a knock forced him out of his cot.

"Sev."

There was concern in Folin's tone, no doubt stemming from Sev's haggard appearance.

"Folin," Sev replied, somewhat relieved to see his friend at the door. Had it been almost anyone else—including the Historian—Sev would not have reacted as warmly.

"May I come in?"

Sev nodded, stepping aside so Folin could enter.

"Are you well, brother?"

Sev took a seat and nodded, giving his friend a small smile.

"I'm just tired, Folin."

Folin frowned, clearly concerned.

"The Council works you so?"

Sev chuckled.

"The Historian himself, would you believe it?"

Folin continued to stare at him, unsure of how to proceed.

"Perhaps I will come back another time, when you are less busy..." he began.

Sev shook his head.

"No, Folin, please. What is it?"

Folin hesitated.

"Sev, I come to you about the Arbitration..."

Sev looked up, surprised by the words.

"The Arbitration?"

Folin, in turn, seemed surprised by his reaction.

"Yes, you wanted to talk about it, remember?"

It took a moment for Sev to navigate the fog of his mind, but he did remember: two rotations before the Arrival, he had approached Folin to talk about the situation, but there hadn't been time.

"I meant to bring it up at our last meeting," he added, "but we were interrupted before I had the chance. In fact, I've been wondering when might be a good time to see you, but wasn't sure if you'd have the time. It seems I chose a poor moment. As I said, I can come back another time, when you are not as fatigued."

As his friend spoke, the fog faded, granting Sev a moment of clarity.

"Actually, Folin, I want to ask you a favor."

It was only then—with his presence of mind back to a normal level— that he realized his friend was still standing.

"Please, Folin, take a seat."

Folin sat down, his eyes on Sev.

"What do you need?"

"I need you to look into a local village—one from the Arbitration."

Folin gave him a look bordering on suspicion.

"What are you looking for?"

"Folin, one of the patriarchs came to visit me the evening the Arrival was announced. You recall there was a death, and the accused man was sentenced to a lifetime of servitude? Well—"

Folin raised his hand to stop him.

"Sev, we've already had this conversation. The man was killed under suspicious circumstances only one rotation into his punishment. At the time, I told you I believed it was by men of the Palace."

Sev hesitated, embarrassed. So much had happened, it was hard to keep track.

"Sorry, Folin. I remember, but the situation is more complicated now."

Folin frowned.

"More complicated?"

Sev nodded.

"I visited one of the villages, the one under the eastern ridge, to speak to the family he was meant to serve."

Sev could see a flash of surprise in his friend's expression but didn't give him time to respond.

"As you can imagine, my presence was not taken kindly, though I did speak to the original victim's woman. I promised her the Scholarship would take care of her and left. This was just before the Arrival, and as you can imagine, since then I haven't had enough time to address the situation."

Again, Folin hesitated, processing what Sev was telling him. When he replied, it was cautiously, deliberately.

"You want me to see to it this woman is taken care of?"

Sev frowned.

"I wish it were that simple, Folin, but the situation has complicated even further."

Folin gave him a concerned look, but said nothing.

"Just two rotations ago, the same patriarch came to visit me again. This time, he asked me to remove myself from the situation, as my involvement had caused his village much pain. I tried to figure out what he meant by these words, but the man was unwilling to go into detail."

Folin sighed, looking away.

"I take it you want me to find out what happened?"

Sev nodded.

"I believe the Palace—or at least this soldier—is retaliating for my actions."

They sat in silence for a moment, and Sev could see his friend struggling to respond.

"Sev, I think you should listen to the patriarch."

Folin looked up at him, a sadness in his eyes.

"We both know what happened here. The soldier probably killed the accused, but even if he didn't, your visit—one you yourself claim was tense—caused a reaction, this pain he spoke of."

Sev stared at Folin, incredulous.

"You think we should do nothing?"

Folin sighed again, and for the first time, Sev noted his friend looked almost as haggard as he did.

"Sev, I have to take some responsibility for what has happened, since I encouraged you to act on what you thought was right, but I think this has gone as far as it can go. I know you crave justice for these people, but what good will my presence do? Even with irrefutable evidence the soldier was involved with the accused's death, what can the Scholarship do? Inform the Elector? No, if I go to this village to investigate, not only will I not find any such evidence, at best I will bring more pain."

For a moment, Sev sat in silence, trying to find a hole in Folin's theory. But the moment of clarity was gone, washed away under a wave of frustration and fatigue. It was so overwhelming, Sev smashed his fist into the table.

"Damn it all!"

Folin's eyes widened, though he didn't flinch. Sev gave him an apologetic look.

"I'm sorry, Folin, it's just—"

But Folin lifted his hand and shook his head.

"No, Sev, there is nothing to apologize for. I feel the same frustration, the same pain—that is why I was so encouraging before."

He flashed a sad smile.

"I will say I'm proud of you, Sev. When we first had this conversation, you refused to admit the possibility of the Palace's guilt, but now you said it yourself—they, or at least one of their soldiers, are almost certainly responsible for what has happened. It's a shame, truly. If the Palace would uphold justice within its own ranks the way it claims it does, maybe this wouldn't be such an issue."

Sev nodded absentmindedly, aware of a thought on the periphery of his mind, something seemingly important but well beyond his current state.

Folin stood with a sad smile.

"I will see what I can do about the woman, Sev. At minimum, some good may yet come of this."

Sev stared at his friend in admiration, surprised by his unflinching optimism.

"Go with Olius, brother," he said.

Folin smiled.

"And you."

And with that, he exited the chamber, and Sev carried himself back to bed, falling asleep instantly.

***

Sev woke the next rotation physically rested but mentally restless. The same questions plagued his mind, with the added burden of the Arbitration piled on top. He had tried to do what was right and failed while the soldier had acted outside the limits of his authority and would get away with it. Even during the Historian's Visit, when the power of the Scholarship for once outranked that of the Palace, the men in purple and black could act without repercussion.

Sev reeled in this line of thought, shocked. Where had such treasonous ideas come from? Eight revolutions he had been with the Scholarship, but before that, he himself wore the purple and black. Back then, he had worked for the Palace, for Primus. He had stood in the same place this soldier now stood, with a hotsword on his belt and a thirst for glory.

He tried to imagine himself in the same position, with the same temptations—if such a word could even be used. Would the old Sev have done what this man had done? He wanted to deny it, to claim he would never disrespect the process of Arbitration, not even for his own pride, but was that really the case? Or was this the new Sev, the white and gold Sev, speaking louder than the old one?

But was this Sev really all that new? Had the pride really disappeared? Every rotation, he struggled with patience, with honesty, with the ideals of Olius. What madness had brought him here, to a place at the stone table?

Eight revolutions ago, Sev left the Palace of his own volition—an incredibly rare move, and one that was normally impossible. He thought back to his last rotations in purple and black: the pending promotion, the growing disillusionment. The Scholarship represented his only chance of escape, and part of him still couldn't believe it had been approved. Unless, of course, his detractors were right, and the Elector considered him a spy, a tool within the ranks of the white and gold.

No, Sev thought to himself, this was absurd. These treasonous thoughts had to end. He had left the Palace for a reason, but he had joined it for a reason too. If the Scholarship was the beacon of truth, the Palace was the beacon of justice, and the supreme leader stood for justice for all Primans...

And then it came to him—the thought in the back of his mind, the one spurred by his conversation with Folin—and he realized what he needed to do.

***

Two rotations later, Sev stood outside the audience chamber of the Grand Palace, wondering what exactly he thought he was doing. Yes, he himself had requested the meeting, but why?

A part of him would claim it was to fulfill the mission assigned to him, to determine if the Elector was withholding information from the Scholarship regarding Secundus, but this part of him was lying. If anything, the Historian's task was the reason it had taken him two rotations to act on his initial thought.

No, the real reason Sev was here was to prove he hadn't wasted the part of his life he couldn't seem to escape.

"The Elector will see you now, High Scholar."

The servant opened the chamber doors, and Sev stepped into the grand hall, his heart in a frenzy. What if the supreme leader knew about his conversation with the Historian? If the Elector found out he had broken his oath...

"Welcome, Sev of Primus."

Sev reached the bottom of the throne and fell to knee and hand.

"Thank you for granting me an audience, Elector."

"Rise, High Scholar. State your business."

There was an eagerness in his voice that worried Sev, but he was already here, there was no turning back.

"Elector, I come to you regarding a matter of personal importance."

The Elector eyed him curiously.

"You have my attention, High Scholar. Explain this matter."

"Thank you, Elector. In the rotations before my promotion, I was part of an Arbitration between two local villages. The Arbiters passed their judgement, but in the time since, I've learned our decision has been openly ignored."

"The villagers have disobeyed the edict?"

Sev shook his head, his heart still in a frenzy. What he said next could be dangerous, but he had come this far—there was no turning back now.

"No, Elector. The other Arbiter—the soldier."

The supreme leader hesitated, and Sev tried to read his expression. Though he dared not take his eyes off the Elector, Sev felt the presence of the personal guardians, knew how close they stood, how quickly they could reach him...

"High Scholar, this is a serious accusation you bring forward."

The Elector leaned back in his chair.

"After this audience, we will arrange a meeting with the presiding general and you have my word the matter will be dealt with appropriately."

Sev allowed himself a deep breath—while he wasn't sure how a meeting with the man's general would go, to hear the supreme leader himself assure the matter would be dealt with...

"Before we can address this issue, however, I have a question for you, Sev of Primus."

The Elector paused, and Sev's momentary relief disappeared.

"Yes, Elector?"

"Has the Historian asked you to share any knowledge regarding Secundus?"

A sharp, cold terror came over him, and Sev felt frozen in place. This was it, he thought. He no longer stood near the possibility of death, but with it fully.

As the silence dragged on, the Elector's expression hardened, a frown forming in response to Sev's hesitation. But just as he was about to lose all hope, just before he caved and admitted to breaking the oath, instinct took over, formulating an obfuscated reply.

"Elector, it is worse than that. The Historian has asked me to determine if you are withholding information from the Scholarship related to Secundus."

The Elector's frown deepened.

"He has?"

Again, Sev felt an impeding and unavoidable doom. He had barely escaped revealing his own treason, but he was not yet free.

"Yes, Elector. The assignment was given to me not long after your audience in the Room of Council."

The Elector nodded slowly, the frown no less present.

"And do you plan to fulfill this assignment?"

And there it was—the question he could not avoid, the answer he could not obfuscate. Either he was going to act the part of High Scholar, or he was wasting his time. The being of Olius himself had presented him this task, this ultimate test. If he was not willing to put his life on the line for the truth, he had no place in the coveted twelve.

"I do, Elector."

A flash of anger came over the man's expression.

"Sev of Primus, have you come here to commit treason against the Palace?"

Sev dropped to knee and hand.

"Elector, I am a High Scholar. I am here to let you know of the task I was assigned, and I am also here to follow the Historian's line of inquiry in the hopes I may be formally inducted to the Council. I am following the word of Olius, as is my duty. I apologize if you have taken offense, none was meant."

His eyes were pressed shut, and Sev hoped for a quick end. He had heard death by hotsword was swift, especially at the hands of the guardians—a strike through the neck, ending his life and his misery.

"Rise, High Scholar."

There was a change in the Elector's tone that surprised Sev, and when he rose and looked upon the supreme leader, he saw the anger was gone.

"Sev of Primus, did you say you have not yet been formally inducted to the Council?"

Sev stared at the supreme leader, wondering how he wasn't yet dead. What had happened? What had changed?

"No, Elector."

Sev expected the anger to return but it dissipated further.

"Very well, Sev of Primus, I will help you in your task."

Even though the anger had vanished, there was something in the Elector's tone that didn't quite match his words. Sev tried to find the meaning between the lines, but it was lost on him.

"You may return to the Scholarship and let the Council know the Historian was right. There is information the Palace is withholding from the Scholarship regarding Secundus."

Part of him was astonished at this announcement, and he reacted in shock.

"Elector—"

His response was cut short by the Elector's raised hand.

"This is a matter for the Historian himself. Arrange another audience and tell him I am prepared to share the information he seeks."

***

Sev stepped out the audience chamber in a daze, ready to analyze this latest development on his return to the Scholarship, but a servant blocked his path.

"High Scholar, the Elector has asked me to arrange a meeting between you and one of the generals."

Sev was so preoccupied with what the Elector had said, he stared at the servant as if he didn't know what he was talking about.

"If you follow me," he continued, "I will take a detailed account of the incident, and we can determine which general is in charge of the soldier you speak of."

Finally, Sev snapped out of his trance.

"Yes, yes. Lead the way."

The servant took him through the ornate halls, and Sev struggled to keep his focus. The Elector admitted to hiding information from the Scholarship... Sure, everyone knew it was true, but why had he admitted it?

They reached a small chamber with a desk, and the servant asked Sev to sit at the table while he grabbed his pen and parchment.

"Please, High Scholar, you may begin your account."

Sev did his best to clear his head and focus, explaining the series of incidents related to the Arbitration as accurately as he could. There were certain details—especially that of his nighttime visit—which brought him a measure of embarrassment, but he thought it best to share as thorough an account as possible, and the servant showed no outward judgement. Once he was finished, Sev was escorted to the exit, and the burning questions returned.

The Elector's statement—while not surprising—was troubling. There was something odd about the way he had suddenly changed tone, the way he had agreed to help. Did the supreme leader aim to grant Sev a formal induction on the Council by agreeing to this conversation with the Historian? It seemed like a rather high price to pay for a relatively small reward, and Sev knew there was something here he didn't yet understand.

There was a reason the Scholarship had stopped compiling data on their neighbor, and that reason was security. Though they were not technically at war, and while trade was active and constant, there remained quite a bit of tension between the two worlds. And in a time of such heightened tension, information was power, including information about information. By keeping all knowledge of Secundus inside the Palace, their enemy was unlikely to know how much Primus knew.

Sev thought back to old conversations he had overheard about Secundan missions seeking intelligence on Priman security measures. If Secundus somehow learned all of Primus's defense capabilities, it could incite an all-out war. And with the Historian potentially visiting their neighbor sometime in the future, it was no surprise the Elector preferred not to show all his cards.

But the Historian wouldn't share this data with Secundus. Above all else, the being of Olius was a being of peace, and no doubt he knew better than to make an exchange that might lead to war. What worried him more was the Scholarship of Primus—not that there were any traitors among them, but that the secrets of the Palace would become common knowledge. Data tomes were open and available to all, what would stop such information from traveling, even as far as Secundus?

The light of Olius was beginning to fade, but Sev made no attempt to hurry. He tried to peek into the future, to discern where this new meeting between Elector and Historian might lead, but no clear path emerged. For now, he had a night's rest before him, and he would need every ounce of sleep he could get.

***

The following rotation, the council began as it always did, and Sev waited for his moment.

"Sev of Primus, do you have any news regarding your assignment?"

It was clear by the Elder Scholar's tone that he expected the answer to be no, but the man was about to be disappointed.

"Yes, Elder Scholar, I do."

It took a moment for the response to register, and Sev reveled in the hesitation.

"Y-you do?"

It was almost too enjoyable, and Sev caught himself before he smiled. He should not hold such animosity for the Elder Scholar.

"Yes, Elder Scholar, I do."

The man peered at him with suspicion.

"Very well then, share it with us."

"Of course, Elder Scholar."

Sev paused, enjoying the attention of the entire Council.

"The Elector has admitted to withholding information from the Scholarship regarding Secundus and is willing to share the knowledge we seek."

Sev turned his eyes to the Historian.

"He has asked for another audience to present this information personally."

The other High Scholars murmured among themselves but the Historian's eyes remained fixed on Sev.

"What was the purpose of your audience with the Elector on the last rotation, High Scholar?" he asked.

Sev was caught off-guard by the question, and it took him a moment to reply.

"Historian, I went to the Palace regarding a matter of Arbitration. Once there, the opportunity to fulfill my assignment presented itself, and I took it."

"A matter of Arbitration?"

Sev hesitated, then dove into the entire story, repeating what he had told the Palace servant. Despite the length of his speech, no one interrupted, and when he was finished, the Historian nodded slowly.

"You believe the Elector will help bring justice to this situation, against one of his own men and without direct evidence?"

Sev frowned.

"I am not sure, Historian, but I thought it worth a try."

To Sev's surprise, the Historian smiled.

"I agree. Well done, High Scholar. After this council, we will arrange an audience for the Elector on the following rotation."

Sev nodded.

"Yes, Historian."

From there, the council returned to normal matters of business, and Sev allowed himself a measure of relief. He had completed an assignment that by all respects should have been impossible—he deserved a little relaxation.

So why didn't he feel accomplished? Why was he still so worried?

***

The Historian invited Sev to sit with him at the mid-rotation meal, and Sev reluctantly agreed. Once inside the Hall of Nourishment, it took some time to get their food, as many Scholars wanted to speak with the being of Olius about matters large and small.

When they finally took their seats—with eager Scholars all around them—the Historian waved a servant over.

"Sev, did the Elector make any special requests regarding this audience?"

Sev thought back to his conversation with the supreme leader then shook his head.

"No, Historian, he did not."

The servant arrived with pen and parchment, and the Historian had him scribe an invitation for the Elector. When he was done, the being of Olius took the paper and signed it.

"Please see to it this arrives at the Palace before last light."

The servant nodded.

"Yes, Historian."

Throughout the course of the interaction, the other Scholars had barely touched their food, and Sev could feel their stares.

"High Scholar, I wish to ask you a question."

Sev tensed, knowing the others were listening in.

"Yes, Historian?"

"In your most recent audience, did you tell the Elector the reason for your visit?"

Sev looked up and saw a benign curiosity in the Historian's eyes, though he was surprised by the question. Why hadn't he asked it in council?

"Yes, Historian."

The being of Olius nodded slowly, then looked up and behind Sev, who turned to see what had caught his attention.

"Sev of Primus?"

An envoy of the Palace, in robes of purple and black. But that was impossible, the message could not have already arrived...

"Yes?"

"The general will meet you on this rotation, if you are available."

Sev glanced back at the Historian, who nodded his approval.

"As you said, it's worth a try."

Sev turned back to the envoy.

"I will join you after my meal."

The man nodded and stepped away, and Sev felt the stares of more Scholars now, though he did his best to ignore them.

"You do not mind if I miss the council?"

The Historian shook his head.

"Join us when you are finished, and let us know what unfolded."

Sev nodded, then took to his meal. He was just as curious as the Historian to see where this thread would lead.

***

Walking along the path to the Palace in the mid-rotation heat, Sev wondered if he should have insisted for a meeting in the Scholarship. Olius was particularly strong at this time, and he was tempted to take shelter in the Hall of Arbitration along the way.

He thought back to the last time he was inside the small chamber, the series of events leading to his current journey. For Sev, the coming meeting with the Priman general wasn't just the next step in the saga: it was a way to alleviate his worries, to prove the purple and black still stood for justice.

Between the disdain the other Scholars held for the Palace and the treason emerging in his own mind, Sev had started to doubt the institution to which he had once sworn loyalty. By bringing this situation to the Elector's attention, he hoped to vindicate the supreme leader, to prove to himself and perhaps even the other Scholars that the Palace fulfilled its stated role, despite its reputation. But what would he do if he proved the opposite?

Sev's head began to ache, a dull throb exacerbated by the stunning heat. He remembered his last revolutions with the Palace, the things leading to his eventual departure: unnecessary ploys, subtle plots, anything and everything to gain a foothold of power over others. These memories brought little hope for the coming meeting, but they also begged the question: was the Scholarship all that different?

For his first eight revolutions, Sev might argue that was the case. But now, at the top of the hierarchy, where he had expected the ideals of Olius to hold the truest, he was peeking behind the curtain, seeing the hints of envy and greed—the way the other High Scholars eyed him when he had the Historian's attention, the way the Elder Scholar disrespected him in the Room of Council...

The stark black walls of the Palace stood before him and Sev quickened his pace. Perhaps he was overreacting, he told himself. Taking all of this too personally. After all, the Council hadn't put him there, the Elector had. Truthfully, Sev held a secret contempt for the supreme leader's promotion, as it had brought him into this mess. He would never tell him that, of course. Truth or not, such words were suicide.

***

The Palace was divided into two main buildings: the Grand Palace, which housed the Elector and his generals, and the Barracks, which housed most of the lower officers and soldiers. In his service to Primus, Sev had spent far more time in the Barracks than the Palace itself, giving the former a hint of familiarity over the latter. Still, Sev felt far from comfortable following his soldier escort through these halls: why had the general chosen to meet him here? He couldn't remember a general ever holding an audience in the Barracks, so why now?

As they walked, Sev recalled the strict schedules and rules within the black walls, wondering how he had ever managed. There was a certain rigidity to the life of a soldier, and not just in their routines—the black and white nature of Palace culture was one of the main reasons he had sought an escape, and he wondered how he would convince this general to see a hint of grey. Then, when they rounded a final corner, it dawned on Sev where they were headed, and he realized he had made a mistake.

The soldier led him into one of the main halls of the Barracks, a place that usually served as a mess, though it occasionally hosted larger gatherings. Sev walked in on exactly such a gathering, with an entire battalion standing at attention inside the chamber, their general waiting patiently at the front.

"High Scholar," he said, smiling.

The general's smile lacked warmth, and Sev knew he had chosen this place to evoke memories of servitude, to remind him who was in charge.

"General," he replied, stepping closer.

Mistake or not, Sev was here now, and he wasn't going to let the Palace intimidate him. At least, no one outside the Elector himself.

"The Elector informed me of certain issues stemming from a recent Arbitration," the man began.

Sev glanced across the crowd of soldiers in purple and black, searching for a particular face. But there were so many of them…

"Indeed, general, it seems as if one of your soldiers has taken justice into their own hands and acted beyond the will of the Arbitration."

He returned his attention to the man in charge, who smiled once more.

"High Scholar, you were once a soldier, were you not?"

Sev kept his frustration in check.

"Yes, general."

"Tell me, High Scholar, is justice not the purpose of the Palace itself? Is it not the very duty of a soldier to, as you say, take justice into their own hands?"

Sev hesitated, contemplating his reply. What if this conversation did more harm than good? What if the general managed to make a mockery of the Scholarship in front of several hundred soldiers? That would be the opposite of what he hoped to accomplish…

"General, as you know, at a certain point I left the Palace to pursue life as a Scholar."

The general eyed him curiously, but said nothing.

"In my eight revolutions with the Scholarship, I have learned a level of nuance I never held as a man of the Palace, the same nuance that no doubt brought the Elector to promote me to High Scholar, and that cemented the very practice of Arbitration in the first place."

The general frowned, but Sev pressed on.

"So while the Palace has always been the arm of justice on Primus, the Scholarship has always been the arm of knowledge. But justice cannot function without knowledge, otherwise it is blind. And that is why I am here on this rotation, general, because I fear justice has acted in good faith, but it has acted blindly."

The general studied Sev intently, sizing up this man of white and gold.

"High Scholar, you are right. Justice cannot function without knowledge, otherwise it is blind. So tell me, what is it precisely you accuse this soldier of?"

Sev felt the stares of hundreds of men, but focused on the eyes of just one.

"General, as you read in my account, the soldier showed visible anger at our eventual decision, though that in itself is no crime. What is concerning is his immediate harassment of the patriarch of the accused, leading to his identification of the accused, as well as his presence at the accused's arrival at his sentence."

The general's smile returned.

"High Scholar, I understand your concerns, but the soldier acted on intuition. According to the Arbitration, the accused man was a killer. The soldier went to identify him immediately, then came to me with the request to be present at his arrival so as to ensure the village's safety should he decide to retaliate. Indeed, later in the rotation, he did just that, and the soldier in question acted to protect the other citizens."

Sev frowned, questioning the judgement that brought him here. Still, he was well in it now, and turning away would only make things worse.

"General, how many deserters have you had in your battalion?"

A subtle change of expression let Sev know he had caught the general off-guard.

"Deserters?"

"Yes, general. In your time in charge of this battalion, how many deserters have you had to deal with?"

For a moment, the man stared at him suspiciously, and Sev thought he might not answer.

"Four."

Sev allowed himself an almost imperceptible smile. The general could have lied and said zero, but Sev had lived in these halls—he knew the truth.

"Four. A rare occurrence of course, but a real one nonetheless. General, these men who attempted to desert, they all took the Palace oath, did they not?"

Now the general caught wind of Sev's plan and his frown returned.

"Yes."

"General, I admit it is rare indeed, but there are men of the Palace who do not uphold their duty to truth. It is possible the soldier in question has broken his oath to the Palace and fabricated his version of events."

Sev knew the soldier hadn't lied at all—in fact, he had told the general everything, including his intention to ignore the Arbitration. But such an accusation would bring the general's character into question, and Sev would be dead before he left the room.

"High Scholar, do you trust the word of the peasants over that of a man of the Palace?"

Gone was the false cordiality, replaced with open malice. Sev knew his options were thinning, the paths before him far more dangerous than they had been moments ago. Why had he done this? Why did he continue to dig a hole from which he might never escape?

"No, general. But a man of Olius must consider all possibilities, lest his own bias blind him from the truth."

The general took a step forward, halving the distance between them. They stood eye to eye much as the Elector and Historian had, one in rich purple and black, the other in bright white and gold.

"To my knowledge, the soldier in question is a man of his word, and there is no reason to doubt his assessment. Does this satisfy you, High Scholar?"

Sev held his ground, unflinching, then turned to the battalion once more. He scanned the faces of the men, looking for the one he knew, the one they discussed, but there was no sign of him. Finally, he turned back to the general and smiled.

"Yes, general, it does. Thank you for your help in the matter, and my apologies for the interruption of your schedule."

Sev turned on his heel and glanced at the soldier who had escorted him.

"Would you escort me out?"

The soldier looked from him to the general.

"Show him out," came the voice from behind him.

The soldier turned around and Sev started after him.

"High Scholar."

Sev turned back to the general, who gave him another smile.

"I hope to see you again soon," he said.

Sev hesitated, then turned back around, following the soldier out of the hall.

***

Although the heat had subsided, Sev's return to the Scholarship was no less troubled. From an outside perspective, he ought to be proud of himself: he had done everything within his power to fix the situation, going so far as to put his life on the line for Hibbon and his people. And despite his inability to bring true justice to those affected, he had managed to uphold the Scholarship's dignity, as evidenced by the general's frustration.

In one aspect, however, he had failed entirely, and this aspect threatened to push his already questionable beliefs into dangerous territory: he was unable to prove the Palace's commitment to justice within its ranks. In fact, quite the opposite.

He tried to defend the general's actions, to find excuses for his behavior, but with each passing rotation, he found it harder and harder to justify the Palace's behavior. Was he being unduly influenced by the treasonous opinions of certain members of the Scholarship, or was he allowing himself to think openly for a change?

Worst of all were the general's parting words. He hoped to see him again soon? Sev knew a subtle threat when he heard one, and it was a stretch to call this one subtle.

He had considered talking to the Elector, letting him know of the menacing remark, but hadn't he just proven the inability of the black fortress to judge its own? No, the person he needed to tell was in the buildings up ahead, no doubt directing another fruitful council. But what could the Historian do? Bring it up to the Elector during his audience?

Sev made an effort to clear his busy mind. What the Historian did was not his responsibility, he only needed to pass along the message. What was of more immediate concern, given the way the situation had unfolded, was the woman in the village. Had Folin had the opportunity to investigate? Several rotations had passed since their chat, but Sev had been far too occupied with the Historian's assignment to check in with his friend—it was time to change that.

With a clear mind and renewed purpose, Sev marched into the Scholarship and scanned the most popular halls. He enlisted the help of two servants, who scurried off in opposite directions to search other buildings on the campus.

Sev had yet to acclimate to the sheer number of people in the Scholarship, and he wandered the corridors with a mix of frustration and awe. On a normal rotation, it might be hard to find Folin, but now? It might be impossible.

Still, it was amazing to see the true size of the institution. The Scholarship tried to maintain at least one Scholar per village, and Sev knew this was a much wider reach than that of the Palace. While the Elector had more men, his forces only occupied villages on or near ore deposits—those involved with mining. But what of the hundreds of other villages, far away from such riches? Were there citizens of Primus whose only authority was the Scholarship, who heeded the words of white and gold over those of purple and black?

"High Scholar."

One of the servants interrupted his search.

"Yes?"

"I've been told Scholar Folin is in the Room of Council."

Sev thanked him and turned around, heading back to the center of campus. If Folin was in the Room of Council, he could report the general's threat and follow up about the woman at the same time. Anything to keep his mind from following another treasonous path…

When he reached the chamber door, Sev hesitated, wondering if he should wait so as to not interrupt. Then he remembered the robes he was wearing and cursed the psychological effect of his continued exclusion.

As soon as he stepped inside, the Historian raised his hand, halting all discussion.

"High Scholar."

Folin turned to see him, but Sev first addressed the being of Olius.

"Historian, I have returned from the Palace."

The Historian nodded.

"Scholar, please excuse us. We will continue this conversation at a later time."

Folin turned back to the Council.

"Yes, Historian."

As he turned to leave, Sev noted the sadness in his friend's eyes. What had happened…? Then, just as Folin passed him by, Sev remembered why he was here and called after him.

"Scholar."

Folin hesitated, turning around.

"Yes, High Scholar?"

"Can you wait outside? I wish to speak to you about the Arbitration afterward."

Folin glanced past him, at the Historian, then back to Sev.

"Yes, High Scholar. I had the same wish."

Sev frowned, noting the same sadness in his eyes.

"Thank you, Scholar."

Folin nodded and left the chamber.

"High Scholar?"

The Historian's voice caught his attention, and Sev turned back to the Council.

"My apologies, Historian."

The being of Olius nodded.

"None necessary, High Scholar. Please tell us of your discussion with the general."

The other faces at the table betrayed a mix of curiosity and frustration, but Sev kept his attention on the Historian.

"Historian, the general attempted to intimidate me by holding our conversation in front of his battalion, but I held firm with the values of the Scholarship."

Sev paused, frowning.

"However, not only was I unable to resolve the situation, the general gave a thinly-veiled threat upon my exit."

The Historian gave him a concerned look.

"A threat?"

Sev nodded.

"As I made to leave, he told me he hoped to see me again. By the look on his face, the meaning behind the words was clear."

The Historian nodded slowly, and Sev shot another glance at the other High Scholars. Gone was their curiosity and frustration, replaced by something closer to fear…

"High Scholar, thank you for your account."

Sev noted a subtle change in the Historian's demeanor, and he paid close attention to the man's words.

"It seems both you and Scholar Folin wish to meet regarding this Arbitration situation. Please take the rest of the rotation to catch up with him on the details and determine the next steps, if any."

There was something hiding behind these statements, a troubling shift in tone and manner that made Sev wholly uncomfortable.

"Yes, Historian."

He dropped to knee and hand, eyeing the Council one last time, then stepped out of the room, the Historian's expression etched in his mind. Could it be possible? Had he seen fear in the being of Olius?

"Sev."

Sev nearly ran into his friend, standing just outside the chamber door.

"Folin," he replied, absentmindedly.

"You wanted to meet?"

Sev nodded.

"Yes, you have news of the woman?"

Folin frowned, and Sev felt his stomach drop.

"Can we speak in your quarters?"

Sev looked around the halls and saw dozens of Scholars moving to and fro.

"Of course."

The two of them made the short journey to his chambers, closing the door behind them.

"Sev, I'm afraid I have bad news."

Sev wondered how the rotation could get any worse.

"What is it?"

"Two rotations ago, I did as you asked and went to check on the woman. The patriarch was hostile to my presence, and for a time I thought the villagers would not allow me to see her. But after some argument, I was allowed to speak with her, though always with the patriarch present."

Sev nodded.

"As it was when I visited. And?"

"Well then I'm sure you know she was clearly coerced by his presence, but I managed to convince her to allow the Scholarship to care for her, at least for some time. I told her I would return on this rotation to bring her to our Hall of Care, and this morning, I made the journey to the village."

He paused, and Sev saw the sadness return.

"When I arrived, the patriarch met me with far less hostility, something that surprised me until I asked to see the woman. He told me she had disappeared that night, and invited me to see her empty home and the tracks leading into the desert."

Folin sighed, looking away.

"I knew something foul was at play, but the man prevented me from investigating further. She might have been taken into another hut or even another village, but I doubt the tracks I saw were actually hers—the gait was nearly impossible for someone of her stature."

Sev felt the frustration threatening to return but he pushed against it, fighting desperately to calm his thoughts.

"Why would they do this? Her coming to the Hall of Care is no threat to them."

Folin's frown deepened.

"Of course not, but this is not about what is or isn't a threat to them, Sev. This is about sending a message, and send one they did."

They stood in silence for some time, both wrapped in thought, before Sev spoke up once more.

"What do you think we should do?"

Folin shrugged.

"There's nothing to do, Sev. We have done everything we could—with the general, with the village—there is nothing left for us to do, at least nothing that won't bring more suffering."

Sev felt anguish on the periphery, an overwhelming and overpowering despair ready to take hold of his very core. But just before it could take root, Folin spoke again.

"I feel your frustration, Sev, but know this: the fight for justice is not won in one step by one person. It is won by the steps of many, all marching in the same direction. And it is precisely when things are at their worst that the decisions made are most important."

He stared at the man before him, astonished at the wisdom in his words. Why were his robes still mixed with the purple and black?

"I must go, Sev, but think on what I have said."

Sev nodded, then took his friend in an embrace.

"Go with Olius, brother."

"And you," Folin replied.

***

On the following rotation, the High Scholars and the Historian greeted the Elector at the entrance of the Scholarship once more. As the supreme leader approached, his personal guardians and a servant behind him, Sev remembered the last time the two men had seen one another—when the Elector hadn't dropped to knee and hand. Would he do the same now, at this introduction? His previous omission was a serious transgression, but to omit the gesture now would be a clear sign of disrespect.

The Elector stopped just in front of the Council, eyeing the being of Olius. After the slightest hesitation, he dropped to knee and hand.

"Rise, Elector."

It was only as it dissipated that Sev noted the tension he had felt not just within himself, but from the entire Council.

"Thank you for granting me an audience, Historian."

The Historian gave him a nod.

"Of course, Elector. High Scholar Sev has informed us you have information to share."

The Elector nodded.

"Yes, Historian."

"We will convene in the Room of Council, Elector, so that you may present this information."

The Historian gestured behind him, into the Scholarship, but the Elector hesitated.

"Forgive me, Historian, but I do not wish to present this information in the Room of Council."

Sev felt the tension rising once more, and a few of the High Scholars shared sideward glances.

"Where would you like to convene, Elector?"

"If I may, Historian, I request we meet privately in your quarters…"

The supreme leader turned to Sev.

"…with only yourself and High Scholar Sev of Primus in attendance."

This time, the rest of the Council did not hide their indignation.

"What is the meaning of this?"

The Elder Scholar took a step forward, anger in both his words and demeanor. Sev watched the Historian's hand come up to the man's chest, stopping him. A wave of heat came over them, and Sev turned to see both guardians in front of the Elector, hotswords drawn.

There was a flash of fear in the Elder Scholar's eyes, staring at the deadly blades. The edges shone red with scorching heat, distorting the air around them. Sev had seen them used many times, had smelt the burnt flesh, heard the terrible screams…

The fear in the Elder Scholar's eyes was quickly replaced by fury, a fury that threatened to aggravate the situation, but the being of Olius's hand held firm.

"Elder Scholar, please."

The Historian's tone was calm, unperturbed. The Elder Scholar's rage subsided, and he took a step back.

"My apologies, Historian."

After a breath, the guardians sheathed their blades slowly, deliberately.

"Elector, your request is unusual, may I ask why you desire this arrangement?"

The supreme leader's eyes lingered on the Elder Scholar for a moment before turning to the Historian.

"Yes, Historian. I will be willing to explain myself once we are in your quarters, as I have requested."

"Very well. Please follow me, Elector."

The Historian turned and walked into the Scholarship, with the Elector and his entourage close behind. For a moment Sev stood with the other High Scholars, stunned by what they had just witnessed.

"High Scholar Sev, will you join us?"

The Historian's voice broke the spell, and shock turned to shame as Sev felt everyone's eyes on him. He knew his former teacher was watching, and wondered if he would ever have a chance for a formal induction after this.

***

The walk to the Historian's quarters was a silent one, and Sev felt more uncomfortable than ever. Was this meeting not meant to mend the relationship between the Scholarship and the Palace? So far, it had not been as effective as hoped.

Sev could not believe the Elder Scholar's outburst. Yes, the Elector's request was offensive, but Sev had never seen the man show true anger. And to speak in such a manner to the Elector? It was unheard of, even for the interim leader of the Scholarship. Had the presence of the being of Olius clouded their judgment? Had they forgotten who wore the hotswords and who forsook violence?

When they reached the door, the Elector turned to his servant.

"Give the tome to High Scholar Sev of Primus."

The servant handed a large data tome to Sev, about three hand lengths tall, one and a half wide, and almost half a hand length thick. It was thicker and heavier than any data tome Sev had ever seen, and noticing the combination lock along one side, he realized it must contain a fail-safe of some kind: a vial of acid which would burst and destroy the contents if forced entry was attempted.

"Wait outside the door."

The guardians took their places by the entrance and the Historian led Sev and the Elector into his quarters.

"Shall we?"

The Historian gestured to the table, where three chairs waited. Sev placed the data tome down in front of them as they sat down.

"Historian, I thank you for your willingness to accept my requests," the Elector began.

The Historian nodded.

"Of course, Elector. I believe I understand the reasons behind your actions, but I do ask that you explain yourself."

Sev's eyes darted from one to the other, his mind trying to process this reality: he was in a meeting with the two most powerful beings in the system. It was exciting and terrifying all at once, but he did his best to focus on their words.

"Yes, Historian. The simple answer is I am trying to fulfill my duty, to ensure the safety of Primus. My motivation is security, not secrecy, but in practice these can be one and the same."

The Historian nodded.

"Of course, Elector. I understand your hesitation."

In that moment, the Historian's conduct was in such stark contrast to the Elder Scholar that Sev allowed himself a measure of hope. Perhaps there could be cooperation between these two men, between the will of Primus and the will of Olius—and perhaps he was on the front line, watching it unfold.

"Thank you, Historian. The information in this tome…"

He gestured to the book in front of Sev.

"…is of a highly sensitive nature. Perhaps the most sensitive that exists on Primus. That is why I have hesitated in sharing it, and that is why even now, as I share it, I do so conditionally."

The Historian eyed the Elector curiously.

"I see. Elector, I understand why you did not share this information sooner, but I do not understand the reason for this private meeting."

Sev also wondered why the supreme leader had requested this arrangement. Any information shared with the Historian would end up being shared with the Council.

"Historian, as a gesture to Olius, I invite you to look over the contents of this tome. However, I have requested this private meeting because I do not yet feel comfortable leaving the tome in the Scholarship, or sharing this data with the Council. Once you have looked over its contents, I will return with it to the Palace, and I ask that its contents remain strictly between the three of us."

The Elector gestured to Sev.

"I have asked High Scholar Sev of Primus to join us in case you have any desire to analyze it in the future. He will act as the sole liaison between us for this tome, as a matter of security."

Now the supreme leader was out of line. His language had shifted from desire to demand, and while the Elector was entitled to such a vocabulary with every being from the planet of Primus, this being was not of Primus.

The Historian considered the Elector's words, and Sev felt terror overtake excitement. He had little desire to be here and was more than willing to give his place to the Elder Scholar. But he had no freedom here. He could only wait with growing unease.

After a long pause, the Historian answered.

"Elector, I admire your commitment to your duties. As we both understand the relationship between the Palace and the Scholarship is in need of repair, I will agree to your terms. I only remind you I will need to copy all of this data before the Departure."

"Of course, Historian."

The being of Olius sat up straighter.

"Very well, time is of the essence. Could you please open the tome, Elector?"

"Yes, Historian."

The Elector pulled the tome in front of him and entered a combination on the lock. A loud click let them know it was safe to open, then the supreme leader pushed it back to Sev, who placed it in front of the Historian.

"High Scholar Sev of Primus, I ask you to look over the contents as well, provided you agree to the terms I asked of the Historian."

Sev looked up at the Elector, unable to read the thoughts behind the harsh lines in his face. There was something more to this situation, something beyond his knowledge, but once again he knew he had no choice.

"Yes, Elector."

Sev turned back to the pages of the data tome and looked on as the Historian scanned through the contents.

Data tomes were divided into sections, and this one seemed to have several related to interplanetary relations: shipping routes, trade agreements, cargo manifests—a comprehensive description of the last link between Primus and Secundus. At first, Sev wondered why the data in this tome was such a high matter of security: the Scholarship also had access to most of this data.

But when the Historian reached the last sections, Sev realized the reason for the Elector's caution. Buried underneath the records related to Priman-Secundan trade were hundreds of entries regarding the Palace's military relation with Secundus. Every specification an enemy could ask for was listed, including the nature and status of research ventures, offensive and defensive tactics, and a detailed log of the entire operational fleet.

Sev's eyes went wide and he glanced up at the Elector, who remained wordless and patient. Perhaps, he thought, the supreme leader was not overreacting. But why had he been chosen as the liaison? Yes, clearly the Elector had a certain trust toward the man formerly of the Palace, but this was crossing the line. Why have a liaison, even a trusted one? Wouldn't it be better if fewer eyes saw this information?

Sev felt danger on the horizon, but he hoped with all his heart his intuition was wrong.

***

Following their meeting, Sev expected the Historian to request he stay, but he was dismissed immediately after the Elector. With his mind reeling from the bizarre sequence of events, Sev got no sleep that night. He contemplated the precarious nature of his position, the way the Elector and the Council pulled him back and forth in a tug-of-war. Was this all politics? Was the Historian part of this too?

Most disturbing of all, Sev had trouble establishing where his loyalty lied. Ever since the Arrival, it was as if he could no longer serve both Primus and Olius—he had to choose. But who did he choose? His first instinct was to say Olius; after all, he had left the Palace eight revolutions ago and now wore the robes of white and gold... or did he? Who had actually given him those robes? Why had they allowed him to leave the Palace?

No, he thought to himself, he had done his part to prove himself worthy. With the sharing of the tome, Sev had done exactly what he had promised to do: seek the truth and find it. The other Scholars may never see him as deserving of his title, but he knew what he had done, the risks he had taken. Whatever happened next was out of his hands, and he preferred it that way.

So why did he find it so hard to accept this conclusion? Why did he feel like the truth hadn't been found? Was his job as a High Scholar really complete? Try as he might, Sev could not ignore these questions, and he tossed in his bed, dreading what the future held.

***

The next rotation, as soon as he joined the rest of the High Scholars in the Room of Council, Sev knew something was different. All eyes were on him, and everyone waited patiently for him to take his seat. As he made his way to his chair, the tension in the air exacerbated his worry.

"Welcome, High Scholar Sev of Primus."

Sev locked eyes with the Historian, unable to read his expression. The other High Scholars were easier to decipher: apprehension… fear, even.

"I begin this rotation's council with an apology, Sev. An apology to you on behalf of myself and the other High Scholars."

Sev's mind raced through all kinds of possibilities, some absurd, some realistic, but all terrifying.

"You see, this rotation is a pivotal one in Primus's history. A rotation that will no doubt go down in history."

These words only heightened Sev's anxiety, but he kept his eyes on the being of Olius.

"This rotation is the rotation Primus will restore—"

The Historian's words were cut short by a yell and a shriek in the hall. All eyes turned to the arched entrance as a Priman general marched in, two soldiers on either side, hotswords out and ready. Two of the men were familiar to Sev: the general he had met only two rotations ago, and the hotheaded soldier, now standing in the Room of Council with a streak of blood along his blade.

"High Scholars of Primus and Historian of Olius, you are hereby charged with treason by the Elector of Primus. You are ordered to the Grand Palace to receive Judgement at once. Any resistance will be met with deadly force."

Before Sev could truly comprehend the words, the Room of Council erupted in chaos. Several of the High Scholars stood and shouted in fury at the three imposters.

"Leave this place at once!"

"How dare you throw such accusations!"

"You have no authority here!"

The general watched their reactions then turned to his soldiers and gave a signal. The two men came around either side of the table, and Sev watched the bloodstained hotsword approach him, the hunger in the soldier's eyes, and he knew the end was here, only steps away...

"Enough!"

The Historian's voice had not made such an impression since the Arrival, and even the soldiers stopped in their tracks.

"We will come without struggle."

The High Scholars looked at the being of Olius with fear in their eyes. But as the soldiers sheathed their hotswords and returned to the general's side, Sev knew they didn't have a choice.

***

They stood in a line of thirteen with the Historian in the middle, in the same arrangement as their councils. Behind each of them was a soldier, so close they could feel the warmth of their blades. In front of them was the same high chair Sev had seen so many times before, with the Elector in his place and the guardians on either side. The Priman general stood next to one of the guardians, eyeing the line as a hunter would eye his yield.

"Welcome, Historian and High Scholars. As the general has surely informed you, you are all charged with treason and are here to receive your Judgement."

"What is the meaning of this!?"

The Elder Scholar's defiant query brought a frown to the Elector's face.

"Elder Scholar, I remind you that during a Judgement, the accused may only speak when asked a direct question."

"You have no authority to arrest the Historian!"

The Elector turned to his guardian and nodded. The warrior leapt forward with such speed Sev barely noticed he had unsheathed his hotsword. The blade came down upon the Elder Scholar's left shoulder,

148

cutting straight through his arm. The limb fell to the floor and the man let out a shriek of horror, collapsing in shock and pain.

"I hope I have made myself clear."

The Elector paused after his statement, scanning the line for anyone else that desired to speak. But the only response he got were the wails of the Elder Scholar, writhing on the floor. Sev stared at the scene in horror, unable to comprehend what he had seen.

"Many rotations ago, agents of the Grand Palace uncovered a communication network operating between the Council and Secundus via our trade ships."

The eyes of the Elector fell upon Sev just as the smell of burnt flesh reached his nose, and a nausea came over him, a sickness that made his head pound.

"Over time, agents of the Grand Palace took over this network to monitor and control it. Earlier this rotation, one of these communications was intercepted and deciphered. Namely, the information on a data tome shown only to the Historian and High Scholar Sev of Primus."

It was too much—Sev leaned over and purged the rotation's sustenance onto the chamber floor. He coughed several times and looked up at the supreme leader, who had paused his speech. Terror gripped him, and the smell of the Elder Scholar's wound mixed with his vomit, drenching his senses. Sev thought he would drown in the repugnant odor, he thought the guardian would leap in his direction to punish him for spoiling the Palace floor.

But after a moment, the Elector continued.

"The information on this tome was of a highly sensitive nature, and the data was not allowed to proceed to its intended destination. But most incriminating of all were instructions attached, evidently by the Historian himself, to use this data to plan an effective coup of the Grand Palace of Primus by forces of Secundus."

The Elector's gaze fell upon the being of Olius, and Sev felt the nausea swelling up once more. The Historian, plotting against Primus? Impossible...

"And so this brings us to the first question of this Judgement, and perhaps the most important: Historian, did you attempt to communicate the information contained within that data tome to agents of Secundus with the explicit intent that those agents of Secundus plan an attack on the Grand Palace of Primus?"

Sev looked at the being of Olius, standing directly in front of the Elector's chair.

"Yes, Elector."

His answer was calm, matter-of-fact. A silence took hold, with only the Elder Scholar's moans echoing in the chamber. Sev tried to process what he had just heard, what he had just learned. The general's face mirrored his own shock, and even the Elector's guardians, ever stoic, betrayed a hint of surprise. But there was no surprise in the Elector's expression, only a deepening frown that morphed into a scowl.

"You admit to treason against Primus, Historian?"

"No, Elector."

If the Historian was searching for the perfect response to infuriate the Elector further, he had found it. The supreme leader of Primus stood from his seat, rage in his eyes.

"You do not admit to treason, Historian?"

"Not against Primus, Elector."

Sev watched in disbelief, his nausea temporarily forgotten. The Elector's frown was more dangerous than any hotsword, but he was well beyond frowning. Sev was sure he was about to witness the Historian's demise at the hands of one of the guardians, the slaying of the being of Olius before his very eyes. But once again, the Elector surprised him, sitting back down in his chair, his fury subsiding.

"Not against Primus, Historian? Do you admit treason against the Grand Palace and the Elector of Primus?"

"Yes, Elector."

The Elector turned and nodded to his guardian. Sev watched the hotsword flash up and across, cutting straight through the Historian's neck. His head tumbled to the floor, and there was a thud as the body hit the ground. The head came to a stop a few paces from Sev, and he vomited once more.

Anguish

The voice was hard to hear, as if muffled or far off. Sev knew darkness was close and let himself sink deeper, closing in on her sweet embrace. With her there would be no worry. With her there would be no fear.

But then the hilt of a hotsword slapped his face and he was forced to hear the words clearly.

"Sev of Primus."

He was still in the audience chamber, still in the nightmare that proved all too real. He had collapsed into his own vomit, filling his nostrils with a putrid odor mixed with that of burnt flesh.

He jerked up, spitting out what had gotten in his mouth and retching—wanting to puke but no longer able. Grabbing a fold of his robe, he wiped the mess off his face, soiling the white and gold pattern. All eyes were on him: every High Scholar, every soldier—and the Elector himself.

"Sev of Primus, did you attempt to communicate the information contained within the data tome to agents of Secundus?"

The supreme leader eyed him curiously—not with anger, not with pity, but with something entirely different.

"No... no, Elector."

He was surprised to hear his own voice, to be able to speak at all.

"Sev of Primus, were you aware the Historian was attempting to communicate the information within the data tome to agents of Secundus with the explicit intent that those agents plan an attack on the Grand Palace of Primus?"

The words rang untrue, even as the man's head lay within reach. The being of Olius, executed before his very eyes...

He turned to look at the rest of the Council. The Elder Scholar's cries had stopped, and he lay crumpled on the floor, staring at the Historian's headless body. Was this the truth that Sev had been searching for?

"No, Elector."

He turned his attention back to the supreme leader of Primus, the same curious look in the man's hard face. Sev tried to read the meaning behind the expression, to determine if these moments would be his last.

"Very well. You are judged innocent of treason by the Grand Palace, High Scholar Sev of Primus."

The Elector turned his attention to the other members of the Council.

"I now direct the same question to the rest of the Council. Were any of you aware that the Historian was attempting to communicate with agents of Secundus?"

No one responded, and their silence was another twist in Sev's stomach. The Council? It couldn't be true…

"The Historian once told me the only thing that mattered was the truth. Do none of you have an answer to my question? Is it not the duty of the High Scholars to speak the truth?"

The Elector paused, eyeing the line for anyone who may yet wish to speak. But none did.

"Very well. While this accusation against you cannot be proven, each of you have been implicated in the illicit communication network operating on our trade ships. Therefore, by decree of the Palace, you are all charged with unlawful communication with Secundus. Do any of you deny these allegations?"

Sev glanced at the others, hopeful, eager that they would object, that they would tell the Elector this was false, this was a lie. But all of them were silent, eyes locked on the lifeless corpse of the being of Olius.

"Very well. All of the High Scholars of Primus save for High Scholar Sev of Primus are judged guilty of unlawful communication with Secundus by the Grand Palace. Your titles and your citizenship are hereby revoked, and you are sentenced to a life of imprisonment."

The Elector signaled to the soldiers and they prodded the other High Scholars towards the door. The men walked in a daze, their eyes glazed over in abject horror. Only the Elder Scholar didn't move, even after a slap on the face—the man was either unconscious or dead. A pair of soldiers bent over to pick him up, and together they carried his body out.

Sev watched them leave, blood still dripping from the Elder Scholar's arm—or what was left of it. When the door closed behind them, he returned his attention to the supreme leader. A numbness had replaced his nausea, and part of him hoped to return to darkness permanently, to leave this reality behind.

"Sev of Primus, it is time I explain to you the reason you were promoted to High Scholar."

The smell of blood and vomit had only gotten worse, but Sev's growing detachment helped to keep his composure.

"As I just announced to the former Council, a communication network was discovered between the High Scholars and Secundus many rotations ago. While the existence of such a network was in itself illegal, it was the content of the messages that was truly worrisome. I'm sure you can imagine the distress this caused—learning the Scholarship itself was plotting against Primus."

Everything was beginning to make sense—the rift between the Scholarship and the Palace, his promotion, his exclusion...

"When news of the Arrival came, there was a significant increase in communication, and I decided the Palace needed a stronger link to the Scholarship, lest the Council try something unthinkable. You were that link, Sev of Primus. That is why I took the risk of promoting you without their input, and that is why you've gone without a formal induction. At the time I allowed myself to believe it couldn't happen—it wouldn't happen—yet here we are."

There was a softness in the Elector's tone that only made the situation more surreal. In a strange way, Sev was reminded of the way Zoph used to address him. Zoph—the man he had known for so many revolutions, the man who was a traitor to Primus. He recalled the wisdom his old teacher had shared regarding the colors of their robes and frowned. Every interaction he had had, every conversation he could remember was now colored by the events that had just transpired...

"Now that Primus has been saved, the true work begins. The Historian is dead and eleven members of the Council are imprisoned. It will be up to you to do as the being of Olius intended: let the Scholarship know the truth. From there, it must be rebuilt."

The Elector gestured to a servant.

"You will stay in the Palace this night, Sev of Primus. You have a lot of work ahead of you, Elder Scholar."

***

Sev lay on a lavish bed in a lavish room, disgusted and confused. There was food on a table by the door, but he wasn't sure he would ever regain his appetite.

The image of the Historian's head falling from his shoulders replayed itself in his mind more times than he could count. How was any of this possible? How was any of this real? And the Elector's explanation... could it be true? Had the Historian plotted against Primus? Sev's gut reaction was denial—he wanted to chalk this up to a plot by the Palace, a way for the Elector to take over the Scholarship. But the being of Olius had admitted it himself!

Except he hadn't, Sev noted. He had admitted to plotting against the Elector and the Grand Palace, but not Primus. What did that mean? What was the distinction? The Palace was Primus, for better or worse, and there could be no treason against the Palace that was not treason against Primus...

Then there were his peers—all of them were in on it. All of them had communicated with agents of Secundus in the time leading up to the Arrival. The rest of the Council, the Elder Scholar, even Zoph.

Sev felt a sickness coming on and turned to his other side, as if he might find comfort in a different position. What if the Scholarship was simply power hungry? What if everything he had tried to leave behind at the Palace—the politics and the greed—had been in the halls of the Scholarship the whole time?

No, he thought to himself, that couldn't be true, not to this extent. What did they have to gain by overthrowing the Palace? Most of all, why open the door for Secundus? Secundus, a planet of farmers and Primus's source of food—not to mention their sworn enemy. The Palace dealt with the occasional hostilities in secret, but even in the Scholarship, where such actions were concealed, there was widespread disdain for the second planet. The Priman people had shunned their neighbors for over a hundred revolutions, what could the Council expect to accomplish in opening their world to these outsiders?

There was only one rational explanation Sev could come up with: the High Scholars had been seduced by false promises made by agents of Secundus in order to sow chaos, and they had just accomplished their mission in spectacular fashion. Except for one thing: how had they seduced the Historian himself? Surely the being of Olius was beyond such human deception?

He felt a sudden urge to read these communications the Elector claimed to have, the evidence behind the massacre he had just witnessed, but the thought of further proof of this plot only worsened his nausea.

He tossed to the other side and cursed every single step that had brought him to this place. Despite the blasphemy of his thoughts, Sev wished he were in the Historian's place, his head on the Palace floor. He didn't want to be alive to face the coming consequences.

***

A knock jolted him awake, and for a moment, Sev wondered how and when he had managed to fall asleep. Then images flooded his mind, vivid memories that made him retch.

"Elder Scholar?"

The voice behind the door caught his attention, and he sat up, ignoring the nausea within.

"Come in."

The door opened and a servant walked in with a meal. He glanced at the food left untouched on the table and placed the new dish alongside.

"Elder Scholar, the Elector requests to see you at your earliest convenience."

A second servant came into the room, carrying a new robe of white and gold, clear of vomit or blood. He tried to remember what had happened to the old one, but it was lost in the haze of nightmarish memories.

"I will see him now," he said, getting out of bed and taking the garment.

"Very well, Elder Scholar."

Sev paused halfway through dressing, eyeing the servant.

"Do not call me that."

The servant seemed surprised by the reaction, and struggled to respond.

"…yes, sir. I will let the Elector know you are ready to receive him."

Sev paused a second time, watching both servants leave and close the door behind them. The Elector was coming to him? Not vice-versa? This was a strange reversal, one that made him anxious.

Left alone with his thoughts, Sev could feel the encroaching despair, an overwhelming feeling ready to swallow him whole…

Another knock at the door made him jump.

"Elder Scholar?"

The supreme leader's voice was inquisitive, almost respectful. Sev stumbled to the door, opening it.

"Elector."

He dropped to knee and hand before the supreme leader.

"Stop, Elder Scholar. You have no need for that gesture any longer."

Sev returned to a stand, more flustered than ever. What was going on?

"Elector, you requested my presence?"

The Elector glanced inside the room.

"May I come in?"

Sev stared at the hardened face, thrown off by the manner he was being addressed. The Elector gave no one such respect.

"Y—yes, Elector."

He stepped out of the way and the supreme leader came inside. Only then did Sev note his guardians were absent, or at least out of view.

"Shall we take a seat?" the Elector asked.

Sev glanced at the untouched food, wondering if he should be embarrassed.

"Of course."

The supreme leader took one of the chairs and Sev took the other, still trying to process what was going on.

"Elder Scholar, we need to discuss your plan of action."

Sev frowned, remembering the man's plan to rebuild the Scholarship. But that wasn't possible, not after what had happened. The Historian was the Scholarship—there was no white and gold without the being of Olius.

"Elector…"

But the supreme leader raised his hand to stop him.

"I know what you are thinking, Elder Scholar, but this line of thought does you no good. You have two options moving forward: allow the Scholarship to fall into disarray and perish, or take what is left and bring it back to life. Which option do you choose?"

Sev stared at the man before him, the Historian's executioner. He should feel unbridled rage at this person, a fury with no bounds, and yet he felt nothing—or more precisely, he felt lost. Lost as to why he was being treated this way, lost as to what the future might hold, lost as to why the man who had just cut the head off of the Scholarship had any interest in bringing it back to life. Was it because it no longer posed any threat to him? Because Sev was a puppet to be controlled?

"This morning, you will address the Scholarship. All of it. I have prepared a speech for you, which you may edit as you please. But before you can do this, Sev, you must accept the role you have been given, despite the circumstances. The Scholarship needs you. Are you going to answer the call?"

Sev stared at the Elector, frowning. He knew what he was trying to do, but the words missed their mark. There was only one path he could see ahead: a complete breakdown of the Scholarship, the end of the institution and its people. Soon, Sev would take the pain and suffering he had just experienced and share it with the rest of the Scholars.

"Yes, Elector."

He answered without conviction, more as a reflex than with thought or meaning. At this point, someone else was pulling the strings.

***

The Scholarship had gathered in the Garden once more, but in place of the Arrival's collective excitement, a troubling silence held them still. The Elector stood at the pulpit the Historian had once used, his personal guardians on either side.

"Greetings, Scholarship of Primus."

Sev stood just behind the supreme leader in his new robe of white and gold. Behind him were the other High Scholars, draped in the grey robes of prisoners, their hands and feet shackled. Only the Elder Scholar was missing, for reasons Sev did not know. He was glad the other Scholars were spared the sight of the old man—their wisest member—beaten and armless, but given what had occurred, did any of this even matter?

"On the previous rotation, the entire Council was arrested for treason against the Grand Palace."

There was shock in the crowd's eyes, and hushed conversation broke out across the Garden.

"Eleven of the former High Scholars, including the former Elder Scholar, were implicated in unlawful communication with agents of Secundus, and have been imprisoned for their crimes."

The murmur grew in volume, and Sev saw anger in the Scholars' eyes.

"I understand these allegations are upsetting, but I invite these prisoners to deny my claim, to renew their freedom if the truth is in their favor."

The Elector turned to his side, speaking to the crowd but looking at the prisoners.

"Do any of you deny the charges against you? Do any of you deny that you communicated unlawfully with agents of Secundus?"

For a brief moment, Sev hoped for an objection, for an explanation that would clear their names and reverse this nightmare, but none came. The Elector turned back to the Scholars in the Garden.

"Unfortunately, this is not the worst news I bring you, Scholarship of Primus. The Historian himself admitted to communicating with agents of Secundus and treason against the Elector of Primus. For these crimes, he was executed."

The murmur erupted into a roar, a mix of disbelief and anger. Sev saw the guardians tense, but none of the Scholars made a move. The Elector raised his hand for quiet, and after a moment he was able to continue.

"Again, I ask any of the men behind me, men supposedly of Olius and of truth, to deny these allegations, to deny the Historian himself admitted to treason against the Grand Palace."

The Elector glanced over his shoulder. Again, the prisoners said nothing, their sad expressions confirming the truth of the supreme leader's words. After a brief silence, the Elector returned his attention to the crowd.

"Scholarship of Primus, there remains one sliver of hope in this time of darkness."

He gestured to Sev.

"High Scholar Sev of Primus proved innocent of all charges, innocent of all knowledge of these plots. The Scholarship has suffered a terrible blow, but it is not a fatal one. Scholarship of Primus, despite the overwhelming evidence to the contrary, I do not wish to interfere in your proceedings any more than is necessary for the safety of Primus. I now give the pulpit to Elder Scholar Sev of Primus."

The Elector stepped aside and gestured to Sev. With a deep breath, he stepped forward, taking his place behind the pulpit and looking out at the faces of the Scholarship. Some were confused, all were angry.

"Greetings, Scholarship of Primus. I know the news you have received from the Elector is shocking and upsetting."

The memory of the beheading flashed before Sev's eyes once more, but he pushed on.

"This is perhaps the most daunting challenge we have ever faced, but we must face it all the same. In the coming rotations, a new Council will be inducted, and we will resume our duties to Olius. I ask for your patience and aid in this process, and that we remain focused on our mission despite the tumultuous events that surround us. The Scholarship's mission is to the Historian, but above all it is to Olius and to the truth. It was by the grace of Olius that we discovered this truth, and we must accept the consequences, as difficult as they may be. The light of Olius still shines upon us, and a new rotation has begun. Always remember what has happened, but do not forget we must move forward."

There were no cheers, no applause. The faces continued to stare at him, unchanged by his speech. Sev looked out at them and empathized. His words sounded hollow, the product of frantic rehearsal and absence of faith.

In that moment, the absurdity of where he was and what he was doing came over him, and his legs began to shake. How could the Scholarship exist without the Historian? This was a farce, a waste of time, why was he a part of this?

A hand on his shoulder made him jump, and he felt a sudden wave of heat. He turned to see the guardians backing away, the Elector's hand placed firmly on his shoulder.

"Time to go, Sev of Primus."

***

They walked to his quarters in silence, the faces of all the Scholars fresh on Sev's mind. So much anger, so much despair...

He stepped into his chamber and stood by the table, barely noting the Elector's parting words or fading presence, his mind a blank and his thoughts empty. Just the faces, hundreds of them, unchanged and unavoidable. The faces of a lost and perished people.

"Sev."

Sev whirled at the familiar voice behind him, startled and confused.

"We need to talk."

Folin eyed him with concern, and Sev glanced around the room, wondering how long he had been standing there, unmoving. He noticed a data tome on the table, the table he had been standing next to. Had it been there when he came in?

"Sev!"

Sev jumped a second time, surprised by the urgency in Folin's voice.

"What?"

Folin frowned.

"Sev, have a seat. We need to talk."

Sev glanced at the chair beside him then back to Folin. For some reason, his friend's words were making him angry.

"Why?"

Folin's frown deepened.

"Sev, I know you've been through a lot, but—"

Before he realized he was doing it, Sev caught himself laughing, cackling in a way that made him uncomfortable. Each sound was worse than the last, yet he couldn't stop himself, he had no control…

A sharp pain in his cheek brought his laughter to a stop, and he stared in shock at Folin's outstretched hand.

"Sev, you need to get a hold of yourself."

Sev brought a hand up to rub the spot where he'd been slapped, feeling the warmth of the blow.

"I…"

He searched for a reply, but Folin gestured to the chairs.

"Take a seat."

This time, Sev obeyed, sitting down. Folin walked around the table and did the same, gesturing to the tome.

"What is that?"

Sev looked at the book and shrugged.

"I don't know."

Folin gave it a suspicious look then returned his attention to Sev.

"Sev, we need to talk about what happened at the Palace."

Suddenly it all came back to him: the Council in a line, a soldier behind each of them… the Elder Scholar's wails, the growing pool of blood beneath him… the flash of the hotsword, the tumbling head…

"Sev!"

Folin snapped him back to reality.

"Is what the Elector says true?"

Sev stared at his friend, unable to speak.

"Did the Historian admit to treason against the Palace?"

Folin's gaze was more intense than Sev had ever seen it, yet he struggled to reply.

"Sev, did the Historian admit to treason against the Palace?"

Finally, with considerable effort, Sev nodded.

"And did the Elector execute the Historian for this treason?"

The image flashed before his eyes once more, but Sev nodded all the same.

"And the rest of the Council, did they admit to treason against the Palace?"

Sev hesitated, then shook his head.

"They didn't?"

Sev shook his head once more, with emphasis.

"If the Council didn't admit to treason, why were they imprisoned?"

With a deep breath, Sev found his voice.

"Because... because they were communicating with Secundus."

Folin stared at him with unwavering intensity, and Sev began to feel uncomfortable.

"And you? Why were you spared?"

There was no suspicion in his words or expression, but Sev felt an incredible anger at his question.

"What are you implying?"

Folin's gaze softened, and he frowned.

"Sev, I'm not implying anything, I'm just trying to verify what the Elector said. I don't trust him, but I trust you."

There was a sincerity in the words that extinguished Sev's anger.

"I was spared because I wasn't communicating with Secundus."

Folin nodded, leaning back and looking away, deep in thought. Sev watched him sitting there, thinking, and wondered what could possibly be going through the man's brain. In fact, how could Folin be so level-headed right now? The Historian was dead, the Scholarship was dead... how could he sit here and think when there was nothing to think about?

"Very well," he announced, bringing his eyes back to Sev. "You're right: we need to resume our duties to Olius."

Sev hesitated, confused.

"What?"

Folin frowned once more.

"Sev, you just addressed the entire Scholarship in their time of greatest suffering, and this is what you said. I know the words may have come from the Elector, but it was you who spoke them, and it will be you who follows through on them. We must rebuild the Scholarship."

He stared at him, surprised to hear his friend agree with the Elector's plan.

"But Folin, the Historian is dead."

Folin nodded.

"He is. But tell me this, Sev: what would he have wanted us to do in this situation? Would he want us to sit idly and let the Scholarship die, or would he want us to act, to put forth more effort than we ever had before and bring this institution back to life?"

Sev heard the words and agreed with the sentiment, but he couldn't help thinking that was all it amounted to: words and a sentiment.

"I see the despair in you, Sev, and I feel it too. But you've been appointed Elder Scholar, and the Historian is gone. You are our leader now. The Scholarship lives or dies with you. If you let this despair take you, then you let it take the Scholarship too. So ask yourself what you would do for all of those people out there, the ones who had to stand and listen to the speech you just gave. Are you going to follow through on your promise? Are you going to give them hope when they have none?"

Their faces flashed before his eyes once more, the expressions of hundreds of Scholars on the verge of breakdown. Like it or not, as usual, Folin was right. And before he realized he was doing it, Sev caught himself responding.

"I will."

***

The two of them spent the rest of the rotation discussing what needed to be done, starting with the induction of a new Council. With Folin's guidance, they came up with a list of eleven candidates, though Sev had to overrule one of them in favor of Folin himself. His friend tried to protest, but Sev shot him down.

"Don't argue with me on this point, look at what you're doing now."

With the list ready, Folin suggested Sev go to the Hall of Nourishment and announce the candidates, inviting them to accept their new positions in the Room of Council. Before he could overthink the idea, Sev marched out the door, parchment in hand. There was no time to waste, not when the future of the Scholarship hung in the balance, not when he himself was on the verge of giving up.

As he walked, Sev ignored the hushed comments and sideward glances from passing Scholars, but he couldn't ignore the questions plaguing his mind. What would these eleven Scholars think, being promoted to the Council like this? Most of these names belonged to individuals with whom he shared a certain level of friction—would any of them even recognize him as Elder Scholar?

Of course, these distractions did nothing to help the already monumental task ahead. So as he took his place at the front of the Hall of Nourishment, as a tense silence took hold of the people before him, Sev spoke without thinking, without allowing emotion to interfere. He called the eleven names on the list, asking them to meet him in the Room of Council at once. A murmur spread through the hall when he stepped down, but he ignored that too, walking with purpose to the heart of campus.

When he reached the door he paused, eyeing the stone in front of him with a frown. For dozens of rotations he had approached this threshold with a mixture of excitement and frustration, ready to enter a place he never quite felt at home but one full of wondrous knowledge. Now that knowledge—or at least the embodiment of it—was gone, and he was all that remained.

When he stepped through the door, his heart sank even further. Never had he seen all of the chairs empty, and as his eyes locked onto the center seat, the nightmarish image returned, a memory he knew he would never outrun. He could smell the searing flesh, hear the inhuman thud…

"Elder Scholar?"

Folin's voice startled him, and he whipped around to see two other Scholars.

"You asked to see us?"

The two candidates eyed him cautiously, but there was no disdain in their expression.

"Yes, Scholars, thank you. Please, wait here while the others arrive."

The two gave each other a look and Sev frowned. He knew what they were thinking because he shared their thought: would anyone else show?

But these questions did him no good at a time like this. Sev walked around the stone table and took his former spot at the end—there was no distinction between the seats of the Elder Scholar and the other High Scholars, and he had no intention of sitting any closer to the Historian's place.

"Elder Scholar, may I return to the hall to make certain the Scholars you called forth heard your message?"

Sev eyed Folin thoughtfully. It was a thinly-veiled euphemism, but it meant the world at a time like this.

"Yes, Scholar. Please do."

He took his leave and Sev watched the other two shift their weight uncomfortably. How much convincing would Folin have to do to get the others to come? Did any of them fear retaliation, perhaps expecting Sev to call in help from the Palace?

He frowned. How could he ever convince the Scholars they were in control? The best he could hope for was a straight coup—for the other Scholars to demote him—and even though neither Folin nor the Elector would ever allow it, Sev welcomed the thought. Still, what did any of it matter when the Historian was gone?

Moments later, the door opened a second time, and everyone took their places in front of the stone table. Sev sat up straighter, eyeing the faces before him. Several did nothing to hide their reluctance, but all were present, and for now that was the best he could ask for.

"Greetings, Scholars."

He hesitated, scanning the faces a second time. This was no time for pomp or authority, this was time for exactly what the Historian would want: truth.

"I know you're angry, and I know there's nothing I can do to change that. But I intend to save the Scholarship, and I can't do it without your help."

Most remained skeptical, but Sev pressed on.

"If we don't act now, the Scholarship will collapse. It's happening as we speak. I have chosen the lot of you to fill the chairs around me in an attempt to make right what can be made right. We can't fix what was broken, but hopefully, we can prevent anything else from breaking."

Again, Sev saw little change, and he paused, deciding to take a different route.

"Listen, I agree: I'm not fit to sit here, not fit to lead this Council. I never claimed to be, the Elector put me here. I'm asking you to give this a chance—not me, but us. With your help, we might be able to put some of the pieces back together. This is not an order, it is a request. Take the rest of the rotation to consider if you must, but give me your answer before last light. You are dismissed."

Most of the Scholars made to leave, but Folin spoke up right away.

"I accept, Elder Scholar."

Another—one of the two he had originally brought—also spoke.

"I also accept, Elder Scholar. May we bring the Scholarship out of this chaos and back into the light of Olius."

The rest of the candidates stood awkwardly in place, half-turned toward the exit, eyeing one another with furtive glances. Folin addressed the lot of them.

"Think on this brothers: if you do not accept this position, someone will. By accepting, you have a say in the future. Is that not worth a chance, however fleeting?"

Sev looked on his friend with admiration. What would have changed if Folin was in his shoes now, if the Council had actually been able to choose Dren's replacement? Folin deserved his current spot, but not with the circumstances now attached to it.

"Then I accept as well," another announced.

Sev nodded, ignoring the omission of his title. At this point, he actually preferred not to hear it.

"I also accept," came another. Then a third. Soon, they had all turned back to face the stone table, each one accepting their new role as High Scholar of Primus.

For a moment, Sev ignored the doubt inside of him, accepting this small victory. He had no idea if there was a future for the Scholarship, but at least they had the present.

***

On the next rotation—the second following the Historian's death—the new High Scholars convened in the Room of Council. The rest of the previous rotation had been spent in the Hall of Nourishment with formal inductions, something Folin had suggested might help bring a degree of familiarity to the stressful situation. Though the atmosphere was anything but festive, it was an opportunity to demonstrate the leadership's unity and give the other Scholars a modicum of hope.

That night, the new High Scholars were tasked with researching everything they could about their role so they could transition smoothly into the first council. Judging by their disheveled appearance that morning, Sev knew they had taken the task seriously.

"Welcome, everyone."

A few of them eyed him curiously, no doubt those who had already witnessed the opening of a council. This was not the normal greeting employed by the previous Elder Scholar, but Sev's change of address didn't stem from a lack of experience. Rather, he was trying to avoid the terms High Scholar and Elder Scholar in a show of respect for the fallen. Whether the others would pick up on it or not, he didn't know, but it was more for him than for them.

"I would like each of you to propose what you consider to be our current major priorities, after which we can come to an agreement and begin discussing ways to address these issues."

He gestured to his colleague on the other end of the table.

"We will begin with Aso, if you don't mind?"

Aso hesitated, then nodded. He was one of the reluctant ones, and Sev hoped giving him the floor would ease his acceptance.

"Council, it is my opinion that our highest priority is the Ascension."

He looked at Sev directly.

"However, I have never known the true procedure, and as I understand, only the Elder Scholar has access to such knowledge. Do you have this information?"

Though there was no outright malice in his tone, Aso's question had the potential to undermine all of Sev's authority. This was the key distinction between the Elder Scholar and the other High Scholars: knowledge of the process of Ascension. And yet, critical though it might have been, Ascension was an obscure and near-legendary subject. The replacement of a Historian? The idea seemed unnecessary, impossible even.

So in that moment, when this key piece of knowledge was most necessary, and as Sev felt the eyes of the Council upon him, he realized he had completely forgotten such a thing even existed. Nearly two rotations had passed now, and instead of jumping to the most important item, he had fumbled about blindly, clearly unfit for his new role.

He glanced at the faces before him and sighed in shame. At the very least, he would emulate the Historian's teachings.

"My brothers, I have a terrible confession."

Some of the faces hardened in anticipation, and Sev looked away, unable to keep their gaze.

"In my grief and confusion, I forgot the Ascension entirely."

And then reality hit him, and Sev shot up out of his seat.

"I will rectify this immediately."

He looked upon them again and saw the surprise in their faces.

"High Scholars, I leave you in charge of the council. Please determine our other priorities and do whatever you feel is necessary. I will return as soon as I have the information we seek."

With that, he sprinted around the table and out the door.

***

Sev reached the Palace drenched in sweat, the white and gold robes sticking to his body and hindering his movements. Although it was early in the rotation, the path to the black fortress was uneven and unkind, and his pace had been anything but gentle. The soldiers by the door gave him an odd look but he ignored them, heading straight for the cool air inside.

"Elder Scholar, we were not expecting you," a servant announced, approaching him.

"I need to see the prisoners," Sev replied.

The servant frowned.

"You will need to speak to the Elector about this, and he is occupied at the moment. I suggest you return—"

Sev shot up a hand.

"I will not return. Please inform the Elector of the urgency of my request."

He could hardly believe the words coming out of his mouth, but they seemed to make the intended impression.

"Of course, Elder Scholar. Please, come with me."

The servant led him through the intricate halls, and Sev let the conditioned air flow over him. If only he could have some water as well… but he didn't want to deviate from his goal, not until he had what he needed.

How could he have been so careless, so forgetful? It didn't matter. What mattered was finding the information he needed and replacing the Historian. Aso was right, this was the top priority. This was the true way to rebuild the Scholarship, the only way.

At first, the reminder had given him hope—maybe there was a way out of this after all—but Sev was quick to temper his expectations. What if the Ascension required the former Historian? What if the knowledge was lost? There was a chance this would save them, but there was also a chance they were beyond saving.

"Please wait here, Elder Scholar."

Sev came to a stop in the same spot he had waited so many times before, just outside the audience chamber doors. The memory of those visits were as fleeting as they were strange: how much his life had changed since then…

"The Elector will see you now, Elder Scholar," the servant announced, opening the chamber doors.

Sev gave him a nod and marched inside, but a sudden and potent nausea stopped him in his tracks. The sight before him brought all the memories back, and although the stains had been cleaned, Sev swore he could still smell the burnt flesh.

While he stood rooted in place a few paces from the entrance, the Elector rose and come down the steps to the floor. The man's approach snapped him out of his trance, and Sev started to drop to knee and hand.

"Stop, Elder Scholar. I told you already, you have no need for that gesture."

He returned to a stand, disconcerted by the change in ceremony. He wondered what ulterior motive the Elector had for this gesture, but hearing the man use his new title helped him focus on his mission.

"Elector, thank you for seeing me."

The supreme leader came to a stand just two paces away, and if it wasn't for the pronounced presence of the guardians, Sev would have felt as if he were chatting with one of his peers, or even an old friend.

"Of course, Elder Scholar. How can I help you?"

Sev hesitated. Again, a tone that was friendly—helpful even. But he needed to focus.

"Elector, I need to see the prisoners. Specifically my predecessor."

A shadow of a frown crossed the man's face, and Sev tensed.

"Why is that, Elder Scholar?"

"The Ascension, Elector. I cannot find the data regarding the replacement of the Historian, and he will know where this information can be found."

Concern turned to confusion, and the supreme leader eyed him curiously.

"You were unable to find it in the data tome provided?"

It took a split second for Sev to remember the data tome on his table, the one waiting for him after the speech in the Garden. They had moved it aside in his meeting with Folin and then…

Sev stood up straighter, frowning, and the Elector noted the change in demeanor.

"What is it, Elder Scholar?"

"Elector, are you referring to the data tome placed in my chambers after my speech?"

The supreme leader nodded and Sev closed his eyes, concentrating his efforts on the memories from the night before, when he was most recently in his chamber.

"Did you read it?"

The Elector's question broke his focus, and Sev shook his head.

"No, Elector. It…"

He hesitated, searching his memory once more, but he was sure of it, there was no doubt.

"…it disappeared."

The Elector gave him a concerned look.

"Disappeared?"

Sev nodded.

"It was on my table after the speech, but last night when I returned from our induction ceremonies, it was gone."

The Elector's frown returned.

"None of the Scholars or servants found it?"

Sev shook his head.

"If they have, I haven't been notified."

For a few moments, the supreme leader looked lost in thought, then his gaze returned to Sev.

"Elder Scholar, the Palace archives contain copies of many tomes, some dating from hundreds of revolutions ago. I ask that you wait here while my men search for a copy of this lost tome. I cannot be certain, but I believe a book of that importance would have a sister in our vault."

Sev nodded slowly, taking care with his reply.

"Thank you, Elector. Do you not think it would be faster if I spoke with my predecessor?"

The Elector shook his head.

"While this might be the case, it is not wise. We are operating in a critical moment, and I'm afraid he may share false information with you that may yet undermine our goal. I know you have many tasks awaiting you, but the Scholarship is in capable hands without you, is it not?"

Sev nodded, knowing there was no argument to be won here. He would just have to wait.

***

When the light of Olius began to fade, Sev was still pacing the lavish waiting room. A servant had brought him here with offers of food and drink, but Sev only requested a glass of water. He hadn't felt this restless in a long time, and the thought of the rest of the Council working tirelessly in his absence didn't help: they probably thought he was just visiting with his good friends at the Palace, perhaps plotting their next move against the Scholarship.

Sev ignored these thoughts as best he could. The one positive that came from this extended wait was the autonomy he had given his peers, and he hoped that was enough to impart some sliver of faith in his intentions.

"Elder Scholar?"

Sev whirled around to face the servant.

"Yes?"

"The Elector will see you now."

They marched the corridors of the Palace back to the audience chamber, and the Elector met him just outside the chamber doors.

"Elector."

He caught himself just before dropping to knee and hand, and if the Elector had seen it, he chose to ignore it.

"Elder Scholar. My apologies for the delay."

Sev fumbled for a reply, surprised by the man's words. The supreme leader of Primus, apologizing? This was something he had never heard of, not in his revolutions at the Palace nor in his revolutions at the Scholarship.

"Of course, Elector. I understand this may have been a complicated task."

The Elector nodded.

"Indeed it was, and unfortunately our work is not yet finished."

Sev felt some of his excitement wane, and the Elector continued.

"We located the data tome you seek, the one regarding the Ascension."

He gestured to a servant, who brought out a data book. Sev eyed the object intently, and now that he saw it up close, it was clear there was something different about this one, something strange. It resembled the tome the Elector had brought more than any of the tomes currently in the Scholarship: thicker and fatter, with a combination lock along the side.

"Unfortunately, we haven't been able to unlock it yet."

Sev continued to stare at the tome, then turned to the Elector.

"The Elder Scholar?"

A frown came over the Elector's face, and Sev was quick to correct himself.

"The former Elder Scholar?"

The Elector nodded slowly, his frown unchanged.

"He might know the combination, but it's not as simple as asking him to open it. He may input the wrong code and destroy its contents."

Now it was Sev's turn to frown. The Elder Scholar, risking the knowledge of the Ascension? Even in these conditions, even given what had happened, would he dare do such a thing?

"Not to worry, Elder Scholar. My technicians will unlock it, though it may take some time."

Sev's frown deepened. All that waiting, and now he had to wait some more?

"In the meantime, I urge you to continue your search within the Scholarship—a tome of such importance shouldn't simply disappear."

Sev nodded, ignoring his intuition and its dark implications.

"Yes, Elector."

The supreme leader eyed him for a moment, then put a hand on his shoulder.

"Elder Scholar, I hope this begins a new era of cooperation between the Scholarship and the Palace. While the previous Historian was wrong about a great many things, he was right that the two pillars of Primus have separated much too far."

Sev nodded, all too aware of the weight on his shoulder.

"Yes, Elector."

The Elector's words seemed gracious enough, but Sev couldn't keep his eyes from wandering to the doors behind him, the doors that led to the nightmare he would never forget.

***

Upon his return to the Scholarship, Sev ignored his pronounced hunger, heading straight for the Room of Council. The light of Olius had gone out, and he hurried through the halls to try to catch the end of council. But as he approached the stone chamber, a servant caught his attention.

"Elder Scholar?"

"What is it?"

"The High Scholars have asked me to inform you of the termination of the council."

Sev glanced at the door ahead of him with a frown, but the servant wasn't finished.

"They have left a parchment for you in your quarters."

Sev gave the servant a nod and went straight to his chamber, where the paper lay rolled up on his table next to a warm meal. Before looking at it, he glanced around the room, searching for the lost book. Where could it have gone? Had a servant cleaned it unknowingly? No, they wouldn't move an Elder Scholar's things.

Did someone hide it on purpose? Other than Folin, Sev didn't know of anyone who had been inside his chamber between their meeting and his return that night. Still, the door wasn't locked, and as he already knew, some people didn't respect the unwritten rules…

The memory of the soldier's unannounced visit morphed into that of him wielding his hotsword, ready to strike Sev down, but his descent into the nightmare was halted by a realization nearly as terrifying as that recollection: the general's prescient words at the end of their meeting. Had the man already known of the plans to arrest the Council? Had Sev walked into the Palace unaware of the bounty on his head?

Sev took a seat, nausea threatening to take over. How blind could he have been, to have the rest of the Council actively communicating with Secundus and he not know? Only now did some of the pieces begin to fall into place: the tasks assigned to him, the missed council, the omission from late night deliberations.

He had longed so much for inclusion yet exclusion had saved his life. Sev thought back to the way both Zoph and the Historian had prodded about Secundus, the way they had forced him to break his Palace oath. Were they trying to get him on their side, to commit irrevocable treason? If he had, would he have been officially inducted? Would they have shared with him the truth, made him a part of their plan?

Or was it simply a ploy for information, another way to inform the agents of Secundus? Had Zoph tried to use his connection to the Palace to help their plot? What about the Historian? No, Sev thought to himself, that was impossible. Wasn't the being of Olius committed to peace?

Somewhere in the recesses of his psyche, a terrifying proposition tried to take root, but Sev fought against it, battling his subconscious for control of his thoughts. If the Historian was the embodiment of Olius, was the overthrow of the Palace the will of Olius?

This was the fundamental issue, the one he could not rectify no matter how he arranged his thoughts. If there was any disagreement between the word of Olius and the word of Primus, the path to follow was clear: Olius was above Primus, always—even if that meant appealing to Secundus. And yet the Historian was dead, killed at the hands of the Palace.

Sev slammed his fist into the table, sending parts of his meal into the air. These were dangerous thoughts for any citizen to have, let alone the Elder Scholar. He held an unfounded optimism that this secret tome might hold answers to these questions—answers that would justify everything that had occurred.

Of course, he knew the opposite might also be true—that the information contained within its pages would prove them all heretics. So far, the quest for truth had led to nothing but disaster. Perhaps it would be better, he thought, if the tome were never found and its sister never unlocked.

He grabbed the parchment before him and tried to focus on its content, but it took several false starts to actually process what he was reading. Only then, after immense internal struggle, was he able to distract himself with what was written.

They had done it, he thought. The new Council had taken the reins and acted admirably, delegating crucial tasks to the right persons and handling more or less everything they needed to handle. Based on what he read, they were probably active even now, moving about the Scholarship and attending to its needs.

A rumble in his stomach reminded him of his lingering hunger and Sev nearly jumped at the food, throwing portions in his mouth with no regard for cordiality. It wasn't that he was that hungry—he had been through worse—but he was in a hurry to join his peers, to get out there and do whatever he could to help. Not necessarily for them or for the Scholarship, but for himself—anything to distract him from the overwhelming doubts.

***

By the next rotation, Sev was able to ignore the questions in his mind and focus on his role as Elder Scholar. Unfortunately, this came at the cost of his initial assessment of the Scholarship's future.

"How many?" he asked, as if it might change the answer.

"At least a hundred, Elder Scholar."

The new Council sat at the stone table, a cloud of uncertainty hanging over them. Sev locked eyes with High Scholar Teero, trying to process what he was being told.

"And they have returned to their villages?"

Teero shrugged.

"I assume so, Elder Scholar."

Sev frowned, contemplating the development.

"Many of them renounced your leadership as an affront to Olius," Aso interjected.

"High Scholar!" Teero objected.

"What?" came the retort. "Do you prefer we obfuscate the issue? Are we not the messengers of truth?"

Teero glared at his colleague with contempt, and Sev felt the cloud above them darken.

"Elder Scholar, if I may."

Sev turned to his friend's voice, hoping beyond hope that he might have an answer, a solution to this madness.

"Yes, High Scholar?"

"The Scholars are confused and afraid—we all are—and this is a normal, human reaction. But if we do not act soon, others will follow."

Sev frowned a second time. Folin was right, but his words did nothing to solve the problem. Was there even a way to solve it?

"Have all the books been accounted for?" he asked the Council.

Several of them nodded.

"Yes, Elder Scholar. The tome you seek is not within our halls."

Aso scoffed.

"So it's in the hands of the Palace then? We fall apart while they deny us our future?"

Sev shot him a stern glare.

"The Palace is working on unlocking their copy."

He scoffed a second time.

"The Elder Scholar can open it for them. Why not just ask him?"

Sev frowned, catching the sideward glances of his colleagues. Should he address the misuse of the title?

"Be that as it may, we do not have access to him. What else would you have us do?"

180

Aso met his gaze.

"Without the path to a new Historian, the Scholarship is finished. If we cannot prove this path exists, then our purpose is forfeit."

He paused, looking at the others.

"In fact, if we cannot find this information, I will no longer sit at this table."

Several High Scholars objected loudly, and Sev watched them descend into yet another argument. He shared a sad glance with Folin, then stood.

"Enough!"

Most of the ruckus subsided, but a few choice words by Aso prompted someone's reply, and now the man prepared to react.

"I said enough!"

Aso whirled to Sev.

"Who are you to say enough? I recognize your position only for the sake of the Scholarship!"

Before the others could chime in, Sev responded with as even a tone as he could manage.

"I understand, but if you wish to save the Scholarship, this bickering does nothing."

The two eyed one another for a moment, then Aso flashed a false smile.

"And what if your friends at the Palace took the tome themselves? What if the reason we can't find it is because they stole it?"

"Why would they do that?"

"To prevent the Ascension, to end the Historian and the Scholarship forever."

Sev closed his eyes, taking a deep breath. This conversation was wearing on him, but the others were watching, waiting to hear his response.

"If the Palace wanted to end the Scholarship, they could have imprisoned me with the rest of the Council. Or better yet, ask me to join them—as you may assume I wish to do—and let the campus rot from the inside. Instead, we are allowing that to happen here on our own."

He took his eyes off Aso and scanned the room.

"Look at us, listen to what we are doing. We're allowing this tragedy to rip us apart. High Scholar Folin was right: this is normal, this is human, but unfortunately, we don't have the luxury the Scholars have. We cannot afford to let these feelings destroy us. I've asked each of you to join me at this table to find the solution, not to worsen our situation. If any of you do not feel up to the task, please, for the sake of the Scholarship, stand down. But if you do, we need to find a way to retain our numbers, at least until we have the information we seek."

There were a few nods of approval, and Sev allowed himself to sit back down, calling on Folin to lead them to the next task. But as they moved forward with the council, he could feel the cloud above them darken, its shadow creeping ever wider.

***

It wasn't until the following rotation that a ray of light broke through the cover. A servant came to council, announcing the arrival of an envoy from the Palace.

"Bring him in," Sev replied.

While the servant turned to obey, Sev shot a glance at his colleagues, noting a shift in the room's atmosphere. There was hope yet, even this far down… if the man came with news of the Ascension, this could be a turning point.

The envoy stepped inside, his purple and black robes evoking terrible memories.

"Council of Primus," he said, locking eyes with Sev.

"You have news for us?" Sev asked, ignoring his dark thoughts.

The envoy nodded.

"Yes, Elder Scholar. The Grand Palace has determined the Scholarship is in danger."

Sev's heart sank.

"Danger?"

The man nodded a second time.

"Yes, Elder Scholar. News of the Historian's execution and unrest in the Scholarship has reached many of the local villages. Our agents tell us some of the patriarchs plan to take advantage of this weakness and pillage the campus."

"What?"

"Impossible!"

Sev glanced at his incredulous colleagues then back to the envoy, equally shocked.

"Pillage the Scholarship?" he asked.

The envoy seemed unfazed, nodding yet again.

"Yes, Elder Scholar. The Elector sends his concern, and offers the Grand Palace's protection. A battalion has been mobilized and is ready to guard the Scholarship before last light."

"No!" Aso announced, making to stand. "This is another—"

"The envoy is a messenger of the Elector," Sev interrupted, his tone sharpened by uncharacteristic aggression. "And our guest need neither hear nor see our internal discussions."

He met Aso's glare with fierce resolve, but there was defiance in the High Scholar's expression. Sev hoped he wouldn't act on it—this was not a show of authority, this was an attempt to save his life.

"Thank you for your news," Sev replied, turning back to the envoy. "We will deliberate the matter with haste and send our reply as soon as possible. You may return to the Elector and present the Council's thanks for his warning."

The envoy held his gaze for a moment, shooting a quick glance at Aso before responding.

"As you wish, Elder Scholar."

With that, he stepped out of the Room of Council, and Sev turned his attention to the agitator.

"High Scholar, if you do not watch your tongue—"

"Do you threaten me with silence!?"

Other voices joined the conversation, some chiding their colleague for his disrespect, some demanding he be allowed to speak. When a small break emerged, Sev took the opportunity.

"I threaten you with nothing, High Scholar, but the Palace does not take treason lightly."

"If they dare—"

"They dared to kill the Historian!" another interjected.

This seemed to rein in Aso's crusade, and once again Sev used the pause to his advantage.

"Treason will ruin us, not save us."

Aso scoffed.

"Treason? Treason to what, the Palace? What about treason to Olius?"

Sev ignored his remark, addressing the Council as a whole.

"This decision needs to be made, and quickly. If the villages are planning an attack, we are defenseless."

"You would allow the same people who murdered the Historian to guard our walls?"

Again, he ignored Aso, looking to the others for input.

"I'm not sure this is a wise idea," Teero proposed.

Sev gave him his full attention.

"Why is that, High Scholar?"

"Elder Scholar, if the Scholars see soldiers all over the campus... well, there are rumors bubbling underneath the surface, and if soldiers arrive, these rumors will grow beyond control. We will lose at least a hundred more before the next rotation dawns."

Sev frowned, aware of the rumors Teero was referring to—the same ones Aso seemed to believe.

"You're right, High Scholar Teero. But if what the envoy says is true, how do we defend ourselves?"

Teero hesitated, but Folin provided an answer for him.

"Elder Scholar, if I may."

Sev nodded to him.

"Yes, High Scholar Folin?"

"Elder Scholar, I believe the envoy's assessment is true, but how many citizens would willingly raise a hand against the Scholarship? We have educated their children, healed their wounded, and spoke for them in disputes across village lines. No doubt some of them see an opportunity here, but are we going to stoop to the level of the soldiers and think of them as peasants? These are the citizens of Primus, not some mindless mob."

There was a murmur of approval across the table, though some of the High Scholars weren't fully convinced. Sev knew what came next.

"I propose a vote on the matter. Does anyone have any last comments?" he asked.

No one did.

"Very well, those in favor of accepting the Palace's offer?"

Three hands went up.

"Those in favor of rejecting the Palace's offer?"

Eight hands went up.

"The majority has spoken, we will reject the Palace's offer."

Another murmur of approval swept the room, but Sev barely noticed it. Aso's eyes were glued to the three dissenters, unmistakable hatred in his expression.

The cloud was back now, darker than it had ever been before.

***

The rest of the council was spent deliberating precautionary measures to defend against a potential incursion of citizens. Scholars and servants alike were asked to patrol the walls and man all entrances, but Sev wondered what good they could do with no training and no weapons.

Still, Folin had a point: how many citizens would turn on those who treated them with respect, who actually cared for their well-being? There were always a few power-hungry instigators, but to paint all the villagers with one brush? That was a disservice. In fact, when Sev finally allowed himself to get into bed, his mind was not preoccupied with the enemies beyond their walls, but rather those within.

Things had moved at such incredible speed he was only beginning to realize just how different the current High Scholars were to their predecessors. Beside Folin, all of them seemed either nervous or agitated, and none seemed to grasp the proper procedures of council. Part of this was Sev's fault, to be sure—he still didn't like being called Elder Scholar, so he made no effort to correct them—but proper nomenclature was the least of their worries.

Aso's open defiance and aggressive nature threatened to rip them apart. Every discussion it seemed to worsen, and every rotation he wondered how much longer it might last... and this after just three rotations. Sev knew he was not exaggerating with his threats: if the tome on the Ascension didn't come soon, Aso would step down from the Council, no doubt taking a few with him. But how much longer could his patience stretch? Even if the Palace came through in time, would that be enough to change his tune?

A knock at the door startled him, and Sev sat up in his cot.

"Come in."

The door opened to a wide-eyed servant.

"Elder Scholar, we are under attack!"

Sev jumped out of his bed instinctively, rushing toward the door. Just before the exit he paused, remembering he wasn't a soldier anymore— there was no hotsword for him to grab.

"Have they entered the complex?"

But Sev heard the answer in the halls: a growing commotion, the combined shouting of dozens of people. Before the servant could respond, Sev jumped out the door and saw two of his colleagues rooted in place, confused and afraid.

"What do they want?"

Sev went to the next closed door and knocked on it.

"Teero! We are under—"

"They're here!"

Sev whirled to see three villagers turn into their hall, each in the typical tattered robes. They held handmade weapons, clubs and batons already tainted with blood.

"Well well, if it isn't the Master Scholars!"

The door beside him opened and Sev darted past his colleague, grabbing one of the chairs and bringing it back outside. Already, two more villagers had joined the group, and when they saw him wielding the chair, they burst into laughter.

"The man of the book thinks he can fight?"

But even as the words left the villager's mouth, Sev was charging forward, swinging the heavy furniture at an unprepared foe. The chair struck the man's head and broke in two, knocking him to the ground. While his friends watched in shock, Sev threw the remaining pieces at the nearest assailant and grabbed the club that had fallen out of its owner's hand.

Reality snapped the men into action, and the remaining four came at him. Sev stepped back and away, keeping his distance from the two that had clubs and focusing on the ones without weapons. The wood in his hand did not wield like a hotsword, but he hadn't so much as touched a weapon in eight revolutions, so it made little difference.

One of the unarmed men came around his right and Sev feigned ignorance until he saw a jump out of the corner of his eye. With practiced but rusty reflex, Sev's club met the man's neck, a loud crack announcing the end of his life.

The realization of what he had just done stopped him in his tracks, and Sev watched in horror as the man's body crumpled to the ground. Then a club made contact with his side, and he cried out in pain, dropping his weapon and collapsing onto the corpse.

For an instant, everything slowed down, and though his eyes were open, Sev saw nothing. Instead he felt a question, one that surged from the very core of his soul. Had he done his best, for the situation he had been put in? Would any of this matter?

An inhuman scream brought him back to reality and Sev smelt the telltale odor of burnt flesh. Despite the tremendous pain in his side, he wriggled off the body and turned to see what was happening. The villagers stood back to back, surrounded by three soldiers with hotswords drawn. A general came around his men and crouched next to Sev.

"Elder Scholar, are you okay?"

There was concern in his expression, and it took Sev a moment to process what was happening.

"What…"

The general offered him a hand, and Sev took it. As the man brought him to his feet, he winced in pain, grabbing his side.

"You've been injured."

Sev nodded, breathing heavily. How different this general was to the one who had arrested them.

"Why… why are you here?"

The general stared at Sev's side with a frown, then looked him in the eye.

"The Elector received word the Scholarship was under attack. We came as fast as we could."

Sev looked at the cornered attackers, terror in their eyes. How quickly the tables had turned.

"What are your orders?"

"The Elector has put me at your command, Elder Scholar."

Sev could not believe his ears, but before the shock could properly set in, a pain shot through his side.

"Ah!"

He felt the general's hand on his shoulder.

"Elder Scholar, are you okay?"

Sev took a few quick breaths to fight the pain, then looked the general in the eye.

"General, remove the attackers without injuring them and post guards at all entrances. After the threat is removed, no soldiers within the walls unless absolutely necessary. Once you have completed these tasks, report to the Room of Council."

The general hesitated.

"Elder Scholar, your orders will be met, but you need medical attention."

Sev took a few more breaths, trying to ignore just how right this man was.

"I will have a medic attend to me in the Room of Council."

He nodded.

"As you wish, Elder Scholar."

While the general turned to address his men, Sev struggled to stand, wincing in pain. An arm came around his shoulders, and he saw his friend's face next to his.

"Elder Scholar, you must rest."

Sev absorbed the scene before him: the entire Council was out in the hall, doors open and surprise in their eyes. How much had they seen? Had they seen him…

"High Scholars, we must convene for emergency council at once."

He did his best to project authority, but Folin's arm kept him from stumbling to the ground.

"Elder Scholar, I—"

Sev locked eyes with his friend.

"Folin, now is not the time. Help me to the Room of Council."

Two other High Scholars were already around them, and he heard someone calling for a medic. The chamber of the stone table was less than a hundred paces away, but by the time they were inside, the commotion in the halls had long subsided.

The High Scholars led Sev to his chair, and the medic—another Scholar—began to inspect him. While the rest of the Council got situated, Sev started to speak.

"High Scholars, we need to address this situation immediately. How do we maintain the trust of the Scholars given—ah!"

The medic had pressed a little too hard and Sev shot him a glare before moving on.

"Given what just occurred?"

The question hung in the air, and no one made to answer. Having been distracted by the death of the citizen, it was only then Sev realized the gravity of what had just occurred. How much time did they have left? How long before the Scholarship fell apart? Maybe this was all a farce to begin with, maybe the Scholarship was already dead.

Sev shot a desperate glance at Folin, but his friend seemed agitated, frustrated. It was a strange thing to see from someone who was always so calm in the face of adversity, and it served to emphasize the severity of their situation.

"Elder Scholar."

Sev turned his attention to the entering servant.

"The general is here to report to you."

"See him in," he replied.

The servant turned around and Sev tried to sit up straighter, but the pain made him double over. He closed his eyes, cursing the wound on his side.

"Please be careful, Elder Scholar," the medic whispered.

Sev heard the general's footsteps and took a deep breath before opening his eyes.

"General, have you removed the threat?"

The man nodded.

"My men have done so, Elder Scholar."

"Without any further injury?"

The general hesitated.

"Yes, Elder Scholar."

But Sev heard the hesitation, saw the frown.

"General, I understand this is against your regular protocol, but you must remember the Scholarship follows a different code than the Palace."

The general's frown was unchanged.

"Elder Scholar, if I may."

Sev hesitated, sensing a challenge.

"Go ahead, general."

"Elder Scholar, this is shortsighted. Your orders were followed, but having known no punishment, these men will return."

Sev considered his words.

"No punishment? General, were there any injuries before you found me?"

The general stood up straighter.

"Yes, Elder Scholar."

"How many?"

The general hesitated once more, his frown deepening.

"Seven dead and twelve wounded, Elder Scholar. But theirs were not the only injuries."

Sev felt a pit in his stomach.

"What do you mean?"

"We found two Scholars and five servants dead at the villager's hands, Elder Scholar, and a further twenty-eight injured."

The words hung in the air, shocking the Council into silence. The High Scholars looked at one another in disbelief, and Sev felt his head spin. Shortsighted... was their original decision to reject the Palace's help also shortsighted? Was their current leader, their imposter Elder Scholar, unfit to lead?

"You—the injured are being tended to?"

The general nodded.

"By your own medics, Elder Scholar."

"And your men?"

"Outside the walls as commanded, guarding all entrances. I am the only one of the battalion still inside."

Sev scanned the faces around him once more, seeing both fear and frustration. He didn't have much time left.

"General, I must send a critical message to the Palace. Can I entrust you with this task?"

Perhaps, Sev thought to himself, the general could get the Elector's ear, even at night. What other way to find the status of the locked tome? But the general shook his head.

"Elder Scholar, my apologies, but the Elector gave me a direct order that in the event of an attack on the Scholarship, I was to protect you at all times. I have been standing guard outside the Room of Council while my men have completed your orders. I cannot carry this message, but any number of my soldiers can."

Sev heard the words and understood their meaning, yet it took him some time to comprehend what he was being told. A Priman general, acting as bodyguard to the Elder Scholar? This was beyond unheard of.

"Very well. We will get a servant to retrieve your soldiers to pass along the message."

He turned his attention to the Council.

"High Scholars, I will ask the Elector to place all possible effort into opening the tome. Until then, it is on us to ensure the Scholarship survives. We will retire to our chambers now, but I will see you all back here at first light to discuss our path moving forward."

As he spoke, Sev began to feel light-headed, his breath shortening. The medic had long since stopped examining him, and was no doubt waiting for permission to treat. But there were a few more words to be said, he wasn't done yet.

"Council of Primus, I know this night we suffered an unimaginable loss, but the dawn of our salvation is near. We cannot give up when we are so close. Council dismissed."

As soon as the words were out of his mouth, reality crept away, the voice of the medic and his concerned colleagues fading into the distance.

***

When he opened his eyes, Sev was in bed, the light of Olius creeping through an opening in the ceiling. He shot up in surprise and immediately regretted it, a stabbing pain reminding him of the night before. He let out a yelp and pressed his hand into the affected side, feeling a dressing attached to his skin.

Memory flooded his senses, and he glanced at the rays of light once more: late morning, perhaps halfway to the mid-rotation meal. Were the others meeting without him? He needed to reach the Council at once…

There was a knock at the door.

"Elder Scholar?"

"Come in."

Although he remembered the general's words, Sev was still shocked to see him enter. Had he really been outside his room all night?

"The Elector asks your status."

The Elector!

"What of my message?"

The general frowned.

"Elder Scholar, the message was conveyed, and the reply has already been given to the rest of the Council. The Grand Palace has made your request its top priority."

So they hadn't opened it yet, Sev thought.

"They are in council now?"

The general nodded.

"Yes, Elder Scholar. Per the medic's recommendation, you were left to rest without interruption."

Sev frowned and stood. There was no time for this.

"Thank you, general. You may let the Elector know I am feeling better."

As he put on his robes, Sev could see the general was unconvinced.

"Elder Scholar, the medic recommended you stay in your bed the entire rotation—"

"General, what would you do in my place?"

The general hesitated, then nodded.

"I understand, Elder Scholar."

Sev gave him a look, then walked out of the room. Though he didn't need the general's assistance, he had to be careful with his steps, making his way to the Room of Council with care. After a few paces, he could hear the men inside shouting, and he hurried to the door, ignoring the pain in his side.

As soon as he stepped into the chamber, the shouts came to a halt, all eyes locking on their leader.

"Elder Scholar!"

"Elder Scholar, are you alright?"

"Elder Scholar, should you not be—"

Sev raised a hand to silence them, then made his way around the table to his chair. He took a seat and relaxed, alarmed at how difficult the walk over had been.

"High Scholars, my apologies for my late arrival."

The rest of the men gave each other concerned looks.

"I understand the Palace's message was received?"

Most of them nodded.

"Very well. In that—"

"Is this what it has come to?"

Sev sighed at the all-too-familiar voice.

"Do we openly cooperate with the men who murdered the Historian?"

Aso stood, fury in his eyes.

"There is a Priman general standing outside this very room and we do not question the relationship between Sev and the Palace?"

Several voices rose in objection, but Aso shouted over them all.

"Are you blind? Do you not see what is happening before your very eyes?"

Sev mustered some of his remaining strength and found the voice to reply.

"High Scholar, we need the Palace to open the tome."

Aso threw his hands up in frustration.

"The tome!? You and the Palace have taken the tome and destroyed it, to prevent the rise of the next Historian!"

"Enough!"

All eyes turned to Folin, and even Sev was surprised by the tone of his voice.

"You claim the Elder Scholar is working with the Palace against the Scholarship. Where is your evidence? That the Palace asked one of their generals to protect him? Do you think the Elder Scholar asked for this treatment?"

Aso himself seemed taken aback by Folin's reaction, but while his tone was tempered, he remained standing.

"How did the soldiers arrive so quickly?"

Folin frowned, and Aso continued.

"See, you know it too! A battalion, here before they breached the Room of Council? We all know the distance from the Palace to the Scholarship. These men were already nearby when the attack began, yet that was not what we voted for."

All eyes turned to Sev, who did his best to conceal his thoughts; namely, that Aso was right. They had to have been close to respond so quickly.

"I cannot control whether the Elector complies with our requests, High Scholar."

Aso scoffed.

"Yet the Elector controls you."

A handful of objections took over the chamber, but Folin shouted over them.

"Silence! What has become of this Council?"

Again, his words caught everyone's attention. No one had ever heard him speak this way.

"Are we going to sit here and bicker over conspiracies or are we going to try to keep this institution alive? Yes, there is a general outside our door and a battalion outside our walls, but ask yourselves: why are they there? How did we reach the point where our own citizens turned against us?"

The questions hung in the air, weighing on each of them with terrible desperation. Everyone seemed to hope someone else would have the answer, that someone else would have the key to fixing the unfixable.

Then Aso let out a bitter laugh, cutting the silence short.

"We all know why there is a battalion outside our walls and why our citizens turned against us. The Scholarship is already dead."

He started to walk toward the exit, but Folin called after him.

"What are you doing?"

Aso turned around and smirked, pointing a finger at Sev.

"I watched this man kill another last night, and now I see he has killed the Scholarship. There is nothing left for me here."

With that, he walked out of the room, leaving the Council speechless.

***

Sev walked the halls of the Scholarship, oblivious to his surroundings. The morning council had ended with half-hearted attempts at reorganization, as well as a call to search for Aso's replacement. But Sev knew as well as anyone no replacement would come.

His mind replayed Folin's poignant questions, on how they had reached this point. The silence that followed was more profound than any Sev had yet experienced, and in that moment, he had thought back to the

Arbitration, to the consequences of his quest for justice. Now, in the face of stark reality, with his naivety beaten out of him by a club-wielding villager, Sev could face the truth: the Scholarship never had any power, the Palace was always the primary force on Primus, and even the Historian could not stand up to its might.

Sadly, he had known all this before, in a past life, but he had spent the last eight revolutions unlearning what he had learned, covering the bitter truth with an absurd idealism that bordered on the fanatical. How could he be so blind? How could he be so naive?

The general walked a few paces behind him, an ever-present reminder of the true power on Primus, and Sev tried in vain to understand the Elector's plans. Why had the supreme leader given Sev the Scholarship? If he intended for it to die, why not let it die with the Historian?

He reached the Hall of Nourishment and paused, looking at the mess before him. All around there were signs of recent struggle: broken chairs, spilled containers, even some blood. Where there was still room to sit, Sev counted maybe half as many Scholars as he would see on a normal rotation, or less than a quarter of what he had seen during the Arrival. No doubt many more had deserted after the attack, spurred by fear or despair. How long until they were all gone?

"Elder Scholar!"

The commotion caught the attention of all inside, and Sev turned to see a servant approach, sweating and out of breath.

"Elder Scholar, the tome—it's been found."

Sev stared at the servant in disbelief.

"It waits in the Room of Council with two of the High Scholars. The Council has been notified."

There was an excitement in the man's eyes, an excitement that dared to ignite hope within him, and Sev did something he hadn't done in a long time—he smiled.

***

They sat at the stone table in silence, all eyes on Sev. The tome lay before him, within arm's reach, yet he frowned.

"Is this everyone?"

Some of the others frowned in turn. At the table sat nine total, including Sev. Where Aso and the other two had gone, no one seemed to know.

"It appears so, Elder Scholar," Folin replied.

Sev looked to his friend, wondering if they shared the same thought. Had salvation come too late?

He cleared his throat, still frowning.

"Who found it?"

Again, Folin spoke.

"The servant who sent for you, Elder Scholar. While cleaning after the attack."

Sev peered at the book, wondering how it had gotten lost in the first place. It had been on his table the rotation of his promotion to Elder Scholar, then suddenly, it was gone. What if it had been tampered with? What if the vial was broken and the pages burnt?

"Elder Scholar?"

His colleague's tone was kind, but Sev heard the subtle impatience.

"Apologies, High Scholar. I am as keen as you to learn the contents of this book, but there is a problem."

He scanned the faces around him.

"I do not know the code."

To Sev's surprise, his colleagues smiled, sharing sideward glances.

"Elder Scholar," one of them announced, "it is already open."

Sev stared at them, dumbfounded.

"Elder Scholar," Folin began, catching Sev's attention, "our apologies for the confusion, let me explain."

Suddenly, the frowns had disappeared, replaced by an enthusiasm Sev never would have expected.

"The servant who found the tome admitted to have opened it upon discovery, attempting to discern its origin."

Folin shot a glance at the others.

"So while our eyes have not yet looked into its pages, his know the text within."

He smiled.

"I dare say his excitement bodes well for us. Even now, he waits outside the chamber for our reaction."

Sev stared at his friend, then looked down at the tome before him. Already open? He thought of the servant's eyes, the joy he had seen in the man's expression. Could they dare to hope once more?

"Elder Scholar?"

The same colleague with the same impatience, though this time Sev had no excuse. He took a deep breath and pulled the book toward him, feeling its weight both literally and figuratively. Carefully, as if he might yet break the vial, he opened the cover, revealing what was inside.

Unlike the sensitive book he had seen the Elector share with the Historian, this data tome contained only one section, one purpose. And as Sev read through the contents, the recently-appointed Elder Scholar felt a wave of nausea come over him. He read and reread the words, aware of their meaning but unable to process them.

Finally, Folin broke the silence.

"Elder Scholar, is everything in order?"

Sev looked up at his friend, concern in his eyes. Without a word, he pushed the tome toward him, and the three High Scholars to his right all leaned over to read the knowledge within. When his friend had finished, the book was passed down the table, and the two of them shared a glance. In that glance, an ocean of meaning passed between the colleagues.

According to the tome, in the event of the Historian's death, the acting Elder Scholar must Depart in Olius's Vessel, to Ascend to the rank of Historian and become the being of Olius.

Ascension

Silence held the Council well after the last High Scholar had read the tome. Over the past few rotations, Sev hadn't had the time to ponder what instructions the book might hold, and ultimately, this revelation was both expected and unexpected. Still, this was the last thing he wanted—he could barely accept his current position, and now he was meant to take the mantle of Olius? This was a cruel joke, a slap in the face to everything the Scholarship stood for.

This was what worried him most—his peers. This tome had been heralded as their salvation, the key to the Scholarship's future. But now that he had read its contents, Sev was inclined to agree with Aso: the Scholarship was already dead.

"Elder Scholar, will you do what needs to be done?"

Folin's words broke the tense silence, and Sev looked up at the Council, all eyes locked on their leader. In their faces he saw a disconcerting helplessness, as if they waited for deliverance at the hands of the Historian's heir apparent. It was too much.

"I'm so sorry."

He dropped his face into his hands, fighting the tears in vain.

"I—I don't deserve any of this, I never did."

He felt himself shaking, the pain in his side flaring with each breath.

"This is an affront to Olius. I shouldn't be here, I shouldn't…"

Emotion overpowered his words, and Sev put his face deeper into his hands, sobbing. His wound objected, but he was past the point of caring. He could not be the Historian, that was going too far.

A soft pressure on his left shoulder made him look up. Folin stood over him, one hand on his back.

"Elder Scholar, we understand this is difficult for you."

There was softness in his voice, equal parts pity and hope.

"These are difficult times for all of us. But if I may share just one thought?"

Folin's gaze was as intense as it had been during their conversation after the Historian's passing. It was a look that pierced Sev's soul, erasing his thoughts and capturing his attention.

"Yes?"

"This very reaction proves more than anything you are deserving of this position."

Sev stared at his friend, emotion swelling within his chest. He glanced at the other High Scholars, every one of them watching him expectantly, and he realized just how critical this moment was.

Ever since the Historian's demise, he had thought the future of the Scholarship was in his hands, but it wasn't. Despite his best efforts—despite all of their best efforts—it had fallen apart, and that was out of anyone's hands.

But this was no longer the case. He wasn't just a man of Primus anymore—he had the power of Olius behind him. Now, for better or worse, the future of the Scholarship was in his hands. And much like these High Scholars before him, he had a choice: take the position and fight for what he believed in, or let it crumble and fall.

He turned back to Folin, grasping his outstretched arm.

"I will do what needs to be done."

Then he looked at the others.

"Will you?"

***

The next morning, Sev did not oversleep. Though the injury stunted his movements, he made sure to give himself enough time to reach the Room of Council before anyone else. Sitting inside the chamber with a torch on the wall and a servant to keep him company, he contemplated the road ahead.

The night before, during the evening meal, the Council had announced the news of the coming Ascension to the remaining Scholars. Sev let the others give the speech in an effort to rest and as a way to hide the presence of his bodyguard—a man who reminded him to send word to the Elector, which he did promptly. He was shocked to have forgotten such a seemingly important task, but his attention was needed elsewhere.

After the announcement, the other High Scholars elected to leave the Scholarship in order to proclaim news of the Ascension to the nearest villages. It was a dangerous mission, but Sev didn't have the physical or mental strength to object. Besides, the idea was sound: what better way to rebuild their image than by promising the coming of a new Historian?

Thankfully, as the light of Olius approached, his peers entered the room one by one, exhausted but alive. By the time the council was ready to begin, there was actually one more at the table than there had been before, though two—including Aso—were still absent. Sev watched them talk amongst themselves, a hint of excitement in their voices.

"Council of Primus, welcome."

The murmurs came to a halt, and all eyes went to their leader. As he spoke, the first rays of Olius pierced through the chamber opening.

"A new dawn rises on Primus, and a new dawn rises in this Scholarship. May this be the beginning of our revival, and let us do all that we can to allow our people to thrive once more."

Leading up to this rotation, Sev would never address the Council in such a manner—it would have seemed fake or patronizing. But now, given the most recent developments, it rang true—necessary, even.

"I suggest we begin with the logistics of the Ascension."

The others nodded in agreement.

"Our first order of business is when and how."

Sev turned to one of his colleagues.

"High Scholar, have any of our Scholars had a chance to examine the Vessel?"

The man frowned.

"No, Elder Scholar. A few have tried, but the technology is beyond our understanding."

Sev frowned in turn. He knew the Palace technicians might know more about Olian technology, yet he hesitated to admit this fact to the Council. Why? He was the Elder Scholar now, shouldn't his only priority be the Scholarship under his care?

"Elder Scholar, there may be a simple solution."

Sev turned to Folin, surprised at his interjection.

"Yes, High Scholar?"

"The original Departure was scheduled to be four rotations from now. Perhaps if you enter the Vessel at the time the previous Historian was meant to leave, it will take you instead."

This was something Sev had considered, but was he really going to board a ship no one understood? What if something went wrong?

"Perhaps, but we cannot know for certain."

He turned back to the man charged with investigating the Vessel.

"High Scholar, I want a team of Scholars to try to understand that which you claim is beyond our understanding. After the completion of this council, I ask you to lead this investigation yourself. Even if High Scholar Folin's hunch is correct, I would prefer not to enter the Vessel blind to its inner workings."

Sev knew these investigations would lead nowhere, but what choice did he have?

"Of course, Elder Scholar."

"Thank you, High Scholar. Now do any of you have reports from your night's work?"

Many of them nodded.

"Indeed, Elder Scholar. Though the numbers are uncertain, it seems several dozen Scholars have returned to their duties."

Sev hesitated, contemplating how to best word his next query.

"And what of our two colleagues? Is there any word on the High Scholars missing from this council?"

The men shot inquisitive glances at their returned colleague, but he shook his head with a frown.

"Very well. If they are not in attendance by the next rotation, we will induct our next two candidates. High Scholars Teero and Eyr, I put you in charge of this task."

"Yes, Elder Scholar," they replied in unison.

"Have we received a reply from the Elector?" Sev asked.

"We have, Elder Scholar," one of them answered. "He requests a private audience with you this evening."

Sev nodded.

"Accept his request and ask him to bring the Palace's copy of the tome."

For the first time since his promotion to Elder Scholar, Sev ran a council that mimicked those he sat on before the execution. Titles were stated, conversations were respected, and decisions were made with no yelling or shouting.

It was an astonishing transformation, one that should have given Sev hope for the future. Yet even as the proceedings continued in orderly fashion, doubt still hung over his head, the same cloud taking on a new color. To be sure, the shadow no longer covered his peers, and when it came to the Scholarship itself, Sev dared to be optimistic. He wasn't worried about the institution, he was worried about himself.

What was Ascension? Replacing a Historian was a profound subject, but only in hindsight. Even after the execution, when such knowledge was most critical, it had taken an outside source to remind Sev of its existence. Before then, he had assumed the Historian was immortal, and why bother with contingencies for a being that lived forever?

Of course, he proved less immortal than expected, and now the future of the Scholarship hinged on this obscure procedure. Even the tome which claimed to hold the answers held very little, sharing only two pieces of information: the method of appointment and the appointee's destination. There were no details on the process, no explanation of what happened in between.

Part of him still wondered on the authenticity of the book. Where had it disappeared to for those few rotations, and how? He hoped by meeting with the Elector and comparing the Palace's copy, he might lay his doubts to rest… or upend the whole thing, driving the Scholarship back into ruin.

But even if the tome was authentic and its contents could save the Scholarship, could they save him? Secretly, he wished the Departure was further away, that his team of Scholars might crack the Vessel's code and give him some warning of what was to come. After all, if the Vessel was taking him to Olius—the bright star that filled their rotations with light—was that not suicide? Was there something that happened within the confines of the ship that would allow him to survive such an ordeal, or was this all a misunderstanding of ancient directives?

This was what terrified him most, but which he dared not say out loud: the Scholarship had been on the brink of death and was only functioning thanks to its blind belief in the words of a historic tome, one that Sev had never seen or heard of before. Even assuming it was real, what if there was symbolism they were missing?

At this point, he told himself, it didn't matter. If he entered Olius's Vessel to Ascend, he could not ensure his own survival, but he would ensure the survival of the Scholarship itself. And what other purpose did he have, as Elder Scholar?

***

That evening, Sev received the Elector in his quarters. They took a seat at the table, facing one another in the candlelight of the darkening room, and only then did Sev realize he hadn't dropped to knee and hand—perhaps he was getting used to these changes after all.

"Elder Scholar, I believe congratulations are in order."

Both books sat in front of them on the table, and Sev glanced from one to the other.

"Elector…"

The supreme leader looked him in the eye, a hint of curiosity in his expression.

"You wish to check our copy?"

Sev nodded, eyeing the book before him.

"I want to verify its contents, if you don't mind. The sister should have the same combination, should it not?"

The Elector glanced at the tomes and back at Sev, nodding.

"Indeed it should."

Sev tried to ignore his curious looks, grabbing the Palace's copy and turning the dials. When the last digit was set, a loud click let him know his hunch was right.

Already, Sev let out a sigh of relief. If the tome found at the Scholarship had been a fake, it wouldn't share the same combination. Still, it remained to be seen if the contents matched.

Sev grabbed the sister's cover and pulled it open, revealing the data inside. He was met with a familiar text—the same text as what he had read in the Room of Council.

"And?" the Elector asked.

Sev looked up.

"They are one and the same."

He pushed the book to his guest, who kept his eyes on Sev.

"Are you prepared for the Departure?"

Sev hesitated, remembering his doubts.

"I'm not sure."

In the back of his mind, he imagined this reply might frustrate the supreme leader, and in rotations past, such a thought would paralyze him with fear. But something about their relationship had changed since the execution, and he found himself able to speak far more freely with the Priman leader.

"You're not sure?"

Indeed there was a degree of frustration in the man's tone, and Sev could see the same in his expression. But it wasn't threatening, not as it once had been.

"I'm not sure," he repeated, looking down at his hands.

The Elector frowned, contemplating his response.

"Elder Scholar, the future of the Scholarship depends on you."

Sev nodded, still looking down.

"I know, Elector. I will do what must be done."

He looked up.

"But the future of the Scholarship also depends on you."

The Elector gave him a curious look.

"You mean their relationship to the Palace after your Departure?"

He nodded, relieved to know the man was aware of his concerns.

"Elector, you and I have enjoyed a strong relationship, one that has quite literally saved the Scholarship. But with all the recent changes, I worry about the future."

The Elector nodded, then spoke.

"Indeed this has been a turning point for the connection between the Scholarship and the Palace, and it is one I intend to maintain. So long as the Council allows it, I plan to build this bridge together, securing the future of Primus for all."

There was no specificity to his words, but Sev knew it was the best he would get. For now, he would plant the seeds of cooperation as best as possible, but once he boarded Olius's Vessel, there would be nothing he could do.

"Sev of Primus."

At the mention of his old name, Sev looked up, intrigued.

"There are things you must consider before your Departure. Things of paramount importance."

The supreme leader paused, peering at him.

"Do you know where the Vessel will take you?" he asked.

With this question, the Elector seemed to tap into his doubts.

"Olius, Elector," he replied.

The Elector nodded.

"Yes, but after that?"

He hesitated, holding the supreme leader's gaze. Then it clicked.

"Secundus."

The Elector nodded once more.

"If the ancient texts are to be trusted, then at certain points in your tenure, you will visit Secundus."

This was two steps ahead of anything Sev had considered, as he was more focused on what the man opened with: if the ancient texts are to be trusted.

"If, or should I say when this happens, your life could be in danger."

Sev eyed him cautiously.

"What do you mean, Elector?"

The supreme leader paused, leaning back in the chair.

"Sev of Primus, the network of communication between Primus and Secundus has been eliminated. The agents of their world know nothing of what has happened here, of the execution or its aftermath."

At the mention of the nightmare he had witnessed, memories flashed before his eyes, but Sev buried them, focusing on the supreme leader's words.

"However, the schedule of Olius is a mystery, and we don't know when the next Visit to Secundus will occur. My men have tried to extract this information from our prisoners without success. Did the former Historian mention anything of the sort in your presence?"

Sev shook his head slowly.

"He did not, Elector."

The supreme leader sat up again, leaning forward.

"No matter what, Sev of Primus, you can never let the people of Secundus know what happened here."

The two men held a tense silence, and Sev realized there were still limits to how freely he would speak. That the man was trying to command the future behavior of a Historian was worrisome, particularly as it went against the very core of Olius's teachings, and while Sev knew now was not the time to bring this up, he could not ignore it entirely.

"I am to lie to the people of Secundus?" he asked.

The Elector nodded.

"If you do not, you will suffer the fate of your predecessor."

Here was a death Sev had not imagined: execution at the hands of the Secundans. Was history bent on repeating itself?

Then another thought came to mind, one even more terrifying than the last.

"And what if they do not recognize me? What if my predecessor visited recently, and the people of Secundus see an imposter exit the Vessel?"

The Elector frowned.

"I've considered the possibility, but it's unlikely. Nearly two hundred revolutions separate us from his last Visit on Primus, a time span of multiple generations. Why would it be different on Secundus?"

Here was another question on Sev's mind: the Historian's longevity. Would the process of Ascension grant him hundreds of revolutions of life? If it could make him survive the surface of a star...

"Even if that is the case, you need not worry. The Secundan people are simple farmers, and while a few might disagree, you need only win over the populace to secure your fate."

Sev thought back to the ancient texts, the ones describing a world of crops. According to the old books, the people of Secundus tended their fields much like the peasants of Primus tended the mines. Clearly their neighbor had advanced if there were hostile encounters in space, but perhaps the Elector was right: if their planet looked anything like Primus, access to such technology was scarce.

"More importantly, no matter the circumstances, the same rule applies: you must never speak of the execution. If you do, it will only seal your fate."

They stared at one another for a long while, the candle's flame still burning strong. As the current Elder Scholar and upcoming Historian, Sev knew truth was paramount, but a rejection here would spell his doom. Thankfully, he remembered that which the Palace lacked—nuance, shades of grey. His priority was the preservation of truth in the future, even if it sacrificed the truth of the present.

"Yes, Elector."

The supreme leader studied him once more, then stood from his chair. Sev did the same.

"Thank you for your time, Elder Scholar." Then, after a pause, "And good luck."

The Elector stepped out, and Sev contemplated their exchange. A trip to Secundus? Would he finally see the planet no Priman citizen had seen in over a hundred revolutions?

But these questions were premature—first he needed to survive Olius, and before that the Vessel itself. For all they knew, he would never make it into space, let alone Secundus.

Of course, if the tome was accurate and this was his Ascension, then Sev had an even bigger problem: he was going to become the Historian, responsible for the future of the entire system. Perhaps it was better if he died in the ship?

***

How three rotations could simultaneously drag for an eternity and pass in the blink of an eye, Sev did not know, but that was exactly what happened following the meeting with the Elector. Each council brought with it uplifting news for the Scholarship—the return of more Scholars, the departure of more soldiers, the induction of two new Council members—but no respite for Sev.

The team charged with investigating the Vessel had no leads, and he couldn't decide which fate terrified him more: death in space, or Ascension itself. Oddly, the thing which brought Sev the most comfort was also what had brought him the most pain: the Historian's execution.

This evidence of mortality humanized the being of Olius and gave Sev hope—both to survive the journey and to take on the role—though this hope struggled to suppress his fears. As the Departure approached, he grew more and more agitated, and on the eve of his journey, he contemplated running off into the dunes, disappearing forever.

A knock at his door interrupted his thoughts, and Sev went to open it.

"Folin."

The two shared a short embrace and Sev gestured inside.

"Please, come in."

Folin smiled, stepping past him.

"I thought you might need some company."

They took a seat at the table, and Sev returned the smile.

"You know me well, Folin."

His friend shrugged.

"I think anyone in your position would need some company right now. I know I would."

The two shared another smile, then Sev looked away, gathering his thoughts.

"I have to admit I'm afraid. I'm afraid of what will happen when I get on the platform: whether the Vessel will take me, where I will go if it does…"

He paused, remembering his role.

"Still, there is one thing that brings me comfort."

He looked at Folin.

"The Scholarship is in trusted hands, and I'm hopeful for the future."

To Sev's surprise, Folin frowned, a sadness coming over his expression.

"Indeed…"

They sat in silence, but Sev's curiosity got the better of him.

"What is it, Folin?"

His friend sighed, forcing a sad smile.

"Sev, I almost let the Scholarship fail."

Sev stared at Folin in disbelief.

"You? Folin, I don't mean to take credit away from you but I was in charge when we fell into the burning fire."

Folin managed a small chuckle, but his eyes were elsewhere, deep in thought.

"Folin."

His friend looked up.

"You know as well as I do you'll be my successor."

He nodded slowly, but Sev saw the doubt was still there. Was he nervous about the responsibility?

"Folin, there is no one more fit for the role. Certainly not me."

He laughed a second time, but it was a weak laugh, one overshadowed by insecurity, and Sev realized he was looking at a reflection of himself, the same person who broke down in the Room of Council a few rotations ago.

Sev stood from his chair and came next to his friend, placing his hand on his shoulder. Folin looked up at him, a hint of fear in his eyes.

"Someone much wiser than me once said this reaction proves you deserve the position."

Folin forced a smile, and Sev frowned. Why was this so difficult for him?

"Sev."

The two of them stared at one another in the fading light.

"Promise me something."

There was something different in his tone, something vulnerable.

"Promise me you will follow the path of Olius, and you will keep an open mind."

Sev held his gaze for a long while, trying to understand what he meant. Why would Folin ask this when his Ascension was around the corner? Still, the look in his friend's eyes told him now was not the time for such logic—now was the time for comfort.

"Yes, Folin. I promise."

Folin placed his hand on Sev's and the two shared a moment of silence. Sev realized this was it—he would likely never see these people again, or even their descendants. If he survived this Ascension and came back in a hundred revolutions, the Scholarship as he knew it would be dead.

"I will miss you, Folin."

He glanced down and noticed the tears on his friend's face.

"And I you, Sev."

And Sev felt the burning in his eyes.

***

The next rotation, a crowd had gathered around the platform once more. Sev looked at the citizens of Primus, the light of Olius coming out from behind the clouds, and saw before him only a fraction of what he had seen at the Arrival.

This did not surprise him. The Scholarship was still rebuilding, with nearly half of their number yet to return to the white and gold. And when the peasants saw the man in the robe of Olius was missing, most of them ignored the ceremony, returning to their homes.

But Sev was not concerned with the Departure's attendance, he was concerned with his life. His conversations with the Elector and Folin had given him a modicum of relief, but that modicum was short-lived, overshadowed by the formidable scene before him. He had forced himself to accept his fate without enough time to understand the implications and now, as he stood within reach of Olius's Vessel, he once again contemplated an escape.

Sev glanced at the large, grey sphere, wondering what awaited him inside. What happened if it didn't open? Part of him secretly hoped for failure, though he knew that would bring its own complications...

A familiar noise came from deep within the craft, cutting Sev's thought process short. As the sound came closer, louder, Sev felt a cold fear in his stomach, its strength growing with each rumble.

A loud snap made him jump, and he saw the recession in the surface—the same recession he had witnessed the rotation of the Arrival. This time, it was empty.

He realized he should say a few words before he entered, and he turned to face the crowd.

"Primus…"

His eyes scanned from the peasants to the Scholars, along the rows of the newly appointed Council, all the way up to the Elector and his guardians. And as the silence dragged on, he realized he didn't know what words to say.

"…goodbye."

He turned back to the Vessel, stepping up and into the recession. Immediately, he had the urge to jump off, to return to the platform, but a loud snap brought darkness all around him. He felt the floor beneath him moving forward, into the Vessel, and braced for impact with the wall in front of him. But the wall moved out of the way, each snap opening a section in front of him and closing the one behind.

His stance relaxed. Fear would not help him now, he was past the point of no return. He let the Vessel guide him forward, feeling the tremor of each thunderous snap in the mobile floor. This continued for tens of iterations, until finally, his vision was restored.

In front of him was a small room with a chair, surrounded by all sorts of protrusions and gadgets the likes of which Sev had never seen. He glanced at the machinery along the walls, unsure of himself, then clambered into the seat.

When his weight hit the chair, lights illuminated all around him. The colors were mesmerizing, but their message was lost. Some of it looked like script, but he could not decipher it. He froze, wondering if these were controls, if he was meant to do something…

A low rumbling caught his attention, not as loud as the snaps but growing in volume. The lights continued to change, continued to dance. The rumbling grew from a noise to a sensation, and he felt a pressure on him, pushing him into the chair. Some of the mechanisms along the wall began to move, items coming toward his torso, his arms, his face.

He felt a sharp sting on both sides of his neck then fell into darkness.

***

Sev woke with a start. He was in a room, the same room—the Vessel. The lights were dancing, their meaning as foreign as ever, but the pressure was no more and the mechanisms had receded.

Sev eyed the recession from which he had entered. Was he still on Primus? Or was he already on Olius?

It didn't matter. Elder Scholar though he may have been, Sev had no knowledge of the technology of this Vessel. He clambered to the recession and stood on the floor, assuming it would bring him back out. He felt the slow forward motion begin, verifying his theory.

After another round of darkness and thunder, he regained his vision in a grand hall, larger than any he had ever seen. Just in front of the Vessel was a raised platform, on which stood three individuals. A combination of shock and disgust came over him as he noticed the surroundings and the people matched in brilliant white and stunning blue—the colors of Secundus.

Part II: Secundus

Appeal

The scene before him was so unexpected that Sev lost his footing, stumbling out of the recession onto the platform below. Helping hands reached out to stop him, but he jerked away.

"Don't touch me!"

He regained his composure and stood, noting the troubled stares of the crowd before him. They were gathered in a hall unlike any he had ever seen…

"Our apologies, Historian."

The title struck him like a blow to the chest, and for a moment his surroundings were forgotten.

"The Senate is eager to speak with you regarding your time on Primus. With your permission, we will take you there now."

He stared at them, trying to understand what was happening. They called him Historian—was this a mistake? He glanced over his shoulder at the Vessel, the recession already gone from its surface. Had he already been to Olius? Had he completed his Ascension?

He turned back to the greeting party, his eyes scanning the rest of the hall: it was double the size of the Palace's audience chamber, with walls of glass as tall as ten men. But more surprising than the room were its occupants: the crowd was clean and orderly, their heads raised high.

Perhaps this was Olius? This couldn't be Secundus. Everything he had ever heard about their neighbor contradicted this image. They were meant to live in huts, not buildings, farming the land for Primus's crops. He had assumed the people would be ignorant and weak—much like the peasants of his home.

But all of these assumptions were just that: a product of his imagination, a placeholder for knowledge the Scholarship lacked. Sure, Secundus might have been a primitive world at the time of the Great War, but that was eons ago. Had they really advanced so far since then? Perhaps this was all for show, he thought. Or perhaps this was the ruling class. But even the Grand Palace was not as impressive as this hall.

His eyes returned to the men directly before him and, seeing the confusion in their expressions, realized they were waiting for him to speak. It was like the Arrival on Primus, except Sev now stood on the other side of the parade, in the biggest shoes he ever feigned to fill.

The silence dragged uncomfortably long, and embarrassment turned into fear. What was he doing here? Was he really the Historian? He didn't feel any different, he hadn't noticed any change…

"Historian?"

The man in the middle spoke up, more concerned than excited, and Sev had a moment of clarity. The Elector had warned him of this very possibility, of what a visit to Secundus would entail. If the people here realized he was an imposter, his fate was sealed.

"Greetings, Secundus."

The words were quiet, almost forced, and Sev felt a cold fear come over him. Was he really about to do this? Was he about to fake the role of Historian?

He saw the eager expressions before him and pushed away those questions. He had followed the writings in the ancient text and entered the Vessel for his Ascension. Was it so hard to believe the process had taken place? He had no way of knowing how long he was asleep, and that might explain what he was seeing now: what if hundreds of revolutions had already passed, and this was his first Visit?

The silence grew long and Sev rushed to speak.

"My apologies, as I have had a long journey."

He tried his best to recall the Arrival on Primus, the words he had heard that fateful rotation.

"Thank you for your warm reception. I am excited to fulfill the mission of Olius and the Scholarship during my Visit."

The statements stumbled out of his mouth without grace, but no one seemed to notice: the crowd watched him wide-eyed, amazed at just his presence.

"With the help of your Scholarship, I hope to learn as much as I can in my short time here."

He hesitated, his momentum waning.

"Thank you."

His attention shifted to the three men in front of him, and they seemed to pick up on his body language.

"Historian, the Senate is eager to speak with you regarding Primus. With your permission, we will take you there now."

Sev tensed. The Senate? What was that? Just as the fear started to take root, he noted a sliver of gold in their outfits.

"Are you the Scholars of Secundus?"

The three nodded.

"Yes, Historian."

Sev looked around the hall once more. Was this the Scholarship? He wanted to ask but was afraid it might reveal him an imposter. But was he even an imposter? Did a new Historian inherit the knowledge of his predecessors?

Sev's mind was spiraling out of control, and he closed his eyes to calm himself. He needed time to think, time to understand...

He opened his eyes and looked at the men before him.

"Take me to my chamber."

The three of them glanced at one another.

"Historian, the Senate insists—"

"Now."

He did his best to mimic the force of the Historian's voice, an outward confidence to mask his inner worry. The three Scholars of Secundus hesitated for another moment, then brought their chins to their chests. What this gesture meant, Sev did not know, but when they turned around and started walking, he assumed his message had gotten through.

The crowd parted as they made their way through the grand hall, and Sev continued to admire his surroundings. How much time had passed in the Vessel? In his mind, it had been no more than a blink of an eye, but out here?

"Your chamber, Historian."

The three men turned to him and indicated a portal in the wall. Sev glanced over his shoulder; Olius's Vessel was still in sight. Was this the Scholarship of Secundus, built around the landing site? He took a closer look at the grand hall's decor, noting the subtle golden accents among the white and blue. It was a far cry from the stone corridors of the Scholarship of Primus, and yet it had a similar austerity to it, a kind of benevolent authority.

He opened the door and looked inside. His chamber was large, with amenities that far surpassed the Historian's chamber in the Scholarship of Primus. He noted several objects he did not recognize, but made a point to hide his surprise. The far wall was the same thick glass, overlooking a lush garden of green, with pathways and trimmed hedges. He had never seen anything like it in his life.

"The terminal is ready, Historian."

He spun around to see the three men had followed him in. They gestured toward a seat with some sort of machine directly in front of it.

"What is that?" he asked.

They eyed each other before responding, and Sev felt a shot of fear. Had he asked too much?

"The terminal, Historian. The repository of our history since the previous Visit. If you need any assistance we can—"

"No, thank you. Please leave."

They eyed each other once more then dipped their heads and exited the room, the door closing behind them.

As soon as they were gone, a minor panic came over him, and Sev took a deep breath to calm his racing mind. He had made it off the landing site and into his chamber. As far as he could tell, the Scholars thought he was the Historian—and there was a chance this was true. But what bothered them were his questions, the way he seemed confused by their building and what was inside of it. If Sev wanted to survive, he needed to adapt to his surroundings, to learn more about this place and its technology and—most of all—to hide his surprise.

Sev approached the chair and examined the machine. Its shape and structure were reminiscent of the interior of the Vessel, but he saw no sharp items that might stab his neck. Whatever this was, it was as foreign to him as everything else. Still, the men had said it was a repository of history. Perhaps this was their version of a tome?

He realized there was no time to waste and sat in the chair. As soon as his weight hit the seat, the apparatus created a floating picture much like the one in the Vessel, and a new set of lights danced in front of him. The only difference was the scripture: it was legible.

He reached out instinctively and the image responded, surprising him. He had never seen technology like this before, yet he knew immediately that his guess was right: this was a data tome. An interactive and three-dimensional data tome.

After a few false starts, Sev learned to control the terminal and found he had access to the full history of Secundus: not just the revolutions since the last Visit, but to a time well before the Great War. The information danced before his eyes in a seemingly endless stream, and he had trouble concentrating on just one part of it.

As he began to comprehend the scope of the device, Sev realized it might be able to answer more than just his questions about Secundus. He navigated the information before him, searching for a timeline tied to the Great War, but the answer he found baffled him.

When he had left Primus, 175 revolutions had passed since the Historian's Visit and the end of the conflict. But according to this terminal, only 147 revolutions had passed. Did Olius's Vessel travel through time as it did through space? Was he now in the past?

It only took a moment for Sev to realize his ignorance. These were Secundan revolutions, not Priman—each planet had its own path around Olius. He dug a little deeper to find the conversion factor, then calculated the Priman equivalent—175.

He closed his eyes, blocking out the interface to clear his thoughts. According to what he was reading, very little time had passed since his Departure—less than a revolution, perhaps only a handful of rotations. On the one hand, this was reassuring: he hadn't executed some unbelievable jump in time, and his friends and colleagues were still alive and well.

But when he opened his eyes and saw the interface once more, he knew this news brought its own set of problems. This was the contemporary state of Secundus? How could such a radical difference between the planets go unnoticed?

Unless, Sev realized, it was designed that way. The interplanetary trade was devoid of human contact, and the trade ships lacked windows. Was Secundus hiding in plain sight? Did the Elector know? Given the skirmishes in space, wouldn't the Palace be aware?

But Sev had an even bigger problem: his Ascension. If so little time had passed since his Departure from Primus, had the Vessel even stopped by Olius? Was he actually the Historian now, or was he exactly what he had feared: an imposter?

Sev felt the panic taking hold and wondered why he had ever agreed to this mission. The tome had directed him to take the place of the being of Olius, but it had not directed his predecessor to be executed, or the immediate replacements to be imprisoned. The only reason Sev was here was because of the Elector—was that the influence of Olius or of Primus?

He tried to focus on the interface in front of him, scanning the library of Secundan knowledge. But where he hoped to find answers, he only found more questions, as the description of their world was simply unbelievable. This was not a planet of farmers, this was a planet of wealth, a wealth he had trouble understanding. How could this be possible?

A mention of his home planet caught his attention, and he zoomed in to examine it. It was some kind of public proclamation made by the Senate of Secundus, announcing the Historian's Arrival and promising a new era of cooperation between Primus and Secundus. According to the text, the Historian's Visit was meant to renew the relationship between the worlds, shedding the distrust of the past. But this was not the only thing explained in the proclamation, and Sev felt dread pile on top of fear.

He stood from the chair and the interface extinguished, the knowledge of Secundus vanishing from the air. His eyes scanned the chamber once more, amazed and confused by the things he saw. Yet in this moment, having read what he just read, the strangeness of these surroundings only made things worse.

The proclamation was filled with talk of unity and peace, but there was one part that stood out to him: how the renewed relationship with their neighbor started with the removal of the Priman dictatorship, as it was called, in order to free the Priman people.

Was this related to the treason of the Council? Was this proof of the collaboration leading to the Historian's demise? If so, how much did the people of Secundus know? Clearly they knew nothing of the execution, but did they know of the planned coup?

Sev knew he would need to re-enter the terminal and search for these answers, but there was an even more pressing matter: the Senate—what he could only assume was another kind of council—wanted to see him as soon as possible. If the entire planet of Secundus had expected something to happen during the Historian's Visit to Primus and it hadn't, how was he supposed to explain that without mentioning the nightmare in the Palace?

***

Though he wasn't sure when he had managed to fall asleep, Sev woke well into the rotation, surprised by the comfort of the cot and the softness of its covers. He sat up and looked at the terminal, the memories of the previous rotation coursing though his mind.

He had spent the night poring over the terminal, and of all the things he had learned, one proved most important: no one on Secundus knew what had happened on Primus. Once he was thoroughly convinced of this fact, he allowed himself some rest, knowing he would need all his energy to face the unknown future.

He noticed a meal on the bedside table and dug in. The food was familiar, similar to what was eaten on Primus, but after a few tentative bites, Sev couldn't deny it was richer—fresher. Of all the surprises Secundus held, this one shocked him the least: these were local foods, of course they were fresh.

As he finished his meal, the chamber door opened and a woman stepped inside. She dipped her head before speaking.

"Historian, I hope you were able to rest."

With her statement he realized just how rested he felt—he had never had a better sleep in his life. Was this another quality of Secundus? Perfect slumber?

"I was, thank you."

She smiled, and Sev noted her robes were the same as the ones he had seen on the three men. Could it be possible? Did Secundus allow women in the ranks of Scholarship? For some reason, the thought troubled him, and he felt a vague discomfort in her presence.

"The Senate requests your presence as soon as possible," she continued.

He tensed, the panic threatening to take root, but he had expected this, planned for it. Having studied the terminal, he now knew the Senate was like a hybrid of the Council and the Palace, a governing body wherein each territory was represented by both a Senator and a specially-appointed Scholar. The intricacies still escaped him, but he had noted an imbalance of power: the Senators decided most matters alone, with the Scholars only voting on matters of Olius itself.

This disparity could prove critical, since Sev hadn't let his guard down completely—not yet. Yes, there was nothing in the terminal about the execution of the Historian, but the former Council had been communicating with somebody on Secundus. More likely than not, it was either the Scholarship, the Senate, or both.

In any case, there was one group whose voice could overrule them all: the people. Meeting the Senate was as dangerous as it was inevitable, but it was just as the Elector had said: you need only win over the populace to secure your fate.

"I wish to speak to the people of Secundus."

The woman frowned, and Sev eyed her cautiously.

"What do you mean, Historian?"

Her tone was more confused than frustrated, but Sev proceeded with care.

"I want to take a tour of the neighboring districts, to see the progress of Secundus in person."

She hesitated, and Sev grasped at a new insight.

"I trust most of the work has already been completed," he continued, gesturing at the terminal, "so I wish to spend my time among the citizens."

In his tenure on the Council of Primus, Sev had learned quite a bit about the Historian's collection of knowledge. Tomes deemed most important were brought to him, after which the being of Olius would study them and ask for clarification or further information on specific matters. As far as Sev could tell, the man never transcribed a word or kept any books, so how this knowledge was actually retained, he didn't know.

One night with the terminal proved such procedure unnecessary on Secundus. In fact, Sev wouldn't be surprised if the technology of Olius's Vessel and that of the terminal were compatible, and all of the data could just be transferred over. He cursed himself for not looking this up before, but he would find the time to check later.

"That is true, Historian."

The reluctance in her voice made him uncomfortable, but no sooner did he notice the discomfort that he realized it was misplaced. Why worry about her reluctance at all? Was he not the Historian? He ignored his doubts and announced his plan.

"I want you to take me to the neighboring districts. Do not alert the Senate or any of the Senators. In fact, I want you to tell as few people as necessary to make this possible. I want to avoid overcrowding or a change in behavior on my account. If I can see Secundus in its true form, I will have completed an important part of my mission."

The change in tone seemed to do the trick, as the woman reacted positively.

"Yes, Historian. I will assemble a few more Scholars to help me and we will take you on your journey."

She made to leave then hesitated.

"Historian, may I inform the Senate you will not be coming?"

Sev pondered this for a moment, then shook his head.

"No. I will address them when the proper time comes."

The woman bowed her head and left. After the door closed, Sev stared at the spot she had stood, trying to figure out why her voice sounded familiar. Then, realizing what was about to happen, he jumped out of bed and into the terminal.

***

It wasn't long before the woman returned, the original greeting party in tow.

"Greetings, Historian."

All four dipped their heads, holding them there for a moment, and Sev realized this was their equivalent of dropping to knee and hand.

"Greetings, Scholars."

He glanced at the woman as the title came out of his mouth, but she didn't seem to notice.

"Historian, we've been told you wish to postpone the Senate visit?" one of the men asked.

Sev nodded.

"Yes. I want to visit the local districts instead, to get a first-hand view of Secundus."

The man frowned, and Sev eyed him warily.

"Is there a problem, Scholar?"

The man caught his mistake and stood up straight, dipping his chin into his chest.

"No, Historian. Please forgive me. We are not used to your presence, and we are not used to denying the Senate. But if this is your wish, it shall be done."

Sev nodded slowly, still eyeing him with suspicion.

"Lest I was not clear before, I do not wish for the Senate to be denied. I do not want them to be informed at all. Any knowledge of my plan will soil it."

"Historian, the people of Secundus would never falsify their livelihood before you."

This rebuttal was one too many, and now Sev wondered if he had an enemy before him.

"Scholar, while I trust the people of Secundus, I also understand the desire to exaggerate. If you let the people know I am coming, they will prepare. This is not necessarily deceit."

The man nodded reluctantly.

"Very well, Historian. When do you wish to leave?"

Sev glanced at the woman, suddenly wishing she had kept this to herself.

"At once, Scholar."

"As you wish, Historian."

They dipped their heads once more, and Sev followed them out of the chamber, into the grand hall. The light of Olius shone through the glass walls, illuminating the interior like no building he had ever seen. Scholars walked every which way, stopping to dip their heads as he passed. Now that he had seen one, Sev noticed many women in the robes touched with gold, interacting freely with their male colleagues. It was a concept so simple yet so foreign, he couldn't quite wrap his head around it. Did the women start as Pupils as well? Who cared for the infants and cooked the meals? He tried to imagine men performing these tasks, but the thought made him uncomfortable.

The Scholars led him toward a door on the outside wall, and Sev marveled at the green beyond the glass. As they crossed the threshold to the outdoors, Sev braced himself for heat and was shocked by the cool breeze that met him instead.

"Historian?"

The word from the Scholar broke his stupor, but as they continued down the path, he couldn't help looking around in awe. It was like something out of a dream: green all the way to the horizon, laid out in beautiful order. Though he had seen it from his chamber, it was one thing to see and another to feel...

A flutter of activity caught his attention—several groups of birds, flying every which way in plain abundance. Again, he found himself rooted in place, staring in wonder. In all his revolutions on Primus, he had only seen a handful of these creatures.

"Historian?"

Now there was a hint of concern in her tone, and Sev realized he needed to get his act together.

"My apologies, Scholars. This is such a change from Primus."

They glanced at one another, then the suspicious one spoke.

"Historian, if I may ask you something."

The others eyed him uncomfortably, and Sev wasn't sure how to proceed.

"Yes, Scholar?"

The man locked eyes with him.

"Did something happen on Primus?"

Sev hesitated, alarmed by this line of inquiry.

"What do you mean, Scholar?"

The man seemed shamed by Sev's reply, but before he could continue, the woman chimed in.

"We do not think you are here by chance, Historian. Your last Visit culminated in the treaty that ended the Great War. The Senate claims you are here to bring peace and cooperation to our worlds once more, but rumors abound that something went wrong. Is that true?"

At first, Sev felt a flutter of panic, but he maintained his composure. Rumors that something went wrong? He wanted to learn more, but now was not the time—now he needed to promote his assignment and win over the people.

"No, Scholar, nothing went wrong. My mission has not changed, only its execution."

The irony of this choice of words gave Sev pause, but he ignored it, continuing his reply.

"That has always been our mission, the Scholarship's mission, Olius's mission. That is why we are here."

They eyed him curiously, no doubt wanting to ask about the change of plans, but now was not the time—not yet.

"I know you have many questions, but time is of the essence. Please, lead me toward the nearest district."

***

The garden's dictated order soon gave way to the chaos of nature, but if anything, their surroundings were greener and lusher than before. Sev found himself in awe of the plant life around them, its density hard for him to grasp. The path they followed was shaded on all sides by a canopy of green the likes of which he thought impossible. It took great effort not to stop and stare, and even in his attempt to act natural, he could sense the Scholars's concern.

This, at least, didn't conflict with his limited knowledge of Secundus—it was an agricultural world after all—but he was unprepared for the scope. How could a planet be so rich with life? He had thought that beyond the garden there might be more scarcity, but it was the opposite. Did this type of vegetation cover most of the surface?

Before them, the path opened up, and Sev saw a number of structures built out of what looked like wood—a rare commodity on Primus—each one about the size of a village hut on Primus. People walked among the homes, some of them stopping to stare at the approaching strangers. These were not the farmers he had expected, and nothing close to the peasants of Primus. These men and women stood as proud as the Scholars escorting him, wearing their own robes of vivid color. There were no tattered rags, no dusty faces, no shy glances.

"Is—is there a place of congregation?" he asked the Scholars, suppressing his shock.

"Yes, Historian. The village square. You wish to be taken there?"

He nodded.

"I will address the people there."

As they approached, many of the villagers stopped and stared while others ran off excitedly, shouting for their friends. Sev's eyes jumped from one to the other in awe, and their expressions matched his own, some of them whispering frantically to the person next to them.

The square consisted of an open space encircled by wooden buildings, and already a crowd was forming. Sev placed himself at what seemed like a natural focal point, the Scholars standing around him. Before he knew it, the crowd had doubled in size, and he could feel the suspense in the air.

"Citizens of Secundus."

The words were a bit forced, but everyone fell silent. Now began his most important work, something that could spell the difference between life and death.

"I am here, as you know, on a mission of peace. A mission to mend the relationship between Primus and Secundus."

He wondered, for a moment, how many were in tune with current events. Did all of them know of the the Senate's proclamation? Was it normal for the people of Secundus to keep up with such news? At this point, he was willing to believe almost anything.

"As I walk these paths, I am amazed by what I see. Amazed by these plants, amazed by these people. Amazed by the things you may take for granted. But I ask you to never take them for granted again."

One thing he did know was their knowledge of Primus: having searched for data on his home world, Sev was certain the people had a vague idea of its status, but the information was painted with a political brush. Now, he thought, it was time to add his own strokes to the canvas.

"These riches, this wealth—they do not exist on Primus. Theirs is a dying planet, and their people struggle."

Sev paused, surprised by the conviction in his tone. Suggesting Secundus was superior to Primus in any way was treason... but was it treason if it was truth?

"We are all one under Olius, are we not? Since the Great War, Secundus has flourished, it has blossomed, yet your brothers and sisters on Primus have not had the same luck. Is this in line with the teachings of Olius? Citizens of Secundus, is it fair what has happened on Primus?"

Sev looked out at the crowd before him, surprised by what he saw. He had expected frowns or looks of disapproval, but what he saw was nodding and looks of consent. While the hardest part was yet to come, this was already working better than expected.

"In my time on Primus, I have come to a deep understanding of the problems they face, and I've realized there is but one true path to prosperity: each and every one of you."

The villagers eyed him curiously, and Sev continued.

"The relationship between Primus and Secundus depends on you just as it depends on your brothers and sisters. The Scholarships of each world can guide the way, but peace and harmony will take root only if it is the will of the people."

He paused again for emphasis, scanning the faces before him.

"Citizens of Secundus, I ask you to follow the teachings of Olius and lay down any prejudice, any hate, any frustration. It is time to heal this divide, to help the people of Primus and, in so doing, lift all those under the light of Olius. My only question is, will you help me in this mission?"

There was a moment's silence as his words hung in the air, then the crowd erupted into applause. Sev smiled at the reaction, a sliver of hope taking root within him. If he could convince the people of Secundus to help Primus in a way that didn't eliminate the supreme leader, not only would he create an explanation for the Senate, he might even live up to his new role.

***

The rest of the rotation was spent exploring the neighboring districts, and Sev began to acclimate to the wonders of Secundus. Shaded paths guided them between villages, where he did his best to interact with as many citizens as possible. Each time, his confidence and his understanding of the situation grew, and slowly but surely, the mechanics of his plan fell into place.

By the end of the rotation, he was preaching a message of grassroots action, something he hoped might not only diffuse the danger of the Senate, but perhaps even justify his impersonation of the being of Olius —assuming it was impersonation, a topic he suppressed for the time being.

Out of caution, he avoided any mention of the Palace or the Elector, worrying such a step was still too drastic—after all, he didn't know if someone on this planet knew the truth. The constant presence of the Scholars in his periphery didn't help, but as far as he could tell, they—and the citizens—considered him the Historian—he shouldn't have to fear them. Of course, that's what his predecessor had thought…

He had to wonder why the original Historian hadn't taken this route. Had the agents of Secundus infiltrated the Council of Primus so heavily that as soon as the Historian arrived, they pressured him to remove the Palace from power? Surely Sev wasn't the only one to realize a popular movement was more in line with the teachings of Olius?

There was more to this story, something either the Elector didn't know or hadn't told him. Perhaps the truth lay within the Senate, the same body he currently avoided? But he couldn't avoid them forever, and it didn't take long for this reality to catch up to him.

"Historian…"

They were entering another village—one of the last of the rotation—when the woman spoke his name. Up ahead, Sev saw a crowd had formed, and he turned to her.

"What is it, Scholar?"

As odd as he might find a female Scholar, thus far he trusted her most. Of course, he made this judgment more or less arbitrarily, so it was hard to say if his gut was right.

"The Senate has caught up to us."

He looked at the crowd but couldn't see its focus.

"How do you know?"

Just as he asked the question, he saw her: a woman dressed in the robes of a Scholar, but with a different flourish of gold mixed into her blue and white. Sev was a stranger to Secundus, but he had spent enough time in the terminal to know this was a Senate Scholar, a member of both the Scholarship and the Senate.

"That is the Scholar of the Premier Territory," the Scholar replied.

Sev nodded, noting the expectant look in the woman's eyes.

"I will take full responsibility for the change of plans," he announced.

They closed the gap quickly, the crowd's excitement growing with their approach. Perhaps this wasn't so bad, he thought. He could spread his message and push agreement from a member of the Senate.

"Greetings, Historian."

The Senate Scholar dipped her head when they reached her, and Sev watched her expression closely.

"Greetings, Scholar."

He had to fight the urge to call her a High Scholar—though she was in some ways above the other Scholars, Secundus didn't recognize such things with official titles. Only the robe and her duties gave away her seniority.

"You have made an unprecedented entrance, Historian."

There was no malice in her tone, but Sev knew better than to trust this political figure in front of her constituents. Thankfully, two could play her game.

"My apologies, Scholar," he said, turning toward the crowd. "As soon as I landed, I knew I had to see the citizens of Secundus before I saw the Senate."

The people gave a cheer, and Sev smiled, turning back to the woman. Again, he saw no change in her expression, nothing to give away any frustration or anger. Instead, she nodded with a smile.

"I have to admit, Historian, you are right. The people come first, and we were wrong to summon you so quickly. But we can talk about these things later. As you said, you are here to see the people."

She gestured to the crowd and they cheered once more. Sev gave her one last glance, then turned to the smiling faces. If she was going to give him an opening, he was going to take it.

"Citizens of Secundus, by now I trust you have heard the message I am preaching, but I will speak it just once more with the support of the Senate."

He dove into another iteration of his speech, proclaiming the need for a popular movement to bring peace to the two worlds. At this point, he

234

had said the same things in so many ways he was running out of fresh sentences, but the message lost none of its punch—if anything, it was growing stronger. With each iteration, Sev felt more and more truth in his words, belief giving way to passion. This was no longer just a way to save his life, this was a way to save many lives.

At the right moment, he paused, eyeing the proud and alien people before him. Could these people be the key to peace? Could they bring prosperity to Primus?

"So I ask you all now, will you help me in this mission?"

The crowd erupted in applause, and Sev smiled. As the noise died down, he turned to the Scholar.

"I trust the Senate will support us?"

The woman hesitated, then smiled.

"Of course, Historian."

She turned to the crowd.

"Together, we can forge a new path not just for one planet, but for a system united under Olius!"

The crowd erupted once more, but Sev's reaction was subdued, his attention on the Senate Scholar. As the villagers dispersed, many of them queuing up to speak with him, he wondered if he had done enough to protect his mission.

As far as he could tell, there were three paths forward. The first was the optimistic path, wherein he faced no opposition in the Senate and they championed his mission, allowing him to do not only what he had spent all rotation proclaiming he would do, but also keeping the dark secrets of the past.

The second was the pessimistic path, one in which the Senate itself was involved in the communication network discovered on Primus and knew his predecessor had been executed. If they were able to bring this information to light, he would lose his public support and face the fate foreshadowed by the Elector: death at the hands of the so-called farmers.

Unfortunately, Sev knew the true path was likely the realistic one, meaning it fell somewhere between the extremes. But which way was the balance tipped: to the side of success or the side of failure?

As the line dwindled and the citizens headed back to their homes, Sev knew the answer would come soon, perhaps sooner than he wanted. But he had gotten this far, and things were off to a good start.

Once he was alone with the Senate Scholar and his entourage, she addressed him directly.

"Historian, do you have any more stops on your journey?"

Sev glanced to the horizon, where Olius had all but disappeared behind the trees.

"No, Scholar, this will do for the rotation."

She smiled.

"It will indeed. While there remains quite a bit of Secundus to cover, your call to action is already spreading."

Sev managed a polite smile in return.

"I hope I will have enough time to taste as much of this world as I can before my Departure, but I know a thousand revolutions would never be enough."

She nodded.

"Historian, while your word will always have the greatest weight, as I understand your mission is one of haste, is it not?"

Sev peered at her, worried where she might be taking this conversation.

"It is indeed. The faster we foster peace between the worlds, the better."

She nodded again.

"I agree, Historian. But in this case, it would be best to let the Scholarship and the Senate work on your behalf. We can begin the process immediately, there is no reason to wait. Come with me to the Senate and we will broadcast your message across the planet. The Senators will be eager to start organizing a plan of action, and the Scholars will support you in every way possible. They are already in session, awaiting your arrival —they would be thrilled by your presence."

She turned around and started down the path, but Sev didn't move. After a moment, she stopped and looked back at him.

"Historian?"

Sev glanced at the four Scholars, each of them watching with confusion and concern.

"Scholar, while I appreciate your urgency, I must ask you give me time. This is a mission of haste, you are right, but what we need more than anything is a plan, and a hurried mind doesn't forge a clear path. I will take this night to gather my thoughts on the matter and join you on the rotation that follows. There, we will begin the process together, but I urge you and the entire Senate to spend the night as I am, preparing for our discussion."

She stared at him as he spoke, but her composure went unbroken. Any frustration she had was well-hidden.

"Very well, Historian. I will rush to my duties and the Senate will welcome you when the light of Olius returns."

She dropped her chin to her chest and took off in a run, surprising Sev with her commitment to the act—if it was an act. Perhaps the Senate wasn't involved with the attempted coup of Primus, or at least not every member. There were 154 of them in total, could such a large group agree to such drastic action?

Of course, he wouldn't find the answer to this question now, and no matter what path lay before him—the optimistic one, the pessimistic one, or the realistic one—he had only one night to prepare for his appearance before the Senate.

He turned to the Scholars around him.

"What is the fastest way back to the Scholarship?"

The woman gestured the same way the Senate Scholar had taken.

"This way, Historian."

"Lead us. I have a busy night ahead of me."

She dropped her chin to her chest and started off, Sev and the other three right behind her.

Accusation

On the following rotation, Sev barely noticed the surrounding greenery or the birds overhead. He walked with the four Scholars from the previous rotation—the woman he had had to request specifically—his mind consumed by the task ahead.

Even if none of the Senate knew of his ruse—a naive assumption, though he remained hopeful—there was another, more entrenched obstacle in his path: apathy. How many of these Senators would care to help their estranged neighbor? While he hadn't seen the sort of disdain he had seen on Primus, there had to be a reason this planet ignored the other's plight.

Still, while the task before him was daunting, his fear of execution had diminished. The night before, in the terminal, he had seen his speeches circulating among the people of Secundus, with stories of his village visits appearing as recent news. Though he had no idea how that information had gotten into the repository so quickly and thoroughly, it was clear it was spreading, and he had faith in the will of the people—the ultimate safety net.

Over the course of the night's planning, Sev had also considered the supreme leader's role in this ambitious mission. After all, if Sev intended to reverse the Senate's plan to remove the Elector, a new era of peace depended on the Palace as much as it depended on the Senate. Thankfully, if this peace was brokered by Sev himself, it might work—depending on what the Senate sought in return.

This, he realized, would be the hardest issue to resolve. Could he convince the ruling body of Secundus to be generous? Based on the information in the terminal, they seemed to understand the extent of their technological superiority, yet they didn't use their advantage to crush Primus. He considered this a good sign, though apathy could be more damaging than malice.

Of course, not everyone on Secundus was apathetic. Whoever had been a part of the communication network had decided to interfere in Priman matters, and Sev had to wonder: why now, at the same time as the Historian's Visit? That couldn't be a coincidence.

They reached a large structure with a tall glass entrance, a building he recognized from the terminal—this was the Senate. The door opened before them, and Sev looked to his followers. He knew from his readings that unless summoned inside, they would have to wait here. Three of them he didn't mind leaving, but the fourth he would miss. He stared at his entourage for a moment, his eyes lingering on the woman, then he turned and stepped through the door.

The Senate was housed in an immense dome of glass, at least twenty men tall and just as wide, its hundred-plus members seated in concentric circles tapering downward with but one interruption—the passage from the entrance leading to center stage. All of it was either transparent, white, or a stunning shade of blue.

Sev followed the path down the middle, feeling the eyes of Secundus upon him. He returned their gaze, noting—as he had learned in the terminal—that each Senator sat next to their territory's Scholar, the latter distinguished only by the flourish of gold in their robe.

He reached the stage and stopped, his eyes scanning the men and women before him. Sev knew one of these Senators was the acting Speaker—the voice of the Senate—but he didn't know who until a woman stood and addressed him.

"Greetings, Historian. Welcome to the Senate."

He faced the Senator, ignoring his lingering doubts. Presumably, these people thought he was the Historian, and the Historian did not face the Senate of Secundus with fear.

"Greetings, Senate of Secundus. Together, we will work to record this planet's grand history, and we shall use the lessons we learn to plan for the future—a future in which we can achieve peace and prosperity for Secundus, for Olius, and for the entire system."

Once again, Sev tried to repeat the words he had heard in the Garden on Primus, and though his memory was not perfect, it was enough to make the right impression.

"Thank you, Historian. We would like to apologize for rushing you on the prior rotation, we understand you may have been tired from your journey."

"No apology is necessary, Senator, but I thank you."

She brought her chin to her chest and continued.

"Historian, our impatience stems solely from our lack of communication. Specifically, on the ninth rotation of your Visit to Primus, we stopped receiving any news from their Scholarship. May we ask what happened?"

And there it was—an immediate and clear connection between the events on Primus and this very governing body: the Senate of Secundus had been communicating with the Scholarship of Primus. But he wasn't dead yet, so they must not have the full story. Still, if the entire Senate was involved with the plot, it made his mission far more complicated.

Thankfully, fear had driven him to prepare for this possibility.

"Of course, Senator. Agents of the Grand Palace discovered the communication network and shut it down."

The words came out of him before he had a chance to think twice, and there was an immediate stir in the chamber. Small conversations broke out among the Senators, and Sev felt a rush of adrenaline at this small victory: this was the reaction he had hoped for.

"Senate of Secundus, this is why the original plan was not carried out. The events that transpired while I was on Primus have convinced me our peace must come another way."

Their side conversations halted, each member focused on what he had to say. Sev knew he had to tread carefully here, but he also had to make his point. It was now or never.

"Senate of Secundus, due to the communication network set up between yourselves and the Scholarship of Primus, the High Scholars were found guilty of treason and imprisoned."

Most of the assembly gasped in shock, which Sev took as proof of their ignorance. He let his momentum carry him, a mixture of preparation and improvisation propelling him forward.

"It was only through delicate intervention that the Scholarship itself wasn't eliminated, and this intervention included a renewed relationship with the Elector, rather than his removal."

Now he was distorting the truth—he had not negotiated the future of the Scholarship, for one—but he had more immediate problems than his honesty: as he spoke, faces turned sour, and many of the Senators looked angry.

"Historian, are you saying the leadership of Primus threatened to eliminate its Scholarship?"

Sev's eyes returned to the woman, whose expression carried a bridled fury. He considered her question for a moment, some of his confidence slipping away.

"Senator, the Elector is a man acting within the confines of his understanding. What he did was unprecedented, but even he had a point to make."

The Senator eyed Sev with skepticism, and he realized he was losing them.

"What point was that, Historian?"

He averted his gaze, trying to calm the building panic. Something about her tone worried him, and he wasn't the only one—several Senators shot concerned glances in her direction, and Sev wondered if maybe she knew the truth...

There was danger here, of that he was sure, but he needed to reestablish his position, to affirm what he had affirmed to the people. He felt the stares of the Senate on him, and he sighed in false resignation.

"Senate of Secundus, mine is a mission to Olius above all else—above Primus, above Secundus—and one of the key tenets of Olius is non-violence. The original plan communicated to the Scholarship of Primus was not one of non-violence, and what happened with the Elector was punishment—the will of Olius exacting itself upon us, alerting us to the error of our ways. It was a costly mistake, but not all is lost. I have come here with a better plan, a plan more in line with Olius, and one more likely to work."

He finished his speech and looked back up at the Senator, ignoring the overwhelming panic in his mind. He was reaching, making assumptions that might prove incorrect, but he was desperate. With just one question and a specific tone, the Speaker had convinced him of his worst nightmare: some people in this chamber knew far more than they were leading on—perhaps that he was an imposter, or even that his predecessor had been killed.

His heart was pounding, waiting for someone to bring it up, to expose the truth and denounce him, but when a Scholar seated next to one of the Senators stood, his words took a different path.

"Historian, the Scholarship will support you in any way possible. We have spent most of the night preparing for this new course of action, and we are eager to hear your proposal."

Though he did not recognize the man, Sev was incredibly grateful for his interjection. There was a murmur of approval around the chamber, and while many of the Senators still looked skeptical, it seemed the Scholars were indeed behind him.

"Thank you, Scholar."

The man brought his chin to his chest and took a seat. Sev smiled at him then turned to the woman.

"Senator, it is time to forge a peace between the worlds through the will of the people. Shall we begin?"

She eyed him curiously, then dropped her chin to her chest.

"Of course, Historian," she said, taking her seat.

The floor was his, and an incredible sense of relief washed over him, pushing away his fears and doubts. All was not won, but he had passed the first and perhaps most difficult hurdle.

"Thank you, Senator."

He turned his attention to the others, scanning the faces around him. Now came the second part of his plan, of which he was much more confident.

"Senate of Secundus, the first step we must take is simple: spread the word across Secundus, gaining the support of the people. I will take the lead on this task, continuing the work I began on the previous rotation and visiting every district I can."

He glanced at the Scholar who had intervened on his behalf.

"With the Scholarship's help, I will target more reluctant regions first, leaving the rest in the able hands of the Scholars."

The man stood again and brought his chin to his chest.

"As you wish, Historian."

He took his seat and Sev continued.

"Once we reach a threshold of acceptance, our next step is to establish a line of communication with Primus."

Someone on his left stood—a different Senator.

"Historian, do you suggest we try to reopen the old network?"

Sev shook his head.

"No, Senator, this would endanger our mission and destroy any good faith the Palace holds in my presence here."

"Then what do you propose?"

There was a hint of aggression in his tone, and some of the Scholars eyed him with disapproval, but Sev answered calmly.

"Senator, I suggest we form a greeting party—composed of myself and some section of the Senate—to travel to Primus and present our plan."

The man's expression soured.

"You suggest we go to Primus?"

"Historian, if I may."

Sev turned to the Speaker, who was standing once more.

"Yes?"

"I believe my colleague's concern is well-placed. Per your account, there is a great deal of latent hostility toward Secundus on Primus. Even if we go there with the best intentions, there is a high chance of retribution, by either the leadership or the people."

Sev had expected resistance here and responded accordingly, turning to the Senator on his left.

"Senator, your concerns are indeed well-placed, but as far as the risk to our party goes, my presence will serve as protection and assure our safety. If that is not sufficient, I will first travel to Primus alone to establish a line of communication, after which we can determine the best course of action."

The man seemed unconvinced, but it was the Speaker who responded.

"Historian, there is one variable we have overlooked."

He turned to her.

"What is that, Senator?"

"As we understand it, the people of Primus know little to nothing of the wealth of Secundus. This is true, is it not?"

Sev hesitated, then nodded.

"Yes, Senator, it is."

She nodded in kind, a soft smile appearing on her lips.

"Our wealth is the key to saving Primus, and even with one of our ships on Priman soil, perhaps even with your word, it would be hard to convince the people of our ability to help them. But if the Priman leader were to visit Secundus itself and see our world firsthand, his account would be taken as truth, would it not?"

Sev frowned.

"You want the Elector to come to Secundus?"

She nodded again.

"This would give him definitive proof of our ability to help. And if you assure the Priman leader of our goal and of his safety, that should be enough, should it not?"

Sev's frown deepened, though he made an effort to hide it. This was a trap, but he knew it would be a mistake to disagree too enthusiastically.

"Even my assurance may not suffice, Senator. Unfortunately, the Elector's suspicion runs deep."

The Speaker nodded.

"Undoubtedly. However, you must understand we share the same doubts—not with regards to you, Historian, but with regards to the Priman leader's intentions."

Her clarification was handled deftly, but Sev saw through the facade. She had chosen her words carefully, and their meaning was clear as could be: some of the Senate did not trust him. The question was how much?

"Of course, Senator. We will have to table this discussion for the time being, until the communication avenue between Secundus and Primus is established. Right now, the support of the Secundan people is my primary mission."

The Speaker nodded, and Sev saw the man sit down out of the corner of his eye.

"Very well, Historian. We do not wish to delay you any more than necessary. The Scholarship will work with you to determine the most efficient use of your time, while the Senate will procure a ship for your departure to Primus when you inform us of your need. Is there anything else you ask of the Senate, Historian?"

Sev eyed the 154 people in front of him, searching their expressions for a friendly face. Most of the Senators seemed concerned or confused, though the Scholars watched him with nearly undivided attention. This battle was far from won, he realized.

"Yes, Senator. Senate of Secundus, I ask for your full support. I sense an alarming amount of hostility toward Primus within this chamber, and while I understand its cause, I worry your attitude will interfere with the mission of Olius, the mission of peace. Never forget we are all united under its light, and our mission reflects this unity."

He scanned the faces one last time.

"Thank you, Senate of Secundus."

And before anyone could respond, he turned around and walked out of the building.

***

His entourage stood outside, waiting patiently beside the entrance. On his approach, each of them brought their chin to their chest.

"We trust your meeting was fruitful, Historian."

Before he could answer, Sev heard footsteps behind him and turned to see a handful of Senate Scholars exit the building, led by the man who had stood up for him.

"Historian, if you are ready, we will convene in the Scholarship to determine our course of action."

Sev smiled.

"Thank you for your support in the Senate, Scholar."

The man gave him an amused look.

"Historian, it is our duty to serve Olius and the Historian, but your thanks are appreciated."

He gestured down the path.

"Shall we?"

Sev glanced back to the entrance and saw more Senate Scholars on their way out. Would all of them be joining? Changing locations to begin another meeting seemed redundant, but he had to remember the political structure on Secundus was different than Primus: here, the Scholarship was not independent.

Was such cohesion possible on Primus? Sev tried to imagine the Palace working in harmony with the Scholarship, but he couldn't even form the image in his mind. Part of the problem was how much the Scholarship had changed in the rotations leading up to his Departure: a new Council, and after his exit, a new Elder Scholar…

Had the Elector maintained a healthy relationship with the Scholarship as promised? Was such a thing even possible, after what had happened? By most accounts, the supreme leader had killed the institution. Yes, Sev had done what he could to resuscitate it, and with the help of his colleagues, there was a semblance of hope for the future. But even now, he found it hard to think of the entity he left behind as the Scholarship. To him, the Scholarship was Zoph, it was the former Elder Scholar, it was all of the men imprisoned for their crimes…

And, for a brief time, it was the Historian. The man executed for his conversations with the very people Sev now stood amongst. If anything, perhaps his time here could answer some of the questions weighing on his mind. He still couldn't understand why his predecessor—a title he used loosely, given it implied he was rightfully in his place—would secretly plot against the Palace. Surely there was a better way…

"Historian?"

The Senate Scholar gave him a concerned look, and Sev replied with a sad smile.

"Apologies, Scholar. I have a lot on my mind. Please, lead the way."

He shot another glance at the mass of people behind them and noticed they were all Scholars—each one had the flourish of gold in their robes. Had the Senators stayed inside to deliberate amongst themselves? Were they plotting against him away from the ears of the Scholarship?

He shook his head in an effort to clear it, walking side by side with the Senate Scholar. These ideas were overly paranoid—sure, he hadn't managed to achieve everything he had wanted to, and yes, there were clearly a few individuals less than happy with his decisions, but he had to consider his visit to the Senate a success.

"Historian, I must say your actions after the Arrival were surprising, but they make perfect sense given what happened on Primus."

The man's words brought him back to reality, and Sev nodded.

"I did not mean to startle or offend the Senate, Scholar. I only wanted to perform my duties as quickly and efficiently as possible."

The man nodded in turn.

"Historian, your actions are our guidance. There can be no offense taken."

Sev eyed him cautiously, then responded in a quiet voice.

"True, but some might take offense all the same."

The man gave him a knowing look, and Sev knew his message had gotten across.

"Historian, I feel as I should warn you…"

The man paused, glancing around before continuing.

"You must allow the Senate some patience. It has been many revolutions since our last Visit, and certain members have gotten used to their position of power."

Sev nodded gently. The man had a point, but was it enough to explain the tension he had felt in the chamber?

"Don't worry," he added. "The Scholarship will support you without reservation."

Sev forced a smile. While the man's words were honest, they were probably naive. Sev already had reservations about the Scholar of the Premier Territory. Could he really count on the entire Scholarship, or were there enemies there as well?

***

When they reached the Scholarship, the man led him into a grand room with a large table—large enough to seat all 77 Senate Scholars with room to spare. There was nothing to distinguish this room as unique or special, and Sev had not delved into the terminal deep enough to learn the details of how this Scholarship functioned, but this seemed to be their version of the Room of Council—albeit with six times as many people.

The man showed him where he could sit, and the rest of the Senate Scholars filed into the other chairs. Sev noticed his entourage was welcome here, and they took four of the closest spots. As the last few individuals took their seats, Sev wondered if he was meant to open the discussion, but the man next to him spoke first.

"Scholars, I trust we all understand the Historian's mission and are ready to do what is asked of us."

He turned to Sev.

"Historian, we do not wish to waste your time. Per your words in the Senate, you want to visit more reluctant districts yourself, while we help spread the message of peace elsewhere, correct?"

Sev nodded, then turned to speak to everyone at the table.

"I assume there are regions of Secundus that will require more persuasion than others. Is that the case?"

Most of them nodded, and another Scholar down the table spoke up.

"Yes, Historian. In my district, for example, you will meet resistance. But I am happy to help you on your mission. Olius must come above Secundus."

Sev stared at the woman, surprised by her demeanor. A few rotations ago, he would never have expected a female to speak so clearly or fit into a leadership role so easily. Secundus was turning his world on its head, and part of him thought it might be for the better.

"Thank you, Scholar. This is a good point—if I can have the local Senate Scholar accompany me to these difficult districts, it may help with my message."

He paused, a thought coming to him.

"Scholars, before we move on, I must ask: are there any here who hesitate to accept my mission? Do any of you have questions or doubts?"

Most of the men and women shook their heads, but Sev saw a few shy glances.

"Scholars, please. I beg of you the truth. I felt the disapproval of the Senate, and I do not wish to feel that here—at the least, I want us to speak to one another without reservation or fear. My time on Primus altered my plans dramatically, and I am open to all viewpoints."

Again, Sev didn't know if every face before him was trustworthy. But where the approval of the Senate felt unattainable, the approval of the Scholarship was within reach. And if he could get this approval in a manner appropriate of his role, it would solidify the support even further.

"Historian…"

His eyes locked on another Senate Scholar, only eight seats away. A few of his colleagues shot surprised glances, and Sev saw his confidence falter.

"Scholars, please do not judge your peers into silence. If you are hostile toward these differing opinions, we cannot have open discourse."

The man gave Sev a thankful look, taking a deep breath to prepare.

"Historian, I am trying to understand what you told us in the Senate, why the plan changed."

"Scholar, you mean to ask why I no longer suggest the removal of the Elector?"

The man nodded, still hesitant to speak.

"Yes, Historian. I… forgive me, as I mean no offense…"

Sev put up a reassuring hand.

"Scholar, speak your mind clear. Olius is the path of truth, there are no compromises in that path."

The man nodded again.

"Yes, Historian. I'm asking if the change was reactive or proactive. Was it because the communication network was discovered and the High Scholars imprisoned, or because you yourself thought it wrong?"

Some of his peers shot disapproving glances at the man, and Sev returned the favor.

"Scholars, I have asked you to keep an open mind. Please do not allow your personal feelings to obstruct the truth."

"Our apologies, Historian," they said. Then, turning to their colleague, "Our apologies, Scholar."

Sev watched in fascination, amazed how in tune they were to one another. There was a depth of communication here beyond anything he had ever seen in the Room of Council, which only made answering the question all the harder. How would he explain what had happened without revealing his predecessor's demise—or existence?

"Thank you, Scholars," he said. Then, returning his attention to the man who had spoken up, "Scholar, I admit the change was reactive. This plan did not occur to me until after the network was discovered and the High Scholars were imprisoned. But since then, I have come to understand this is the right path, and I hope to convince you of the same."

Sev felt a stab of guilt at his slippery words. Yes, this was technically the truth, but after having preached to these Scholars the importance of honesty he still avoided it. Such a sin would only be forgiven if he was successful: if he could actually bring peace between the worlds. Only then could he consider telling the full story...

"Thank you, Historian," the man replied. "And I will support your mission to the fullest, as I support Olius to the fullest."

Sev smiled.

"Thank you, Scholar."

He scanned the faces before him and saw a more unanimous front, but he knew this was his best opportunity to win over the Scholarship.

"Scholars, I don't wish to address this topic a hundred times but I do have one more thing to say: the will of Olius cannot be forced upon a people, it can only be suggested. Do we wish to save the people of Primus or do we wish to let them save themselves? The removal of the Elector may have sparked a rebellion of some kind, or caused underlying resentment. How would you feel if the Scholarship of Primus removed the Senate from power? Clearly these examples are very different, but the similarities are worth considering. Are we treating Primans as equals worthy of the lives held by Secundans, or are we treating them with pity, as if they were below us?"

All eyes were on Sev, and not one of them broke their focus.

"Scholars, I ask you to reflect on these questions, but now we must return to the task at hand."

He turned to the man who had led him here.

"Let's establish a list of districts for me to visit and begin the process at once."

The ensuing discussion formed a clear plan of action, and soon they had Sev's schedule mapped out. With these first steps out of the way, he felt a measure of relief, but only if he didn't think too far ahead.

What would happen when they needed to establish a line of communication? Or when a delegation from one planet had to go to the other? Or when the Senate exposed him for what he really was?

No, he thought to himself, that wasn't going to happen. If they had wanted to do that, they had missed their window. The question was why they allowed him to continue: was it because so few of them knew the truth? Or was there another motive?

***

Over the next few rotations, Sev visited districts by light and explored the terminal by night. As his journeys grew in distance—to the point where a shuttle was necessary—his exploration of the information held within the machine grew equally extensive. Each rotation he returned to his chamber thoroughly exhausted but unable to rest, diving into the digital tome to soak up as much as possible.

What he read continued to defy what he had assumed. According to the terminal, Secundus was prosperous, its people comfortable and wealthy—so much was visible on his travels. But he found no mention of a lower class, no discussion of peasants. The menial work was left to machines, machines the likes of which Sev had never imagined. It was all shown to him, displayed holographically inside his chamber, and occasionally he would encounter these foreign creations during his missions, proving what he had seen or read.

Rotation after rotation, he delved deeper into the planet's history and saw the development and emergence of each stage of technology. As he traced back ten, fifty, even one hundred revolutions, he realized Primus was not only well behind, it was stuck in place. Why didn't they have machines in their quarries, digging the rock and mining the ore? Why had they not advanced to this degree, or even half of it?

Part of the answer was there in the terminal, in the period after the Great War. At first, he had focused on the attack on Primus—the infamous event which ended the ceasefire and closed their borders. Here too, what he saw did not match what he knew. According to the terminal, it was not Secundus that broke the truce but a rogue terroristic group bent on rekindling the conflict. Secundus agreed to honor Primus's decision to close its borders, and even allowed them to control the trade—with windowless ships and fully Priman crew—so no citizen of Secundus could ever step foot on Primus.

But it was what happened just before the attack, toward the end of the temporary peace, that hinted at an answer to his biggest question. Here, the data was sparse, but it wasn't hard to piece together. Secundus had done what the Palace was trying to do—they had tapped into Olian technology. But where Primus still struggled, Secundus had succeeded, and remarkably so.

Ever since the closing of the borders, one planet had accelerated at an exceptional rate while one had stagnated, and Sev failed to understand the discrepancy. Yes, Secundus was mastering the technology of Olius, but most of their advancements came through the precious metals mined on Primus. Why hadn't Primus been able to take advantage of these assets in the way Secundus had? If they were the source of the raw materials, should they not see the greatest share of the wealth?

He reached further back in the timeline, to the Historian's last Visit to Secundus, the Visit that brought about the end of the Great War. Here, the holograms were artist's depictions, as Secundus was far from their technological achievements of the present. For this, Sev was relieved—if there was an accurate depiction of the Historian on record, he would have been found and charged on the spot.

As he read about the historic Visit, another question came to him, one that had been festering in his mind for some time: what was the Historian's true purpose? He had been told over and over the Historian was meant to collect the knowledge of the planets and ensure the people of Primus and Secundus prospered. According to what he saw, the second part was undoubtedly true, but the first? The terminal made no mention of any collection of data or processing of history, it only spoke of the peace agreement.

Sev thought back to the paradox of the Historian's data collection on Primus. Here on Secundus, the terminal housed all knowledge and could connect to Olius's Vessel, but on Primus? During his time on the Council, the other High Scholars had had lengthy discussions with the Historian and showed him many tomes, but the being of Olius took no notes. He had assumed the man would need to transcribe all of their data, but he had never seen or heard of it actually happening. True, the Historian must have had a good memory to convey the contents of the sensitive tome, but a memory good enough to hold the history of a planet's people?

These thoughts reminded him of the most terrifying doubt in his mind: whether or not his Ascension had taken place. Shouldn't he know these things himself now? Shouldn't he have an infallible memory and incredible longevity? He had already searched the terminal for data regarding Ascension—anything to ease his conscience—but there was nothing to be found.

Then a thought struck him: if there wasn't any information about Ascension itself, maybe there was something about a succession of Historians from hundreds of revolutions ago? He tried to delve deeper into the past, to go beyond the last Visit, but the Great War marked the edge of the terminal's content. There was a loose timeline of previous Visits, but these were mere lines on a prehistoric chart, with no accompanying details or clarification.

Sev felt the familiar frustration of being incredibly close to an important revelation, but not close enough to see the truth. How long would it take for him to see the full picture? And when he saw it, would he know what to do?

***

"Historian, if I may?"

It was the sixth rotation since his Arrival, and Sev sat at the same large table, all 77 of the Senate Scholars accompanying him. Many other Secundan Scholars stood around them, some as part of their duties, others out of curiosity. More and more observers had joined these meetings, and despite some initial trepidation, Sev welcomed their presence as a way to spread his message.

"Yes, Scholar?"

He turned to the Scholar of the Premier Territory, hiding his hesitation with a half-smile. He had a feeling he already knew what she was going to bring up, but he played along all the same.

"Historian, I believe it is time we discuss the opening of our line of communication with Primus. We are closing in on the threshold, and I don't think it would be wise to procrastinate on this task."

She was right, of course. With each passing rotation, Sev felt the pressure mounting. How much longer did he want to spread his message? How many more districts needed to hear his words in person? Soon, it would be time to charter a ship and fly to Primus, to speak with the Elector and try to bring about a new peace.

But there was a problem: he still hadn't found a way to convince the Senate to send the peace party to Primus. They wanted to bring the Elector to Secundus to sign the treaty, but Sev thought this far too dangerous. If some of the Senate was working against him, bringing the Elector to Secundus would allow them to wipe out the leader of Primus and the being of Olius in one swoop.

Of course, as he couldn't share these insights, he gave the Scholar a small smile.

"Of course, Scholar. Do you have a proposal?"

She nodded.

"Indeed I do, Historian. I suggest this mission be handled solely by the Scholarship, given the relationship between the Priman leadership and our world. You would select whatever Scholars you thought appropriate, and the Senate would procure the ship. I suggest we decide on the crew and ask the Senate to have the ship ready."

Sev felt the eyes of the Scholarship upon him and gave a reluctant nod.

"Very well, Scholar. I will decide on the crew. Will you handle the craft?"

She brought her chin to her chest.

"Of course, Historian."

***

Two rotations later, Sev was on another shuttle heading to another district, his four trusty Scholars in tow. This time, they were heading to a trading hub—one of the locations where trade ships would land and offload ore deposits before loading agricultural products.

One of the Scholars was explaining the trade ships to him, but he wasn't listening. His mind was racing to find a convincing argument for the leaders of Secundus to go to Primus. It wasn't just that the Elector would never come to Secundus—Sev didn't even trust this first mission, the one meant to open communication. Yes, he had been allowed to select his crew, but this didn't preclude any foul-play. The only way to ensure his journey to Primus was safe was with the Secundan leadership aboard, and he was running out of time to make it happen.

"Since the closing of its borders, Primus has not allowed any crew to leave their ships. In fact, no citizen of Primus ever interacts or sees a citizen of Secundus. The ancient ships have no windows, and the interior is separated into two distinct sections: the cargo hold and the living quarters. After they land, the crew convenes in the living area, closes off the cargo hold, and opens the cargo door. Then we board the ship, remove their shipment, and load our own. Once ours is loaded, we notify the crew via a lever, then they close the cargo door, check the hold, and leave."

Sev picked up on a few words and glanced at the Scholar. How did they know the interior design of the trade ship? But the answer was already on its way.

"When we were communicating with the Scholarship of Primus, we would load everything except the last item, put one of our people in the cargo hold, then notify the crew we were finished. The Priman crew always sends one member to check the hold before takeoff, to make sure the entire shipment is there. This was the person we had an arrangement with. Our person would pass along whatever information was necessary, then the crew member would return to the living quarters and say the last item was missing. The cargo door would reopen, our person would leave, the last item would be loaded up, and we would notify them once more."

Sev nodded.

"It was always the same Priman checking the hold?"

"Almost always, yes. The crews have very specific roles, and changes were decided well in advance, so we would typically get fair warning. If an unknown crew member appeared, we would use the last missing item as an excuse, but that was a rare occurrence."

As the man spoke, Sev couldn't help but address his curiosity.

"How did the communication network start?"

"These arrangements were made just after the closing of the borders, as the new rules came into effect. The Council of the Scholarship of Primus wanted to maintain contact with us, but it was strictly forbidden by the Grand Palace. As new generations have taken over, the Council has continued to solicit the help of the trade crews. Of Primus's twelve ships, we still had arrangements with ten of them just before we lost contact."

Sev let these words sink in. This was not some fresh network: there had been generations of contact between the Scholarship of Primus and the Scholarship of Secundus. Why hadn't they shared the knowledge of Olius? How had this technological gap grown to such an unfathomable size?

"And when you lost contact, how did that unfold?"

The man frowned.

"It was a difficult series of rotations. An unexpected crew member came to check the hold, and our person had to feign ignorance, though I assume at that point Primus knew our deceit. Especially because this happened three times before we realized it was a global issue."

A harsh tone came from the walls of the vessel and the Scholar looked around, startled.

"What is it?" Sev asked.

The man rose from his seat and walked to one of the walls.

"My apologies, Historian, it seems the Senate has rerouted our ship. This must be a mistake. Give me a moment and I will rectify the situation."

Sev watched the Scholar interact with a small hologram similar to the terminal and shook his head in disbelief. How had Primus had fallen so far behind—and why?

Then another realization came to him: the Council must have known about the superiority of Secundus, which might have played into their treason. Perhaps they saw the removal of the Elector as the safest way to bring this technology to Primus—but why wait until now? To get the Historian's blessing?

And what of the Elector, he wondered. How much did he know? How long had he spied on the communication network, and how much had he learned?

All these small questions led to one big question: if they knew, why keep it a secret? To preserve Priman pride? Sev could see this from the Palace but not from the Scholarship. He felt as if he was on the verge of a discovery, just moments away from an important realization—

"Hm."

The Scholar's tone caught Sev's attention.

"What is it?"

"I apologize again, Historian, but the Senate has assured me they are not mistaken. They wish to see you at once. Our ship is headed back now."

***

He entered the immense dome of glass and walked down the path to the stage. Off to the side he saw a man, clearly malnourished, his garments mangled and his body dirty. But even under the grime, even behind the ripped robes, Sev recognized his face.

"Sev!"

In all the revolutions he had known him, Sev had never heard such fury in Zoph's voice.

"Why are you here?"

He could have asked him the same question.

"Former citizen of Primus, I ask that you show some respect. You are speaking to the Historian."

At these words from the Speaker, a wave of shame came over him, drowning him in the memory of the nightmare on Primus. The smell of burnt flesh, the wails of pain, and the image seared into his soul forever—that of a hotsword slicing through the Historian's neck.

"The Historian?" Zoph asked, giving the Scholar an incredulous look. "This man is not the Historian. The Historian is dead."

Assistance

A tense silence followed Zoph's announcement, and Sev's mind raced, trying to understand how his former mentor was on this planet. He looked like he had just stepped out of the Palace prison, yet here he was in the Senate of Secundus.

"High Scholar Zoph, please."

Sev's eyes darted to the Speaker above them.

"At this time, the man before you is still the Historian in the eyes of Secundus," she continued. "Though the claims you have made are urgent, we must follow protocol."

Surprise turned into panic, and Sev searched desperately for absolution, for some explanation to save him from what came next.

"Historian."

The Speaker looked him in the eye, but he couldn't hold her gaze.

"Earlier this rotation, High Scholar Zoph was found hidden in a Priman trade ship. When discovered, he informed our citizens of his identity and his escape from Primus, asking for asylum on our world."

He stared at Zoph, incredulous. Escaped from Primus? From the Grand Palace? Impossible.

"Upon further questioning, he told us the Priman leader not only put them in prison, but executed the Historian for treason."

Then it hit him, and Sev cursed his naivety. Escaping the Grand Palace was impossible, but what if he had had some help?

"We let him know the Historian was among us, but he was adamant this was not possible. This is why we had your ship diverted, and we ask your forgiveness as this may postpone our attempts at reestablishing the line of communication."

She dropped her chin to her chest, and while he doubted the gesture's authenticity, it didn't matter. The eyes of 154 Senators and Scholars were upon him, all of them waiting for an explanation. But he didn't have one —Zoph was telling the truth.

How could he have committed such a grave miscalculation? He had underestimated his enemies, the same enemies who had convinced the former Historian to promote a coup. And now? Now the silence dragged on, sowing doubt all around him. This was it, he realized. It was over.

Unable to bear it any longer, he dropped his eyes to the ground and spoke.

"Senator, everything this man says is true."

Conversation erupted all around him, a roar of activity that startled him. Almost immediately, the Speaker raised her hand and brought it down in a swift motion, her gesture causing the entire dome to emit a harsh tone, halting all conversation.

"Historian, you will forgive our outburst, but what you say is impossible. This man claims the Historian was executed, yet here you stand before us."

Her tone was calculated, convincing. Sev was sure she was toying with him, yet her confusion seemed genuine. He glanced at his former teacher, saw the rage in his eyes.

"The Historian is dead," he announced, not looking away.

This time, Senators and Scholars alike stood from their seats, shouting over one another in the ensuing confusion. Sev heard voices of anger and doubt, their volume rising until the harsh tone returned. With it came an invisible force, like a gust of wind, pressing everyone back into their seats.

"Senate of Secundus! We must have order!"

A few of them spoke some choice words, many of them grumbled, but everyone remained seated. Sev didn't have time to marvel at the details of this mysterious technology—his attention was on the man before him, the man who had done the impossible, the man who would bring an end to any chance of peace.

"So you claim everything High Scholar Zoph has stated is true? That the Priman leader executed the Historian for treason against the Palace?"

The memory, the nightmare—it threatened to come back to him once more, but even that could not outweigh the terror he now felt.

"Yes, Senator."

The grumbling grew in intensity, but the Speaker spoke over it.

"So you are not the Historian?"

Her question silenced the chamber, and once again Sev felt the stares of all those present. This was it, he thought. He would lose the people's favor and any protection he had had.

"If he is not the Historian, how is it he arrived in Olius's Vessel?"

A familiar voice caught his attention, but before Sev could look up, Zoph interjected.

"He was on the Vessel?"

The Speaker shot him a stern look.

"High Scholar Zoph, we must insist you do not interrupt or you will be silenced."

She turned her attention to the Scholar.

"Scholar, please take your seat, as—"

But the Scholar ignored her, addressing Sev directly.

"How did you arrive in Olius's Vessel?"

And then it came to him, a ray of light in the darkness: the data tome. Could it absolve him? Could he explain everything away? He decided to give it a try…

"At the time of the Departure, I had been promoted to Elder Scholar —"

"Elder Scholar?! How dare you!"

Zoph lunged at him with unexpected quickness, but before he could reach his target, he fell to the ground in convulsions.

"High Scholar Zoph, this is your final warning. If you cannot maintain order you will be removed from the Senate. And you, Scholar," she said, whirling to face him, "It is not your turn to speak. Please take your seat, or you will be asked to leave."

Zoph's convulsions stopped, and Sev's eyes darted up to the Speaker. How had she managed to incapacitate him from such a distance? The High Scholar stumbled to regain his footing, breathing heavily, and despite everything that was happening, Sev felt a hint of anger take root—anger at the treatment of his former teacher.

"This is a matter for the Scholarship," the Scholar continued, still standing. "We deserve to know the answer to these questions."

Sev glanced up and saw defiance in the man's eyes. The Speaker hesitated, and when she replied, it was with contempt.

"Very well, Scholar. We will follow your line of inquiry. Please take your seat."

The Scholar glared at her then sat down, and the Speaker turned back to Sev.

"How is it that you came on Olius's Vessel?"

Sev shot a glance at the Scholar, but his eyes were still fixed on the Speaker.

"Senator, I came on Olius's Vessel as part of my Ascension."

Another outburst took over the chamber, though this one was less raucous than the last. The Speaker brought her hand down, silencing the other voices—including Zoph's. Sev saw his former teacher grasp at his throat in pain and felt the same mix of wonder and anger—wonder at the technology of Secundus and anger at its Speaker. Was this how they treated a High Scholar of Primus?

"Explain yourself, and do so quickly."

Sev looked up at her, suppressing his growing indignation. Now was not the time to defend Primus's honor.

"Yes, Senator. As I said, at the time of the Departure, I had been promoted to Elder Scholar."

He glanced at Zoph, but the man said nothing, eyeing him with a silent hatred.

"How is it that you were promoted to Elder Scholar?"

He turned his attention back to the Speaker.

"I was promoted when the Palace discovered the communication network and imprisoned the rest of the Council. I became the Elder Scholar because I was the only High Scholar left on the Council."

The Speaker digested his words for a moment.

"So you were not just a Scholar of Primus, you were a High Scholar of Primus, a member of the very Council on which Zoph sat?"

Sev glanced at his former teacher once more.

"Yes."

The silent hatred reached a crescendo, and Zoph turned to the Speaker.

"Senator, if I may?"

His tone was sharp, bordering on demanding, and the Speaker eyed him warily.

"Go ahead, High Scholar Zoph."

Zoph turned his attention to Sev.

"His promotion was never recognized by the Council except in an attempt to avoid hostility from the Palace."

"And why is that?"

"Because he was promoted by the Elector directly only a few rotations before the Arrival."

She turned to Sev.

"Is this true?"

There was no more deceit in her tone. Malice had infected her words, a malice that made Sev both terrified and angry. He wasn't sure if he wanted to cower in fear or leap up and attack her, but he couldn't do either—not now, not when everything hung in a delicate balance.

"Yes, it is true."

"And this is not in following Priman protocol?"

He hesitated.

"It is… but it is not in following Priman practice."

She nodded.

"Very well. You were promoted to High Scholar and then to Elder Scholar. How does this relate to the Ascension you speak of?"

Sev almost let out a sigh of relief: finally, he could set the record straight.

"Senator, the Elder Scholar possessed a data tome which contained the instructions for Ascension in case of the Historian's demise. According to this tome, the acting Elder Scholar would take the place of the Historian."

"What? This is false!"

Sev turned in time to see Zoph collapse to the floor once more.

"High Scholar Zoph, as you are unable to maintain your composure, you are asked to leave the Senate at once."

At this point, Sev could not bear it any longer.

"Is this how you treat a man of Olius?"

The Speaker met his gaze.

"I ask that you respect the sanctity of this chamber," she announced, but Sev could hear the hesitation in her words—a hesitation he couldn't ignore.

"And I ask you respect the sanctity of Olius. This man is a High Scholar of Primus, equivalent to any of the Scholars who are a part of this chamber. Is this the way to treat such a man?"

For a brief moment, Sev had her—the Speaker was speechless, struggling to respond. But just before he could finish the deed, just before he could take control of the situation, his former teacher lashed out once more.

"Don't use me for your personal gain, traitor!"

He turned to Zoph and frowned. The man looked like he hadn't had a real meal in many rotations, and the Speaker's invisible attacks had all but erased his remaining strength. Yet he had enough in him to fight this battle, to bring them both down before the Senate.

"How dare you pose as the Historian! You carry his blood on your hands, and the blood of the Scholarship! You are a shame to Olius itself!"

At these words, Sev's hopes collapsed—not just of outward success, but of inward belief. His former teacher had done what he never could: he had told the truth—the cold, hard truth—and now they would face the consequences.

"Citizen of Primus."

He winced at the Speaker's words, knowing full well what they signified. She had regained her composure and authority, and this marked the end of his journey.

He had had the audacity to describe the fall of the Priman Scholarship as Olius's retribution for the Secundan plot, but that was a lie. Now, in this very Senate, came Olius's retribution: the punishment for what had happened in the audience chamber of the Grand Palace. Soon, he would face the same fate as the true being of Olius, only this time, death was deserved.

"By your own admission, you were promoted by the Priman leader to High Scholar of Primus, after which the same leader executed the Historian and imprisoned the rest of the Council, making you Elder Scholar. This, according to you, made you rightful heir to the position of Historian. Is that true?"

He looked up at the Speaker, whose self-doubt had been replaced by an almost smug satisfaction. Around him was silence; there was no more grumbling, no more side conversations. All eyes were focused on the Speaker and Sev.

"Yes, Senator."

"Citizen of Primus, the Senate of Secundus does not recognize this Ascension. You have committed crimes against Secundus and crimes against Olius. As Speaker, I bring forth a motion of judgement against you, and suggest the punishment of death for your willing impersonation of the Historian. The Senate will vote now, all—"

"Wait!"

All eyes turned to the Scholar of the Premier Territory, who jumped up to speak. Sev felt another pang of dread, wondering what she could possibly say now.

"Senator, I beg your pardon, but it is not up to you to recognize this Ascension. This is a matter for the Scholarship alone."

It was clear from the Speaker's face this was just as surprising to her as it was to Sev.

"This man rightfully claims the position of Historian, and—"

The Speaker finally got a hold of herself and gave the Scholar an incredulous look.

"Scholar, you have no right to—"

The Scholar turned to Sev.

"Why was the Historian executed?"

Some of the Senators gaped, astonished by the proceedings.

"Scholar, I must ask you to leave the Senate. You have breached the—"

But as she spoke, the grumbling erupted once more, with most of the Scholars standing and shouting to let Sev answer. The Speaker dropped her hand with particular resolve, and everyone was forced back into their seats—including the Scholar of the Premier Territory.

"Senate of Secundus! We must have order! You!"

She pointed to the Scholar.

"You must leave at once."

The Scholar stood, dropped her chin to her chest, and left through a small portal in the wall behind her. The Speaker watched her leave, then turned back to Sev.

"Now, as I was saying, I bring forth a motion of judgement against the citizen of Primus who stands before us. For the willing impersonation of the Historian, the punishment of—"

She stopped mid-sentence, shock in her expression, but Sev never managed to see what she was looking at. He barely felt a hand on his shoulder when he lost consciousness, falling into darkness.

***

Sev woke with a start, confused and disoriented.

"Where…?"

He lay on a bed in a small chamber. To his right sat a Scholar he did not recognize.

"Historian, how do you feel?"

Historian? Had it all been a bad dream? Zoph denouncing him in the Senate, the order of execution... was it just a nightmare?

"What—what happened?"

The Scholar frowned, shaking his head.

"The arrival of the High Scholar of Primus has caused quite a stir, Historian. Your very life is in danger, I'm afraid."

Of course it wasn't a dream, Sev thought. Why would he be in a different chamber?

"Where am I?"

"You're safe in the hands of the Scholarship."

He sat up and looked around, noticing another difference between this chamber and his own: there were no windows here.

"What happened in the Senate?"

Again, the Scholar frowned.

"The Scholar of the Premier Territory removed you from the Senate to save your life."

The Scholar of the Premier Territory? Had she come down and grabbed him?

"She saved me from the Senate?"

He nodded.

"At great risk to herself and the other Scholars, but it had to be done. The Senate was proposing a punishment of death for you, Historian."

Sev could no longer ignore the title.

"Scholar, I am not the Historian. Were you not there? Did you not hear?"

These words brought an even greater frown, and the Scholar was hesitant to reply.

"I was not there but... I was listening. You came on Olius's Vessel, did you not?"

Sev sighed, a sadness coming over him.

"Scholar..."

The door in front of them opened, and his savior walked in.

"Historian, how do you feel?"

He stared at the woman, suspicious. Had this woman truly saved him? This woman he had originally pegged as an enemy, like the Speaker...

"Historian?"

Her persistence snapped him out of his trance, and he answered with a hint of frustration.

"For the last time, I am not the Historian."

She stared at him for a moment, then turned to the other Scholar.

"Will you leave us?"

The Scholar got up and walked out the door, closing it behind him.

"What is your given name?" she asked.

"Sev of Primus," he answered.

"Would you prefer if I referred to you by this title?"

He nodded.

"Yes."

"Very well."

She walked over to the side of the bed, sitting where the other Scholar had sat.

"Sev of Primus, may I ask you a few questions?"

He gave her a curious look, part of him still wary of her presence and intentions. Still, if she had saved him from execution...

"Yes, Scholar."

"Thank you. Sev of Primus, according to the data tome you mentioned, you were meant to board the Vessel and become the Historian?"

He hesitated.

"Yes, but Ascension happens on Olius and I arrived here on Secundus."

She frowned.

"You traveled directly from Primus to Secundus?"

He mirrored her frown, wondering if he was about to shatter her hopes. Had she saved him out of misguided faith? Part of him considered feeding her desire, but he shut the thought down quickly—the time for lies was over.

"I believe so."

She gave him a curious look.

"You believe so?"

He sighed, pitying her tone.

"I do not mean to give you hope, Scholar. I am almost certain that was the path of travel."

She peered at him, unfazed.

"But you are not fully certain?"

He sighed a second time.

"When I boarded the Vessel on Primus, some kind of device was activated and I was knocked unconscious. I woke upon my Arrival here on Secundus."

She nodded slowly, then looked away.

"Sev of Primus, I understand your doubts, given the circumstances…"

Her eyes returned to him.

"…but frankly, these doubts are unfounded."

He stared at her with a mix of disbelief and frustration, but she didn't give him a chance to respond.

"I do not claim to know the inner workings of Olius, nor those of the Vessel, but I know one thing: you followed the information in an ancient data tome for rightful succession—information similar to what we have here."

He hesitated, his frustration replaced by surprise.

"Similar? What do you mean?"

She gave him a small smile.

"Sev of Primus, we too have a process of succession for the unlikely passing of the Historian, and the process is simple: the Senate Scholar attached to the acting Speaker at the time of the Historian's death is meant to board Olius's Vessel."

He stared at her, a hint of the old suspicion returning.

"But I've searched for this information in the terminal…"

She nodded.

"And it is not there. Indeed there is some knowledge we keep hidden, if only to prevent political interference in the matters of Olius."

Sev remembered one other item he couldn't find in the terminal: the skirmishes in space, the small-scale battles reported by the Palace. Was this another piece of hidden knowledge, that their planets were in sporadic but active conflict?

"Now, Sev of Primus, allow me to pose a different question."

He snapped out of his train of thought, giving her his full attention.

"Did the data tome on Primus describe the process of Ascension? Did it explain in any fashion what would happen or how?"

He shook his head slowly.

"No…"

She nodded encouragingly.

"And neither does ours, Sev of Primus. There is no information here or on Primus that explains Ascension in detail, and I doubt that knowledge is kept anywhere in the system."

Finally, Sev began to see what she was trying to prove, but he didn't agree.

"Scholar, wouldn't a Historian know they had Ascended? Shouldn't I have changed in some way?"

A flash of frustration crossed her expression.

"Again you try to decipher the workings of Olius! Do you not think it might be beyond understanding?"

Sev frowned, impatience beginning to eat at him.

"But if I am the Historian, should I not understand? Shouldn't the being of Olius be able to decipher its will?"

She gave him an incredulous look.

"Sev of Primus, don't you see? You cannot decipher its workings, but you have already deciphered its will. In fact, you have been preaching its will for several rotations now, a will that has resonated with the people and brought new life to the Scholarship."

There was fire in her eyes as she spoke, and Sev found himself wrapped in her words, unable to look away.

"The will of Olius has always been equality between the worlds and their people, an equality we haven't seen since the end of the Great War. This is neither a secret nor a surprise, and I do not claim to have been blind to it before your Arrival, but your presence has changed an idealistic proposition into a potential reality, all in a matter of rotations. Is that not the role of the Historian? Is that not the role you are filling?"

Despite the appeal of her statements, Sev struggled to agree.

"No, Scholar. I am filling the same role you are, one of a Scholar. The fact that this idea is emerging is simply a product of the population's perception, that they believe I am the Historian."

She stared at him, frustration giving way to anger.

"What else is the Historian if not a platform of faith? Do you wish to know the secrets of the universe before you allow yourself to accept the position?"

He stared at her blankly, surprised by her sudden fervor.

"Sev of Primus, we are at a turning point now, one that will go down in history, and you question your pivotal role. Do you not understand why the Senate is condemning you?"

He hesitated, and she continued.

"The powers that be have seen what you are doing. They have seen the public opinion shifting, and they're making a clear and decisive attack to stifle this uprising. Your presence threatens their superiority, threatens the superiority of Secundus over Primus."

He stared at her, shocked to hear the words come out of her mouth. How could she admit to such a thing against her own people, against her peers? She was a member of the Senate, was she not?

"I have another question for you Sev of Primus, and this one is important. You said your promotion to High Scholar was unconventional, and yet you also said it was according to protocol. Was there anything illegal in your promotion, or did you knowingly attempt to secure the position for un-Scholarly reasons?"

"No…"

"And when the Historian was executed and the rest of the Council imprisoned, were they guilty of their crimes of which they were accused?"

"Yes…"

Sev thought he knew where this was headed, but suddenly she leaned forward, a sadness coming over her expression.

"Sev of Primus, why was the former Historian executed?"

He hesitated, caught off-guard by the change in subject.

"The Historian was executed because he admitted to treason against the Elector."

"And he admitted to this treason?"

"Yes."

"What was this treason, Sev of Primus?"

"There was a data tome with sensitive military information… the Historian tried to share this information with Secundus so they could rout the Grand Palace."

The Scholar listened, nodding as he spoke. It was clear to Sev this was the answer she more or less expected.

"Tell me, Sev of Primus, does this not seem like the most important question of all. If the former Historian is dead, shouldn't we be asking why?"

He nodded slowly, trying to ignore her use of the word former.

"Do you know why the Senate didn't ask you this question? Do you know why they didn't want me to ask you it either?"

He shook his head. The thought had not occurred to him, but she had a point.

"Because the Senate of Secundus is just as much to blame for the death of the Historian as the Elector. We asked him for this information, we assured him the security of our communication, and we failed. It was not the Historian that wanted to rout the Palace, but Secundus. The Historian was quite reluctant to agree, but the Senate ran with his approval, ultimately ending in his death."

Sev stared at her, wide-eyed. Clearly, the woman before him held answers, answers to questions he had had since the Historian's execution.

"The Senate was responsible for the plot to attack the Palace?" he asked.

She nodded, and Sev pressed on.

"Why? Why did Secundus want to rout the Palace?"

She sighed, giving him a knowing look.

"Power, Sev of Primus. Why do humans do anything? The Senate wants direct access to Priman metals. The Palace used to give them such access unhindered, but in the last dozen revolutions, your Elector has made things more and more complicated."

Again, Sev was speechless. Here she was, telling him every dirty secret the Elector had hinted at or wondered about. How could she be so brazen, so open?

Then a thought came to him.

"If the Senate wanted to remove the Elector, why haven't they done so? The technology of Secundus is clearly well beyond that of Primus."

The Scholar smiled.

"Because of Olius. Olius is the grandest power in the system, and it is one of peace."

Here, Sev didn't follow.

"But the Historian himself helped Secundus set up an attack on the Palace. Clearly, Olius was on their side."

"Yes, but as I've said, this was a reluctant agreement. The former Historian realized the Palace was beginning to threaten the Scholarship of Primus, actively fighting against the truth. When the Historian saw this firsthand, he realized he needed Secundus to intervene—not for power, but for truth. Not for the metals of Primus, but for the Scholarship of Primus."

The pieces of the puzzle were finally coming together. The Historian had committed treason against the Grand Palace, but he refused to say he was committing treason against Primus itself. This was why.

"The Senate of Secundus doesn't dare act without the will of the people, and the will of the people is almost always behind Olius. With your arrival and the spread of your message, this is more pronounced than ever, and the Senate realizes this. Whether they admit it or not, you are a threat to them, and unfortunately, you just gave them an excuse to eliminate you."

She looked him up and down, leaning back in her chair.

"Sev of Primus, the Senate of Secundus views itself as a beacon of enlightened thought, but it is in fact quite similar to the Grand Palace of Primus. Each of these entities desires power, desires control. The only thing standing in their way is Olius and the Scholarships, our fragile connection during these troubled times. According to the Council and yourself, it seems the Palace has successfully dismantled the Scholarship of Primus, and now, the Senate is looking to dismantle the Scholarship of Secundus. They have turned a blind eye to their own guilt and you have given them an opening."

He was moved by her words, but there remained a major inconsistency.

"Scholar, you claim the Senate is looking to dismantle the Scholarship, but is the Scholarship not an integral part of the Senate? Aren't you a member yourself?"

She nodded, frowning.

"You're right, of course, but things are never so simple. At this very moment, the Senate is almost evenly split, and order is all but lost. The Senators are calling for your judgement and death while the Scholars defend you. Normally our powers in the Senate are limited, but this is a matter specific to the Scholarship which only confuses the situation further. This is uncharted territory, and there is a very real threat that the Senators will use this situation as an excuse to remove the Scholarship from the Senate once and for all."

She took a deep breath and leaned forward again, her gaze intensifying with its proximity.

"Sev of Primus, in your eyes you have been more or less placed into the position of Historian by the Elector, and this is the source of your guilt, is it not?"

Her eyes stared so deep into his own Sev wondered if she could read his thoughts.

"Yes, Scholar."

She leaned back a bit, looking away and granting him a moment of reprieve.

"I will not lie to you, Sev of Primus. Your concerns are valid. It is clear you are conflicted, and I know you do not want to be the Historian. But if you reject the position, you will have changed nothing. Instead of the Elector of Primus, it will be the Senate of Secundus that chooses the next Historian. More to the point, the Senate will take your impersonation as an act of war by Primus. Olius has always been the grandest power in the system, and one of peace. If we cave now, another Great War will begin, and if both Primus and Secundus no longer bow to the will of Olius, this war may not end until Primus is extinguished or enslaved. In the meantime, the Scholarships will fall, and with them, the light of Olius will fade."

Then the moment of reprieve was gone, and her eyes pierced his soul once more.

"Primus and Secundus are counting on you, Historian."

***

The Scholar's rousing speech was not enough for Sev to believe he was actually the Historian, but it was enough for him to accept the role a second time. Doubts still plagued him, but she was right—this was bigger than him, and it was not just his own life on the line. But how was he meant to fulfill his mission with the political situation on Secundus?

After further discussion with the Scholar, he learned he had been placed in a secret, secure location, known only to a few of the top Scholars—another bit of information hidden from the terminal, no doubt. The good news was he was safe, but the bad news was he was stuck. According to the Scholar, if he left he would be spotted, and if he was spotted, he would be arrested, judged, and executed.

While the Scholarship had vowed to protect him, the Senate would take any overt resistance from its members as treason, thereby opening a path to their removal from the Senate. In other words, if any Scholar was discovered actively helping Sev, they would be treated as a criminal. And if enough Scholars were removed from the Senate, the path to Primus's takeover was as simple as framing Sev's impersonation of the Historian as an act of war.

Given the circumstances, the Scholar of the Premier Territory advised him to stay in the chamber, and while he agreed with her counsel, he didn't like it. Sitting in the windowless room, Sev felt restless and frustrated, and he wrestled for a way out, for some kind of solution to the problems he was responsible for. In the meantime, the Scholars gathered intelligence and reported to him, everyone working collectively to find a solution.

On the second rotation of his confinement, the Scholar visited him once more, and there was a brief moment of excitement as she entered the chamber. As soon as he read her expression, however, the excitement vanished. Something was wrong, very wrong.

"What is it, Scholar?"

She dipped her chin to her chest.

"Historian, it turns out you were right."

Sev felt a pit in his stomach, knowing the answer to his question before he even asked.

"What do you mean?"

"According to our sources, Zoph's escape from Primus was no accident —agents of Secundus performed a delicate mission of extraction in order to bring him here."

As terrible as this news was, he couldn't say he was surprised. This had been one of the key issues he had asked the Scholars to investigate: had Secundan agents helped Zoph escape? Now that his suspicions were confirmed, it made the situation much more complicated.

"Does the Palace know?" he asked.

The Scholar shrugged.

"As far as we know, no. But even if they don't know, they may make the assumption."

The pit in his stomach deepened. If the Elector thought agents of Secundus were responsible for the escape of a prisoner, he would consider it an act of war.

"Is there still no way to reach him?" Sev asked.

The Scholar shook her head.

"No, Historian. The Senators have him isolated, and he refuses to speak with the Scholars because of our position. But even if we could get ahold of him, he may deny this rumor. It is possible the agents of Secundus performed the rescue in a way that made him believe he had escaped on his own."

Sev nodded, his mind racing.

"So it's possible the Elector is preparing for war?"

She nodded.

"And if he declares it, or makes any sort of move against us, the Senate will view that as just cause to retaliate."

His eyes widened. What happened when Priman pride encountered Secundan technology?

"So as you can see, we do not have the luxury of time. The Elector may not blame Zoph's disappearance on Secundus, but that is not a risk we are willing to take. We must assume retaliatory action is imminent. If we sit idly much longer, your vision of peace will disappear forever."

Frankly, Sev was shocked the supreme leader hadn't made a move already. He remembered his rotations at the Palace, the way they had reacted to any threat or slight… what if there were already Priman ships on their way to Secundus? Surely Secundan technology would be able to track any incoming threats? After all, they probably tracked the trade ships.

Suddenly, Sev experienced a moment of clarity, one that pieced together a plan of action, something that might actually work. Finally, he knew what needed to be done.

***

After some time, his eyes adjusted to the dark and his nose adjusted to the smell, but Sev could not ward off the cold. He shivered in his robe, the involuntary trembling exacerbating his discomfort—this mattress of vegetables wasn't quite the same as a Secundan cot. Still, it shouldn't be much longer, he told himself. Soon, the top would be lifted and he would be set free. After that, the real work would begin.

It was three rotations after the hearing in the Senate, and Sev's plan was underway. The Scholarship had been hesitant to accept his proposal—the risk was enormous—but they soon realized it was necessary: if there was indeed a chance of Priman retaliation on the horizon, only the authority of the Historian could stop it.

The first steps had gone according to plan: two Scholars had guided Sev out of his secure hideout on a nightlong journey across Secundus. This was the most dangerous part of the operation, and they had taken many precautions to assure safe passage. Ship transport was out of the question, meaning they had to walk, but they also had to avoid all roads and paths, trekking through the wilderness instead.

Despite the hood masking his face, Sev stole glances as often as possible. He still couldn't get over the view—trees in every direction, seemingly infinite in number. He knew from his travels and his studies the entire planet was this green, this lush, this rich in life, and yet he still had trouble believing it. Of course, even if he hadn't expected Secundus's technological progress, Sev should have expected their abundant vegetation: how else could they harvest enough crop to feed two worlds?

Now he lay in a temperature-controlled crate full of these crops, waiting for the approach of the Priman trade ship. That was his grand idea: to return to Primus, where he was officially recognized as the Historian, and stop any attempt at war. This trip could also serve as an opening of communication between the worlds, or at least between the Scholarships, and even rekindle his ambitious project of peace.

At least, that's what the optimistic side of him thought. The other side wondered if there was already a battalion of Priman soldiers on the way, perhaps hidden on the very trade ship he was meant to board. Or if the same Secundan agents who had helped Zoph perform a similar maneuver were now expecting this escape plan, lying in wait at the port.

Even if neither of these scenarios were true, and assuming he managed to make it to Primus, how would the supreme leader react to Sev's attempt at authority? Could he tell the Elector Secundus helped Zoph escape and in the same breath ask him not to retaliate in any manner, and instead accept an offer of peace?

A thud reverberated through the crate, breaking his train of thought, and Sev felt himself lifting up off the ground. Finally, the crops were being loaded onto the ship. A machine carried him up the ramp and into the cargo hold, placing him beside the other crates. He listened as the other crops were loaded around him, then the machine rolled back down the ramp.

The sound of the cargo door closing made his heart rate spike, and Sev forgot all about the cold. This was it, he thought. Someone was walking through the hold right now, checking the crates. Any moment now, he would—

The top of the crate swung open and a Priman crew member stood over him. As a combination of confusion and shock came over the man's expression, Sev sat up and spoke with all the authority he could muster.

"Citizen of Primus, I am the Historian. I am in danger and need help and safe passage back to Primus."

The man took a few steps back, glancing at the door to the living quarters.

"The Historian…?"

Sev noted the terror in his eyes and found solace in the reaction—this was no agent of Secundus.

"Citizen of Primus, you must trust me. I am the Historian. I am here because I am in danger and need to speak with the Elector."

Sev was wearing the robes of the Scholarship of Secundus, and though the man before him would not recognize them, he would certainly understand the white and gold. But they were not the robes the Historian had worn on his Arrival on Primus, and perhaps worst of all, they included the blue of Secundus.

"The Historian…?" the man repeated, still eyeing the door.

Sev dared not make a sudden move, but he knew he had to act fast. If the cargo door was reopened, he would be standing in the Senate before the end of the rotation.

"Yes, the Historian. I was a Scholar in the Scholarship of Primus, and a Pupil before that. I have sat at the stone table in the Room of Council and was in the audience chamber of the Grand Palace when the previous Historian was killed for his treason. The forces of Secundus have learned this history and are plotting against me."

There was a hint of recognition in his eyes, but suspicion still marred his expression.

"What… what was your name, your name before the Ascension?"

Sev hesitated, surprised by the question.

"Sev of Primus, I was known as Sev of Primus."

At these words, the suspicion disappeared.

"Sev of Primus… the Historian…"

The man dropped to knee and hand in such a hurry Sev was afraid he might hurt himself.

"Forgive me, Historian. I did not mean to doubt you."

Sev sat up straighter, his conviction restored.

"Rise, citizen of Primus—you are forgiven. Will you help me?"

The man stood and nodded.

"Of course, Historian."

Asylum

Their flight lasted three Priman rotations, and Sev found the living quarters of the ship only marginally better than the crate. The space was cramped, having been designed for a specific number of people, and privacy was unheard of. Despite the conditions, he did his best to hide his discomfort—the crew were desperate to please the being of Olius and tended to him with alarming resolve: strict rations were shared without complaint, and they insisted he sleep on a makeshift cot, forcing the rest of them to wedge their bodies into whatever corner possible.

During the waking hours, there was little for the crew to do—the ship piloted itself, guided by the technology of Olius—and Sev could tell they didn't know whether to keep him company or give him space. He tried his best to be friendly and kind, engaging the men in conversation without touching on forbidden topics. In the end, while their reverence brought him some measure of guilt, it also brought relief—if the rest of Primus felt this way, it would make his job much easier.

Time was of the essence, so as soon as they landed, Sev was by the cargo door, watching it open. The heat washed over him—a stifling, heavy welcome—and the light of Olius reflected off the orange lands below. What a contrast, he thought. It all seemed so… dead.

The trade port was connected to the Palace grounds, and he saw the black fortress ahead. As he came down the ramp, the workers outside gaped in bewilderment, catching the attention of the nearest soldiers.

"What is the meaning of this?"

The two men pressed their way through the crowd, hands on the hilts of their hotswords. When they reached Sev they paused, eyeing the strange man of white and gold.

"Soldiers of Primus, I am the Historian."

He wondered how he might convince these two, but a flash of recognition was followed by a drop to knee and hand.

"Historian. Our apologies."

Seeing the soldier's humility, all of the workers dropped to knee and hand, and Sev felt a familiar discomfort—he was not worthy of such respect.

"Please, rise, all of you, rise."

The workers got to their feet and Sev directed his attention to the soldiers.

"I must see the Elector immediately."

They nodded.

"Certainly, Historian. We will take you to him at once."

The two men cleared a path, leaving open mouths and stares of disbelief in their wake. On Secundus, the citizens had shown him muted admiration, but here on Primus, people looked at him as if he were a god.

He realized he considered the Secundans more dignified, more intelligent even, and the thought brought him great shame. How could he feel that way? These were his people, his world. And if their ways were indeed primitive, whose fault was that?

Sev had contemplated the disparity between the worlds many times on Secundus: how it could have stayed hidden so long, whether the Council or the Elector knew… all important and interesting questions, but what of the future? If this peace were ever forged, how would the technology be introduced in a fair and just manner—a manner which allowed Primus to rise to equal Secundus, rather than remain beneath its benevolent will?

These were pressing questions worth his time, but when he reached the looming black walls of the Palace, Sev shelved these thoughts, focusing on the task at hand. One step at a time, he told himself.

Their entourage walked into the Palace, and Sev took a deep breath of the cool air. This, he thought, was the closest thing to Secundus on the entire planet.

A servant approached them, and Sev saw the same look of confusion on his face.

"What is the meaning of—"

But his sentence was interrupted by one of the soldiers.

"Servant, show some respect! This is the Historian!"

The servant dropped to knee and hand, tripping over himself in shame.

"Historian. Welcome to the Grand Palace. My apologies, I did not—"

Sev glared at the soldier, then cut the servant short.

"Rise, you are forgiven. I must see the Elector immediately."

The servant jumped up and nodded.

"Of course. This way, Historian."

As he followed the servant through the halls of the Palace, Sev saw his surroundings with new eyes—eyes that had seen the wonder of Secundus, and eyes that were no longer impressed. When he looked closely, the purple and black on the walls was fading. But before this defamation of Primus could develop any further, his attention shifted to the path they were taking—this was not the way to the audience chamber.

"Historian, these are the Elector's private quarters."

The door before them was black as night, a dark and imposing portal. On either side stood the Elector's personal guardians, hotswords at their hips. Seeing them brought terrible memories, and doubt crept into his mind. What was he doing here? He had no right to visit the Elector in his private quarters…

But just as he was fighting these invasive thoughts, the guardians dropped to knee and hand, and the tone of the situation changed completely. With this simple gesture, much of his confidence was restored.

"Rise, guardians. I am here to see the Elector."

They stood and knocked on the door, and Sev had but a moment to prepare himself before it opened.

The harsh lines in the Elector's expression painted a fluid picture of his thoughts. Frustration became confusion, which in turn became concern. But Sev barely saw the man's face, barely registered his presence. Right now he was focused on the length of this silence, on the delicate affair unfolding before him. What happened next could mean the difference between success and failure, and the fate of Primus hung in the balance.

Finally, the Elector brought his right knee and right hand to the ground, and Sev let out a sigh of relief.

"Historian, I…"

"Rise, Elector."

He could not believe the words that came out of his mouth, but he said them all the same. This was not about him—this was about the entire system.

"May I speak with you in private?"

The Elector looked him up and down then stepped back from his doorway.

"Of course, Historian."

He walked into a chamber that would have impressed him in the past: the size, the decor, the amenities… but nothing could compare to what he had already seen, to what he had already experienced.

The Elector gestured to a small table, and the two of them sat down on either side.

"Sev of Primus, I have to say your visit is a surprise…"

There was a hint of suspicion in his voice, but Sev was more concerned with the title. He appreciated the Elector's public display of respect, but now that they were in private, he realized it was just that—a display.

"I understand, Elector. I know you have many questions, and I will answer them all now. I only ask that you are patient, as there is quite a bit to share, and that you are understanding, as a good deal of it may be difficult to hear."

The Elector nodded, but Sev could see the suspicion deepening.

"Go ahead."

He took a deep breath, gathering his thoughts. He had spent much of the trip over imagining this encounter, plotting the various ways their conversation might go, but all of those imaginary meetings took place in the audience chamber. He wasn't sure if being in the supreme leader's private quarters was better or worse, given his mission.

"Thank you, Elector. First, I must ask, are you aware of how High Scholar Zoph escaped?"

A shadow came over his expression, and Sev was surprised by how little it affected him.

"How do you know of his escape?"

He hesitated.

"Because he boarded a trade ship and landed on Secundus."

The Elector's surprise made it clear—the supreme leader had no idea Zoph was on Secundus.

"That's impossible…"

Sev nodded.

"Normally, yes. But he had help."

The supreme leader leaned forward, the suspicion returning.

"Help?"

Sev nodded again, hesitating. He knew what his next words might cause, and he needed to be careful.

"Agents of Secundus secured his escape."

The Elector's face hardened, his frown morphing into a scowl.

"They brought him to Secundus to discredit me, to explain what happened here in the Palace and to reject my claim as Historian."

The Elector eyed him curiously, some of the scowl disappearing.

"And you were forced to flee?"

Sev shook his head.

"Not entirely. The Scholarship of Secundus stands behind me, as do most of the people. As you said, the populace is a powerful ally. But where Primus has its Palace, Secundus has the Senate, and a good deal of them are doing everything in their power to bring me down."

The supreme leader looked away, processing his words.

"You're saying this Senate helped Zoph escape to discredit you?"

"Yes, at least part of it. And while I have no proof, I believe they knew what had happened here on Primus, but they needed Zoph's proclamation to give the accusations credibility."

The Elector nodded slowly.

"I see... yet despite this, you managed to get the support of the people?"

"Yes, before Zoph's arrival. I'm sure their attempt to discredit me has had some success, but I believe I still have the support of the people."

The supreme leader eyed him curiously once more.

"If you have the support of the people, why are you here?"

"First, to dissuade you from any retaliatory action. I know they committed an act of war, but we cannot attack them."

As expected, the Elector's expression hardened once more.

"Why not?"

Again, Sev hesitated. This was another key moment, one where he needed to tread carefully.

"If we are forced into a war with Secundus, we will lose. Theirs is not a planet of poverty and filth, it is a planet of wealth and riches. Their technology is unlike anything I have ever seen. The little I've learned about their military tells me we are woefully outmatched."

As he spoke the words aloud, Sev tried to read the Elector's face, to discern if he already knew the truth. But where he expected to see surprise, he saw growing disapproval.

"So you've come to make sure I don't make any rash decisions?"

The hint of anger in his voice didn't go unnoticed, but Sev kept his calm.

"Elector, my mission to Olius is compromised, as is the future of Primus. There are individuals working to discredit me in any way possible, and those same individuals are hoping you will react. Anything to give them the war they want, a war they know they can win. But I am here to deny them that. I am here to make sure Primus emerges the victor."

These words caught the Elector's attention, and the frown softened.

"Go on, Sev of Primus. What do you propose?"

He sighed in relief. This was the opportunity he had hoped for.

"I propose we spearhead a peace agreement between the worlds. Let Primus be the one to lead this charge, let us be the ones responsible for the will of Olius."

He tried to frame his scheme in a way that might be attractive to the supreme leader—one that might erase his frown entirely—but his words had no discernible effect.

"And how do you suggest we bring about this peace agreement? Do you propose a meeting between the leaders of both worlds, as there was at the end of the Great War?"

Sev nodded.

"Yes, Elector. You and whatever delegation you see fit, along with the Council of the Scholarship of Primus, will join me and travel to Secundus."

Traces of anger appeared in the supreme leader's expression, but Sev continued.

"There, we will meet with the leaders of Secundus and come to a binding agreement, one that will bring peace and prosperity to both worlds. If we travel together under a directive of peace—the directive of Olius—this warmongering faction will have no choice but to accept."

Sev saw the frown return and prepared himself.

"This is what you propose?" the Elector asked.

He nodded.

"It is not only what I propose, Elector, it is the will of Olius. A will you must obey."

The supreme leader stood from his chair, incensed.

"Watch your words, Sev of Primus!"

Sev met his glare with surprising indifference, and found himself responding with a calm he didn't know he was capable of.

"Elector, as of now, I am the key to the survival of Primus. As long as the Secundan Scholarship is on my side, the Senate will not attack you. But if we allow the Senate to have their war, it won't be you who chooses the next Historian."

He saw a flash of rage in the man's eyes and knew he had pressed too far.

"You are out of line, Sev of Primus. Guards!"

Sev heard the door open and felt the heat of a hotsword at his neck. The same men who had just dropped to knee and hand were now prepared to execute him. Given their history, this should come as no surprise—it could almost be expected.

"Do not forget who put you in those robes, Sev of Primus. Outside this chamber, you are the Historian and I am the Elector, but only one of us controls the other. I removed your predecessor, and if it seems in the best interest of Primus, I will not hesitate to remove you. Is that understood?"

The man's glare emphasized the truth of his words, and Sev knew if he answered incorrectly it would be the last answer he ever gave.

"Yes, Elector."

His response was correct, but the tone was still calm, relaxed. This was clearly not what the Elector had expected, and for once, Sev saw something behind the hard lines of the man's face: he was processing this reply, trying to decide if it was insubordination. This momentary hesitation humanized him, and Sev realized why he had never displayed such uncertainty before—there was no room for doubt in the Palace, only action. The Elector wouldn't be where he was with patient analysis. So why was he thoughtful now?

Finally, he nodded, gesturing to the guardians.

"Leave us."

The heat dissipated with their departure, and the Elector took his seat.

"Now explain to me your plan, and do so swiftly."

***

Their meeting concluded more or less on the same note, and while the Elector hadn't given an official opinion on his plan, Sev was asked—or told, depending on the perspective—to stay in the Grand Palace until further notice. The supreme leader said nothing regarding the reason for this pseudo-imprisonment, nor if anyone else would be notified of his arrival. Still, hundreds of peasants and workers had seen him—he couldn't imagine word not reaching the halls of the Scholarship. If it did, how would the Elector explain his confinement?

For a brief moment, Sev contemplated an immediate and dramatic escape. His plan was contingent on the faith of the Priman people, a faith based on the Historian's supremacy, one already in question. If the general populace found out he had returned and was being held captive, support would weaken, and his mission would fail.

What if he made his way into the country, as he had on Secundus, and secured the backing of the villages? Then, with their aid, he would return to the Scholarship and make the Palace bend to the will of Olius.

As quick as the thought came to him, so too did its absurdity. This was not Secundus. These people were not independent and critical thinkers, and even if they were, they knew who controlled the food supplies and just how ruthless the man in charge could be. Any attempt to organize a coup would meet resistance, regardless of its leader. And since the execution and the sacking of the Scholarship? Forget it.

Besides, Sev had not preached rebellion on Secundus, just peace. If he tried the same thing here, some of the Scholarship might agree outwardly, but he knew what the majority of Primus thought of their neighbor. He could not do on Primus what he did on Secundus—he had to find another way.

So Sev paced the length of the room he had been placed in—the same one in which he had waited for the locked data tome so many rotations ago—contemplating his next steps. Had he made a mistake coming to Primus? What if the Elector was preparing a warship to retaliate for the escape of the High Scholar?

A knock at the door broke his train of thought, and Sev looked up.

"Yes?"

A servant came inside, dropping to knee and hand.

"Historian."

"Rise, citizen. What is it?"

The man did as asked.

"Historian, the Elector humbly requests your presence in the audience chamber."

Sev had to surpress a scoff.

"Of course."

As the servant led him down the Palace halls, Sev tried to calm his beating heart. The meeting with the supreme leader didn't scare him, but he had hoped he wouldn't have to step foot in that room—not again. Unfortunately, the Elector was cunning, and having them meet in the audience chamber was a great way to remind him who held the actual power. But when the servant led him inside, Sev realized he had underestimated the supreme leader, and a pit formed in his stomach at the scene before him.

At the base of the Elector's platform stood a soldier, hotsword drawn, towering over a kneeling figure. It was a sickeningly accurate reproduction of that nightmare of a memory, right down to the attire: the man on his knees wore the robes of a Priman High Scholar. And even though there was only one member of the Council in the room rather than thirteen, it was the identity of the kneeling figure that made this all the worse: the Elder Scholar, his best friend—Folin.

Sev hesitated, looking from the Elector to the soldier to Folin. For the second time, he saw the leader of the Council at the mercy of the Palace, and it was a horrid sight. The memory flashed on the edge of his conscience but he fought against it, trying to focus on the present.

Was this the end of his mission, he wondered, or even the end of his life? He wanted to shoot a glance behind him, to make sure he wasn't about to join his friend, but he suppressed the urge and continued forward. If the Elector had wanted him on his knees, he already would be. So what was this about?

As he approached, the Elector stood from his seat and made his way down the stairs, stopping at the base of the platform next to Folin. Sev watched him intently, confusion temporarily replacing fear, until he was within a few paces of them both. After a pause, the supreme leader dropped to knee and hand.

"Historian."

He stared at the lowered figure, baffled. What was going on?

"Rise, Elector."

The supreme leader stood, and Sev shot another glance to the men at his side. The soldier eyed him warily, while Folin seemed calm, unperturbed. Nothing about this scene made sense, and even after the Elector's display of respect, suspicion outweighed acceptance.

"Historian, I apologize for the scene before you, but it was necessary given the circumstances."

He returned his attention to the supreme leader, surprised again by his behavior and tone. Apologizing before this audience? Was this some kind of trick?

Then, as if a switch had flipped in his mind, he realized he needed to take advantage of this opening. It might be a trap, but if there was even a chance the Elector was allowing him to act the part of Historian, he needed to act it—his mission depended on it.

"What is the meaning of this?" he asked, gesturing to Folin. "Why is this man being threatened?"

The Elector gave him a curious look, then answered calmly.

"Historian, I suggest you listen to what he has to say."

Sev stared at the supreme leader then turned to Folin.

"Elder Scholar, what is the meaning of this?"

The two shared a glance, and once again Sev saw his friend's calm, his patience. Despite the hotsword hovering behind him, he showed no fear.

"Historian, I too must apologize."

At these words, Sev noticed something more, something hidden: Folin was ashamed.

"I have come to the Palace to reveal a plot against you, Historian."

Sev hesitated, trying to understand the source of his friend's guilt.

"A plot against me?"

"Yes, Historian. Agents of Secundus have been directed to ensure your assassination here on Primus."

He stared at him, dumbfounded.

"Agents of Secundus?"

Folin nodded.

"Yes, Historian."

Now the shame emerged in his tone, and Sev struggled even more to understand.

"Tell him how you know," the Elector interrupted.

Sev glanced at the supreme leader, confused, then turned back to Folin.

"How do you know?" he asked, the pit in his stomach returning.

"Historian, I know because I myself am an agent of Secundus."

A silence followed, and Folin looked away, unable to contain his shame. For his part, Sev was dumbfounded, trying to process what he had just heard.

Folin, an agent of Secundus? Yet another of his brethren ensnared in this affair, and this time, it was his closest friend. Sev wondered how the Secundans had seduced him, what they had promised... but he didn't need to think far. He had just seen their people, their planet. Perhaps it wasn't seduction, perhaps it was simple logic...

He remembered where he was and glanced at the Elector. These were treasonous thoughts he was having, and they were becoming more and more common. What had happened? When had he allowed himself to become a traitor?

"Historian, I came to the Palace immediately and voluntarily, revealing my identity to protect you from this plot."

Sev looked back at Folin, but he didn't know how to reply.

"Historian, this is true," the Elector added. "This man came to us and explained both his work for Secundus and the nature of the plot against you."

He nodded, but his eyes never left Folin.

"Whose plot is this? Who directed you?" he asked.

Folin sighed in defeat.

"Certain members of the Senate, Historian."

Sev digested this information with growing disgust. They were after him here as well?

"And you yourself were given this mission?"

Folin nodded.

"Yes, along with my associates."

"Associates?"

"The other Secundan agents on Primus," he replied.

Sev stared at him, struggling to comprehend all this information.

"How many other agents are there?"

Folin frowned.

"Historian, I prefer not to say."

Sev frowned in turn, shooting a glance at the Elector. Had they already had this discussion?

"And these other agents, do they agree with you or do they intend to fulfill this mission?"

Folin hesitated.

"Historian, I cannot be certain. If I knew for a fact any of them were a threat to you, I would have already revealed their identities to the Palace. The problem is we are divided. I am here because I agree with the Scholarship—the Scholarship of Secundus—and I know many of my peers do as well. But I don't know who, and it would be irresponsible of me to put innocent lives in danger."

"No spy is innocent," the Elector opined, but Sev ignored him.

"If you will not expose your brethren, how can you assure my safety? Do you know the details of their plot?"

He frowned again.

"No, Historian. There were no specific instructions, only two directives: that you be eliminated, and that the elimination be made to look like the Elector's doing."

Sev's eyes widened.

"The Elector's doing?"

"Yes, Historian. This would give the Senate grounds for a declaration of war."

Of course, Sev thought. The Historian's death at the hands of the Elector might sway even the Scholarship's opinion.

"Do you know which members of the Senate are responsible for this plot?"

Folin shook his head.

"No, Historian."

Sev frowned. This was the key: who were these people? How much of the Senate did they actually control? It couldn't be a strict number of people—certainly some were more involved than others, and while many might desire war with Primus he couldn't imagine most sought the Historian's demise. How would he find out which was which?

"Your orders came from someone, did they not?" the Elector asked.

"Yes," Folin replied, "but not directly from a Senator."

"From one of your compatriots here then?"

He didn't answer, and the Elector turned to Sev.

"Someone must know, Historian. If we follow the information to its source, we will find the group responsible for this plot. This is the same group that threatens your mission of peace, is it not?"

Sev nodded slowly, staring at his friend. The man he had known so long and thought he had known so well...

He turned to the Elector.

"What is to become of this man?"

The supreme leader's expression hardened.

"Historian, his fate is in your hands, but he has committed treason against Primus and is therefore worthy of execution."

Sev met the Elector's stare, noting the subtlety in his tone. He was meant to accept the supreme leader's judgement, but he couldn't, not after what he had heard.

"Elector, may we speak in private?"

The Elector hesitated then gestured to his guardians.

"Of course, Historian. We will convene in my chambers, if that suits you?"

"Yes," Sev answered.

The Elector turned to the soldier behind Folin.

"Put this man in a cell."

"Yes, Elector."

The soldier sheathed his hotsword and gave Folin a kick in the back.

"Up!"

"Soldier!"

The soldier turned with eyes wide, shocked by the anger and authority in Sev's voice.

"This man has acted on behalf of Olius. He is a prisoner, but you are to treat him with the respect worthy of someone who has just saved the Historian. Is that understood?"

The soldier dropped to knee and hand.

"Yes, Historian. My apologies, Historian."

"As you were."

Sev turned and started walking toward the door, avoiding the eyes of the Elector at all costs.

***

The silence between Sev and the Elector carried through the halls, with only the sound of footsteps bouncing off the decorated walls—and not just their own. As the light of Olius faded, servants ran about lighting candles, and Sev watched their frantic movements with a frown.

They went through this routine every night, lighting every hallway, then in the morning, the same servants would go around extinguishing the flames. Every once in a while, a candle would run out, and a new one would replace it. This went on rotation after rotation, in a seemingly endless pattern.

Not on Secundus. There, light emerged from seemingly nowhere—small objects on the floor, the walls, and the ceiling shone like miniature stars all through the Scholarship. It had been a fascinating sight for the first few nights, then he had gotten used to it. So used to it, in fact, that it had taken him a full rotation in the trade ship before he realized it also contained this technology.

So when they reached the Elector's chambers and took their seats, Sev found himself distracted by the dancing shadows cast all around him. If the trade ships had this technology, and if the Palace was investigating it, why didn't the Elector's private chambers have such light?

"Sev of Primus, you are testing my patience."

The supreme leader's harsh tone snapped him out of his train of thought.

"Elector, that man may lead us to the cause of our problems, but he defects because he believes in my mission. If he does not see the influence of Olius here on Primus, we may lose his trust."

This sidestepped his true intention—to protect Folin as a friend and as the Elder Scholar of Primus—but it seemed a more convincing argument.

"You would suggest leniency for treason?"

Sev knew the Elector understood his reasoning, but even a slight subversion of authority put rational thought on hold.

"Elector, I would suggest we do everything in our power to find this group of Secundan citizens who plot against Primus."

The supreme leader eyed him with disdain.

"And if he leads us astray? If this is another part of the plot?"

Now the Elector was reaching, yet Sev had no choice but to entertain his notions.

"If there is any indication of treachery, his life is in your hands. But if we want his help, we need to tread softly."

The Elector leaned back in his chair, contemplating Sev's proposal. Finally, he gave a slow nod of approval.

"Very well. We will be lenient with the spy so long as he leads us in the right direction."

Sev felt a measure of relief, but the supreme leader wasn't done.

"Once we know the individuals responsible for this plot, we will eliminate them."

The Elector leaned forward, eyeing him with a hint of curiosity.

"After all, we must fight for the will of Olius, for peace between our worlds. Is that not true?"

Sev hesitated, choosing his next words carefully.

"Elector, we must fight for the will of Olius, but I'm not certain this will includes such drastic measures…"

The Elector shook his head.

"Sev of Primus, here you are clearly wrong. Was it not the will of Olius that this Palace be routed? Does that not qualify as a drastic measure?"

Sev frowned. Of course it qualified as a drastic measure, but look what happened when they tried.

"We will fulfill your mission of peace, Sev of Primus, and I will indeed accompany you to Secundus. But this cannot be accomplished without the removal of our enemies from the Secundan government—and from the Priman Scholarship, if need be. Once they are gone, peace will come easy."

The Elector stood from his chair, and Sev was forced to mirror him.

"Following this meeting, your old bodyguard will accompany you at all times as a precaution. This is at the suggestion of the prisoner, and here I am forced to admit he is right."

The supreme leader paused as if expecting a rebuke, but Sev said nothing. While he didn't necessarily like the idea of having a Priman general at his side, if what Folin said was true, it made sense.

"Now you will go back to the Scholarship and announce your mission. Tell them of your time on Secundus, of everything you learned and your attempts at peace. But make no mention of the plot against you—we have to stay one step ahead of our enemies, and there may be more traitors on the Council."

Sev frowned a second time. Did the Elector really think there were more Secundan agents among the High Scholars?

"How am I to explain my arrival? I am here because of this plot."

The Elector hesitated.

"You can explain anything known to the Secundan public—the rift between the Scholarship and the Senate, even the escaped prisoner and his role in your retreat. But not how he managed to escape."

Sev nodded, still frowning.

"And the Elder Scholar? How am I to explain his absence?"

This time, the Elector didn't hesitate.

"Tell them you sent him here to work with me, as a show of unity between the Scholarship and the Palace. But at no point will you mention the assassination plot, his status as a Secundan agent, or anything giving away our knowledge of such. Is that understood?"

He met the Elector's eye and saw a hint of curiosity underneath the harsh expression, as if he thought Sev might actually deny him. But Sev knew better than to risk the peace of the system on an ultimately insignificant power play.

"Yes, Elector."

Or, he thought to himself, what seemed insignificant. Only time would tell.

***

Sev walked to the Scholarship under the darkness of night, with only the general in his company. According to the Palace, no one at the Scholarship had been officially notified of his return, and he was happy this was the case—the more his appearance adhered to his own terms, the better.

Besides, the bigger question now was not how they would handle his appearance, but how they were handling Folin's absence. Had he left the evening council with an excuse, or had he simply disappeared? He wasn't sure how well the Council would accept the Elector's lie, but even that was easier to believe than the truth.

His friend's confession replayed in his mind, and try as he might, Sev could not wrap his head around it. Folin, an agent of Secundus? How was it always the people closest to him, and how could he be so blind, again? At this point, he wondered if there was a member of the Council who wasn't collaborating with the enemy...

But was enemy the right word? He struggled to place his feelings, his judgement on everything he had seen, everything he had learned. Secundus was not what he had expected—far from it. And while there was a small group intent on striking him down, the majority of the population was more in line with the word of Olius than Primus had ever been...

The stone walls appeared on the horizon, lit by a handful of torches along the perimeter, and Sev found himself wishing he had come here first. The Scholarship would follow his guidance, they would offer support without the number of conditions imposed by the Palace. But the reality was their help was worthless. Whether he liked it or not, the Scholarship of Primus was nothing like its cousin on Secundus—its power was more ceremonial than useful.

It could be worse, he realized. At least the Scholarship was still functioning, and apparently with some degree of autonomy. What if he had returned to a gutted institution? What if the Elector had reneged on his promises?

He found himself wondering if this peace could be the beginning of something different, the start of a new chapter in the history of Primus, one which could change the world's power structure. Yes, Secundus was a wholly different planet, but the balance seemed to work there—at least enough to keep him alive. Could a rotation ever dawn where the power of the Palace was checked by the will of the Scholarship?

"It can't be!"

Sev turned to see a Scholar on a nearby dune, scrambling to his feet then dropping to knee and hand.

"Historian."

"Rise, Scholar."

The man stood up, eyes wide with wonder.

"The rumors are true, Historian?"

Sev peered at him in the darkness.

"What rumors, Scholar?"

"You have returned!"

He smiled, the man's excitement clearing up his mood.

"I am indeed here. Could you help me with something?"

The man stared at him in disbelief.

"Help you? Ye—yes, Historian. It would be my honor."

He stumbled down the dune to the path, wiping the sand off his robes.

"What do you need, Historian?"

"Could you assemble the Council for me, Scholar?"

He nodded enthusiastically.

"Of course, Historian. I will do so at once!"

Just as he was about to take off, Sev put up his hand.

"Yes, Historian?"

"Everyone except the Elder Scholar."

The man hesitated, then nodded again.

"As you wish, Historian."

And with that, he turned and ran inside.

***

Eleven familiar faces sat in eleven familiar chairs, while two were empty. Concerned glances at one answered Sev's question—they didn't know about Folin—but this concern was overshadowed by the other, or rather its rightful occupant, who preferred to stand on the floor than sit in a chair of which he felt unworthy.

"Council of Primus," he began, noting the mix of surprise and confusion before him, "I have returned to Primus under difficult circumstances, but I believe these circumstances can yet turn in favor of Olius."

One of the High Scholars was a new appointment, made after his Departure when a spot had opened up. But even if he was new to the table, Sev knew him well, and he was impressed by the judgement of those around him—despite the tragic conditions that had brought this particular set of individuals to this place, he had trust and faith in their stewardship.

"Council, I will not mince words, but I warn you there is a lot to digest, and most of it will be difficult."

He hesitated, wondering what kind of theories were running through their minds.

"First, our image of Secundus is decidedly inaccurate. The planet is abundant not just in natural resources, but in wealth and technology. Their lives are far more advanced than our own, and I am ashamed of the ignorance we have held up to this point."

These words caused the intended stir, and though a few individuals prepared to comment, he raised his hand to stop them.

"I understand this will come as a surprise or even an outright lie, but I assure you this is the case, and it is far worse than whatever you may imagine."

"How can that be?"

He turned to the one man unable to contain himself.

"High Scholar, think on your question. The Palace has long withheld knowledge of Secundus, but based on my experience, even they aren't aware of the extent of the gap—perhaps the Elector himself knows, but even that is unlikely. Our trade ships run blind on purpose, and this blindness has lasted for almost a hundred revolutions. In that time, Secundus has advanced at an unprecedented pace, and Primus has all but stagnated."

Sev could tell the High Scholar didn't fully believe him, but he was not here to to convince them of the truth—he was only here to explain it.

"Once I understood the depth of inequality between our worlds, I realized it was time to promote the reopening of Primus's borders and the start of a new, proactive peace—a peace that could heal this Scholarship's wounds, but also a peace that would bring prosperity to Primus, as is the will of Olius."

Some of the High Scholars were nodding along, their focus devoted to his words. Others shot skeptical glances at one another, but he ignored them. Again, he was only the messenger.

"Unfortunately, not all of Secundus agreed with my mission. While the Scholarship gave its full support, the most powerful governing body—the Senate—disagreed and sought to suppress my voice, to remove my influence."

"Were you banished?"

The same man raised this second question, and one of his colleagues shot him a glare.

"High Scholar, remember who you address."

The man bowed his head in shame.

"Historian, my apologies."

But Sev smiled at him.

"Teero, no apology is necessary."

It was true, the man had omitted his title, but if the Elector himself was dropping to knee and hand—at least in public—Sev had no reason to worry about these ceremonial details.

"In a way, you are right. I was not banished, but I was made to flee. You see, as the Senate and the Scholarship debated, something unforeseen happened: High Scholar Zoph arrived on Secundus, having escaped the Palace prison."

This revelation caused another stir, and the High Scholars muttered words of disbelief.

"Upon his arrival, the High Scholar denounced me in the Senate, and the Scholarship had to take me into hiding. There, I came up with a plan, a plan that could bring peace and prosperity according to Olius, and which required my return to Primus."

The news regarding Zoph had reset their attention, and he had the unbroken focus of all eleven.

"I arrived earlier this rotation and went directly to the Elector to secure his support, and he has agreed to join me on a mission of peace to Secundus. I now ask all of you to accompany us as a united delegation of Primus to sign an agreement with our neighboring world—an agreement of peace and prosperity under the light and command of Olius."

A few of them shared excited glances, but most still eyed the empty chair, waiting for an absent leader to guide them.

"Historian…"

The High Scholar spoke with apprehension, and Sev knew what he would ask before the words came out of his mouth.

"…my apologies for the digression, but where is the Elder Scholar?"

Sev cursed himself for trying to avoid the subject. Of course they were going to ask about Folin, did he think they would simply ignore it?

"The Elder Scholar…" he began, then hesitated.

Several thoughts hit him at once: the general outside the door, his promise to the Elector… but also the title he currently held and the mission he was trying to accomplish.

Finally, he cleared his throat.

"I've asked the Elder Scholar to work with the Palace on this mission. He is there now, as the Elector's guest."

With a glance toward the door, he stepped forward, just in front of the table. When he spoke again, it was quieter, almost a whisper.

"Council, what I say next must remain between us, is that understood?"

The men at the table leaned forward and nodded, eyes wide with intrigue.

"What I have just said is a lie. The Elder Scholar is not working with the Palace."

They stared at him, absorbed by the sudden reveal.

"Per his own admission, Folin has acted as an agent of Secundus."

He watched their shocked reactions, gesturing to the door as a reminder to stay quiet.

"I understand this may seem more unbelievable than anything else I've told you, but there is more. Folin worked as an agent of the Senate, who informed him of my arrival and ordered him to interfere with my mission. He defied these orders and went to the Palace of his own accord, admitting his treason to Primus in order to alert them of the plot against me."

Sev shot another glance behind him, wondering if the general had noted the change in volume. Would the man report it to the Elector? Was this a terrible mistake?

"Folin risked his life for this mission, for peace between our worlds. The Elector has imprisoned him, but I have made sure he will not come to harm. If all goes to plan, he may yet be set free."

He took a step back and gave them a knowing look. When he spoke again, it was at full volume.

"So I ask a second time, will you join me on this mission of peace?"

Most of the men were still reeling from his revelation, but at least one understood what was necessary.

"Historian, it would be an honor to accompany you on this historical mission."

Sev smiled at him, then scanned the rest of the faces.

"High Scholars, if anyone objects, please speak your piece. I cannot and will not force you to join me."

There were a few more shared glances, but no one objected. Despite a series of astonishing disclosures, Sev had his delegation.

***

The Council retired soon after, and for the first time since his predecessor's passing, Sev found himself in the Historian's chambers. It was a sad contrast to the amenities on Secundus, and even now, almost a full rotation into his arrival and in the dead of night, he had yet to acclimate to the heat.

He tried to take advantage of the moment of respite, either to sleep or at least to process the situation, but his mind refused to cooperate, juggling an endless list of burning questions.

The Council had accepted his words with minimal hesitation—the call to action, the technological superiority of Secundus, even the treason of their Elder Scholar. From an outside perspective, it was everything he had hoped for—the people of Primus believed in his role, his position—but Sev knew this was a superficial assessment.

The High Scholars were clearly troubled, no doubt filled with burning questions of their own. Should he have told them the truth about Folin? Part of him worried about what might happen if the Elector found out—or worse, if he was right and there was another Secundan agent among them—but his main worry was the way they had reacted.

Should they trust him blindly, even with such outlandish claims? Yes, the Historian's words were truth, especially in the Scholarship, but there was something troubling about their acceptance of his testimony. Given the circumstances, they couldn't really question him on Folin's situation, but what about his public condemnation by Zoph? Shouldn't they ask why the former High Scholar denounced the current Historian?

Worse yet was what this could mean for the future. Was this the destiny of the Priman Scholarship, quiet obedience? For the being of Olius, this might make sense, but what about for others with power? The Palace already walked all over the Scholars, the last thing they needed was to tip the scales further.

He frowned, staring at the empty table with its three empty chairs. This was where it started, he thought, this descent into darkness. All it took was one meeting and a very specific data tome—that was enough to indict the Historian and turn the world upside down.

But that wasn't true, he realized—it had started much earlier than that. The Elector knew about the communication network well before their fateful meeting—he explained as much during the Judgement. Was the data tome simply a trap, a way to prove the Historian's treason?

Sev realized just how dangerous this train of thought was and tried to convince himself otherwise. The Elector hadn't used the book as a trap, but as a test—he was trying to prove the Historian's innocence, not his guilt, but things took an unexpected turn.

Then another question dawned on him, and a pit formed in his stomach. How long had the Elector known about the network? Had he known before High Scholar Dren's passing? Could he be involved in the late High Scholar's death?

Try as he might, Sev could not repress these treasonous thoughts, and they plagued his mind all night. Once again he wondered if the quest for truth was worth it, if the path of Olius wasn't simply a path of death. To think he had left the Palace just before a promotion only to have the Elector promote him all the same—a cruel twist of fate.

A knock at the door interrupted his thoughts, and he jumped to answer —perhaps this was a High Scholar coming to seek clarification.

"Historian."

The pit in his stomach returned—it was a Palace envoy.

"The Elector requests your presence after your first council on this rotation."

Sev looked him up and down with a frown.

"Very well. Let him know I will be there."

He closed the door and felt the fatigue of the night hit him all at once. This would not be an easy rotation.

***

The morning council was a fruitful if not frenzied affair, and Sev had to commend the High Scholars's restraint: it was clear they wanted to ask about their imprisoned leader, but discussions remained formal and on topic. While Sev would have gladly answered their questions, he knew another bout of whispering might make the general suspicious—it just wasn't worth the risk.

In the meantime, he took the opportunity to address one of his primary concerns: he asked the High Scholars if the relationship with the Palace had improved since his Departure, or if a more productive partnership was possible. The replies he received were vague, but their hesitant glances provided a more honest answer. He wanted to ask for clarification, to see if the Palace was overstepping its boundaries, but again, now was not the time—not with his bodyguard outside the door.

They had scheduled a speech before the mid-rotation meal, and Sev requested a tour of the grounds just prior. He used the opportunity to inspect the campus as thoroughly as possible, and once in the Hall of Nourishment, he examined the gathered Scholars, taking note not just of their number, but of their appearance. Altogether, his investigation confirmed his suspicions: the Scholarship was stable, but its condition was critical.

While these findings troubled him, Sev wasn't sure what he could do. The institution wasn't in total ruin, but it wasn't any better than when he had left it—in fact, with the recent loss of the Elder Scholar, it was worse. Unfortunately, there was no time for him to address these problems—right now, the future of the system was at stake.

After his speech, he made his way to the Palace for his meeting with the Elector, the state of the Scholarship still on his mind. If this peace mission was a success, could the Scholarship of Secundus help its sister on Primus? If the will of Olius was backed by the power of Secundus, could there finally be equality between the pillars of Primus?

When he stepped inside the black walls and felt the wave of cool air, Sev frowned. Even if they could achieve equality between the Palace and the Scholarship, could they ever achieve equality between Primus and Secundus? Was such a thing even possible between a desert and an oasis? Regardless of technological advancement, if Primus didn't have the rich life found on Secundus, could it ever truly prosper?

His train of thought came to a halt as soon as he stepped into the audience chamber. Before him was the same scene, with Folin and the soldier in their respective places. This time, he marched forward without hesitation, stopping at the base of the chair. As he stood there waiting for the Elector to drop to knee and hand, Sev felt a surprising amount of impatience at all this ceremony.

"Historian."

"Rise, Elector."

The man stood and met his gaze.

"I apologize for taking you away from the Scholarship, but the prisoner insisted he would only answer questions in your presence."

He gave the Elector a curious look. Had he really accepted such a request?

"No apology is necessary, Elector."

He turned to Folin and frowned.

"Stand up, for I will not converse with you on your knees."

Folin got to his feet, and the soldier shot a glance at the Elector.

"Have you been treated well?" Sev asked.

His friend met his gaze.

"I have been treated as a prisoner, Historian, but I have not been abused in any way."

Sev turned to the Elector.

"What are your questions, Elector?"

The supreme leader peered at him, and Sev could see a subtle frustration behind his eyes.

"Thank you, Historian."

He turned his attention to Folin.

"How did you learn of the Historian's arrival and this assassination plot?"

Folin glanced at Sev then back at the Elector.

"While the trade ship liaison has been shut down, there remains another method of communication."

"What method?"

Again, Folin glanced at Sev.

"I prefer to discuss this matter with the Historian alone."

Sev frowned.

"For his continued safety, that won't be possible," the Elector replied.

Folin turned to Sev.

"Historian, I beg you. I have critical information I must share with you, and you alone."

Sev's frown deepened.

"Again," the Elector interjected, "given the current situation and the plot against the Historian, we cannot allow it."

Folin's expression betrayed uncharacteristic torment, and Sev felt a cold fear come over him. Why was he so desperate to speak alone? Sev knew the Elector feared an elaborate trick, but Folin? This was his best friend.

"Why can't you share this information now? The Elector is a part of our peace delegation, and he has allied himself with the Priman Scholarship to ensure the success of this mission."

His words felt hollow, and Folin's frown only added to his shame.

"Historian…"

He bowed his head and sighed in resignation.

"I have been untruthful."

He raised his eyes to meet Sev's.

"I am a citizen of Secundus."

Sev stared at him, incredulous.

"A citizen of Secundus?"

"Yes, Historian."

"You were born on Secundus?" the Elector interrupted, as surprised as Sev.

Folin turned to the supreme leader.

"Yes, Elector. I was born on Secundus."

For a moment, both Primans were speechless. Sev tried to process this disclosure and failed. How could a Secundan citizen infiltrate their world to this extent? So many questions came to mind, he wasn't sure where to start.

"How long have you been on Primus?" the Elector asked, two steps ahead of him.

"Eighteen revolutions."

Eighteen revolutions, Sev thought. Not only had his best friend been born on a different planet, half of his life story was an outright lie.

"You were never a Pupil?" he asked.

Folin turned to him and frowned.

"Never, though I had a similar upbringing on Secundus."

"Why did you come to Primus?" the Elector asked.

Folin turned to the supreme leader.

"The Council and our Scholarship came to an agreement: we would send a young Scholar over to join your Scholarship so both worlds could learn more about the other. While the communication network was functioning, it was always considered dangerous and slow. My presence helped bring each planet's knowledge up to speed."

Sev continued to stare at him, unable to keep up with all this information. Did this prove the former Council knew of the technological superiority of Secundus? That would explain why they were so sure of their plan to overthrow the Palace…

"How did you arrive on Primus?"

While Sev reeled from each successive revelation, the Elector's line of inquiry remained clear and decisive.

"I was dropped off by one of our ships."

Sev glanced at the Elector then back to Folin.

"You weren't spotted?" he asked.

His friend gave him a curious look.

"Our ships are capable of avoiding detection by Priman technology."

Sev frowned, thinking back to the small skirmishes he had heard about as a soldier. Why would there be battles if the Secundans could avoid detection?

"Are there more like you on Primus now?" the Elector asked.

"Yes—this is why the Historian's life may be in danger, and the only reason I cooperate now."

The Elector turned to Sev with a knowing look, but Sev was too busy looking at his friend, struggling to see more than the man he had known for eight revolutions. Folin, a Secundan citizen?

"Then this method of communication relies on Secundan technology?" the Elector asked.

Folin nodded.

"A device we call a communicator. It allows me to communicate with Secundus directly."

He turned to Sev.

"It could allow you to speak to the Scholarship before your arrival on Secundus."

Sev's eyes went wide.

"We can communicate with the Scholarship of Secundus?"

Folin frowned.

"Unfortunately, it is not so simple. The device is made to contact only one other device, a device owned by the same people who plot against you. But I should be able to modify it, allowing us to send a public message—not just to the Scholarship, but to Secundus itself."

Sev stared at his friend in shock. A way to communicate with the people of Secundus? This could give them quite an advantage.

"This device," the Elector began, "where is it?"

Folin frowned.

"If you confiscate my communicator and attempt to use it, you will destroy our only chance of speaking with the Scholarship of Secundus."

Before the Elector could reply, Sev interjected.

"We cannot risk losing such an important link, Elector. The right message could keep us from being shot down in orbit."

The Elector's face hardened.

"Historian, I understand the risk, but if we learn how this device functions, we will be able to communicate with Secundus as freely as we wish."

"No, Elector," Folin interjected, "you will not. Primus is not capable of understanding this technology."

Sev saw the Elector's face harden even further, and wondered how much protection Folin actually had. At a certain point, it didn't matter what Sev said—if the Elector wanted him dead, he'd have him killed.

"What makes you so certain?"

"We know the extent of the Palace's knowledge, Elector. You have not deciphered the communications relays on the trade ships, even after transplanting them into your military craft. This device is a far more advanced version of the same system."

There was a flash of surprise in the supreme leader's expression, then the hard lines took over once more.

"The Palace will choose how or how not to use the device. I ask again, where is it?"

Folin looked to Sev, who turned to the Elector.

"Elector, I must object. This device may be key to our success, and this man knows how it functions. I have seen Secundan technology firsthand, it is well beyond that of Primus."

The Elector met his gaze with a scowl.

"Historian, we cannot trust this man. He may use this device against us in some manner, perhaps in a way we won't even understand. Only by allowing Palace technicians to examine the device, can we be sure of its safety."

Sev knew he couldn't let his frustration get the best of him, but the Elector was testing his patience. Was this really the right move, even for him? If the peace mission succeeded, he would have access to much more than one device.

He turned to Folin with a sudden revelation.

"You said there are more agents on Primus now?"

Folin nodded.

"Yes, Historian."

"And these agents, they also have communicators?"

Folin hesitated, frowning.

"Yes, Historian. But I will not willfully disclose their identities."

Sev frowned in turn.

"Folin," he began, addressing him by name for the first time, "you have shared the truth to support my mission, have you not?"

At Sev's change in tone, Folin returned the favor, looking him up and down as if looking at a stranger. Yet there was clear respect in his eyes, respect that gave Sev hope.

"Yes, Historian."

Sev nodded.

"For that, and for possibly saving my life, I am thankful. But it is not enough."

Folin sighed.

"Historian…"

Sev raised his hand.

"You and I both know there is a faction within the Senate intent on bringing me down. Since the arrival of High Scholar Zoph, my position has weakened, and my mission is in danger. The Council and the Elector have agreed to join me as delegates of peace, but what good is a delegation if the Historian is dead? By your own admission, these other agents may be working against me, and some may plot to kill me. Even if you refuse to give their identities, do you not have any information that can help? Do you not have a chain of command from which you received these instructions, a chain we can follow to discover our enemies?"

Folin frowned.

"The will of Olius is one of peace, Historian, not of violence. Why else do you think I am here, rejecting my orders?"

Sev sighed, frowning in turn.

"Was the plan to rout the Palace free of violence? Did you reject your orders then?"

Anger entered his friend's expression.

"Why do you think I hesitate to speak freely, Historian? If I was talking to you and you alone, you would already know the identities of these agents, this chain of command you seek. But this man here," he said, gesturing to the Elector, "is a man of violence, and one I do not trust to seek peace. The plan to rout the Palace was meant to remove such violence."

Sev nodded slowly, considering his words.

"I understand. In fact, I agree."

He wanted to shoot a glance at the Elector, but he controlled the urge.

"I was here, in this very chamber, the rotation where we lost my predecessor. I watched it happen with my own eyes."

The memories came back and a nausea welled up inside him, but he fought against it, pushing through his reply.

"This man sought the execution of the Historian and succeeded."

He knew he was out of line and could only imagine the fury in the Elector's eyes, but it wasn't important—not now.

"Yet now we have another group of individuals with the same goal, a goal of equal violence, and you wish to protect them? Is there not a measure of hypocrisy in this?"

The two of them held an intense silence, and for a moment, it was as if the soldier and the Elector weren't there—just Sev and Folin, two friends standing in the audience chamber of the Palace. And in this moment, the friendship evolved, its dynamic shifting.

Folin looked away with a sigh. When he spoke again his voice was soft, almost hard to hear.

"You're right."

He looked back up at Sev.

"Historian, I will help you in this mission, but I want your assurance that whenever possible, the men responsible will face judgment on Secundus—not on Primus."

Sev nodded.

"You have my word."

"Historian."

There was a sharpness in the Elector's tone that almost made Sev jump. He turned toward the supreme leader, masking any inner fear.

"May we speak in private?"

The man was on the verge of open hostility, and Sev knew better than to argue.

"Of course."

***

The door to his chamber had barely closed before the Elector made his opinion known.

"Sev of Primus, you have gone too far."

Surprisingly, Sev was unmoved—he wondered if he was growing too comfortable calling the shots, as if his life didn't depend on the whims of this belligerent ruler. The personal guardians were just outside the door, yet he was unafraid.

"Elector, I understand your anger, but this is the only path to success. Secundus is one excuse away from eliminating me, and the support I have on their planet is the only thing preventing them from interfering in Priman affairs as they please—and again, based on their technological superiority, there will be nothing we can do to stop them if they wish to do so."

He saw the fury bubbling up a second time, but he had had enough. Before the Elector could react, he lashed out with surprising vigor.

"Spare me the rebuke—I know you cannot stand the idea of not being in total control, but this situation is out of your hands. If you want to execute me for insubordination or what have you, do so, but I assure you if I fall, so will Primus. I am not asking for you to abdicate nor am I asking for you to bow to me as you have already done several times. All I ask is that you do your job and protect Primus, rather than your ego."

It wasn't until he was finished that Sev realized how aggressive his words had been, and for the first time ever, he left the Elector speechless. For a moment neither spoke, and as had happened when the supreme leader first laid eyes on him one rotation ago, the man's expression painted a picture of battling emotions: anger, confusion, rage, doubt… and finally, to Sev's surprise, acceptance.

"Very well, Sev of Primus."

The Elector let out a sigh, and it was as if an immense weight came off his shoulders.

"We will follow your plan to the letter."

Then he looked at Sev with a hint of intensity.

"But you are never to speak to me like that again, is that understood?"

Sev smiled.

"Very well, Elector."

Aggression

Three rotations later, Sev was in space once more, on the final approach to Secundus. In place of the cramped quarters of the trade ship, he had a private chamber aboard the Priman flagship, the Feat of Primus. Yet despite the comparative luxury, he felt more trapped than before.

He had not expected to arrive in a warship. In fact, he had fought against the idea, but it was one of many compromises he had had to make over the course of endless deliberations and countless meetings. Yet the amount of negotiation he had endured paled in comparison to the frustration caused by the Palace's secretive nature: every discussion was riddled with omissions, and now that Folin had revealed the extent of Secundus's reach, the Elector refused to share anything even remotely related to military secrets.

In theory, this secrecy was well-founded, but in practice, it was useless. Even with two squadrons of Priman fighters flanking either side of the ship, the Feat of Primus was at the mercy of Secundan superiority. Put short, if the enemy wanted to destroy them, no amount of secrecy would be enough.

In fact, Sev was beginning to think this secrecy was the root of Primus's problems. The more he contemplated the origins of the technological divide, the more he came to the same conclusion: on Secundus, the Scholarship had led the way, researching Olian technology and sharing it with their citizens. But on Primus? On Primus, the Palace controlled the trade ships and the hotswords, hoarding them for power.

These weren't thoughts he shared aloud—lest his bodyguard tell the Elector—but he knew he couldn't keep them to himself. Assuming they made it to Secundus and succeeded in their mission, this would be an important topic of conversation—the recalibration of power on Primus. While he still considered the idea optimistic—naive even—he figured now was a good a time as any to be hopeful. After all, would they even make it to Secundus?

There was one factor working in their favor, the only part of the plan that gave Sev a measure of confidence: Folin's modified device. Before their departure, they had broadcast a message to the Secundan people announcing their intentions and approach.

Unfortunately, they didn't know if the message had reached its intended audience. According to Folin, their enemies would move quickly to block the signal, and they had no way to know how many of their words had reached Secundan ears.

Here too, the Palace's involvement proved frustrating. To permit his use of the device, Folin was made to identify the other agents on Primus. Thankfully, the Elector had kept his reluctant word, and these agents—along with Folin himself—were currently aboard the ship, on their way to Secundus for judgement. But the Palace had confiscated their communicators, handing them off to their technicians for analysis.

Sev couldn't understand what the supreme leader intended to do with such foreign technology. When Folin had first made a comment regarding communications relays, Sev had no idea what he was talking about, but after two rotations aboard the Feat of Primus, he understood: the men inside the warship were able to speak and hear the men inside the fighters, despite the thick hull and openness of space separating them.

According to Folin, the Palace technicians found these relays incomprehensible, and they were but a primitive version of the communicator. If they couldn't decipher such ancient machines, what use was the latest iteration?

Despite all the research it had put into Olian technology, the Palace was as ignorant as ever. Even this warship, the best Primus had to offer, looked like a combination of trade ship engineering and haphazard upgrades. If only the Scholarship had pursued this avenue sooner, Sev thought, maybe things would be different.

But they hadn't, and now the High Scholars were the only ones impressed by their surroundings, gaping at the lights in awe. Sev watched their reactions with a hint of shame, hoping this mission could change the course of their planet. Ultimately, he realized, it had to—either they would share in the wealth and prosperity of Secundus, or they would be dead.

"A ship approaches."

The pilot's announcement cut his thought process short, and a tense silence took over the flight deck. Sev and the rest of the Council had the honor of sharing the deck with the Elector and his pilots, and he intended to use this position to stop an all-out war. Of course, if a dispute arose between the Historian and the supreme leader, it was hard to imagine the men of the Palace siding with Olius.

"Do not engage unless fired upon," the Elector declared.

Sev let out a sigh of relief. He had been painfully clear about the importance of a non-confrontational approach, but he wasn't sure the man understood the concept.

"There seems to be some kind of—"

The pilot was cut short by the appearance of a holograph in the middle of the control room floor—that of a Secundan Senator.

"Priman warship, you are violating the terms of the peace treaty. Please exit Secundus's space-zone or your intrusion will be taken as an act of war."

The holograph switched to a schematic, showing the Feat of Primus crossing into the space-zone.

"Our holograph cannot hear or see you. We await your immediate reply over any channel."

Sev shot a glance at the supreme leader, who stared at the display in confusion and shock.

"Elector, they seem to be using our communication relays."

The pilot's announcement did nothing to break the Elector's attention. After a moment's hesitation, Sev turned to the pilot.

"Can you reply?"

He shot a glance at the Elector then back at Sev.

"I don't know, Historian."

At least they were still alive, he thought. Their only hope now was the message they had sent. But even with the combined pressure of the Scholarship and the people, it would be difficult to convince the Senate to allow a Priman warship to land.

"Elector, we must respond," he insisted, but the man was fixated on the dancing lights.

"What is this technology?" he asked.

"Only the beginning, Elector, as we will soon find out if we do not reply."

Sev watched him with a frown, wondering if he would have to step up and take control. What would he say? Would the crew listen to him? But just as these questions ran through his mind, the Elector turned away from the hologram and addressed the pilot.

"They are on our relays?"

The pilot nodded.

"Yes, Elector."

The Elector turned to the relay near his seat, leaned forward, and pressed a button.

"This is the Elector of Primus. I come to Secundus on a mission of peace with the Historian and the Council of the Scholarship of Primus. We ask permission to land on Secundus and meet with the Senate and Scholarship of Secundus in order to sign an agreement of peace between our worlds."

A silence followed, and Sev glanced nervously around the flight deck, noting the hushed conversations of several technicians into their own relays—were they talking to the fighters, or had those communications been blocked? Had the Elector's message gone through? He cursed the Palace for their amateur understanding of Olian technology.

"If the Historian is aboard, have him verify his presence."

A new voice came out of the relays, seemingly familiar. Was it a Scholar? Had they gotten the Elector's response? Sev turned to his own relay and pressed the button.

"This is the Historian. We come on a mission of peace. We request permission to land on Secundus and meet with the Senate."

Another silence, punctuated by even louder snippets of conversation. As the Elector listened in, a frown spread across his face. Something was happening, but Sev wasn't sure what. Apparently no one was.

"Prepare the weapons."

Sev's eyes went wide.

"Elector—"

"You do your job and I will do mine."

His tone left no room for argument, and Sev felt his heart racing. Why hadn't they responded yet? Maybe they had thought wrong—maybe their replies weren't being received.

"Weapons ready, Elector."

Though this ship lacked windows, he could paint an imagine in his mind: a lone Secundan craft floating somewhere nearby, weapons ready. Based on what he had read in the terminal, they were severely outmatched. And yet, hadn't other Priman ships survived? What about all those skirmishes he had heard about?

"Prepare to fire," the Elector announced.

Before Sev could react, a voice came over the relays.

"Historian!"

The cry made his stomach drop, and Sev knew what came next.

"Fire the—"

The Elector's order was cut short by a loud crash, and the entire flight deck went dark as they lurched to the right. Sev felt himself lifting out of his seat, gravity no longer restraining him, and scrambled to strap himself into his chair.

"Sitrep!" the Elector cried.

"All systems unrespons—"

Another crash sent them hurtling through the darkness, and he tucked himself as compactly as possible, a cacophony of chaos going off around him. Several collisions were accompanied by screams of pain, some of which he recognized.

"Historian!"

High Scholar Teero's voice reached him, horrified and confused, but just as he was about to reply, the flight deck came to life—light returned, as did gravity, and objects and humans alike fell to the floor in a deadly mess. Blood splatters painted the walls and ceiling, and men crumpled to the ground with cracks and thuds, screaming in pain.

"Sitrep!"

The pilot turned away from the horrifying scene and tried some buttons.

"Systems still unresponsive, Elector, but we are back on—"

A new hologram appeared on the flight deck, and this one he recognized—the Scholar of the Premier Territory, the woman who had saved his life.

"Historian, you are in grave danger. Board the—"

The hologram stuttered then disappeared, and a stern voice came over the relays.

"Warship of Primus, you have violated the terms of the peace treaty. Any evasive action—"

"Fire on the Secundan ship!" the Elector proclaimed.

Sev shot him an incredulous look.

"Elector, all systems are unresponsive, including weapons."

Before the supreme leader had a chance to reply, Sev was out of his chair, scrambling to tend to the wounded.

"Is there a medic aboard?" he shouted, but no one seemed to be listening.

A loud crash from the bowels of the ship cut all of their conversations short, and Sev grabbed at the nearest secured object. For an instant he wondered why the ship hadn't moved, then the sound of footsteps made things clear—they had been boarded.

The Elector's personal guardians leapt from their posts, unsheathing their hotswords and facing the exit. Sev scanned his surroundings in dismay, wondering why he had ever agreed to this mission. The entire power structure of Primus was aboard this ship, and he knew the Elector's personal guardians were no match for the approaching footsteps.

Unless, he thought, this was—

"Historian!"

He looked up at the source of the noise: an unknown figure in an exotic outfit of white and blue—something more metal than cloth, with no part of the body uncovered. While he had never seen one in person, he recognized the Secundan warrior from his time in the terminal—these were their soldiers, their keepers of the peace.

Just as he was processing this information, the guardian's hotsword came down from above, meeting the warrior's helmet. But for the first time in his life, Sev witnessed the unthinkable: the weapon jammed into the top of the metal suit, unable to cut through. The guardian, as surprised as Sev, lost his grip on the blade, and both men tumbled to the ground below. As soon as they hit the floor, two more warriors entered the flight deck, and the second guardian prepared to attack.

"Enough!"

The Elector's command stopped him in his tracks, but he kept his hotsword raised, challenging them to make a move.

"Where is the Historian?" one of the warriors asked.

Sev sat up straighter.

"I'm here."

The man turned to him and dipped his chin to his chest.

"Historian, we are here to remove you from this ship and take you to safety."

"On whose authority?" the Elector asked.

The warrior ignored him, taking a few steps toward Sev.

"Please, Historian. We must leave now."

Sev glanced behind the man and saw his companion get back on his feet, an extinguished hotsword stuck to his helmet. The Elector's guardian also stood, exposing and igniting his second blade.

"We act on behalf of the Scholarship of Secundus."

These words brought his attention back to the warrior in front of him.

"We must leave now, Historian, there is no time."

Sev looked at the people around him—some still alive in their chairs, most dead or mangled on the floor.

"What about the men?" he asked.

The man frowned.

"Historian, a second boarding party is en route, and they do not act on behalf of the Scholarship. We must leave now or risk a confrontation we cannot win."

He was rooted to the spot, cognizant of what the man had told him but unwilling to face such a reality.

"Historian," came a raspy voice to his left, "You must go."

His eyes turned to the source and found High Scholar Teero at his side, his body twisted into an unnatural position. How long had he sat next to one of his own High Scholars and not noticed?

"You must go!" he repeated, then broke into a cough, spattering blood over Sev's robes.

Sev looked down and watched the red stain spread, swallowing the white and gold. He grabbed a fold of the soaked cloth, feeling the warmth between his fingers.

"Historian, accept my deepest apology."

He barely registered the voice behind him, noting only a light pressure in his shoulder before losing consciousness.

***

Sev jolted awake, clarity washing over him like ice water.

"Teero!"

He was inside another ship, strapped into another chair, but this was no Priman vessel.

"Historian, how do you feel?"

A woman's face leaned over him, visible behind a pane of glass. There were at least a dozen other warriors around him, every one of them eyeing him with concern.

"Where is the Council?" he asked.

The woman frowned.

"Historian, four members of the Priman Council are aboard—"

"And the others?"

The woman's frown deepened, and she dropped her chin to her chest.

"Historian, we had no choice but to evacuate, the—"

At the thought of the rest of the Council—and especially of Folin—Sev could not contain himself.

"You left them to die!?"

The woman stumbled backward in shame.

"Hi—Historian, we did everything we could. If we hadn't hurried, you might be in the hands of the Senate."

Her head was still bowed in respect, but Sev's anger grew.

"Take us back immediately, I order it!"

She hesitated, and someone else replied in her stead.

"Historian, if we return, the Senate will take you and everyone aboard. You will be tried and executed for treason and incitement of war."

He paused, catching Sev's eye.

"As will we."

This last bit caught him off-guard, and he shot the man a confused look.

"You will be tried for helping us?"

The man nodded.

"And executed."

Sev stared at him in shock.

"Executed?"

He nodded, and the woman rejoined the conversation.

"Historian, we have committed high treason in the name of the Scholarship. The Senate will not forgive us unless peace is established under your command."

Sev processed these words, his anger fading.

"By saving me you have committed high treason?"

She nodded, a hint of shame still in her eyes.

"Historian, once the peace was breached and the fighting began, many of us were forced to fight our own sisters and brothers. It was the only way to save you."

His eyes widened, grasping the gravity of the situation. The Secundans had fought their own, for him? In hindsight, it made sense—how else could they have survived?—but the thought of what he was responsible for was too much to bear, and he bowed his head in shame.

"What have I done…"

"You have pledged to bring peace between the worlds, Historian."

The reply was immediate and unquestioning, but its irony only served to deepen his guilt.

"Yet all I have brought is war."

There was a momentary silence, and Sev considered the consequences of his actions. He remembered what had happened after the Arbitration, where his quest for justice had led. Was this but another example at a much larger scale? Had he failed the entire system?

"No."

The soft objection caught his attention, and he looked up at the woman.

"Historian, you did not bring this war, the Senate did."

He made to reply, but she cut him off.

"Did you order any offensive action against Secundus or Primus?"

Even behind the glass of the helmet, her stare was piercing.

"No."

"Then why do you put this burden on your shoulders?"

He wanted to respond, to string together a coherent explanation as to why this was all his fault, to tell her every detail from his first promotion to his most recent blunders, but something about her gaze had hypnotized him, and he couldn't find the words.

"Historian, we have made sacrifices of our own volition. Do you still intend to bring peace between the worlds?"

There was another moment of silence between them, but Sev no longer felt the weight of his actions—rather, he felt the weight of responsibility, the weight of purpose. He tried to ignore thoughts of Folin, of the crew on the Feat of Primus… perhaps they had survived, perhaps not, but now was not the time to think on this. After all, they had risked their lives for this very mission, was it not his duty to complete it?

"Yes, citizen of Secundus, but only with your help."

He turned to one of the others.

"Where are we headed?"

"The Senate."

The answer was calm and unassuming, and it took a moment to sink in.

"Is that wise?" Sev asked, masking his doubt as much as possible.

The man shrugged.

"We don't have a choice, Historian. We are on the brink of full-fledged war between the planets, and the longer we wait, the harder it will be to stop. We must act now, and we must act decisively."

He took a deep breath, contemplating the implications of this course of action. The man was right, of course, as much as Sev didn't want him to be.

"Very well. What is the plan?"

"The Scholarship will explain their proposal to you."

As he finished his statement, a hologram flickered into existence before them: the Scholar of the Premier Territory.

"Where is he?" she asked, her eyes scanning the deck before locking on Sev.

"Historian."

She dropped her chin to her chest.

"I cannot express the depth of our regret at what has happened…"

As she spoke, Sev knew he must channel the same energy that had just saved him.

"Scholar, none of this is your doing. Right now we must focus on the future. What is your plan?"

The Scholar frowned.

"Historian, the Senators have locked down the Senate and stripped the Scholarship of its powers, ejecting us from the proceedings. While we haven't been formally accused of treason, it is only a matter of time. We need to get inside and end this conflict before it gets out of hand."

He nodded, contemplating her words.

"If we approach the Senate, will they attack us?"

"It's possible, but it's a risk we have to take. We can only hope your presence, and perhaps the presence of the Priman peace delegation, will persuade the Senators to reconsider their position."

He nodded again, then turned to the woman in metal.

"How much of the delegation was saved?"

She winced, but there was no anger in his words.

"The Priman leader, his guards, and four members of the Council."

"Where are they?" he asked.

"In the passenger hold," she replied.

He wondered how the supreme leader had taken his exclusion from the main deck.

"Bring the Elector here, please."

She brought her chin to her chest then passed the assignment to a colleague. Sev turned his attention back to the hologram.

"Where are you, Scholar?"

"Also on my way to the Senate, with the rest of the Scholars not protesting outside the walls. We plan to present a united front under your guidance, Historian."

A pit formed in his stomach, but Sev kept a brave face.

"Very well. Is there any way to speak to the Senate?"

She frowned.

"They won't accept any of our signals but I'm certain they will send a message before we arrive."

"They know we are coming?"

She nodded.

"While there may be a rift in Secundus, our technology remains intact. We couldn't hide if we wanted to."

The sound of approaching footsteps caught his attention, and Sev turned to see the Elector enter the main deck, a Secundan warrior on either side. It was odd to see the man flanked by these soldiers of white and blue, and there was unmasked discomfort in his expression.

"Elector, please join me."

Sev gestured to a nearby seat, but for a moment the man didn't move. His eyes scanned the room with a mix of suspicion and awe, pausing on the hologram in the middle. Sev watched the scene unfold and wondered what was going through his mind—was the man reconsidering everything he thought he knew?

"Historian."

The supreme leader came within arm's reach and dropped to knee and hand, confusing Sev. Why do that now?

"Rise, Elector. Take a seat."

The Elector did as asked.

"Elector, this Scholar acts as a representative of the Scholarship of Secundus."

Sev gestured to the hologram, and the woman dropped her chin to her chest. It occurred to him this might be the first time the Elector had seen a woman in a position of authority, but this was the least of his concerns.

"Our plan is to go directly to the Senate under a united front," he said. "Olius, Primus, and the Scholarship of Secundus. Are you still committed to the mission of peace?"

The Elector glanced at the hologram then back at Sev.

"We're going to the Senate?"

Sev nodded.

"Yes, Elector. We cannot afford to let this conflict last any longer. The only way to save Primus is if we make a stand for peace right now. Will you join us?"

Again, the Elector glanced at the Scholar before answering.

"Do I have a choice?"

There was a hint of anger in his voice that did not go unnoticed.

"Elector, you told me you were ready to join me on this mission of peace, that you would stand behind a treaty between Primus and Secundus when the time came. Have you changed your mind?"

He peered at the supreme leader, curious where this conversation would go. Unfortunately, the man was right—he didn't have a choice. And backing someone as proud as the Elector into a corner—for example, the confines of a Secundan ship without his personal guardians—could have undesirable consequences.

"Historian, I agreed to a peace treaty, and what I got was a war."

Such a calm, truthful statement had a much stronger effect than any outburst could have had, and Sev found himself speechless.

"I took an immense risk coming here, and now the fate of Primus rests in their hands," he said, gesturing to the others. "Do you think these people want to see our planet thrive? Even these supposed allies, these Scholars, when have they helped our citizens? How long has our neighbor had the technology to bring us wealth and prosperity, and why have they waited until now to act?"

Sev stared at the supreme leader in awe. The man had never proven himself such an eloquent speaker, and certainly not such a measured one. He felt as if he was hearing the words of the old Historian, not the man who had him killed.

"Elector, your words ring painfully true, and we have no excuse for our past," the Scholar replied. "But the present gives us only two options: a war Primus will certainly lose, or a peace in which this prosperity you seek may be possible."

The supreme leader met her gaze with a frown.

"Be that as it may, my participation in this mission will require the Scholarship's unwavering commitment to share all of Secundus's technological knowledge with Primus."

Now it was the hologram that frowned, and Sev watched their interaction with intent curiosity. Was this another ploy by the Elector? Even if it was, the man had a point: the only true path to equality was full transparency. If Secundus kept a portion of its knowledge to itself as leverage, it negated the entire purpose of the peace.

"The Scholarship of Secundus is committed to this mission of peace, and to the equality of our worlds. So long as Primus agrees to use this knowledge to further such peace, we will share it."

The Elector nodded.

"Your terms are acceptable, but you must make this directive clear, and you must promise the Historian, not me."

The Scholar hesitated, then turned to Sev.

"Historian, the Scholarship of Secundus will adhere to the Elector's request: if this mission of peace is a success, we will divulge every detail of our technological research to Primus."

Sev noticed the hesitation in her tone and couldn't help but frown. Even these individuals—the ones he considered above petty prejudices— clearly held some. The worst was the Elector's poignant argument: why hadn't this technology been shared sooner? Did they really need the Historian to make it happen? But now was not the time for these questions—they had a job to do, and no time to waste.

"Your words have been heard, Scholar," he replied. Then, turning to the Elector, "And your terms have been accepted, Elector. Do you agree to help us?"

The supreme leader looked from the Scholar to Sev and nodded.

"I will do everything in my power to convince the Senate to end this conflict, including the promise and fulfillment of peace from Primus."

"And not a moment too soon," the Scholar announced. "We are on our final approach."

Just as she finished her statement, another hologram appeared beside her—the same Senator who had greeted the Feat of Primus. His eyes scanned the interior of the ship, pausing on Sev and the Elector, then continuing to the nearest Secundan soldier.

"Warrior, you are in direct violation of your orders. These two individuals have committed acts of war against Secundus. They must be brought before the Senate for judgement of their crimes."

The woman dropped her chin to her chest.

"Senator, we respectfully decline these orders in the name of Olius, the only one above Secundus."

The hologram scowled.

"This is not the being of Olius, this is an imposter! The Historian was killed by that man right there," he said, pointing to the Elector.

"Senator, these men are indeed on their way to the Senate," the Scholar remarked.

The Senator turned his attention to the hologram beside him, and Sev was once more awed by the technology of this world. Could they communicate like that?

"But they come as messengers of peace, not as prisoners," she added.

The man's scowl worsened, and he turned back to the warrior.

"A party will meet you outside the Senate. You are to hand over the two prisoners without resistance, and after they have been dealt with, your insubordination and the insubordination of your peers will be judged in turn. Think on the consequences of your actions."

With that, his image vanished, leaving only the Scholar, who turned her attention to the warrior.

"Ensure the safety of the Historian above all else, and restore the weapons to the Elector's guardians so they may help our mission."

The warrior dropped her chin to her chest, and the hologram turned to Sev.

"I will see you on the ground, Historian."

She brought her chin to her chest then disappeared.

***

As the ship came to a hover, Sev looked out the window with a frown. A small crowd of Secundan warriors awaited them, each outfitted in the same white and blue suit, each somehow far more imposing than the ones sharing their flight deck. This was no welcoming party, that much was clear.

"Where is the rest of the Scholarship?" he asked.

The warrior next to him pointed out the window toward another ship. As he watched its descent, a light pressure let him know their own craft had touched ground, and he felt the weight of his imminent, unescapable reality. This was about to happen whether he liked it or not, and it was not just his own fate in the balance: the fate of the entire system was in their hands.

"Historian, we've landed," the warrior announced.

Sev knew it was time to remove his straps and get up, but he hesitated. How did they intend to bypass the soldiers on the ground? Even if the other ship had just as many warriors as their own, they would be outnumbered two-to-one.

Finally, noting the growing tension around him, he rose from his chair.

"Lead us to the exit door."

The warrior brought her chin to her chest.

"Historian, should we bring the other survivors with us?"

Sev glanced at the Elector.

"His guardians will join us, yes?"

She nodded.

"Yes, but what of the others?"

"Bring the High Scholars."

She brought her chin to her chest again.

"Yes, Historian."

The walk to the exit door made the ship seem enormous, but Sev knew it was mostly in his head. What was he going to say to these soldiers on the ground? How could he convince them to put down their arms and let them speak to the Senate?

When they reached the exit door and came to a halt, it became clear just how much depended on the being of Olius: everyone, including the Elector, stood a few paces behind him. Some of the warriors were speaking, perhaps even to him, but he couldn't hear anything over the pounding in his head. He feared his own mortality to be sure, but to hold the future of two civilizations in the balance? Several well-meaning individuals had managed to convince him of his ability to take this role, but standing where he did then, he disagreed with all of them.

The exit door swung upward, and he shot a glance to his left. The other ship was much closer than he had expected, its door also open and a handful of Scholars coming down the ramp. What he didn't see were any more of the white and blue suits, and he understood why none of the soldiers on the ground bothered to intercept them.

"Historian, we await your guidance."

The gentle reminder from the warrior to his right brought his attention back to the ramp before him, the few pieces of metal separating them from the Secundan surface. He looked at the approaching warriors and frowned. They would reach the end of their march any moment, and Sev knew he couldn't stay in the ship forever.

But before he could lift his foot and take his first step down, Sev froze in place, confused. The warriors on the ground had crossed the threshold where he had expected them to stop and were making their way onto the ramp. At the same time, the warriors behind him stepped forward, putting themselves between Sev and the aggressors.

"What is—"

A flurry of movement and light answered his question before it could leave his mouth. Sev had spent enough time in the terminals of Secundus to learn about the weapons of this world, but if the warrior's standard method of attack had escaped his comprehension when he had read about it, seeing it in action did little to clear things up.

By some technology he couldn't grasp, the metal suits gave their owners the ability to create temporary hotswords along any portion of their body—the forearm, the shin, the head, wherever a strike was about to be made. The end result was a complicated and coordinated dance as warriors on either side jumped and attacked, blocked and dodged. Contact was frequent but often harmless—the suits themselves shielded from such attacks, but they weren't invincible.

A shriek behind him caught his attention, and Sev whirled to see one of the Elector's guardians cut clean in two, both halves of his body collapsing to the ground. As he processed this horror, the other guardian met a similar fate, and the attacking warrior prepared to strike the supreme leader himself.

"No!"

Sev's voice thundered with all its might, but only those closest to him heard it through the chaos. The warriors around him paused, turning to see what he was yelling about, but it was too late—the Secundan soldier swung his outstretched arm straight through the Elector's neck, killing him without hesitation.

"Historian!"

The cry behind him came just before a hand locked on his shoulder, pulling him into the arms of the aggressors. Another hand grabbed his leg and resisted, but then an arm went around his torso, yanking him away.

"Historian!"

It was too late. The warrior holding his torso pulled him well into the mass of opposing soldiers, beyond the reach of his allies.

"Stand down! Stand down!"

Sev screamed at the top of his lungs, hoping his followers could hear. The warrior pulled him to his feet and let go, but Sev dropped to his knees in pain, grasping his stomach. He wished for a quick end, for a hotsword to cut his head clean off, but he knew this wasn't the fate that awaited him —not yet. These warriors would take him to the Senate, where he would be formally denounced. But did it even matter?

Much like the Elector, Sev had come on a mission of peace and found war. This would mark the end of his legacy, the end of the Historian, the end of the Scholarships, and the end of Primus. He was the reason the original Historian was dead, and now he was the reason the Elector was dead. His own death was long overdue. If only it could come sooner.

Alliance

Sev lay crumpled on the ground, waiting for someone to pull him up or drag him forward, but no one laid a hand on him. Finally, after what felt like an eternity, he opened his eyes and saw a forest of metal legs. Behind them, he could just make out the other ship—the one with the rest of the Scholars—but there wasn't a soul in sight.

What had happened to them, he wondered. Had they scattered in fear?

"Can you stand?"

The warrior's voice was gentle, and Sev looked up at her, confused.

"Yes," he answered, forcing himself to his feet.

She eyed him with a hint of pity.

"We must take you to the Senate."

He stared at her, hesitating. Was there reluctance in her tone?

"If you take me to the Senate, I will be executed."

She frowned.

"Your fate is in their hands, not ours."

Before Sev could respond, she turned to the warriors around him.

"Take him to the Senate without harming him."

Two hands pulled him gently forward, and Sev saw the familiar dome ahead of them, about a thousand paces away. He shot a glance behind him, where a second group of warriors surrounded the other captives. Everyone was on their knees, and the captured warriors had removed their helmets. What would happen to them? Would they be executed, as they had predicted?

His eyes shot back to the second ship, and an unbearable guilt came over him. Would the Scholars face a similar fate? Is that why they had disappeared? Could they find refuge among the people?

Behind the ship was a forest, and Sev knew what lay among those trees: towns, villages, gathering places of the citizens of Secundus, the same places he had grown to know during his stay. He remembered his first speech in such a town, the men and women with their heads held high...

Even now, as he marched to an almost certain death, he had to admire this planet's society. When was the last time Sev had felt such confidence and freedom? Perhaps in his revolutions as a Scholar, but all that was destroyed with the Elector's promotion.

He thought back to that fateful rotation and shook his head. How could so much suffering come from such a positive gesture? He wanted to resent the Elector for what he had done, but if the supreme leader was guilty of incredible sins, he had just paid for them.

Did he deserve his fate for the execution of the Historian? An eye for an eye, as it were? Sev realized these thoughts were mere distraction—whether the man deserved it or not, what had happened had happened, and now the situation was beyond saving.

How could they have thought this plan would work? There was nothing left to save Primus: the supreme leader was dead, and the already fragile Council was broken beyond repair. Their only hope, the beacon of peace between the worlds, was on a path to judgement and execution, and Primus would share his fate.

Somewhere deep inside of him, Sev was relieved. Relieved that it was over, that the final chapter was coming to an end. It hadn't even been a revolution since his promotion, yet that rotation felt like a lifetime ago. Too long had he felt himself an imposter, too many times had those around him had to convince him of his worth, of the importance that he continue, that he fulfill his mission. This conclusion was long overdue.

Some hushed chatter caught his attention, and he looked up. About three hundred paces ahead, between their entourage and the Senate, a line of people was forming across the field. These were no warriors—most wore the clothes of Secundan citizens, but there were a few in familiar robes of white and gold.

Within moments, several dozen turned into over a hundred, body after body emerging from the forest. Sev could hardly believe what he was seeing—the people of Secundus, guided by their Scholars, were forming a wall between his escort and the Senate, blocking their path. Somewhere deep inside of him, a spark of hope emerged, a ray of light shining in the darkness.

The wall filled in as they approached, and he saw some familiar faces—not just the Scholars he knew well, but citizens who had attended his speeches. All of them watched the soldiers approach with surprising composure, and Sev once again realized just how different this planet was to his own. On Primus, their soldiers would cut through such defiance—literally. But based on the way these citizens carried themselves, it didn't shock him when the warriors came to a halt.

"Citizens, please make way."

The command was firm but not harsh.

"We will not make way, warrior."

Sev turned at the familiar voice and saw the Scholar of the Premier Territory take a step forward, separating herself from the pack.

"We ask that you free the Historian to the Scholarship and the people of Secundus."

She planted herself firmly in place, almost daring the warriors to make a move. Sev could not believe the audacity of these people—if he had acted this way toward the hotheaded soldier on Primus, even his High Scholar's robes wouldn't have saved him.

"The Senate has asked—"

"We are the members of the Senate responsible for the Historian."

"You are not—"

"The Senate has unlawfully stripped our powers in an effort to further their agenda of war. Will you allow them to execute the Historian as well?"

Sev watched their exchange, dumbfounded. These warriors could slaughter the lot of them with little to no resistance, but they let themselves be scolded and interrupted time and time again. Where had they learned such restraint?

"This man is not—"

"Warrior, do you believe the Senate should have the power to decide the legitimacy of the Historian without the input of the Scholarship?"

The soldier hesitated, and the Scholar turned to face the crowd behind her.

"Citizens of Secundus, is this man before us, in the custody of the warriors, the Historian?"

"Yes," came the thunderous response.

She turned back around.

"Warrior, the people and the Scholarship have spoken. I thank you for your unwavering service to Secundus, and I regret the nature of our encounter, but we cannot let you go any farther."

She stepped forward, toward Sev.

"The Historian must be allowed to join us, so that we may go to the Senate and reverse this mess. This is the will of the people, and the will of the people supersedes your orders."

She took another step forward, putting herself face to face with the warrior, the only body between her and Sev. The two women stared at one another, and Sev caught sight of some uncertain glances among the blockade. As the moment lingered, he felt the spark of hope fading, its light returning to the darkness of reality. This was inspiring, but ultimately meaningless, if these warriors had agreed to bring him in they wouldn't—

And then the warrior stepped aside, dropping her chin to her chest and clearing the path to Sev.

"Scholar."

The wall of people gave out a collective sigh, and Sev gaped, frozen in stunned silence.

"Historian," the Scholar said, catching his attention.

With another glance at the warrior, Sev took a tentative step forward.

"Thank you, Scholar," he answered. Then, turning to the warrior, "Thank you, warrior."

The warrior looked at him intently, but said nothing.

"Historian, time is of the essence," the Scholar added.

"Yes," Sev answered, turning toward the Senate. "Lead the way."

***

As the mass of people approached the glass dome, Sev tried to imagine what was passing through the minds of the Senators inside. They had to be aware of the situation, perhaps even watching it unfold, but what were they thinking? Were they reconsidering their actions, seeing the will of the people on display?

It was something he almost dared to believe, but it didn't take long for this fantasy to die. When they were some thirty paces from the door, a contingent of warriors came out to meet them, standing guard just outside the entrance. As they got closer, the Scholar of the Premier Territory addressed him.

"Historian, they will not allow the citizens to enter, but I don't think they'll stop you or us—they want everyone inside as prisoners, and escorting you is evidence of treason, so they will allow it. Just to be safe, we'll keep you protected."

The Scholars formed a circle around him as they crossed the line of warriors, but the soldiers let them pass without issue, blocking only the citizens in their wake. They walked into the glass dome and down the central path, never breaking formation. Even when they reached the Senate floor, they kept the arrangement, as if their presence would somehow guard him from the inevitable. Sev glanced around the familiar walls and was surprised to see over half the seats empty—all of the Scholars were missing of course, but so were some of the Senators.

"So nice of you to finally join us."

The same Senator they had seen in holographic form now stood above them, eyeing them with contempt, and Sev wasn't sure if he preferred this Speaker or the last.

"Senator, you have no right—"

The Speaker dropped his hand and the Scholar of the Premier Territory was silenced.

"Your privileges in this chamber have been revoked!"

Sev frowned at the man's brutal tone. He would have preferred to deal with the previous Speaker, but at least he wasn't the only one frowning: a murmur went up around them, and a few Senators shared uncertain glances.

"You will speak only when prompted, as you have been accused of serious crimes against Secundus. Is that clear?"

He paused, eyeing the Scholars before him with disdain.

"What are these accusations?"

Sev turned to the Scholar, impressed by her resilience. If he had ever had any doubts about women in the Scholarship, she had erased them.

For his part, the Speaker was more angry than impressed.

"You and the rest of the Scholarship have committed high treason. You have supported a false Historian and allowed the forces of Primus to attack Secundus. And now, as this war begins, you sow discord among the ranks, turning our own soldiers against us."

The Speaker paused, eyeing the Scholar as if he hoped she would speak, but all she did was frown. When it was clear she wouldn't reply unprompted, he continued, disappointed by her restraint.

"How do you respond to these accusations?"

"The Scholarship has committed no treason, Senator. This man is indeed the Historian, and we are not the cause of this war—you are."

The Speaker scowled.

"This is treason!" he proclaimed.

"Enough!"

Sev's voice carried weight, its depth and volume commanding respect in a manner that surprised even himself. As everyone's eyes turned to him, he took a small step forward.

"You are out of line, Senator, as you have been since my return."

The Speaker's scowl contorted with rage.

"You have no room to speak here, deceiver!"

He lifted his hand but Sev rushed his words.

"You killed the Elector!"

The Speaker hesitated, a wry smile crossing his face.

"The policy of Secundus is to punish those who kill the Historian," he answered, hand still hovering in the air.

"Then why haven't you been punished?"

The smile vanished, and in the moment it took to process this accusation, Sev spoke his piece.

"The Historian was executed for a plot you encouraged."

The Speaker scowled once more.

"Are you suggesting we are responsible for the Historian's death? It was not our blade that cut his throat!"

Sev glanced at the man's hand, still hanging in the air, and nodded gently.

"Yet it was your blade that cut the Elector's, and it will be your blade that cuts mine."

They held each other's gaze in silence until a Senator on the far left stood up.

"Speaker, this has gone too far. We cannot dismantle the Scholarship—the people will never allow it."

A Senator to the right stood up in turn.

"We don't have a choice! They are the cause of this war, and they continue to undermine our authority!"

"The will of Olius is above all else!" one of the Scholars cried.

"The Historian is dead, Olius is no more," the Senator on the right replied.

"The Historian stands before you!" another Scholar shouted.

Sev felt a pressure in his throat and looked back to the Speaker—his hand had fallen.

"Silence! We must have order in the Senate!"

The Senator on the far left shot back up in defiance.

"I put forth a motion of no confidence in the current Speaker, and suggest we remove emergency powers."

The Speaker glared at the dissident.

"We are in the middle of a war!"

"A war we can end right here, right now," the Senator replied.

The Speaker nodded emphatically.

"Indeed we can, if we punish those working against us."

A third Senator stood.

"Look around you, Senators! The people are outside our building, protesting in favor of the Scholars! Action against the Scholarship will lead to civil war—in fact, it already has! We can't even control our military. Why do you think Primus succeeds in its attack?"

"What attack?" Sev interrupted, confused and alarmed.

The Senator turned to Sev and gave him a derisive look.

"Don't feign ignorance, deceiver. This is as much your doing as the Elector's."

Sev stared at him, incredulous.

"What are you talking about?"

"Your ships are attempting to breach our defenses, and the chaos you've sown is working."

He felt his stomach drop. Priman ships were attacking Secundus? What ships? Why?

"That's precisely the problem, Senator," the Speaker interjected. "The Scholars won't rejoin us without our acceptance of this deceiver, the one who caused this mess."

"No!" Sev shouted, catching everyone's attention a second time. "I know nothing of this attack and have nothing to do with it! I am here on a mission of peace, and peace alone!"

His words were met with skepticism, but he continued.

"You destroyed the Priman flagship, did you not expect their forces to retaliate? Would your military not do the same?"

The Speaker shook his head.

"If this was a mission of peace, why did the entire military force of Primus accompany you? These ships did not appear out of thin air—they were with you on approach, waiting just beyond the space-zone."

Sev stared at him in disbelief. The entire military force of Primus? Had the Elector made alternate plans? Perhaps this was his fallback, if things fell apart. Or—and here he felt a growing nausea, a sort of unfortunate understanding of the supreme leader's persona—was this the plan all along? Create a rift in Secundus and strike?

"You expect us to believe you didn't know?" the Speaker asked wryly.

Sev stared at him, then glanced at the handful of Senators still standing from their seats, all waiting to hear his response. He knew denial would never work—he had to try a different route.

"Senator, it doesn't matter if you believe me."

This answer clearly disappointed them, but Sev wasn't done.

"In fact, it doesn't matter if I knew."

He paused, noting he had their attention.

"Senator, the only reason these Priman ships are making any progress is the division you see here," he said, gesturing around him. "If you reinstate the Scholarship and the Scholars, you regain full control of your military. And once you have that, the forces of Primus won't stand a chance."

Some of the Senators nodded, but the Speaker shook his head.

"No—this is further deception. Reinstating the Scholars means accepting you as Historian. And once you have this mantle of power, you could allow the forces of Primus to do as they please."

Sev had to fight the urge to laugh.

"Do you think your warriors are mindless? Look at what they did when they disagreed with your directive. If you recognized me as Historian and I allowed the forces of Primus to take over Secundus, they would rally behind you and refuse. I would lose my power as soon as I had gained it."

The Speaker hesitated, and one of the standing Senators took the opportunity to voice his thoughts.

"He's right, Speaker. Whether or not he is responsible for what has happened, what you claim is preposterous."

The Speaker turned to the Senator.

"You are willing to let this man parade around as the Historian, sowing discord among our people?"

The Senator hesitated, but it was the Scholar of the Premier Territory who responded.

"How much discord can he sow in eight rotations?" she asked.

Sev glanced at her, incredulous, having all but forgotten his scheduled Departure from Secundus. New versions of old questions surged through his mind—questions about Olius, about Ascension, about his fate—but now was not the time for these questions.

"Eight rotations is still enough time—" the Speaker began.

"Speaker, you are reaching," one of the Senators interrupted, "and don't have time to argue. Suggest a motion for the reinstatement of the Scholars in the Senate, or we will vote in no confidence and do it without you. This madness must end."

Sev watched the Speaker's frown grow, his eyes scanning the Senators around him.

"Is this what we have come to? The forces of Primus are on our doorstep, and we plan to give this man the—"

"I bring forth a motion of no confidence against the current Speaker."

The Speaker glared at the Senator.

"I second this motion," another declared.

"Enough!" the Speaker proclaimed.

He stared at his colleagues with unfiltered anger.

"Very well. Your voices have been heard. Rescind your motion and we will vote to reinstate the Scholars."

The first Senator hesitated, eyeing the Speaker warily.

"…I rescind my motion."

The Speaker glared at him, shaking his head.

"Whatever harm this man causes is on all of you."

He cleared his throat, and the other Senators took their seats.

"As Speaker, I bring forth a motion to reinstate all Senate Scholars of Secundus to their previous positions within the Senate, and thereby reinstate the Scholarship of Secundus. The Senate will vote now, all voices must be heard."

Sev watched the Speaker take his seat, then all of the Senators made one of two motions with their hands, diagonally in one or the other direction. After this brief ritual, the Speaker stood once more.

"Senate of Secundus, all voices have been heard."

He looked at Sev and the Scholars, anger in his eyes.

"The motion has passed."

The Scholars dropped their chins to their chests, then the Scholar of the Premier Territory turned to Sev.

"The Scholarship of Secundus recognizes and affirms your rightful position as Historian."

Sev replied in kind, dropping his chin to his chest.

"Thank you, Scholar."

He turned to the Speaker.

"Speaker, I ask that you subdue all aggressive Priman forces at once, but without harming them—take them prisoner if you wish, but again, do not cause them unnecessary suffering."

The Speaker hesitated, frowning, then gave a short nod.

"Yes, Historian."

The word struggled to leave the man's throat, but once it did, Sev felt a considerable weight come off his shoulders.

"Thank you, Speaker."

He scanned the seats above him.

"Senate of Secundus, I will aid in whatever way necessary to heal this wound, but as soon as the forces of Primus have been stopped and this unrest has ended, we must come to a peace agreement encompassing both worlds."

The Speaker nodded, but Sev could see the anger lingering in his eyes. The hardest battle was over, but the war was not yet won.

***

The remainder of the rotation was spent dismantling the Priman attack on Secundus and discussing the fate of its participants. Sev was on his feet the entire time, standing at the center of the glass dome among the men and women who until very recently would have approved his execution. Not only was this a critical time to display his authority, it was the only way he could see their precarious agreement cement into something permanent.

Still, this wasn't the Council nor was it Primus, and Sev had to delegate most of his power to those who knew the planet well. Thankfully, the newly-reinstated Scholars had returned to their seats, granting him a knowledgable ally to speak in his stead. In fact, it wasn't until the Senate voted against punishing the dissenting warriors that Sev made a noticeable interjection.

"And what of the others?"

His question prompted expressions of confusion.

"What others?" the Scholar of the Premier Territory asked.

"You agree to pardon the warriors, but what of the agents on Primus? I know at least one who dissented, and I owe him my life."

To his surprise, the Scholar frowned, glancing at her peers.

"Historian, the agents you speak of are a delicate matter…"

As she struggled to respond, the Speaker interjected.

"This dissent led to the capture of our other operatives, compromising most if not all of our intelligence operations on Primus."

His tone did little to hide his anger, but Sev ignored it.

"Once this peace is established, these operations will no longer be necessary," he proclaimed.

The Speaker made to respond, but Sev was already addressing the chamber.

"Senate of Secundus, this dissident acted with the same purpose as the warriors, and at a more critical junction. If he had not defected, I doubt I would have made it to Secundus, and this rift might have deepened enough for the Elector to launch his attack all the same—this time with success. I pardon all the other agents without reservation—despite their actions against Olius—and I ask you to pardon the one man who stayed true to the Scholarship and its teachings. Now is the time for unity, not division."

The Speaker hesitated, looking at his peers and clearing his throat.

"As Speaker, I bring forth a motion to pardon the agents of Secundus found on Primus for all actions against Secundus or Olius. The Senate will vote now, all voices must be heard."

He took his seat and the vote began, but Sev noted a change in ambiance. Over the course of these discussions, he had seen plenty of resistance, but there was something different about this. Why had some of the Senators shared sideward glances? Why did even the Scholars seem reluctant?

Before his train of thought could continue, the Speaker stood.

"Senate of Secundus, all of our voices have been heard."

He looked at Sev, and there was something odd about his expression...

"The motion has passed."

The Speaker stood up straighter, looking away.

"We have more updates incoming. As Speaker, I pause our deliberations to hear the message."

Sev hesitated, then stepped to the side. A hologram of a warrior appeared beside him and began explaining the most recent updates, but he wasn't paying attention.

The motion had passed, so why did he feel that familiar pit in his stomach, that mix of anxiety and fear, the idea that there was something important he was missing, something just beyond the reach of his understanding...

But he couldn't dwell on it, not in the midst of leading the most important negotiations in the system. Right now, he needed to focus on the future of Primus and Secundus—he could figure out Folin's future later.

***

The next three rotations were a whirlwind of activity unlike anything Sev had ever seen, beyond even the preparations for their mission to Secundus. With the Priman attack quickly and easily subdued, the Senate could focus on healing its planet, which began in a familiar manner: district visits, only this time as a united front of Senate and Scholarship, and at a larger scale than what Sev had accomplished alone.

The main objective was to get their message out as far and as fast as possible, and Sev experienced a type of expedited deja vu, with appearances at twice as many towns in half the time. This itself was a demanding and exhausting load, but the speeches were the easiest of his duties. It was the time between each visit—as members of the Senate and Scholarship travelled with him from one spot to the next—that the real work was being done.

"Historian, the Senate has every intention of fulfilling its role in this arrangement, but what you're asking for is wildly different than what was agreed on."

Sev eyed the Senator warily. For all intents and purposes, this man—the newly appointed Speaker—was on their side. He was the one who spoke up to reintegrate the Scholarship, and he was just as eager as Sev to see a new era of peace with Primus. There was only one problem: peace was as far as he was willing to go.

"We made no promise to share any of our knowledge with Primus, and we do not intend to divert or lessen the resources of our planet at such a critical time."

"You may not have made a promise, but I did," the Scholar of the Premier Territory replied.

The Senator turned to her with a frown.

"Scholar, we've been over this. Your promise was made at a time when the Scholarship's powers were unrecognized by Secundus. The agreement you made is unenforceable."

Sev shook his head in frustration.

"Senator, there cannot be peace without equality. How can we have peace between our worlds without the free exchange of knowledge?"

The Senator hesitated.

"Historian, forgive me, for I have not been clear. The Senate is not opposed to helping Primus, they're simply concerned about the scale and the methods. If we go over there and explain our technology without careful planning, we invite the possibility of negative and unforeseen consequences. But if we delay the process, if we initiate an educational operation over the course of several revolutions—one with proper oversight—then we have the chance to correctly empower the Priman people."

Sev felt the length of the rotation wearing on him, and the man's resistance did nothing to help. Correctly empower? There was so much prejudice here, sometimes he wondered if they even recognized their biases.

"Senator, some of your words ring true, and for the most part, I agree. Bringing this sort of knowledge to an entire population must be done carefully and effectively. In fact, I agree with the major components of the Senate's proposal—what I disagree with is the implementation."

The Senator peered at him, curious.

"Historian, what exactly do you disagree with?"

"The current proposal gives the Scholarship of Secundus majority control of the Council, with a sizable force of warriors to help maintain order. While this is well-intentioned, it puts too little power in the hands of Primus, and it will lead to an insurgency."

The Senator glanced at the Scholar then back to the Historian.

"This is an eventuality we understand, Historian."

Sev nodded, restraining his frustration.

354

"Senator, forgive me, but you don't. Or at least, not to the extent I do. The resentment sown by this arrangement will fester, and over time, outright rebellion is guaranteed. We have a better idea."

He shared a glance with the Scholar, with whom he had discussed this problem at length. While they thought they had the solution, it would be a hard sell.

"Instead of filling the vacancies on the Council with Scholars of Secundus, we ought to bring the former High Scholars back to their seats."

The Senator hesitated, surprised by the proposition.

"The ones imprisoned on Primus?"

Sev shared another glance with the Scholar and nodded.

"Imprisoned because of their support of Secundus—by putting them back in power, you have reinstated an ally and Primus has reinstated its people."

"Do we know their status?"

Sev frowned.

"Of the ones on Primus, no, and we won't know if they are alive until we see them ourselves. But not all of them are imprisoned on Primus."

The Senator raised his eyebrows.

"You want to reinstate High Scholar Zoph?"

Sev smiled.

"Senator, do you think this is the time or place for grudges? He is the right man for the job, and the first step to making this work. We will propose this solution and see what he thinks, and when our delegation arrives on Primus, we will find the rest of the former Council and give them the same opportunity."

He hesitated, his smile vanishing.

"That is, assuming they are still alive."

The Senator eyed him intently.

"If they are all alive and all agree, will this not overfill the Council?"

"Theoretically, yes, but I know the current High Scholars would gladly make way for their predecessors. I know I would."

The Senator considered his reply.

"And the Secundan Scholars we had planned to send over?"

Sev smiled and turned to the Scholar of the Premier Territory.

"Scholar?"

She returned the smile then answered.

"The Scholarship of Secundus recommends we fill the ranks of the Priman Council if and only if they cannot be filled by former and current members. As this is unlikely, we propose a second, temporary Council be formed—made up of our Scholars—to help advise and support the main Council. The details of their power structure and duties can be resolved amongst themselves."

The Senator nodded slowly, and Sev added the finishing touch.

"Senator, we also suggest a decrease in military presence. The need to maintain order is paramount, but do not forget your technological superiority. Two divisions of warriors should suffice."

He watched the Senator with unbroken attention, his exhaustion put on momentary hold. This was a key development, and he had not expected the conversation to flow so smoothly.

"I will need to confer with my colleagues," he said, "but this proposal may pass."

Sev shared a relieved glance with the Scholar. While these negotiations had only lasted for brief spurts of travel over the last two rotations, they seemed to drag on forever. With the possibility of an accord on the horizon, everyone's spirit was lifted, though Sev was far from relaxing.

"Thank you, Senator. If this measure is accepted, I plan to depart with the delegation on the rotation that follows."

The Senator frowned a second time.

"Historian…"

Sev raised his hand to cut him off.

"Senator, you know as well as I do we are already late. The Elector is dead, as is most of the Council. The generals sit in your prisons with the rest of the military leadership. The planet has been without a Palace and without a Scholarship for almost three rotations now, how long do you think it will take before chaos breaks out, before the remnants begin battling for control?"

He thought back to the sacking of the Scholarship and wondered if there would even be a campus to return to…

"Forgive me, Historian," the Speaker replied. "You are right. I will do what I can do expedite these agreements and make sure your convoy is ready in the morning."

Sev smiled, far more relieved with this victory than the last.

"Thank you, Senator. Can you arrange an audience with former High Scholar Zoph this evening?"

The Senator nodded.

"It shouldn't be a problem, Historian."

Then a thought came to him, and he looked at the Scholar.

"Do we know Folin's status?"

The Scholar shared a glance with the Senator.

"I will look into it, Historian."

"If he is no longer being processed, I would like him to join us."

"Very well," she replied.

They had been so wrapped in conversation, Sev was surprised to feel the ship hit the ground—time for another district tour. They exited the craft, and he saw yet another crowd of Secundan citizens preparing for yet another rousing speech.

As they placed themselves at the front of the audience, he couldn't help but frown. What was he still doing here? This planet had a wound that needed healing, but it was nothing compared to what was needed on Primus. Every citizen before him looked well-fed and, despite recent events, calm. Meanwhile, his home planet was falling apart, and every effort to save it was met with lukewarm approval.

There were good people here, to be sure, but just how good were they? The debate over technology was the perfect example: the Secundans were content to bring the Primans second-hand knowledge, enough to improve their lifestyle significantly. But were they willing to make them true equals, to sacrifice some of their own wealth and prosperity in order to give others a chance to partake?

No, he thought to himself. They were not. Was anyone?

***

That evening, with the tour of Secundus over, the Scholar of the Premier Territory escorted Sev to his chambers.

"The measure was approved," she announced.

He looked at her, pleasantly surprised.

"Excellent. We are prepared to leave in the morning?"

She nodded.

"Indeed."

They reached his door and she gestured toward it.

"High Scholar Zoph is waiting inside."

He nodded.

"And Folin?"

She frowned.

"He is still being processed."

He frowned in turn.

"Scholar, is this normal?"

She shook her head.

"No, Historian. It doesn't make sense."

He felt the familiar pit in his stomach, a foreboding he didn't want to entertain.

"Will you look into the situation? I want him to join our delegation."

The Scholar dropped her chin to her chest.

"Yes, Historian. I will see what I can do."

Sev returned the gesture and watched her leave. Would they dare do something to Folin, even after their peace agreement? Or was he overthinking things, a product of the past few rotations?

He remembered the guest waiting inside his chambers and opened the door.

"Zoph."

His former teacher stood in the middle of the room, clearly irritated. As uncomfortable as he seemed, at least his appearance had improved—he looked far healthier than when he had denounced Sev in the Senate.

"Sev."

He ignored the man's tone, both too tired and too focused to care.

"Take a seat," he replied, gesturing to a chair.

"Why am I here?" Zoph asked, still standing.

Sev took the other chair and gave his old mentor an amused look.

"You know why you are here, why else would you agree to see me?"

A flash of anger crossed the man's expression.

"This was a mistake."

Zoph marched toward the exit but Sev called after him.

"Zoph, wait!"

The man spun around, indignant.

"Do you expect my support, charlatan? I cannot believe I'm standing in the Historian's chambers and you act as if—"

"Zoph, be quiet and listen."

His words were calm but forceful, silencing his former teacher.

"I need your help. I understand you are upset, and I am more than deserving of your anger. The Historian died as part of a political ploy, and I've played a major part. But I did not cut him down nor did I promote myself to his place. I have been a pawn in this game, at least until now. Now I have power, I have leverage, and I have the opportunity to make right what was made wrong."

Zoph looked him up and down as if he didn't recognize who was speaking.

"The Elector is dead, Zoph. The man who killed the Historian has met his fate, and the pillars of Primus are in shambles. I know you know this, and I know you understand the opportunity before us. My Departure is in five rotations. After that, I can no longer interfere in your affairs. Help me get this started, help me bring Primus back into the light of Olius, and leave your hatred and disapproval for when the job is done. This is going to happen with or without you, so tell me now: do you accept your reinstatement on the Priman Council, yes or no?"

For a moment, Zoph was speechless, and Sev saw all manner of emotion in the man's expression: rage, confusion, concern…

Finally, he took two steps forward and fell into the chair with a sigh.

"Very well. I accept."

Sev nodded.

"Thank you."

"And the others?" he asked.

Sev shrugged.

"We won't know until we arrive. Were they alive when you escaped?"

Zoph frowned.

"I don't know. I haven't seen them since…"

They locked eyes in silence, both reliving the nightmare in their memory, then Sev nodded.

"I understand."

He stood, and Zoph mirrored him.

"We leave in the morning. Try to get some sleep."

Zoph hesitated.

"Sev…"

The two shared a moment of silence, then his former teacher turned around and left the room.

***

For the first time in hundreds of revolutions, a Secundan ship landed—officially and openly—on Priman soil. She was flanked by remnants of the Palace's fleet, a precaution that gave them some protection from the skeleton crew inside the Priman fortress, though their approach was not without incident—a few projectiles had to be intercepted, nothing the Secundan ships couldn't handle. The bigger issue on Sev's mind was the delegation itself—or specifically, who was absent.

The Scholar of the Premier Territory could find no trace of Folin, and there was no evidence of his processing or even of his capture. Had he died in the Feat of Primus among the others? If so, why had they found the other bodies but not his? These questions hung over Sev the entire journey, but as the ship's doors opened and the hot Priman air rushed in, he knew he would have to shelve such worries for a time.

They had chosen to land directly by the Palace to meet any remaining opposition, and already a battalion of soldiers had taken formation in front of the entrance. Sev stood at the top of the ramp and watched a handful of warriors move forward, their blue and white suits shining under the light of Olius. It seemed preposterous sending five to battle a hundred, but he knew the odds were in their favor.

He turned around and looked at his immediate company: the Scholar of the Premier Territory, Zoph, and two more warriors. His eyes locked on Zoph, the most important piece of the puzzle.

"Ready?"

He nodded.

"Yes."

Sev turned back around and was surprised by the efficacy of their forces: already the warriors had cleared a path to the Palace.

"Go," he announced.

Sev watched the four of them march down the ramp and across the small expanse, cutting through the dismantled battalion. The warriors covered either side, deflecting the occasional attack with ease, and soon they disappeared into the black fortress.

Seeing the situation unfold before him, it occurred to Sev that despite everything, the original Historian's plan was coming to fruition: here they were, routing the Palace. Zoph and his escort were on their way to the prison, to find and free the former Council. Sev had originally planned to join them, but he decided his presence might hinder their mission. They needed to see the support of Secundus and they needed to see Zoph—they could process Sev's involvement later.

For now, he had his own mission, and as it became clear they had achieved their goal on the battlefield below, he walked to the other end of the platform, into a small opening along the side of the ship—the entrance to a shuttle, attached to the ship's exterior. Inside were another five warriors, along with the surviving members of the Priman Council and two Secundan Scholars.

"Ready?" he asked.

There was a mix of affirmative responses, and Sev took his seat, the door closing behind him.

"Let's go."

With a small jerk, the shuttle detached from the ship, and they began their flight to the stone campus. Sev glanced out a window usually filled with trees and grass and saw a sea of rocks and sand. Again he found himself wondering if equality was truly possible between a desert and an oasis. Maybe the wealth of Secundus could turn Primus green? It would be a preposterous thought, had there not been a time when the Garden was filled with life…

"We're here, Historian."

Their flight was shorter than expected, and already the shuttle was coming to a hover. Sev looked at the people inside—the warriors and Secundan Scholars looking outside with wonder while the Priman Council gaped at the ship's interior—and smiled.

"What a rotation this shall be," he announced.

The ship hit the ground and he stood.

"Olius is shining down on us stronger than ever. Let us do what we came here to do."

The side door opened next to him, revealing the campus perimeter. For whatever reason, the sight brought with it a new perspective, and Sev reflected on the tumultuous path leading up to this moment—every twist and turn, every victory and defeat.

For Olius, he thought to himself, then stepped out onto the sand.

Aberration

"Historian, all prisoners have been processed and are being held in the Palace. We have repurposed most of the chambers into holding cells."

Sev nodded, taking stock of his surroundings. He had sat in the Room of Council many times, but never like this—never in the center chair, and never with the colors of Secundus welcome inside.

"Has the fighting stopped?"

One of the men in blue and white nodded.

"Yes, Historian. The remaining pockets of resistance are being monitored."

Sev turned to the chair to his left, the one closest to his.

"Elder Scholar, your Council will handle communication with these groups?"

A familiar face looked back at him, one he had known and trusted for longer than any other in the room. The last time they had shared this table, it had looked on him in anger. But those rotations were long gone.

"Yes, Historian."

He held Zoph's gaze for a moment before turning his attention back to the Secundan Scholars.

"Very well, it seems my job here is done. I will return to Secundus before last light. Please ready the ship."

"Yes, Historian."

He shared another glance with Zoph.

"Councils of Primus, I know there is much to be done, but I ask you all to take the rest of the rotation to rest. Calm reflection can lead to new insights, and I would prefer to pass what time I have left on Primus without stress."

Many of them smiled, and he smiled in turn.

"All of you are dismissed for the remainder of the rotation, and on the following rotation, the Elder Scholar shall lead the council."

Those in blue and white dropped their chins to their chests and the High Scholars got up from their seats. Scattered conversation broke out in all directions, but Sev had his eyes on one person only.

"Elder Scholar, would you accompany me to the Garden?"

Zoph nodded slowly, gesturing to the exit.

"After you, Historian."

The two of them weaved through the others, making their way into the hall. As they walked side by side toward the Garden, Sev tried to take it all in—the faces of the Priman Scholars, the familiar echo of the corridors, even the grey coloring on the walls.

"I owe you an apology, Sev."

Sev smiled, giving him a look of disapproval.

"An apology? You owe me nothing, Zoph."

The Elder Scholar cleared his throat.

"For eight revolutions I walked with you in these halls, and still I misjudged you. I let anger guide my thoughts, and that was a mistake."

Sev laughed.

"Zoph, you don't need to apologize. This situation has made us all question one another—and ourselves."

They reached the threshold of the Garden and stepped out into the shade. Sev looked around, remembering the Arrival: all of the excitement, all of the hope.

"If anything, I need to be thanking you," he said, turning to Zoph. "Without your help, I'm not sure the people of Primus would have a strong enough voice in the coming alliance."

Zoph nodded slowly.

"I will do what I can."

Sev hesitated, then frowned.

"You must, and not just for the Scholarship. I fear there are still some on Secundus that plot against this peace."

Zoph frowned in turn.

"Still no word on Folin?"

Sev shook his head.

"No. According to the Scholar of the Premier Territory, he is still being processed."

They stared at one another in silence, then Sev gave him a curious look.

"Did you know he was an agent of Secundus?"

Zoph hesitated, then nodded.

"I did—the entire Council knew. But this communicator you speak of, he never mentioned it."

He frowned again.

"It doesn't make sense. Why were we using the trade ships when he had this device? All of this could have been avoided…"

They shared a silence, each one deep in thought, and Sev turned to look at the Garden.

"I also thank you for taking the mantle of Elder Scholar, despite the circumstances."

Zoph let out a sigh, and Sev thought back to their predecessor, the man he would always consider the true Elder Scholar. Somehow, in that moment, he could not recall his harsh manner toward Sev on the Council, only his gentle guidance in the revolutions before.

"May he go with Olius," Zoph replied, quietly.

Sev placed a hand on his shoulder.

"He will, on the following rotation."

Zoph met his gaze.

"You're sure you cannot stay?"

Sev smiled, removing his hand.

"I would like nothing more than to attend his Walk, but Priman rotations are longer than those on Secundus. If I don't leave this evening, I risk missing my Departure."

Zoph gave him a curious look.

"Perhaps in the future, your Visits will be concurrent."

Sev smiled again, having had the same thought.

"If this peace lasts, may it be so."

They shared another silence, and Sev looked out at the Garden once more. He thought dismissing the Council might afford him some rest, but without immediate tasks to complete, the uncertainty of the future took over his mind.

He had done everything in his power to give Primus a fighting chance, but he knew the fate of both worlds lay in the hands of Secundus. He trusted the Scholarship to do its part, but he was hesitant to extend the same confidence to the Senate—at least not all of it. How long would these agreements hold, once he was gone? What would happen when this faction tried to sabotage the peace? Could his vision last, even in his absence?

He took a deep breath, clearing his head. This was his final task—to pass the torch, to hand the light of Olius over to the Scholarships—and he wouldn't question it. Such was his duty, as Historian.

***

Sev left Primus that evening and arrived at a similar time on Secundus, less than a rotation away from his Departure. After a few final meetings with the Senate and the Scholars, he retired to his chamber knowing full well he would not sleep. What he didn't expect was a knock at the door.

"Yes?"

Sev looked the man up and down, wondering why this Scholar seemed so familiar…

"Historian…"

The man shot a glance behind him, into the hall, then back at Sev.

"…may I come in?"

Sev hesitated, then the memory came to him: this was the Scholar from the safe house, the one who had taken care of him at the Scholar of the Premier Territory's request.

"Of course," he replied, stepping aside.

The Scholar rushed in, closing the door behind him.

"Historian, I apologize for the late visit, but I needed to speak with you before the Departure."

Sev noted the creases in his robes, the bags under his eyes—this man had not rested well for some time.

"What is it, Scholar?"

He hesitated, glancing about the room with a frown.

"I—I was asked by the Scholar of the Premier Territory to look into your friend, Folin."

At the mention of this name, Sev leaned forward, intrigued.

"You found something?"

The Scholar frowned again.

"I—I'm not sure, Historian. But I couldn't wait any longer, you're leaving in the morning."

Something about the man's words brought the pit back to his stomach, but he dared not interrupt.

"At first, I tried to access his information myself, but the file didn't appear. This wasn't a surprise—his existence was a secret as was his mission. But when I approached the directors of the Rehabilitation Program, even they couldn't find his file."

The Scholar locked eyes with Sev.

"If he was being processed in one of their Centers, shouldn't they have his file?" he asked.

Sev wasn't sure if the question was rhetorical, but before he could respond, the Scholar continued.

"Next I searched for the others, the ones your delegation brought with Folin, and their files were visible—not to me, of course, but to the directors. I learned where they had been processed and I went to those Centers myself, asking the staff if they had seen Folin…"

The Scholar paused, locking eyes with Sev once more.

"No one, Historian. Not one of them claimed to have seen or heard of him."

The pit in his stomach grew deeper, but the man wasn't done.

"Then I did what I thought was impossible: I tracked down one of the operatives, and I asked him what had happened to Folin."

He paused again, and Sev could hear his own heart racing.

"He claimed not to know what I was talking about, as if Folin never existed."

His eyes begged Sev for an explanation, for guidance.

"I—I don't understand…"

His words hung in the air, and Sev fought to keep his composure.

"Scholar, I…"

Theories swarmed his exhausted mind, each one a nightmare of his imagination trying to explain these loose ends. He knew somewhere in this spectrum of possibility there was truth, but he had no way of knowing where, and no time to figure it out… and frankly, none of that mattered. What mattered was what he had realized in the Garden, earlier in the rotation.

"Scholar."

His confidence had returned, and the change in tone made an impression on his audience.

"Olius is the champion of peace as it is the champion of truth. What you have told me is an affront to both of these, and it is our duty to fight against it."

The truth of these words strengthened his resolve, and as he spoke, his conviction grew.

"I have less than a rotation left among you, but this mission of peace and truth does not end with my Departure—in fact, it continues for as long as Olius shines down on our worlds. There will always be struggles, there will always be conflict. But if Primus and Secundus are to prosper together, all of you must fight for that prosperity—and thousands of citizens are far more powerful than any one Historian."

He leaned forward, eyeing the Scholar intently.

"So do not let this disappear, do not let this go away. Fight for the truth as you fight for peace, because they go hand in hand, and it is now more your mission than it is mine."

The man nodded, but Sev could see the lingering doubt.

"I know your hesitation, Scholar, and I wish more than anything I could assure you of success, but such a thing does not exist. This is a constant battle, a journey rather than a destination, and our fight is but one part of a never-ending process."

Sev sighed, looking away.

"Now I must try to rest, as much as I know sleep will elude me. Thank you for everything you have done, Scholar..."

He looked back at him, locking eyes.

"...and thank you for everything you have yet to do."

The Scholar dropped his chin to his chest.

"Thank you, Historian. I will do everything I can."

With that, he turned around and left Sev, closing the door behind him.

***

The next morning, Sev woke in his chamber, surprised his mind had allowed his body some rest. He sat up in bed, turning his attention out the window. Their arrival the night before had been late, well after Olius's last light, and only now could he appreciate the garden once more.

Despite everything he had achieved in the past few rotations, Sev felt as if he had barely scratched the surface of what he owed the people of Primus and Secundus. There was so much to be done, so many questions yet to be answered—not to mention the number of unforeseen circumstances bound to occur.

He stood and made his way to the table, pushing away these intrusive thoughts. As he had told the Scholar last night, it was out of his hands now, and in theirs. The real question he should be asking himself was where he was heading.

Everything he had learned—as a Pupil and a Scholar, as a High Scholar and Elder Scholar, and even as Historian—pointed to the same answer: Olius, the light of the system and the bridge between the worlds. Now, as had happened on Primus, he questioned not just how a person could journey to a star, but whether the very nature of his being would change.

Was this the true Ascension? Would he be granted an enormous lifespan and find himself returning to these worlds in hundreds of revolutions? If so, what would he find?

A knock caught his attention and the door opened, revealing the Scholar he had met on his first rotation here—the lone woman he had trusted in those troubling times.

"Historian."

She brought her chin to her chest, and Sev smiled.

"Scholar, it's nice to see you again."

The Scholar gave a shy smile in return.

"Historian, the ceremony will begin as soon as you are ready."

Sev nodded.

"Give me a moment, I will be out soon."

She dropped her chin once more.

"Of course, Historian."

Sev watched her leave then glanced out the window a second time. This was it, he thought to himself. The end of his duties, at least for now. Had he done a good job?

***

The ceremony on Secundus was a much more celebratory affair than his Departure from Primus. The entire Scholarship of Secundus—save the handful still on Primus—was present, along with the entire Senate. The Vessel took center stage, as it had on his Arrival, and Sev marveled at how little he had noticed the craft sitting less than two hundred paces from his chambers.

After some parting words from both the Speaker and the Scholars, a loud snap announced the reappearance of the recession, sending a gasp through the crowd. Sev stared at the opening in the Vessel, then turned to the gathered masses.

"Secundus…"

His eyes scanned the faces before him—faces of a foreign world—and he smiled. This time, he knew exactly what he wanted to say.

"This marks the end of my Visit and the end of my journey. I will not see any of you ever again. When I return, Primus and Secundus will be unfamiliar, changed in ways even I cannot foresee. I ask of you but one thing: fulfill the word of Olius. I do not take this journey lightly, knowing the circumstances that brought me here. Primus and Secundus have both endured a great test and they have passed. But it is up to you to maintain what has been built. It is up to you to continue our shared mission, to ensure a peaceful and prosperous future not just for one planet, but for the entire system. Thank you, and goodbye."

He turned around and stepped into the recession, ready for whatever came next. The floor beneath him moved forward, into the Vessel, and he relaxed. Moments later, after the familiar snaps of thunder, he reached the small room in the middle. He glanced at the machinery with a sense of familiarity, then sat in the chair.

The holograms came on, indecipherable as ever. He closed his eyes and heard the rumbling around him, feeling the pressure of takeoff. He tensed his neck in anticipation, and the sharp stings dropped him into darkness.

***

Sev opened his eyes to the same dancing lights and let out a sigh of relief.

Whatever lay beyond the walls of the Vessel, he had survived the trip. He looked at his arms and body, searching for signs of age, then took a moment to compose himself. There was a chance, however small, that many revolutions had already passed, that his trip to Olius was one beyond his conscious mind. If he was now returned to Primus or Secundus, he needed to be ready, to face whatever awaited him as a Historian should.

He took a deep breath and stepped into the recession, letting the ship take him forward. As each thunderous clap brought him one step closer to destiny, Sev felt an unfettered excitement. Olius, Primus, or Secundus, he was ready to do what needed to be done.

And then, darkness gave way to light.

***

Before him was a familiar sight, and Sev's eyes scanned his surroundings with a mix of disbelief and confusion. Tree branches swayed in the light breeze, and the grass below him was the same green as he had seen earlier in the rotation. But he wouldn't have been completely sure of his whereabouts were it not for the three Senators standing before him, flanked by six warriors of white and blue.

"Greetings, Sev of Primus."

A smile crossed the Senator's expression, one more sinister than friendly, and Sev's confusion gave way to fear.

"Where am I?"

The smile widened.

"Why, you don't know? This is Olius, of course."

At these words, the other Senators smiled, eyeing each other knowingly. While they enjoyed their moment, the warriors maintained their composure, staring at Sev with frightening persistence. Something about them brought a chill to his core, and he tried to back up, but there was barely enough room for him to stand in the recession.

"Enough."

At this word from the Senator, the wall moved outward, filling the recession and pushing Sev to the ground. He landed on his side with a gasp, more shocked than hurt, confused as to what was happening. The Senators watched him struggle to his feet, amused.

"What is the meaning of this?" he asked, trying to channel some kind of authority.

His words brought a few chuckles, and the chill cut even deeper. He glanced at his surroundings but saw nothing—the only sign of civilization was a ship about a hundred paces away.

"Why am I here?"

The Senator in the middle took a step forward.

"This is your Ascension, Sev of Primus. A joyous occasion."

Sev looked him up and down.

"Your sarcasm falls on deaf ears, Senator. Have you interfered with Olius's Vessel?"

The Senator turned to his peers with a smile.

"Gentlemen, did you hear that? I think he's caught us red-handed."

"If you mean to threaten me, do what it is you've come to do, but know that when the rest of the Senate catches wind of what you've done —"

The Senator whipped his head back to Sev.

"Catches wind? Sev of Primus, no one will ever know what happens here."

The humor was gone from his tone, and Sev lost any semblance of confidence. The Senator gave him a once over, then continued.

"In a way I pity you, Sev. This was never meant to happen to you, or to anyone for that matter. In fact, the only person responsible for your fate is the late Elector."

Sev stared at the Senator, fear temporarily replaced by curiosity.

"What are you talking about?"

"Your predecessor, Sev: the Historian who arrived on Primus but did not depart. If he hadn't been killed, none of this would have happened."

The Senator's dismissive tone ignited a frustration within him, one he couldn't contain.

"So you would have threatened him instead? How is that any different?"

The Senator stared at him, amused, then shook his head.

"No, Sev. We wouldn't have threatened him because he was one of us."

The Senator took another step forward and this time, the warriors did the same. Sev stumbled backward, colliding with the Vessel.

"You see, Sev, there is no such thing as the Historian. A man that lives forever? Come now, this is clear fiction."

Sev stared at him, incredulous.

"Impossible! The Historian has visited our planets for thousands of revolutions—"

"Were you there?" the man interrupted, catching Sev off-guard.

"Was I...?"

"How do you know the Historian has visited for so long? The Scholarship claims such things, but even our terminals cannot extend that far in the past."

Sev shook his head emphatically.

"This is blasphemy. The Historian was the one who ended the Great War, and your terminals show these records. Do you claim this never happened?"

The Senator shook his head.

"No, Sev. You're right. Some two-hundred revolutions ago, there was a man who went to Primus claiming to be the Historian, and thanks to this man and the influence of the Scholarships, the Great War came to an end. But this was the only Visit ever, and the man who called himself Historian then is long dead."

Sev could not believe what he was hearing—would not believe what he was hearing. These were lies, lies that flew in the face of everything he had ever learned.

"Dead? What are you talking about? The Historian brokered peace between the worlds then returned to Olius."

The Senator gave him a disappointed look.

"Sev of Primus, how do you not understand? The man who ended the Great War was just that—a man. He was a Secundan citizen playing the role required of him."

Sev felt the cold metal of the Vessel pressing against his back and glanced at the soldiers bearing down on him. There had to be a way out of this, he thought. They could not all be heretics.

"Are these the lies you tell yourself? Is this how you justify threatening me?"

The Senator sighed.

"Sev, after everything you have been through, are you yet so blind?"

The pity in his tone only angered Sev further.

"I do not speak on faith alone. Your terminals hold these same records, even if the data is sparse."

The Senator shook his head.

"Not all knowledge is in the terminals, Sev. You of all people should know the power of secrets."

Sev stared at him, curiosity taking over once more.

"What are you talking about?"

The Senator smiled.

"Sev, do you know why Secundus has prospered while Primus has not?"

Sev frowned, and the Senator continued.

"I know this issue is dear to you, and I know you've done your research."

He paused, giving Sev a knowing look.

"But as I said, not all knowledge is in the terminals."

Sev felt the anger returning.

"Enough of this. Explain yourself."

The Senator's smile returned.

"Before the Great War, both Scholarships worshipped the technology of Olius, the ancient gift of interplanetary travel. But it wasn't until the Great War that our ancestors on Secundus took the first steps to understanding this gift and learning its secrets. You see, Sev, war is the greatest inventor."

He paused, eyeing the warrior next to him.

"Unfortunately, our ancestors ran into an obstacle: the materials required for the development of this technology were scare on our planet…"

He turned his attention back to Sev.

"…but abundant on yours."

Sev glanced at the warrior then back to the Senator. There had to be a way out of this mess. One of these warriors had to understand the depth of their sin, one of them had to be willing to save him…

"At the time, both Scholarships believed the Historian would bring peace between the worlds, as the legends claimed he had done in the past. So a small group of intrepid Secundans put together a plan: they would give the Scholarships their Historian and their peace—and with it, a favorable trade agreement, of course."

He smiled.

"After the Great War, Secundus advanced far quicker than Primus, and we knew drastic action had to be taken before Primus found out— renegotiation of the trade terms or a call for technological parity would hinder our advancement. So an event was staged—the attack by Secundan extremists, as you probably know it—that closed Primus's borders and gave the Palace new authority in the name of security. "

Sev watched the Senator with a mix of fascination and disgust. Some of what he said was undoubtedly true—he knew pieces of this history from his own studies—but so much of it was heresy, he couldn't tell the truth from the lies.

"Unfortunately, where the previous Electors abided by our rules, this most recent leader decided to overstep his boundaries."

The Senator frowned.

"He pushed your planet's pride, filling your people with dangerous ideas of military might—ideas that could lead to another conflict. Worst of all, he started looking into Olian technology—and unlike his predecessors, he had some success."

His frown vanished, an amused smile taking its place.

"Granted, success is a term I use lightly, but the point remains—we can't have any threat to our people's prosperity. So we decided to use the most effective tool in our arsenal, our secret weapon of peace—the Historian."

Sev grimaced. Did this man just refer to the being of Olius as a weapon?

"We sent a new Historian to your planet to regain control of the Palace and reestablish order on Primus, but as you know, things did not unfold as planned."

The man's frown returned, and he sighed.

"When the Elector executed our man and made you the Historian, he put us in a tough spot. Our own Scholarship was expecting an imminent Visit, and even if we would have preferred to prevent your Arrival, the ball was rolling too fast to stop. Still, despite your continued meddling in our affairs—and the unfortunate alliance you managed to forge—a peaceful solution is in sight."

Sev shot another glance at his surroundings, praying in vain for some wandering soul to see them, for an innocent bystander to catch a glimpse of this scene and investigate. Something in the way these men stood over him gave him an anxiety he hadn't felt since the night he watched the Historian die.

"Your peace agreement was a wonderful idea, of course, save one detail: we cannot share our technology with Primus, as that would rob of us of our ability to maintain order. Think on it, Sev. Do you really believe the citizens of Primus can responsibility wield what we possess? Do you think anyone—the peasants working the mines or the stubborn generals—could take the power our technology permits and use it sparingly, or for the greater good?"

The Senator shook his head.

"Of course not. But not to worry. We will share a few details, as we have in the past, in order to reestablish our relationship. Then once that is done, there will be another incident—perhaps an attack by Priman terrorists, bent on stealing the military technology of Secundus we so generously tried to share—and suddenly, the Scholarship will realize its errors and the borders will close once more."

He paused, eyeing Sev curiously.

"You see, Sev, very few people know the truth I've just told you. These men here," he said, gesturing to the warriors and the other Senators, "are among the small number privy to this information. The Scholars certainly don't know, or else how could they do their job? It's easier to sell a lie you believe as the truth than one you know to be false."

His frown disappeared, and a small smile crossed his expression.

"So in a way, this is my gift to you—your Ascension. You now know the deepest secret of the entire system, one shared by you and your predecessors and unknown to almost anyone else."

For whatever reason, seeing the Senator smile snapped him out of his fearful daze.

"Enough with this madness! If you are intent on killing the Historian, so be it. Have your soldiers do your bidding and become just like the man you claim to have caused this mess. But at least have some dignity. Don't hide behind elaborate lies, behind a story so far-fetched even I, on my deathbed, see right through it."

The Senator stood up straight, surprised and amused by the sudden outburst. Behind him, his colleagues chuckled, but it was a laugh of boredom, one that robbed Sev of his newfound confidence.

"Sev of Primus, you are a testament to the efficacy of our methods, though I pity your blind faith."

A silence followed, and the Senator contemplated his next words.

"Tell me, Sev, do you know what happened to the man you knew as Folin?"

Sev eyed him uncertainly, the familiar pit growing in his stomach.

"He's missing…"

The Senator frowned again, but there was something different about this one—something pitiful.

"That man knew the truth, Sev, he knew it from the time he arrived on Primus to the time you brought him back here. And he was going to tell it to you too, if he had ever gotten the chance."

The Senator studied him another moment.

"Ironically, we have your Elector to thank for keeping his mouth shut. He wanted to tell you everything, but he couldn't do it with the Elector or the Scholars present—after all, if the Elector knew the truth, he would never agree to any kind of peace, and if the Scholars found out, it would destroy their entire belief system."

Sev barely heard the words, his eyes darting desperately in either direction, searching for some kind of salvation, for some kind of hope.

"Lies… All of it, lies…"

The Senator watched him struggle, noting the despair in his eyes. Here was the Historian, the grandest being in the system, cornered like an animal with no place to hide.

"Perhaps… perhaps I have misjudged you, Historian."

Sev looked up, confused by the change in tone and title.

"You are right—we shouldn't hide behind a story, when already our time grows near."

The other Senators shared confused glances, but Sev was focused on the man in front of him. Something in his demeanor had shifted, and while the threat of the warriors hadn't changed, this shift was enough to quell his anxiety.

"Do you have anything left to say, before you meet your end?" he asked.

Sev stood up straight, locking eyes with his enemy.

"Yes. That you are acting against the direct wishes of Primus, Secundus, and Olius. That you may strike me down here, but what I have forged will not falter. And may you think on the depth of your sins, as they will haunt you for the rest of your lives."

The Senator nodded.

"You're right, Historian. This will haunt me for the rest of my life."

The two men stared at one another, each oblivious to their surroundings, each deep in their own thoughts. Then the Senator made a subtle gesture, and the warrior on his right swung his arm, the hotsword along the side coming to life.

www.ingramcontent.com/pod-product-compliance
Lightning Source LLC
Chambersburg PA
CBHW072111250626
47159CB00007B/2405